About Turn

by
Deirdre Haugh

AuthorHouse™ UK Ltd.
500 Avebury Boulevard
Central Milton Keynes, MK9 2BE
www.authorhouse.co.uk
Phone: 08001974150

© 2008 Deirdre Haugh. All rights reserved.

No part of this book may be reproduced, stored in a retrieval system, or transmitted by any means without the written permission of the author.

First published by AuthorHouse 6/30/2008

ISBN: 978-1-4343-9876-5 (sc)
ISBN: 978-1-4343-9877-2 (hc)

Printed in the United States of America
Bloomington, Indiana

This book is printed on acid-free paper.

For my grandparents

Chapter 1

Sorcha stood on the dirty, broken footpath by the Liffey on the way out of town, tentatively waiting to cross to the south side of the river as cars roared past her in either direction with their headlights flashing in a blaze of electricity. It was early evening in December and already pitch-dark and freezing cold. She tried to avoid the litter that rustled noisily in the dusty breeze, threatening to block her view. The smell of the river was palpable and she covered her nose with her gloved hands to block the stink. Just then, the lights changed and the traffic came to an unwilling halt. She stepped gingerly off the pavement and crossed in a hurry, partly from fear of a lone motor speeding with no warning and partly with a desire to get out of the cold.

She quickly scanned the buildings in front of her. They had said it was down here somewhere, halfway along the quays, and she knew she had taken the correct turn. She had to help set things up for the party and didn't want to be late. She scanned the row of buildings yet again and there it was: the old church nestled in the shadows of the Guinness factory where, later tonight, some of Dublin's poorest people would be given hot food and treated to some entertainment in the season of goodwill.

Sorcha stood at the front door of the building which was padlocked shut. She could hear voices close by – two men having an argument and a can being kicked around violently. She was of medium build with soft brown hair covered by her winter clothes and knew it was a good idea not to hang about outside. She moved swiftly to the side-entrance where Danielle, her tiny dark haired workmate, was picking up parcels of food from a parked van.

"You made it," she said, smiling above her scarf, her breath pouring out like smoke in front of her. "It's through here. Same place as last year."

They stepped briskly down the narrow path to the side door. "What did you bring?" Danielle asked looking at the bags Sorcha was carrying. "Decorations, cheap and cheerful," Sorcha said, holding one bag slightly open and pulling out handfuls of tinsel, balloons and streamers. She had gone to the pound shop after work the previous week and had collected what she could on a tight budget. She knew it had to be more about quantity than quality.

"Well, these dinners have been donated," Danielle said. "I didn't make them myself. I don't think some of these guys would appreciate vegetarian lasagne for Christmas dinner. Despite my persuasions, I could really eat one of these. I'm starving."

Inside, they put their packages down. The cheap tinsel in gold, green and red spilled out all over the shabby tables set in rows throughout the main room. Danielle disappeared back to the van. Sorcha took off her winter woollies and checked out who else had arrived. Isabelle, the French girl, was chatting and smoking with one of the organisers. It was Grainne's last gig before she went on maternity leave. Her department buddies were kidding that she would have made a great Santa Claus but Grainne was keeping her coat firmly tied around her. "I'm only staying until the meal and then I'm gone. I don't like the idea of driving this evening when it could snow any minute." She started to set cutlery and paper hats at each table as her co-worker Audrey jokingly waved a red bauble around.

Isabelle greeted Sorcha, "Hey you, you look really cold. Let me defrost you with my cigarette." She made a gesture with her hand. "Sadly, it's not much better inside," Isabelle said as she shivered in her jacket. "I'm afraid with my coat that I'll burn it. It's the only decent warm one I have."

Isabelle put out her cigarette and helped Sorcha untangle her collection of Christmas décor. They unravelled pieces of tinsel and stuck them to the walls. "If I don't make it, you'll let my parents know, won't you?" Sorcha said, teetering on a table and trying to attach each item to the walls. Grainne stood back and took a look at their efforts. "All we need now is the crib and the Baby Jesus. I think I saw one in the church on our way through but it's not what this is about." She signalled to the girls that it was time to commence the celebrations.

Two of the centre doors opened, revealing a crowd, mostly men, who pushed through into the dining area. They moved hesitantly, taking places at random tables that had been set with a cracker in each place, some holding on to cans of beer. In the case of one or two, they were unable to walk very far and had a helper to take them to a spare seat. Plates of food were handed out and the small group of organisers talked among themselves as the guests began to eat.

"Here, Sorcha, we are going to have to arrange the presents. These bags are a little heavy." Isabelle lifted a couple of sacks onto a spare table at the side of the room. "Just some small gifts for the people who came. I think Grainne and her bunch bought these earlier." She rummaged for a moment in the bags, holding random parcels to her ears and shaking them jokingly. "I wonder what's inside. Christmas seems so far away. I really could do with some things. I need some new clothes. Anyway...."

Although Isabelle had had plenty of boyfriends, she always bemoaned the fact that she could never meet anyone to support her. Mick, her current beau, was not the sentimental type and rarely gave her gifts. She depended on her small income, which was never enough. Like most of the group, she worked for a fundraising organisation and was paid on Community Employment terms with small bonuses here and there.

Nonetheless, Isabelle was old enough and travelled enough to have accumulated a nice varied wardrobe and Sorcha was envious of her whole room in fact, pieces of well-chosen furniture sent from Paris and arty photos and pictures in the right places. Everything was arranged very tastefully and Isabelle managed to keep it clean most of the time. She was a few years older than Sorcha, a raven haired woman with mixed roots, and had come to work for the organisation after stints as a waitress and some time on the dole.

They quickly placed the extra tinsel on the gifts table and waited for the meal to end. The guests were making themselves at home, chatting to each other and discussing their plans for the Christmas season. They were trying to plan some kind of accommodation, as the weather was likely to get colder by late December.

Tea and coffee followed the main course and the clients were asked to line up for the gift presentation. Some of them stayed in their seats, oblivious to the laden sacks. "I'm just asking him to explain why he won't stay there," Grainne said good-humouredly. She was chatting to a middle-aged man whose name was Francis. He had a chance to stay in a secure hostel for a couple of months but made a face each time it was mentioned. He was sceptical of the hostel's ability to protect its clients.

"Every time I stay there, a fight breaks out. Last time someone had a knife. I'd be safer on the street. But it's cold though. I just have to make sure I'm covered up when I sleep outside."

"I really think that's exactly why you should take the place when it's offered to you. At this time of the year?" Grainne remonstrated. "Have you got any other options? I doubt it."

"We'll see," said her companion, and walked away with a present tucked under his arm, singing a Christmas carol under his breath.

A handful of the guests took the gifts, mostly practical items such as clean clothes, socks, handkerchiefs, warm jumpers and received them gratefully. "Well, at least it's not Cartier, or I'd be pocketing some of these. I mean it's Christmas you know. Some of these guys have better treatment…." Isabelle broke off, as one of the men broke away from the group and retreated to a corner.

He was shabbily dressed and began throwing his wrapping paper around and making a fuss in an angry but disoriented manner. "That's Phillip, I think. I was here last year and they told me the story," Isabelle was whispering. "You know, he had a full-time job, happy home life and then one day, apparently, he had an accident on his way to work. He hit his head very severely and has never been the same."

"He has no family?" Sorcha asked.

"Well, he's kind of hard to deal with sometimes so they don't take care of him. I feel sorry for him but it's none of my business."

They watched the scene as a couple of his friends and helpers went over to Phillip to talk him round. He remained in his place, shaking his head and eventually they led him back outside. The entertainment group had arrived and was starting up on the stage. As the singer began his repertoire of Irish songs, Sorcha was reminded of the countless open days at hospitals, senior citizens parties and charity gatherings that she had attended at home as a schoolgirl. Her mother would stay till the bitter end, clearing up dishes and saying goodbye to those leaving, returning the next day to help with the clean up afterwards and moaning how few people were willing to help out.

Here, at least, there were plenty of volunteers, who would not allow the celebration to continue any longer past 10pm. They had socialising of their own to do, or families waiting for them at home in the suburbs.

This was how Sorcha found herself with Isabelle and Danielle and the rest of the posse heading back into town at a late hour, fighting their way along the bitterly cold quayside. Some of the group broke off to visit a pub in Temple Bar but the main core of the group kept going to Grafton Street where they could get access to a late-night club at the Gaiety theatre.

"I've never been in here before after dark," Sorcha exclaimed as they joined the queue to gain entry.

"You'll love it. They have different bands playing in each room. You can pick whatever you want and move on when you get bored. There's also a cinema but I don't feel like it tonight." Isabelle searched in her purse for her admission money.

They paid at the booth and went inside the glass doors where the doorman checked their tickets. The interior was plush red velvet and a tiny sweet shop in the corner was closed for the night. They put their things in the cloakroom and continued up the steps into the main auditorium, which was not in use. The smaller rooms were full of people and each had a different theme: samba, jazz, disco DJ playing alternative records. Isabelle moved swiftly through the crowd, holding a cigarette aloft in her hand. She greeted the rest of the bunch and ordered some drinks. They stood, watching the band perform; the drummer was catching everyone's attention.

"He's really great." Isabelle observed. "Oh, there's Mick." She waved her hand to get his attention. "He said that he might make it down here tonight if he finished work on time." Mick worked independently and freelanced in magazine production. A former heroin addict, he had successfully beaten the habit and was now fast becoming a workaholic. He approached them, a wiry thirty something in denim, hugged Isabelle and nodded at the rest of the crowd.

"What's this rubbish?" he said abruptly in his inner-city accent.

"Look at him. He's wonderful!" Isabelle pointed to the drum kit where the player was hammering out his beats, smiling and laughing at the crowd.

"So, how did the party go?" asked Mick, drinking an orange cordial.

"Fine, it was great. No real problems. Just a couple of disagreements. Little ones. No police calling at the door," Isabelle laughed.

Mick looked around himself. "You didn't bring them with you, did you? I mean, this is a bit of a hip place. You'd never be able to show your face again." He burst out laughing. Isabelle's face was unforgiving. "What a thing to say, you had the same experience one time, don't forget."

Mick's face grew sober and he put his glass back on the nearby table. He motioned to the doorway and said he'd be back. Isabelle was silent. "I'd better go find him," she said.

They returned shortly after, Isabelle looking apologetic. Mick picked up his jacket and said his goodbyes. The band was taking a short break so the girls went to a room further down the hall where the DJ was playing David Bowie and people were dancing. Sorcha kept an eye on Isabelle. Although the French girl was older, she could behave immaturely and had had to make some adjustments in her life to extricate herself from the clubbing scene. Apparently, this meant something a lot more hardcore than the city centre on a late night.

The club closed at 3am so they both took a walk up to a dingy basement café on Dame Street and had a late snack. Sorcha hated this place. It was usually full of people on their way home but the place gave her the creeps. Isabelle was in no better mood. "Shit, I wish I hadn't opened my mouth," she said, pointing to her lips. "I'll just have a coffee, I'm not hungry." She burst into tears and cried quietly into a napkin. "It was stupid of me to say what I said. I have so much respect for Mick. But I can't help having an opinion. I should say it in French in future. He doesn't speak the language as well as he thinks. Anyway...." She rolled her eyes and looked at her companion. "Well, did you have fun?"

Sorcha nodded. "Well, hopefully you won't have to go to any parties with your mother when you go home. Explain to her that you've been there and done that, OK?" Isabelle laughed then said, "Poor you, being dragged to these things, seeing how the other half lives. What if you had to be in a relationship with someone like Mick? He can be very hard to deal with but I love him. This is what it's like in the big, bad city. Believe me, I know."

She wagged her finger at Sorcha and through her tired eyes, the girl looked at someone five years her senior who purported to know it all but didn't entirely convince. She had known Mick for several years but something did not make sense. "Don't worry about it. The argument was silly, it will probably blow over like it always does," she said, reassuringly.

Isabelle shrugged and didn't continue. They finished their meals and went outside to get a taxi. Sorcha had her suspicions about the motives of her French co-worker. They had some good perks at their office, thanks to their PR team but most of the staff had their sights set on something better paid. Such jobs were hard to come by and Mick had contacts all over the city and plans to set up his own production company. Sorcha knew that there was more than one reason why his French girlfriend stayed put.

The taxi dropped off Isabelle at her house just off Pearse Square close to the city centre. The street was a mixture of shabby buildings and council housing, interspersed with more established landmarks such as an old school and a public library. By now, it was pitch dark and Sorcha shut her eyes as they drove to her own flat in Donnybrook. The three storey red-brick on the outskirts of the village was split into ten separate flats. She walked through the stoney pathway to the steps, yawning as she opened the front door. The house was deathly quiet as she climbed the stairs to her room on the first floor. Her flat was basically one room with a bathroom of her own on the landing of the next floor, for all of which she paid £40 per week. She had put down a draft excluder to maintain heat in the room at body temperature. There was a bed in the corner beside the window, which faced onto the street. Sometimes the curtains were no protection against the bitter cold this time of year.

Sorcha paid a quick visit to the toilet on the next level. At least the electricity was billed and there was never a chance of running out of coins. Still cold, back in her room she undressed and covered herself with blankets, glad to finally be able to sleep.

No matter what protection she had inside, like every Irish person she still had to contend with the weather once outside. The next day was Friday and she had to be in the office by 10am. She never really took breakfast and was never hungry first thing in the morning. It felt warmer if she moved quickly, she reasoned, as she sat on the bed and pulled on her boots. Apart from the bed, the furniture was spare. There was a bookshelf overhead with a selection of poetry, humour, biography and stories all of which she meant to read but could never find the time. She had bought them as light reading having finished her studies. The fireplace had been blocked up and a table and chair placed in front. Beside the window was a chest of drawers. On the opposite side of the room a fridge and a small cooker had been installed. Because she spent so much time out of here, it was rarely used. Pulling on a coat and scarf, she let herself out of the room and locked it securely.

Outside, on the steps, she noticed some furniture trucks pulling up. A man and a woman were walking on the gravel of the house next door, intensely discussing the grounds. She had heard the house had been sold from Laurence, the psychology student who lived in the next flat. The morning was overcast but there was no rain in sight, just a cold wind blowing. The sight of half a dozen people standing at the bus stop in the morning usually set her off walking to the end of Morehampton Road onto Baggot Street then round the corner at the end to cross over Baggot bridge.

Taking the right turn, she ended up through the spanking new business blocks of Dublin 4 and came out under a train archway onto Pearse Street. She liked this walk first thing in the morning. From Pearse Street, it was just a quick walk across the Liffey crossing at the City Arts centre to her office.

As she waited to cross the street beside the Customs House, she could see the IFSC gleaming like a big shiny beacon in the early light. A burning flame, a memorial to famine victims, seemed incongruous beside this mass of buildings. Sorcha's workplace was a few minutes' walk to the left. The area was a mixture of old pubs and some new shops and restaurants. The train station was partially boarded up, pending some development work to increase its capacity. She never used this station, her home trips started from Heuston on the other side of the city centre.

As she walked, Sorcha could look across the Liffey at the docks and she could see scaffolding of huge proportions on one side of the river where Citibank was building their new offices, beside a newly completed hotel. There were great plans ahead for the area known as the Docklands. She stopped for a coffee at the small café underneath

Connolly. Sometimes she would grab a sandwich from one of the small shops in the area. There were plenty of places to choose from if she got hungry during the day. Then she buzzed on the door of the office a few doors down the street to gain entry.

Reaching her office involved negotiating a labyrinth of stairs with small rooms branching off each stairwell. She said 'Hi' to one of the office admin staff who was playing receptionist for the morning. Inside, her room was empty apart from Karen who was one of the senior staff. "Hiya, love," she said, grinning. The tall redhead was always in a good mood. Sorcha said good morning and removed her coat.

"I would have bought you one if I'd known you were in at this time. Are you busy?" Sorcha made chatty conversation. The others would be in later and she wouldn't have time. She had a lot to do this morning and would be kept occupied. She switched on her computer and ran through yesterday's work list. Karen asked about the party inbetween puffing at a cigarette and reading an article from the paper. The rest of the staff trickled in one by one. Isabelle seemed to be in a better mood. Gill showed up with her daughter Louise in tow; she hadn't felt well and there was no place to keep her during the day as the crèche was full. She gave her some colouring things and spare paper. The managers didn't seem to mind if there were kids on site and nobody ever seemed to check.

Sorcha concentrated on her phone work, calling potential donors to contribute to their little venture and ticking off the names on her list. She had some typing to do which she tried to squeeze in when she could. At lunch, they visited a new pub The Harbourmaster, which boasted a long history of serving hardworking men in the docks. Today, it was full of financial staff from the IFSC buildings but they managed to find a table, which had just been vacated.

"This is quite nice. The soup here is good value. They give you a great big bowl and as much bread as you want. I've never tried the main courses. We should come here some night for a meal. I wonder what the desserts are like," Gill pondered as she looked at the menu. Her skinny hands ran through a curly dark head of hair which needed a cut and colour.

Isabelle looked at a tall blond leaving a booth on the side of the room. He was talking with a young woman and both were in smart suits. "I was just noticing. It's a nice view out there with the river but I'm watching the people too. Not my type, though. I can imagine I would have to change a lot."

"Not mine, either," said Gill. "Too straight-laced. Makes me nauseous actually. Just reminds me of being back in London."

They discussed the future of the fundraising project where they were employed. Most of the group had been under contract for two years, and renewal for a third year was doubtful. Things were looking up on the jobs market though and they were sure to find alternative employment.

Having contacts through PR meant that they regularly received invitations to events in the city and this allowed them to network a little. Gill was trying to build up her own niche in this area and often attended launches after work. This meant Louise needed a minder after hours.

"You're still able to make it tonight, Sorcha?" Gill asked.

Sorcha dipped her nutty bread in the vegetable soup and nodded.

"Cool, thanks." Gill relaxed in her seat and checked her nails.

"What time do you think you'll be at Mick's tonight, Gill?" Isabelle asked, curiously.

"Eightish, after eight, I should think."

"OK. Well, tell him he's a fuckeur for leaving us in the club last night. I didn't tell you on the way here because of Lou but that's what he did."

"I'm not going to tell him any such thing. He's supposed to help me Isabelle, remember? I've been given notice on my flat and he said he'd help me with that. Tell him yourself."

After coffee, they edged their way down the tiny staircase of the pub to the exit. Isabelle was looking dolefully at her stomach. She had wolfed down a huge cheese sandwich. "Look at my belly. I have the right name for that," she said half-laughing. Gill and Isabelle walked behind with Louise. Karen and Sorcha chatted about their holiday plans as they came back out of the busy centre into the main street again. Outside the station, a young man was sitting collecting coins in a box. His companion wore a tatty tracksuit and spat on the sidewalk as they went past.

Isabelle looked back at them and said, "You have to be careful down here. I hate walking past this place on my own. It gives me the creeps. So dangerous."

The afternoon went pretty fast. Sorcha finished her typing and spent a couple of hours in the photo files, sourcing pictures for a promotional leaflet. She had some more calls to make and had to tidy up her contact listings before the weekend. She left early as she could to catch the number ten bus on O'Connell Street. The journey home dragged and she read a booklet about internet courses. If the company paid for her training, she could get a qualification to create her own websites. She was always on the lookout for things like this. They didn't have e-mail in the office but she had recently opened up her own hotmail account.

Taking a break, she looked out of the window on Kildare Street. It was now close to six pm. There was a dark-skinned old man bent over in the light of the office block just before the Shelbourne hotel. She could make out a bag and he was holding a book in one hand. The scene surprised her but she didn't chance leaving the doubledecker to speak to him. She sat back and laughed at a joke Karen had made that despite all the good press, organic food production was still not such a great option for the chickens.

Back at the flat half an hour later, she made pasta and ate as she watched Sky News. They were about to break into the same hourly report when she noticed the time. She called for a taxi, which was one good thing about living here. There was a pretty good network between the villages so you could get around if you had the money.

This time of night, the inner city streets were full of people setting out on a night of drinking. They walked in various directions down well-known streets to the Long Stone, Kennedys and Ned Scanlon's. Any other time, Sorcha would be doing the same. The taxi drove her away from town and towards Pearse Square where Gill lived next door to Isabelle. Although it was close to eight o'clock, kids were playing in the street, amid the dilapidated buildings and busy neighbourhood shops on either side.

The taxi turned into the square. Gill had moved here from London, following a break-up with her partner. She had a tiny flat on the lower ground floor, which she shared with Louise.

Sorcha paid the driver his few quid and descended the steps to the front door of the flat. She could hear voices arguing inside. Gill turned the latch and greeted her with a great big smile. "Hi!" she said. "Don't worry; I'm just discussing something with my daughter." They entered the living room. Louise had turned her back in a sulk and was playing with a doll on the floor. "Oh, Isabelle was here earlier. She said she'd see you tomorrow. Aren't you going to that market?"

Isabelle lived two houses down in a shared, rented house. They had planned that Sorcha would stay overnight in Gill's place and that they would visit the St Andrew's Resource Centre which had an organic market on Saturdays. "Yes," Sorcha replied. "I'll just have breakfast here and I'll call on Isabelle after that."

Gill had put on a hat and scarf. She grabbed her keys; her daughter was trying to take them out of her hand. "Not now, Louise." Gill edged towards the door and handed her daughter a teddybear. "I don't want to keep my friends waiting. Mike is to help me with my housing application. I need all the help I can get.

"Really not now, Louise. Talk to Sorcha. Haven't you got some books to show her?" She turned to speak to Sorcha, "She's feeling so much better now. I'm not sure she was sick at all but I didn't have the energy to argue."

She unlocked the door just as a car pulled up. It was another taxi. She quickly kissed her daughter goodbye and waved to Sorcha.

She disappeared out of the door, locking it behind her. Sorcha sat Louise beside her and they watched a video together. It was The Secret Garden, starring Gabriel Byrne. She remembered the novel from school. The girl Mary Lennox loses both her parents to a deadly disease and returns to England to her uncle, where she befriends a country boy and his pets.

"Wouldn't you love to have someplace like that to run about in?" Louise nodded her little girl mane of light brown hair and Sorcha noticed her face of freckles. "Maybe they'll clear the park soon."

The square was just a mound of dug-up earth and the entry gates had been locked for months while it was refurbished. Louise looked at her with her deep green eyes and said matter-of-factly, "I don't think so. Anyway we have to move, don't we?"

Her mother was in agreement. Later, they sat and chatted when Louise was asleep in her room. There was only one bedroom and Gill had a camp bed in the living room. She was also doubtful about their future in the area.

"I would love to stay here. I was so lucky to get this in the first place. It was the same thing a couple of years ago. We stayed in a hostel for a couple of weeks then they were arguing that we couldn't stay much longer.

"The girl who owns this building is a single mother and was happy to let me this place. But now she's been offered a packet for the house and wants to sell, leaving me in the lurch. I've made all my phone calls and no-one is willing to let a flat for around sixty quid a month, with a child. On my own, fine, but not with a child."

She gazed out the window at the park outside. "As for the green area, I reckon what they'll do is put all this grass down and a few benches and turn it into a real park for the new inhabitants. Whoever buys the house will be able to sell it for double the amount in a couple of years. This happens all the time in London."

Sorcha was inexperienced at these things and didn't know what to say. "It's just a shame," she offered. Like Isabelle, Gill had spent a considerable amount of time travelling and was nearly forty. She had some family support but wasn't inclined to return home to what she had left behind anytime soon. Mick was a friend who had connections in the city but he had only been able to offer advice on the application. Gill just had to get all her paperwork together and apply for a points rating, which would hopefully gain her a house in the end.

That night, Sorcha slept on the sofa in a flat that was remarkably quiet. She mentioned it to Gill in the morning. "Probably the old walls," Gill said. "You don't hear a thing, despite all the traffic on the main road. These were townhouses at one stage. If you go through the tiny door in the hallway, you'd see a staircase leading to the main house. I have a key for it but we only use it in emergencies. It's not our space. Sometimes the kids play there but it's not used as a rule."

She opened the door and showed Sorcha the darkened stairwell. "We'd better not make any noise or I'll end up being given the push earlier than I thought." She locked it again smartly holding Louise away. Then the doorbell rang and they heard a loud voice. "That sounds like Isabelle."

The French girl came through the door, looking worse for wear. "Before any of you, either of you, ask, this is not the effect of a night on the town, girls." She pointed at her face. "Look, I'm a mess. Those fuckeurs came here this morning at 6.30am and have been drilling ever since. It has been like this for the past two months. I'm not getting much sleep. I had a relatively late night last night and can't make up for it with all that noise. I'm a wreck!!"

Gill patted her arm and went to make her a coffee. Isabelle lit up a cigarette and sat down beside Louise.

"You can't see it from here," she explained. "They're knocking down some of the old houses behind us and are building something. It looks like a big deal. Maybe a gym or something useful for the community but I don't think so. I have my suspicions. Every morning they're here. And Sundays too. I moved here thinking Great! Holy Catholic Ireland. I'll get my sleep at the weekend. Now look what's happening."

She laughed in spite of the situation and gratefully took the coffee in her hand. "Don't expect too much from me today, Sorcha, please understand. I should have a scarf like a fucking movie star to cover up these shadows under my eyes."

Gill's flat was protected from the worst of the noise and she had too much on her mind to worry about its intrusion anyway. She busied herself in the kitchen as the two girls finished their coffee and left the warm flat to cross the busy street to the old school, which was a hive of activity. There was a range of activities including counselling sessions for drug addicts and music lessons for kids during the weekend.

"It's really great," Isabelle observed. "But they have to be careful. You can't mix addicts with young children for one thing. These kids coming in with guitars could make friends with the wrong kind. Not good."

The main room at the back was where they had all kinds of organic produce: honey, oats, chickens, fruits and vegetables. But the prices were off-putting. It was so handy having all of this fresh food next door to your house but they had to resist temptation and just buy what they needed. They bought some organic bread and cakes from a busy guy in glasses and left.

Isabelle invited her friend back to the house for tea. It seemed that most of the occupants of the square were out shopping for the day, as the streets were practically empty. Isabelle lived in the house close to Gill's and shared it in its entirety. The size of the whole house always impressed Sorcha. She couldn't believe the kind of room available for such reasonable rent.

"It's not much more than two hundred a month, I think. Plus I get some rent allowance as the job is part-time, as you well know."

They were sitting in the living-room which had a large couch and a real fireplace, decorated tastefully for the Christmas season. The room was large enough to be split into thirds: one third for the living space, another third for the dining area and the last third for the kitchen. Upstairs, Isabelle had a large room of her own which was probably the size of Sorcha's whole flat. She made some soup and they split the cake.

"What are you doing for the holidays? Any plans, Sorcha?"

"I suppose, just going home. It's not like I can afford to go away. I don't have the money to do much."

"You always say that but you're never short, you're good with the amount you get." She paused. "Next year, you should really try to get a new job and develop yourself. The charity could be a deadend if you're not careful. I don't know how much longer it will last to be honest. It has to compete with so many other interests."

She was checking her plane tickets and lighting another cigarette. "Just one more and then I have to tidy this place. I'm leaving a few days before Christmas and won't be back till the new year. I'm flying directly south to my parents' house. You never seem to be lonely up here but you're so far from home. Are you?" Sorcha shrugged. She mentioned the homeless man she had seen in town to change the subject.

"Yeah, I've seen it too. There's a lot of Bosnians around for obvious reasons. They have a centre of their own just around the corner. They're having a Christmas party but my flight home leaves the day before. I know someone who works there and it's a nice crowd. You should go, no?" Sorcha shook her head.

"And I have seen a lot of Africans around. And Romanians. I think the information is spreading, little by little, that this is the place to be. As much as I like it here, I'm not sure if I'm happy to stay. I like to keep moving. But for some people it's a necessity. You see what happens in Rwanda."

Sorcha stood up to leave. She had a good idea of what Isabelle was planning to do tonight. Later on, she would ring Mick and they would make arrangements for the evening. She took her things and let herself out, Isabelle still chatting through rings of smoke. It was only late afternoon so she felt safe enough to walk home to Donnybrook through the streets. She had lived in the area right through college and knew a lot of shortcuts. The large red-brick homes were a constant reminder of how much ground she had to cover before she could consider herself as having achieved her life's goals.

She still felt regret at not having finished her degree but was making the best of things. No more than the others, there were certain things she didn't have to divulge. She knew that the charity had limited potential and it was struggling to survive with all the different interests vying for attention in the city. The original aim had been to develop a site for use as a market stalls but the proposed site had recently been bought by a consortium with other plans.

It didn't delight her to think of what she would have to do in the coming year: give up her simple life and accelerate her career before it got too late. The start of a new year was seen as full of prospects but she had begun to doubt this more and more the longer she lived in Dublin. She had sent her details to employment agencies in the past but had had very little response. Her parents had hinted more than once that they had other kids and wanted her to get a proper job in a bank or a company to give herself security.

She wasn't looking forward to the journey home for the holidays, either, which meant hours on an old train heading to the country. Her parents never overdid the celebrations and just got through the event with as little fuss as possible. She had bought some small gifts at the markets to prove to her mother that the city was not just a mass of commercial stores, eager to take your money. But it would take some doing to jolt them into the Christmas spirit and she knew it.

She envied Isabelle and her trip to France, although she knew that her parents spent a lot of time at the local golf club and expected their daughter to go with them and listen to their gossip and complaining. Isabelle usually managed to squeeze in a night or two in Paris and would go out with some old friends. She had mentioned how apprehensive she was at the thought of being back in the same crowd again and was hoping to stay on her best behaviour.

Sorcha didn't really have a group of friends like this and was only too aware of her status of being outside most clubs, which worried her a little. Since moving to Dublin, she had made some friends but wasn't sure what she would do if she ended up on her own like some of the people she had seen at the party just recently: wizened faces and weary bodies worn down by street living. From what she had been told, it seemed like it could be too easy to end up like that and it worried her.

In her own way, Sorcha relied on the job and her small network to bolster her existence. There were a couple of cards that had arrived from home and from friends of hers so she put them on the mantelpiece to create a sense of Christmas cheer. The village people walked to and from town on their way home to their own houses and, as she looked out of the large window onto the main street, she felt strangely isolated. She was hoping for the best too as the year came to an end, slowly but surely.

Chapter 2

The sound of French chatter could be heard on the stairwell early one morning as the workforce trotted in for another day. Sorcha was trying out some ringtones on her new mobile phone and waiting for the conversation in the reception room to end. The entrance to their building was shabby but there was a small couch by the window where informal meetings were held. Isabelle was meeting with Nigel who was from the Congo. He had arranged to meet the girl as they both spoke French fluently and he was having difficulty with getting around the city.

"*Au revoir*," she said finally, holding the door open to let him back onto the street, and "*Bon chance maintenant*" as he left the building. The dark-skinned young man was thin and slightly hunched; his clothes were worn and over laundered. He seemed pleasant and smiled back as he walked across the street.

"He was fine," Isabelle said as she walked down the stairs, holding a cigarette she had just lit. "I just had to give him some help with directions – the place he's staying in is not great and he's afraid to take a wrong turn if you know what I mean. He's already had a few things said to him by kids in the flats nearby. And he has a meeting this morning. I had to explain some things. He's looking for asylum."

She paused for breath as they walked upstairs from the coffee room. "He's a nice person but he's been through some stuff."

"What kind of stuff?" Sorcha was curious.

"Never mind. I won't worry you. You might be afraid of those crazies who've been through a war and are now on the streets of Dublin." She laughed at the sight of the phone, which was huge. "Only joking. Come on, we've got work to do."

"It's a billed phone," Sorcha explained. "I was advised to get this as it's easier than using the phone in the flat which is used by everybody."

"You'll be making secretive calls now to possible employers," Isabelle said snidely. "Don't think I haven't read your mind."

They were crossing the street at O'Connell Bridge after work. "Are you coming tonight? The show starts at eight, remember?" They were on their way to see Asian Dub Foundation at the new Temple Bar Music Centre. The band comprised of a collective of young Asians from the UK promoting issues relating to their community through music. They had their own website and publication through which they disseminated information.

"I'll be there." Sorcha answered. She crossed over the bridge and they went their separate ways at the Megastore on Aston Quay. Sorcha didn't feel like going home first to change. She was bloody-minded about always having to look perfect and fresh and didn't think it would matter for once. She was interested in seeing the band perform as Isabelle had seen them before at a festival in France and raved about it.

Little by little, shiny new constructions were replacing the grey decrepit buildings in the cultural quarter but it was tasteful for the most part. Some of the older buildings were being used in new ways, such as the film centre where you could still see the original stone walls inside. Sorcha nosed around its bookshop – there was such an amount of information available on those shelves and she felt overpowered, like she was back at college again.

The streets were usually full of foreign travellers who occasionally asked for directions to a cathedral or an ice cream parlour on a hot day. Today, it was early in the year for all that but there were a few obvious travellers about and numerous more permanent travellers as well. She encountered groups of Asians, East Europeans from Bosnia talking in a language she had never heard, and Africans who had arrived in Dublin amid reports of the economy taking off at last.

The papers were full of stories about refugees entering the country illegally but most of them had to endure horrendous conditions to get here and then wait for approval to stay in the country. Isabelle had seen the same thing happen over the years in France and had been involved in the cause for some time.

She had some money for a snack so walked along the cobblestones, chewing a sausage roll from the deli. The area was a centre of culture: it was evening now but during the day, she could choose from films, galleries, alternative clothes or photography. She stayed close to the venue on Curved Street. There were people already drinking in the pubs, oblivious to the activity outside. Once in a while, a car attempted to drive through the crowd and gathered speed as it reached the quays.

Groups of people began to gather outside the music centre. There were goth-like teenagers in one corner, arguing over who had dressed better and passing a can of beer around. It was eight by now and they trouped into the venue to get the best spaces. Sorcha had long finished eating and was fingering her ticket – where was Isabelle? She could hear the support band being applauded by the crowd inside. As she reluctantly made for the doors, Isabelle came running up out of breath. "Sorry, jesus, I'm so late. Quickly, let's go inside." They gave their tickets to the doorman and were ushered in to the main hall. The music room was fairly full but they found standing room at the front. There was a bar operating in the corner.

"They're not on yet. Let's get a drink. I'm thirsty," Isabelle led the way.

They ordered and Isabelle whispered, "I have some bad news, I'm afraid. That's why I was late. THEY WANT US TO MOVE. WE GOT NOTICE ON THE HOUSE TODAY. THAT'S WHAT HAPPENED. I'M SO ANGRY." She shouted above the crowd then changed tack as she saw Sorcha's mystified expression.

They watched as the Foundation crew bounded around the stage rapping on injustice and what they wanted to do about it. It was hard to understand each song but the crowd seemed to know what the songs meant and wildly showed their enthusiasm. Isabelle left abruptly halfway through then came back, clapping energetically and shrugged her shoulders.

Afterwards, they were walking back onto the main street to get their buses. It was raining and they rushed through the damp footpaths. "I can't bear this. Let's go inside somewhere. This fucking country," Isabelle said.

They went inside a nearby pub which was still open. "You know, France is bad enough. And now it's starting here. I can feel it. People are happily settled in their homes but we want to move you. To think we were planning parties just a couple of months ago and now I will have to watch every penny."

She took a swallow from her drink then said calmly, "Well, it's not so bad. My flatmate already knows a couple of places that we can take a look. But it's just the money. I have to pay a deposit before I get my money back from the house I'm living in. It's a real pain. Nobody really has the money to lend me what I need. I suppose I'll manage."

She looked at Sorcha. "What about you? Have you had any landlord knocking on your door telling you to move yet?? You'll be next, mark my words."

On her way home, Sorcha thought about Isabelle's predicament. She felt like it could be the kick-start the girl needed to get going again. She didn't think that it was a good idea to say this, however, given the French girl's mood.

―――◆―――

They found a small house on the South Circular Road. The rent was not too high but still more than before. The owner had renovated the front room into a third bedroom and they had a small kitchen and living-space upstairs.

"It's very cramped," Isabelle said, "and the rooms are weird. Kind of….what's that word? Topsy-turvy."

"Higgeldy-piggeldy", Sorcha offered.

Isabelle nodded. The good news was the house had a large bathroom, which had been built on the ground level from scratch. Plus it was still close to town, although it meant taking a bus.

"It's OK", Isabelle reasoned, when Sorcha came on a visit. "You know, Gill's new flat is in the same area. Same postcode anyway. I've just finished moving my things in here and now I have to help her move her things next weekend."

Gill had been given a council flat in the Dublin 8 area. "We went to have a look you know. It's vacant right now because the last occupant has died." The French girl laughed. "The area is close to everything although it is rough though, for a little girl like Louise. Some of the buildings on the next street are derelict and there has been no life there for the very long time, so it's not perfect but what can you do?"

―――◆―――

They went out to celebrate that their searches had come to an end, catching a show at the Olympia, with tickets blagged by Gill. The

Afro-Celt Sound System was performing and had been getting rave reviews in the press for their fusion of Celtic and African sounds. Some of the musicians wore traditional costume and beat their handmade instruments in addition to drum machines used to pad out the sound. The effect was mesmerising.

Tina, the office receptionist, had come along for the evening after making complaints that they never took her anywhere. She was moving her over-large body from side-to-side as the girls stood in a line, enjoying the music.

"What's wrong with you? Are you not enjoying yourself? You didn't get the eviction notice too, did you?" She laughed out loud. She looked at Sorcha strangely then moved off.

"At least she didn't say Up Yours this time. That was her catchphrase last time we went out, the cranky cow," Sorcha said, drinking from her pint glass.

Gill tried to talk her round, as Tina had been so supportive over the last few weeks. But Sorcha wasn't interested. Her mind was occupied by other things. She was tired of living on so little and felt her life needed a boost. But she said nothing as the girls started to dance in a group. They were planning to visit a club later. Did she want to come along? She backed out as Tina began to recruit a bunch of men to accompany them for the craic, asking Sorcha what her problem was, and left early on purpose, only imagining what was being said behind her back with Tina egging the others on to dish the dirt.

It was almost midnight by the time she reached the flat. She hadn't been home yet that day. There was a bunch of letters on the side-table in the house: one of which was a note from the landlord with her name on it. She sat down to read it: he was putting up the rent from the next month. Sorcha looked at it silently then tucked the letter into her jacket and went up to her flat.

The following evening, she bumped into Laurence who was taking the issue very seriously. "What he really means is he wants to sell the house. It's common practice. He's probably had an offer like the guy next door and will sell eventually," Laurence said.

"I heard that house went for a quarter of a million," he said matter-of-factly.

There were people on the ground floor that had lived in the flat for years and were taking the news very badly. One of the women worked part-time and had a small flat at the back of the house but the landlord was helping her move.

"So it's true then?" Sorcha looked at Laurence questioningly.

"Well, I objected when I got this yesterday. He told me that he wanted to sell the house."

"How long have we got?"

"Till the end of the month, I suppose. I'm going to stay with a friend. I think some of the guys upstairs have family around here. Have you thought about what you're going to do?" he asked Sorcha.

She didn't know. Most of her family lived elsewhere and she wasn't keen to impose herself on friends who had little space. Luckily, the landlord had not yet found a buyer. He was happy to let her stay for a few weeks until he got a deal.

"Ohmigod," Karen said, when she heard that Sorcha had to move. "That's just happening all the time now, isn't it? Well, you can move in with me and Rob for a while if you want."

They were sitting in her living-room just over the bridge from Isabelle's new house. They had crammed all their things in here and there wasn't really enough room for another person but she would keep the offer in mind. As they sat with the window open, a full moon shone on the Jewish graveyard next door to the apartment block. Visitors had left a number of small stones on the graves by visitors in the Jewish tradition as Sorcha could see in the darkness.

"That's spooky," Sorcha observed.

"I never notice," Karen answered. "I'm usually too busy with college three nights a week. It's nice here but there isn't any place to walk around in, and the park is too far away, so I get a lot done. At least now that Rob has a car, we may be able to do things at the weekends." Her boyfriend Rob, a computer programmer, had bought a second-hand BMW and was happy to regale everyone he met with just how powerful an engine it had. "But it's funny," Karen said, "the other day we were driving back from town and ended up stuck in traffic. I was like, so go on then show us how fast it can go, and really telling him to put the boot down." She giggled. "We're helping Gill move this weekend so let us know if you need it too."

The rest of the girls had been sympathetic but hadn't really said anything. Now that her house was sorted, Gill was focusing on a new school for Louise. Sorcha just tried to avoid Tina by coming in the back entrance, not wanting to hear any more of her banter.

Just sitting on the steps outside of the office door made her feel depressed. The backyard looked onto the nearby railway station, was grey and dank and hadn't been touched in years. Grass was growing from parts of the wall and they only had a rusty railing to cling to if they were using the back exit when going home. She was starting to feel she had to get out of here somehow. She knew that there had to be better jobs out there and didn't feel she could take any more of the jibes about her single status. Seeing Karen's relative comfort made her think she should move on.

Sorcha had been spending her free time on O'Connell Street in an internet café just beside the bridge, the Global Internet Cafe. It had opened just recently and she had gone in there on evening after work to take a look. They had helped her obtain an e-mail address and the office services meant she could work on her CV. Sometimes she just read a magazine.

She often bought the street magazine sold by homeless vendors. She chuckled at the ridiculous articles that had obviously been lifted from other publications. They had stopped writing on serious issues and the cover usually boasted a famous actor. Inside, there were pages of advertising for homes and interior décor of all things. It seemed like it was struggling to survive.

A copy of TIME magazine had a big spread on the Irish capital and its growing popularity as a place to live and work. She had noticed plentiful adverts for staff all over town in shops, on pub windows and café notice boards. But it wouldn't pay her enough – she was after something better.

O'Connell Street was usually full of shoppers crossing over between Henry Street and Talbot Street. Old ladies pushed their carts along the streets trying to avoid a collision as traffic rushed along either side. The tricolour flapped in the wind at the GPO and the rain only added to the grey atmosphere. Sorcha often had to dodge a couple of characters on her way back to the office if it was lunchtime: maybe a skinny couple arguing over a cigarette or a couple of old bowsies throwing slaps outside a pub.

It was hard to concentrate on her work when she had the worries of a new job and home rolling over in her mind. She could also feel unrest from Isabelle who sat beside her.

"What's up?" she asked her one morning as they queued for coffee in the café one morning.

"Not much" Isabelle answered. "I'm just tired. I was out late on Saturday and didn't get much sleep. This coffee is going to be my third today."

Later she admitted that she had been trying to get Mick to give her a job. After two years, she was earning not much more than she had when she'd started. And the expense of the move and the new house had made things tighter.

They were on their way down to Bewleys Café Theatre, not to see a play but to attend the launch of a new record by a mutual friend. The theatre space was on the mezzanine level and sporadically showed theatre productions, running for a week at a time. They went inside and grabbed their comfortable seats. A red velvet curtain separated the performers from the audience before anyone went on stage. The singer appeared shortly and gave a boppy rendition of some songs he'd written while busking around Europe.

Isabelle was chatting with the promoter and taking notes. She was mentioning the name of a PR woman she knew who could maybe help. They had a glass of wine before leaving. "Hey, wait; come up here, this way." Isabelle was taking a right as they left the café. Busy Grafton Street was almost deserted at this time of the evening. "Where are we going?" Sorcha asked.

"I want to take a look, OK, at the Habitat Store. It's just around the corner. Gill was up here at the weekend and said it was great, but very expensive." They took a look in the window at the leather couches and dining tables crammed into the small space. Isabelle was taking a good long look at everything, making mental notes.

Next day at lunch, she was still thinking and said out loud. "You know, I would love my own place. Or even share, if Mick would agree to it. But I've been here a long time and nothing's happening.

"When I see you, Gill, settling in and I have to move to such a small house with the same old flatmates, I think I need to do something."

They were in the local Italian and had just finished their main courses. Gill was looking at Isabelle like she was crazy. "What's wrong with the house?"

Isabelle fiddled with a cigarette. "It's not the house so much. I've told you before, Gill, I'd prefer to be mature and have my own space when I come home in the evening."

"Try living with a five-year-old who doesn't understand the concept of 'my own space', not when it comes to 'my' space anyway."

"Well, I just think my friend Jo is looking for a place of her own. She can't afford a house on a single income but maybe with the Affordable Housing Scheme, she could get a place. They don't really build enough to give you a choice though." She turned to Sorcha. "Jo has a great job and earns enough money but she can't buy the house she wants. Her bank manager told her she would have to change jobs if she wanted to be taken seriously. It's a stupid system."

Gill had an idea. "Tell you what, why don't we go down to the shops after work and spend our pay cheques? Easily done, you just pick out something you like and hand over the dosh. Are you coming, Sorcha?"

"Not this time. I have to look for somewhere to live." This was her cover for spending so much time in the internet centre. They vaguely knew about it but she hadn't discussed her job-hunting with anyone, just to be on the safe side.

She stopped at the centre on the way home and signed up for an evening course in internet design. The training course was covered by the community scheme and materials were included. That evening, she wished she had been telling the truth with her answer as the landlord called round out of the blue. He was curious to know if she'd found a new place yet and she had to reply that no, she hadn't. The encounter left her feeling nervous.

"You should definitely move in with Karen, at least for a while, until you find a place. Have you been looking?" Isabelle asked.

"I haven't found any place I've liked. The rents have gone up a bit in the past year."

This was true as she had checked the papers daily but had not had much luck with her subsequent phone calls. She agreed to move in with Karen and gave the landlord the notice he'd been waiting for. Rob called over to collect her things at the weekend. He was friendly as he helped her take some boxes down the stairs. She had a CD player and some bags but it all fitted in the boot of the car. They drove along the canal at top speed and came to a halt outside the apartment complex.

"I'm just so grateful. I feel like a refugee. I never seem to be able to stay somewhere for more than a few months," she said, packing her things away in the spare room. Karen was working on her computer and Rob had some paperwork to finish in his room but they told her to make herself at home.

―――◆―――

In the morning, Isabelle was waiting for them at the bus stop on the South Circular Road. She normally left later but had made a special effort. They took an IMP into town and walked from O'Connell Street. The traffic was chock-a-block and they had to stand in the passageway, holding on for dear life. Isabelle was telling them the story of her flatmate who had been waiting for the same bus the previous morning.

"This guy, obviously African, not much English, came along and was asking her if she fancied a date this week! Can you imagine?" Isabelle guffawed. "And my flatmate is very picky. She was really angry. That's the thing. You don't do that here; ask someone if they want a date first thing in the morning. But then again, if Mick doesn't wake up, I might be out there tomorrow, all dressed up." She paused. "Only joking, girls."

They passed by the church at Aungier Street where old ladies were hobbling to the morning Mass, dressed neatly and chatting. The bus was going so slowly that they could watch the old women shift their handbags and chat as they put their hands in the holy water font at the church entrance.

They turned the corner at the Olympia theatre and the bus raced on towards Trinity College. It finally stopped over the bridge and they clambered out onto the early morning griminess of O'Connell Street. The council had recently announced plans for a complete overhaul. "Look at the state of it," Isabelle said. "It's no Champs d'Elysees that's for sure. If someone offered me my own monument on this street, I'd refuse. I give my life for my country and this is what I get? I'd say, 'No thanks'."

They crossed the street and went in the direction of the office, looking at cheap offers on boots and bags and household items in the shops lining Talbot Street as they went along.

That weekend, Sorcha was alone in the flat. The guys had gone out for a meal with some friends and she was busy sorting out CVs into piles and putting them into envelopes. There was some warmth at the full-length window at the corner of the living-room. If she turned around, she could look to see the Jewish graves. The Dublin Mountains were visible to the right and if she looked out of the window, she could see the city landscape covered in cranes as the town went construction crazy.

She sifted through the papers looking for job notices, her pen hovering over the pages in anticipation but there was absolutely nothing she wanted. There were notices for sales consultants and an advert for a design assistant but that was it. There were a lot of ads for large finance companies opening up in Dublin though; they were looking for people to 'join the winning team' and 'find a better future'.

One advert showed a group of smiling, happy faces in what was supposed to be an office environment. It looked more like a Benetton ad but these people claimed to be young professionals and loving every minute of their job. 'Can you see yourself in this picture?' the heading said.

Sorcha wasn't sure but she read the text anyway: the company was looking for marketing representatives for their sales office in Dublin. It offered potential employees a great working environment, first class opportunities and a range of benefits, apparently. All she had to do was phone for an appointment. The Dublin offices would be holding open evenings next week. And the phone lines were open between 9am and 9pm even at the weekend.

She called the number and a bored-sounding young person called John took her details. The open evenings were being held on Tuesday and Thursday; which of these suited her? She chose the earlier one; the sooner she got going on this one the better.

So the following Tuesday at 7pm, Sorcha was walking past the Shelbourne on Stephen's Green in a smart suit and a new pair of shoes, towards the offices for her interview. She approached the line of large grey buildings on one side of the green and saw the company's logo on the wall, which confirmed she was in the right place. Inside, the reception area was decorated in marble and gold. Irish paintings hung on the walls, which gave the room a familiar feel, but Sorcha felt the place was a bit much. For half a second, she thought of backing out, but she gave her name to the security guard at the desk and waited to see what would happen next. A group of people occupied the red velvet chairs placed underneath the paintings. Some were young guys with expressionless faces dressed in smart but drab-coloured suits or girls dressed impeccably and absorbed in themselves.

Sorcha was pleased to see a couple of ordinary people dressed in street-clothes who had obviously just come to see what this was all about. There was silence as nobody made any attempt at conversation.

The double-doors at one end of the room opened and a well-dressed man and woman entered. The man welcomed them and introduced himself as the manager of their call centre operation where the vacancies were based. It was situated on the fourth floor of the building. "This is Brenda," he said, indicating his companion who was dressed in a navy suit and looked like she would much rather be somewhere else.

"She works in our HR department and she'll be taking you on a tour of the building. Then you'll be given information and application forms to fill out, depending on what you think of us."

He motioned to Brenda, who came alive all of a sudden. She clapped her hands together, and said, "I'm so pleased to welcome you all to our offices. We'll be going upstairs in a moment but first, I have to issue you all with security passes so you can access the rest of the building." She seemed to be trying too hard as she handed out the badges. Perhaps she'd had a long day and this was unpaid overtime. She clicked her own badge at the security tag by the double-doors and held them open as Sorcha and her group filed through.

Brenda instructed half of the group to take the elevator and she led the others like the Pied Piper up the stairs to the fourth floor. They regrouped and she led them around a large room divided into rows of small cubicles, some of which were occupied by people talking on the phone or writing on pads of paper, talking all the time.

"So this is our call centre. There aren't many people here right now as it's the evening shift but normally it's very busy. We're doing very well which is why we're looking for more people to join us."

She smiled a huge smile at the group as she said this. The group nodded and took in the atmosphere. It all seemed very relaxed and no one paid any attention as the small band of people trotted past. Quotes from great thinkers had been inscribed at key points on the walls to motivate the staff. Brenda pointed at this and smiled again. "Some wonderful quotes there."

She led them to a quiet section of the room, which was full of empty pods. "OK, everyone gather round. This is an example of a script that you would use in here." She held up a sheet of paper.

"Mainly, what we do is call existing customers and ask them if they would be interested in our services. We can send them information if they want. And if they apply, then that's a sale. You would use this script at all times on the phone." She passed round the sheet of paper and then described the desk and its apparel. "Each desk is the same although some people decorate theirs differently." She laughed and held up a furry toy that someone had left on top of the computer.

"And the managers are very approachable. We call each other associates. Everyone is an associate." She said the word again. "Sometimes, if we've had a good day and reached our targets, the managers have even been known to come onto the floor and serve ice-cream to everyone."

She said this like as if it was the greatest thing on earth. Then she clapped her hands together again and said out loud, "Isn't this great? Everybody come together and let's have a group hug!" and she stretched her arms out. She was really getting carried away. Nobody moved. But when it came round to question time, several people raised their hands. A late middle-aged man asked how soon he could start. For all her efforts to convey that the company was a fun place to work, Brenda's smile seemed to disappear when he said this and she told him he would have to apply for an interview first and complete the necessary stages for selection.

They trooped back downstairs again, this time to the boardroom. They could help themselves to refreshments while they filled in application forms. Sorcha took a form and scribbled down as many details as she could. She gave this with a copy of her CV to Brenda who was collecting the forms. Her smile had an edge to it as the time approached 8pm, and as she waved everyone out the door, she almost seemed glad that they were going.

Sorcha didn't feel enthusiastic about the position but needed a start. She wasn't used to the lengthy procedures that companies took to hire staff and knew there could be different stages that lay ahead. But she kept checking the post-box anyway. On Thursday morning, she found a letter with the company's logo on the front. She ripped open the letter, expecting the worst. But it was good news: she was to attend an interview on Tuesday at 2pm. 'Yes!' Sorcha thought, and put the letter in a safe place.

The following Tuesday afternoon, she found herself back in the reception room sitting on a red velvet couch and staring at the marble floor. A neatly dressed blonde woman who spoke with an English accent greeted her. "I'm Rosemary," she said, shaking her hand, "pleased to meet you, Sorcha". They clicked themselves through the double-doors again and took the lift up to the second floor this time. It had the same layout: rows of pods, all of which were empty. It seemed strange but Rosemary didn't bat an eyelid. She took a seat at an empty desk that was not part of a pod and Sorcha sat at the other side, relieved that the meeting was going to be this informal. Rosemary explained that this was a preliminary interview and if she were successful, she would be called for a second interview. Depending on the outcome of that, she would either be offered a job with the company or not.

Sorcha's heart sank but she tried her best in the next half-an-hour to answer questions about her work experience to date and her college achievements, with Rosemary scribbling notes. She hadn't a lot of experience of job interviews, and began to wish she'd practised first. When Rosemary asked her to describe herself in five words, she remembered that Isabelle had once compared her to Phoebe, a character on the sit-com Friends, because of her laidback attitude and immediately said without thinking, "I've been told I'm easygoing." The blonde woman looked up from her notes, and stared at her.

Sorcha thought quickly and scrabbled together a few more words that seemed to be more acceptable like reliable, hard-working, and considerate. The woman asked for examples of this in her behaviour and continued writing. Rosemary seemed to become doubtful and then reality started to set in as Sorcha realised the competition for these jobs could be fierce.

Finally, it was all over. Rosemary gathered up her files and they walked downstairs together. At reception, they shook hands again and

Rosemary thanked her warmly for coming in. Sorcha left the building in a hurry and walked swiftly to the comfort of the busy pedestrian Grafton Street. It hadn't gone well, really, and she knew that she had a slim chance of getting called back. She stood at the window of Thornton's chocolatier and gazed in at the array of sweets. She wouldn't mind guzzling a few handfuls of those right now. But she turned away and continued up the street. The shops were thronged with people searching for the right outfit or some music or health product. Sorcha walked to the end of the street then turned back to go home.

Everyone seemed to be working in recruitment these days. Karen had mentioned that Grainne was planning to join a recruitment agency when she came off maternity leave. She would be a big loss to the charity but her new employers had offered her a nice package. And as Sorcha came onto College Green, she passed by the offices of Marlborough, the largest recruitment company in the country, which had recently been floated on the stock exchange. The property shop in the next building listed steadily growing prices for their houses on sale.

Things were changed slowly in the city and Sorcha knew she had to get moving and couldn't rely on the interview alone. It would be an idea to contact a few of the job agencies around and see what they had on offer. Her first foray into that area had spurred her on to try more.

That evening, she made a list of agencies; some based in town and some in her local area. She delivered CVs and letters to half-a-dozen addresses. Looking around the flat afterwards, she tried to feel hopeful. The room was full of items owned by the couple and she had to admit she had hopes of settling down in the next five years.

A couple of days went past and she'd heard nothing. Thoughts were going through her head like how hard it was to really know what was going on job wise. Her applications could have been binned and she was worried that her endeavours would not pay off. She lay in her room one evening, looking at the white walls, and listening to Dirty Three, a CD she'd picked up after she'd seen the trio play in Whelan's.

The instrumentals were pleasant but her mind was elsewhere and she wasn't getting anything from it. As she switched it off, she could hear the phone ringing in the hallway. Sorcha leapt up and answered it. A well spoken, middle-aged woman said, "Good morning. Can I speak to Sorcha please?"

"This is Sorcha."

"Oh, good evening. My name is Maura McDonald. I'm calling from the finance company. I believe you applied to one of our recent notices."

Sorcha had some recollection of having done so. "That's right. I did."

"Would it be possible for me to run through a short interview with you over the phone?" the woman continued. "It should only take ten minutes."

Sorcha said it would be fine. The woman ran through her experience to date and asked her why she was interested in working for the company. Sorcha heard herself wheel out the old chestnut 'I'm looking for a challenge' but the woman seemed unconvinced, so she plunged into a lengthy explanation about her desire to join a large organisation for the opportunity to grow as a person. This seemed to sit better.

At the end, the woman said, "Well, I have no problem putting you forward for a further interview. But you'll be contacted by us and given details on that later." She thanked Sorcha warmly and then hung up.

Early on Monday morning, Sorcha walked through rows and rows of council housing in the Dublin 8 area, searching for her location. She had walked along by St Patrick's Cathedral first of all but now she was in a residential area, which didn't seem right. Then she saw the modern reddish building: construction workers were still swarming over parts of it, adding some finishing touches. She could imagine herself working here; she could see herself trotting happily to work each day from the bus stop, having taken an IMP into town.

Inside, the receptionist was friendly; obviously, she was new here too and eager to make a good impression. Sorcha took a seat and took in her surroundings. The interior was huge with trailing plants everywhere; she noticed a Basil Blackshawe painting of a horse on the wall this time and remembered an exhibition she'd seen.

A girl in a dark blue uniform approached her and shook her hand. This was Linda, who worked in HR and would be conducting the interview with another woman who managed the call centre. They flew upstairs in a glass elevator; Linda seemed to find it amusing almost as if the lift was just a bit of fun but she kept a tight hold of her folders. Sorcha went along with the joke.

Upstairs, they entered a small meeting room, where a shorthaired woman in a plain dark blue suit sat expressionless and barely made any sign of recognition when Sorcha shook her hand. Linda went through her CV first of all, Sorcha again painstakingly answering questions. The woman's expressionless face changed into a smirk when Sorcha stumbled here and there trying to match her work experience with the requirements of the job.

Sorcha thought on her way outside again that things didn't look hopeful. The role involved dealing with customers for some kind of motor insurance though, so she didn't think she was missing anything. She thought perhaps the stilted environment had made her babble at certain stages of the interview as she tried to fit herself into a role that didn't appeal to her but it was all that was available.

That afternoon, she also had another interview with a sales company near the POD on Harcourt Street. Perhaps in keeping with its locale, this office was considerably more relaxed; a friendly handyman said hello as he fixed a light bulb as she waited for her grilling. The interviewer was again a young woman who took notes in a boardroom downstairs. There were figures on a whiteboard at one end of the table and Sorcha could feel her eyes drifting there every so often. Perhaps her lack of attention was noticeable, as the woman didn't seem too convinced of her interest in the job.

As she left the building and crossed over the street, she reluctantly decided to go to her next and last meeting for the day, which was in a recruitment agency's office in Hatch St, just round the corner. She found the building, a beautiful old three-storey house; inside, it was furnished much like someone was living there, were it not for the continuous stream of people in smart outfits clutching clipboards. Sorcha filled out a couple of forms and was then greeted by Suzanne, a friendly brunette, who took her into what would once have been a family dining room. A huge table took up most of the floor space and expensive pieces of china and silver were visible in glass cases along the walls. Sorcha sat on one of the chairs and Suzanne sat across from her, smiling pleasantly.

"Well, Sorcha, I thought that you might be interested in a start up project which we're recruiting for at the moment. The company has just relocated here and are planning to use Dublin as the base for its European operations," she said.

Sorcha felt like Homer Simpson being asked to locate Sector 7G and prevent a meltdown as the woman continued. The company's plans for their Dublin site were a little more than she could handle at this stage in the day. The company was an internationally renowned organisation dealing in office services. Sorcha had a vague idea of what they did and was carried along by her interviewer's enthusiasm.

"If you're successful, Sorcha, you'll be working for the UK section of the company. They are planning on moving other European country teams over here but that will be a later stage. Do you have any languages?"

Sorcha mentioned her school French and German. But she had spent a lot of time meeting people from different backgrounds in her current job. She thought that something in recruitment would be a good idea. In the changing environment, she thought it would be an interesting role. The girl agreed and put her forward for interview, smiling broadly as she stood on the steps of the building, telling Sorcha she would hear from her soon. Sorcha had had a long day and she hopped on a bus that would take her straight home.

She plodded slowly from the bus stop to the flat and removed her interview uniform. Standing in a cool shower, she closed her eyes and put the power on full blast to rinse herself clean. She started to feel like a person again as she put on comfortable clothes and lay on the bed. She fell asleep without trying and when she woke up, it was dark outside. She had work again tomorrow so she forced herself to sleep till morning.

The girls were discussing what to do for the weekend and had decided to start early by having a long lunch at the local Italian restaurant before looking at the shops. At lunch, Sorcha checked her phone for messages of which there were none. She was suffering from a bad headache and was quite happy not to have to chase around. Nobody had asked any questions about her day off so she didn't discuss it and ate her pasta quietly while listening to the conversation.

She had not pinned her hopes on a job just yet and had resigned herself to working for the charity until something else came along. On her way home in the evening, she stopped at the church off Grafton Street and lit a couple of candles in the hope that everything would go ok. If she mentioned this habit to her workmates, they would laugh at such nonsense but she realised she would need all the help she could get.

Sorcha summarily checked her phone over the next couple of days got a message from the agency in Hatch Street late one evening. She was surprised but supposed that the recruitment agency was working overtime to meet the needs of its client. The message was from Rachel and she had picked up Sorcha's application. She wanted to know if Sorcha could attend an interview that Wednesday. It would be held in an office block just off the South Circular Road. "They have all your details," Rachel said, "You'll be interviewed by a couple of people from the company itself. We're not sure who it will be, but reception will show you where to go."

It turned out that they did have positions for HR administrators as the company was planning a major expansion within Dublin the coming year. Sorcha jotted the details down on a scrap of paper and jumped up and down. Who would have thought that she would be frothing at the mouth like this for a job? It had started to look exciting with official notepaper and the role had masses of potential, no doubt.

She hoped no-one would mind if she took some more time off. She did get annual leave but two days taken this way might arouse suspicion. She shook off any concerns about this and made plans to get to the interview. By now, she was sick of the process but she duly signed her name, took a name tag and waited her turn like the rest of the applicants. But she decided she'd give it one last chance so she donned her uniform again and took a walk down the sunny South Circular to the building.

The company was renting some rooms upstairs from which to conduct interviews; for a giant corporation, it was all very low key. She chatted to a blonde, curly-haired Southsider who was playing receptionist to fill in the time. Every so often, a man or woman in a suit would call to the door and a candidate would be chosen and ushered out the door.

A woman introduced as Mary sat at a desk, taking notes. After a bit of role play and questions, the interviewer Murray asked her about her experience working with the charity. She again highlighted that she had been very much involved with new employees within the organisation and would like to focus on this in her new role. The charity had been a low budget operation and she had met quite a few job applicants and had held informal interviews with them in the meeting rooms downstairs. She had used a database and had some other office skills.

He asked, 'Would you be ready to start tomorrow?' as if her life depended on it, looking at her for any signs of indecision. She wasn't sure of success as she left but the interviewer saw her to the door and seemed reasonably friendly as he shook her hand goodbye.

Suzanne at the agency had said that the company took people in on relatively low salaries and allowed them to develop and grow with the company. Maybe she had a chance.

───◆───

Sorcha followed up on the other jobs just in case but she needn't have worried. On Monday, she found a large white envelope in the post-box. It was a letter welcoming her to the company and wishing her well with her future career there, signed by the HR director. She read it through a couple of times then put it away.

To celebrate her new-found employment and her departure from the charity, Sorcha organised a meal at a new Chinese restaurant in Rathmines. It had been reviewed in the Irish Times but was only half full for the length of the meal. Gill had to leave early so left a small tip for the Asian dreadlocked waitress with the Scottish accent. Sorcha had felt some tension from Isabelle since she'd announced her news. "I just thought you would have said something," she said later.

Sorcha replied, "I just wasn't sure what the outcome would be. You know what it's like. It's touch and go."

Isabelle looked confused. "She means she wasn't sure she'd get the job," said Karen.

"Oh, well, congratulations." She gave Sorcha a hug.

"If there are French jobs next year, I'll put you up front."

"Don't bother. No offence, but I think I'll be looking elsewhere." The French girl grimaced and sucked on a cigarette. She was prepared to work for a living but, having worked for a number of political organisations in France; she was suspicious of the activities of large companies.

They splurged on a taxi home and Isabelle got out first. "Don't forget us. Come over some time and let us know how you're getting on."

They waved goodbye and waited until Isabelle had gone inside then drove over the bridge to the flat. The canal was quiet at night-time. There was no noise apart from a couple of ducks quacking before going to sleep. Back in the flat, they boiled the kettle for tea and chatted quietly. "I hate this herbal stuff," Sorcha noted, "but it's good for digestion. And sleep, I hope."

"You mean you can't sleep, you're so excited about the job?" Karen laughed.

"And nervous. I'm so glad to have the interviews over with. Never again, but I'm joking." Sorcha said. "I'll see where this takes me and I can always leave if it gets too much."

"I really admire you," Karen said, "you have such guts. I can't wait till I'm qualified and I can start working and have a proper set of benefits.

"You'll be able to give me loads of advice. As long as you don't change once you join the corporation. You'll be edging past us in a smart new car while me and Rob are stuck in our shoddy secondhand."

"Hard to say." Sorcha had no idea what was ahead. "You have my permission to tell me if you notice anything. I'm just anxious to get going although it will take me some time to learn everything."

They went to sleep. Sorcha lay on top of her quilt for a while, feeling like the success story of the moment.

Chapter 3

A tinny sound came from the computer just as a miniature envelope appeared on the bottom right of the screen. It was an e-mail from the help desk, advising Sorcha of a password for the database system she had been learning to use. It was a useful way of tracking the work done for the day. Just then, a mobile phone rang. Lisa the manager looked up and quietly told the owner to switch it off. Lorna, another new starter, apologised with a smile and did as she was told. It was just the four of them for now: Gemma was the other girl who had started at the business park that week. They were the HR administration team and shared a floor with the management team and their staff in the main building. They had been warned of keeping quiet at the induction meeting: the managers had attended briefly and were introduced as John the HR director; Alan the General Manager and the Financial Manager Daniel. They had called in quickly on their way to a meeting and welcomed the girls warmly.

Apart from that, the meeting had consisted of an overview of the company and its progress in the world market with a couple of short films showing the new products on the shop floor. They had been introduced to Lisa, a blonde woman who lived locally and had quite a bit of experience in personnel and people management. She was friendly but also watchful of time-wasting. They had a quick training session then were given tasks to do. Sorcha had been filing applications and printing off letters all morning. She didn't really know what to expect and had decided to just go along with the schedule as it was decided upon.

She had had time at the coffee break to chat to her two co-workers. Tall and blonde Lorna was a mixture of sophistication and working-class good humour. Gemma was rotund and prickly but seemed like she could have her good days. The girls had been to college together and knew a lot of the same people.

"Sorcha, you don't mind if we go to lunch at the same time, do you? I know you're new too but I think Lisa said she goes at the same time," Lorna asked her anxiously.

Sorcha shrugged. It didn't matter. She was still finding her way around and didn't feel so insecure that she couldn't chat to someone new. Lisa was at a meeting but they knew that the department needed someone to answer the phones. There were a couple of calls but nothing she couldn't handle. The managers had a PA nearby so if she got stuck she could ask for help. Lisa came back and had a quick sandwich at her desk. "You can go ahead now, Sorcha," she said, smiling, as the girls returned.

She took her lunch on the last break at half past one. She was doubtful that there would be anything left at this stage but they still had most of the main courses on offer. The canteen staff had introduced meals from the home countries to welcome the foreign language teams that were starting up within the company. Sorcha took a quick look at the menu then leaned into the hot food counter area and said, "Swedish meatballs, please." The assistant heaped some meatballs and sauce onto a plate and handed it to her to put it on a tray.

"Anything else?" he enquired. "Rice, potatoes, vegetables?" He pointed at the array of food in bowls and serving dishes on the counter. Sorcha shook her head. She took a bread roll and some butter and went to pay.

The catering staff made friendly greetings as usual, getting in the spirit of things, although the cashier's hat looked worse for wear. They had been at work since early morning and were about to clock off for the day. Sorcha paid and sat at a table with a small vase of plastic flowers in the centre. A girl was already stacking plates onto trays so she ate quickly. There were still some people finishing off their meals. She recognised some faces as people had left their bank details to be processed with the HR office during the week.

The admin team had been taken on a tour of the building after they had arrived. The new recruits were upstairs for the moment but would soon be relocated in the new rooms on the ground floor. The existing office space was undergoing a facelift for the new operations. They heard drilling and hammering constantly although it was kept at a bearable level during the day. There were English speaking teams including Irish people who dealt with the UK service market, and also some Nordic teams. There would be teams from all over Europe eventually, the larger countries like France, Germany and Spain migrating later.

Some of the teams were already live and the agents helped to train newcomers who sat beside them and listened on headphones as they chatted to customers in the home country. The company eventually planned to employ over a thousand people at their Irish base.

As part of the induction process, each new staff member attended a special meeting often attended by a company manager and usually facilitated by the HR Department. The new starters filled out forms as the projector played out the usual presentations on the company's history, current profit status and operations. Each team split into sub-groups for a while to relieve the monotony and act out situations they might encounter on a daily basis with their customers. A large red-haired Corkonian lifted the phone in one corner and chatted in German about a pretend complaint to his teammate who was taking the matter very seriously. Eventually, the Irishman made a quick joke to lighten the mood and everyone who heard him laughed.

The customer service staff had to deal with consumable orders but would also be working on a RCA system to fix machine complaints. To assist with their information, the starters were given a number of hours training on the various products. Most people seemed only too glad to leave the small, airless training room and go back to the office floor or the laidback environs of the canteen. A line of young Irish girls tottered through the reception space after one gruelling day, grimacing and complaining.

"I hate this place," the leader said, her long dark hair tied back in a ponytail. "It's worse than me last job." One of them was still wearing a headset from her practice session and tore it off, handing it to Sorcha who checked it before giving it to the girl's trainer. The supervisor was sitting behind her computer with half a sandwich on her plate. She took the headset with a smile and kept tapping in the latest statistics.

"Working in our department is a great way to get to know people. Don't worry. It seems like a lot of organisation but these guys know what they're doing. They've dealt with these kinds of moves before; John certainly has on a European level." Lisa was upbeat. "There are a lot of opportunities here but I'm not saying any more as I don't want to lose you three to another manager in some department. OK?"

"As if," Lorna said later, as they left for the day. "I wouldn't work in customer services or technical support and there isn't really anything else until they bring in the sales element and that could take a couple of years. They still have some offices running in the UK. What we do is as well paid as the language teams anyway. Plus there should be room for some serious progression once this whole thing gets going."

Gemma usually drove Lorna home as they lived in the same area. Sorcha took the long bus journey into town. She was tired by the end of the week. They had had their meeting at 9am on Monday, but since then it had been 8.30am starts. This meant leaving the flat at 7.15 at the latest. An IMP took her to town where she caught the only bus going in the direction of the business park at the GPO. So far there had been no hitches but it was strange standing there at the GPO at an ungodly hour waiting for a cranking double-decker to take her to work.

"I just wonder what it will be like in a couple of months when the new groups start. You can't have half the workforce crammed onto one bus," Sorcha laughed.

Lorna looked at her with a frustrated look. She had to use public transport once in a while as Gemma went to the dentist or left early for some reason.

"Just as long as they don't drop us in the middle of a housing estate," she said disparagingly as the bus drove past a burnt out car. "This area is a blackspot, you know. It's not safe. I was worried coming out here but I think it's ok if you hop on a bus in the evening and get the hell out." There was a shopping centre but none of them had any real money to spend just yet.

Lisa broached the subject with management following a meeting with the administration group. All of the employees were invited to a short meeting where the matter was discussed. It would be looked into as one of the foreigners had been slightly injured in an accident that very morning. He had been caught in a closing door as an already crowded bus had taken off from town.

Lorna was adamant. She said, "As soon as I'm paid, I'm getting a car. You should move out here, Sorcha. At least you'd be close to work. That's what I'm planning to do next year but I can't afford to right now."

Sorcha checked out the neighbourhood on the way home. They drove through Blanchardstown and Castleknock on the 38 route which was full of 1970s modern housing estates. Moving house would not solve the problem of the limited bus service which was a worry. Karen was home in the evenings sometimes and they swapped stories about the events of the day. Karen was worried when she heard about the accident and encouraged her to look at the papers. She found herself looking through the Evening Herald in her spare time and making appointments to view rooms.

Then she had another commitment. Lisa had announced an Open Day in a city centre hotel to attract new employees. "We're not a very international city yet so we have to recruit within the countries in the case of some languages like the Benelux. But we are having a recruitment drive on Saturday to communicate with the foreigners living here. And anyone else who is interested."

Rob was cynical when he heard and said that the only reason the company had moved here was to cut costs and make use of the government tax breaks. "They always plamas the employees and tell them they're here for the educated young populace, etc.," he said. Sorcha didn't take what he said too seriously and didn't really feel like she had a choice. The job was the best she could find and she had no desire to go hunting again.

The personnel team was obliged to show up at the recruitment fair and would be working in conjunction with the professional hiring team who would be holding first round interviews during the day. Sorcha set her alarm again and arrived at the hotel in the heart of Temple Bar on the dot of 10am. Lisa had been sent to Galway to take care of its recruitment day. Gemma and Lorna soon arrived and they donned t-shirts and caps bearing the company logo.

There were posters and flyers everywhere advertising the company. There were two television sets playing and replaying a short informative film about the company in either corner in the main room downstairs. The girls were put here to catch people as they came through the exhibition. People began to stream in almost immediately and they were kept busy all day, welcoming visitors, answering questions and ushering the interested applicants upstairs for interviews. Sorcha found it hard to cover everything but she did her best.

"What is this job about?" an Italian girl asked her, pointing to an information sheet for customer administration jobs. Sorcha told her as much as possible about the role, that it was phone-based, there was lots of training involved and she would be working within a team with great opportunities.

"How much does it pay?" the girl asked when she had spoken with her friend. Sorcha told her the basic earnings and the Italian made a face. "I'll think about it," she said, and took an application form.

A couple of black guys with French accents approached her at one stage. "Any jobs apart from customer services?" one of them asked. Sorcha didn't know much about some of the areas but she gave it a go. She told him about the openings in IT and technical support. His eyes lit up. "Yes, that's what I'm interested in. And my friend wants to use his business courses."

Sorcha scanned the room quickly trying to locate a familiar face that could talk to them. She noticed one of the IT guys already chatting to a group. "Here, take this information pack and chat to Frank." She pointed to the group. She gave his friend another pack which gave him details on their finance department. They thanked her and moved away.

When the show finally closed for the day, the girls tidied up and had a quick drink in the bar. "I'm wrecked," Lorna said, "I don't think I'll make it home this evening. If I had any money I'd book a room and stay here."

Sorcha agreed with her. "It was like being thrown in the deep end. Thank God it's over."

"I need a foot massage," Lorna said, groaning and holding her feet. "And a back massage."

"There is no way I'm doing this again," Gemma said. "Keep it quiet, but if they had asked me to climb those stairs one more time, I would have gone on a permanent tea break. They almost made us come here today and they know they can get away with it. There are jobs to be had in the future and if you don't play along, they won't happen."

"Some of the people were so rude. You could bend over backwards and they wouldn't care."

"It's probably the language barrier, as they call it. Hopefully next time, they'll have more staff to pick from to work these things. Judging by the amount of applications that we're processing, they'll need to get more people. I think they said some of the jobs were for personnel staff. Fingers crossed."

They went their separate ways. Sorcha walked as it was such a pleasant evening and she needed the fresh air. She planned to take a cab along the way but she was back at the flat in forty minutes. There was no-one about so she took a bath. It would take a mallet to have her relax, she thought, after the activity of the day. Her bags were still unpacked in the temporary room and left to one side. She decided she would check the papers after work on Monday and find a new home. She put all her laundry from the week in the washing machine.

Rob and Karen arrived home together and offered to cook dinner. Rob played the part of chef, like Jamie Oliver, Karen's favourite TV cook, boiling up pasta and emptying a huge jar of tomato sauce into a pan as the vegetables and fish fried on the hob. He took pleasure in doling out amounts of food and checking that they all had equal amounts. "We can't really afford to cook from scratch but we try," Karen joked. She made comments about his culinary skills as Rob sat down. But she was only joking. Rob was her sweetheart and his dark good looks and practical personality meant she had little to complain about. They sat side by side and Rob asked, "How are you getting on, Sorcha?"

Sorcha had a mouthful of pasta. She gave him the thumbs up. He looked relieved. Sorcha told them about the open day.

"That sounds like a busy day," Karen said, tossing her hair out of her food.

"Yeah, a surprising amount of people I've never met before." She had bumped into an old college friend on the stairs but had no knowledge of the other applicants.

"You don't really see a lot of foreigners in Dublin apart from the tourists. It's not like London where every second person is either black or Asian or both," Rob said. "Most people come here on holidays to get a taste of shamrock or the blarney."

"Well, the city has changed a lot even since I moved here five years ago," Sorcha said. She wasn't sure if it was a good thing. But she knew life in some of the European countries could be tough as house prices escalated and average income earners were pushed out of the market.

"We all are after the same stuff, that's it," Rob said. "We'd like to get a house eventually and we'd better hurry before it's all taken. No offence, take your time, but you should get looking for a new house as soon as possible. There are big changes on the way."

On Sunday, Sorcha got up at midday and read the papers all afternoon, the window of her room open as a cool breeze blew through it. Outside, some people were visiting the graveyard and she could hear them talking softly to each other. She left them to it and by evening, she was ready for a good night's sleep. She had enjoyed her time here and would be sad to leave. Her bags were stacked together in preparation for a move and every time she needed something, she had to hunt through all her things. Plus she knew she couldn't impose on her friends for much longer. The Dublin 15 area had plenty of accommodation to rent, mostly estates of three or four bedroom houses. There wasn't a lot of variation and the rent seemed reasonable enough. She found that some of the adverts were linked to Swedes or other nationalities working in the area.

She found a room in a shared house on her second evening of searching. The two guys living there were working in the local branch of an Irish bank. James was the older of the two and had moved to Dublin after a stint in London. Jason had just finished college and was a new recruit. He had the box room. Sorcha was offered the middle-sized room at the back. It had plenty of room and the main road was ten minutes walk. Lorna congratulated her. "It's so much easier living with boys. I'll have to arrange something myself very soon."

"We'll be out to visit and see how you're getting on in the country," Karen's e-mail said. She had opened a new account and had been sending e-mails everywhere on their home computer. They collected her stuff in the evening. James had offered to drive her into town and bring her things to the house.

Sorcha was glad as she was running low on funds. Once she had paid a month's rent and deposit, had covered her expenses at the flat and had bought some new clothes, there wasn't a lot left. She had just a couple of hundred until the end of the month. Even her salary, when it arrived, seemed so small. It was her first real paycheque as she had always signed for the community scheme.

The couple had not come back that evening so they locked the door and Sorcha put the keys back through the letterbox. She had returned the mail, saying she planned to visit when she had time. They drove through the Phoenix Park slowing down at intervals to avoid grazing deer that tended to stray onto the road at night-time.

Her new room was the same as she'd remembered. Together, they took everything upstairs and Sorcha sorted out things that she would need right away. She put a couple of photos on the wall and a vase on the windowsill. The back yard was pitch-dark but she could make out neighbours putting their kids to bed or having a cup of tea in the kitchen. The bathroom was next to her room. She checked the shower times with her new housemates then shut the door.

James dropped her off in the village the next morning but she still had to join the commuter crush on the bus, which was full as usual. There had been announcements made of improved services but it would take time. She met Lorna in the park first thing. She was complaining about the size of her wage packet and had been gloomy all week. This was only her second real job after she had spent four years getting a business qualification. She had decided to stay in Dublin where her family was but the salary scale was miniscule in comparison to what she could have earned in London.

They had spent the past few days processing the recent applications and the department had gone crazy arranging interviews and meeting potential new starts in the little rooms downstairs. There were people sitting there now as they entered the main hall, filling out application forms or staring ahead, looking impatient. Sorcha went back downstairs as soon as she could and made herself a decent coffee. She had finally been trained on the new system which centralised all the aspects of their administration. It didn't reduce the paperwork involved but it meant everything was stored neatly in one place. Fuelled by caffeine, she tapped happily for a couple of hours until her legs told her to take a break.

She was on her way back to her desk when Lorna said excitedly, "Hey, we're going to London next week. Lisa just told me. It's just the three of us. We'll have some training but it means overnight stay in a hotel." She was in her element and was eventually told to calm down by Lisa as the noise level rose.

Gemma told her to shush and giggled to herself as she sensed her friend's enthusiasm. Lisa was also keen to arrange a night out. It could wait until they got back, she said. She left to sit with a manager and

Gemma leaned over her desk and said, "They are going to have to send you home early if you don't quieten down. Look at me, and look at Sorcha. We're taking this all in our stride."

"One word," Lorna said, "shopping." She rubbed her hands with glee.

Lisa returned and the chatter stopped. The next day, they got their travel arrangements. They would be flying into Heathrow and would have to take a taxi to the office which was in the area. The hotel had yet to be decided but would be most likely the Radisson at the airport.

"I can't wait," Lorna said, looking at the documents. "I just hope we get a bit of time to look around the shops. I've got my wages still. I won't be going for that car loan just yet."

Sorcha was secretly pleased. She had hoped that this new job would be the start of better things. But she still had a mountain of paperwork to finish. It was laborious work, tapping in every detail and ensuring that all the correct paperwork had been provided with each application. She was fast becoming an expert on foreign names. It was interesting to note the diversity of the applicants. Some had hardly worked before and others had ten years of experience. She noticed the Corkonian's face again on his photo ID. He had worked in Austria on construction jobs and had obviously come home to settle, choosing an office job as a way to capitalise on his language skills. She was working so fast that she didn't notice the time. The girls chatted as they made their way out of the building at five pm and waved goodbye. There was only one downside to the trip: the fact that they had been booked on the 7.30 flight.

Sorcha woke on the morning of the trip to the sound of a shrill alarm ringing. It was a quarter past five and the taxi would be here at six am. She dressed quickly and grabbed her handheld travel bag which had been packed the night before.

She reached the bottom of the stairs just as the taxi appeared, its headlights glowing in the early morning haze. "That's an early start," the driver said. "Where are you going?" Sorcha explained and he said very little for the rest of the journey which suited her fine. She was nervous that she had forgotten something but she had gone through the list several times. She could always borrow if she needed anything.

Lorna and Gemma had just arrived at the airport when she got there. Gemma was dressed up in a suit, a winter coat slung over her shoulder. Lorna had a long furry jacket on over some smart pants. They both had roller bags and were drinking coffee as they greeted her.

The airport was busy with people rushing to and fro as they queued for their tickets. "I hope to God there's no mix up. I heard that it happened to someone in the finance department. They had to go back to the office for the day. I'd kill them."

"Sadly, she's also the one giving you an appraisal and who'll be getting you a better job when you're here a few more months," Gemma joked.

At last they were off. The plane journey took less than an hour and then they arrived in Heathrow to the sight of dozens of planes taking off to faraway destinations. They negotiated the exit path and took a black cab which drove slowly out of the terminus and onto the main road. It was freezing cold and they huddled in the back seat.

It was well over nine am when they arrived at the office which was a big grey block, one of two; the second had a For Sale sign attached. They signed the visitor's book and waited for their contact to come and get them. The receptionist seemed OK to let them leave their things behind the desk.

"I'd be a bit nervous with all of these Irish people coming over here and leaving their bags around," Lorna said in a low voice.

They stood up as Louise the trainer approached and greeted them. "How are you doing? Did you have a good flight?" She was a twenty something with blonde curly hair and a wide smile. They nodded and followed her through the security gate and upstairs to the training room on the first floor. Louise asked if they wanted coffee before she closed the door. She went to get glasses of water.

Lorna said, yawning, "I can't wait to get to the hotel. I'm just going to get through today and relax this evening. We should go for drinks while we're here."

She stopped talking as Louise returned with a jug of water and some cups. She was in charge of running through the policies and procedures with the personnel staff. She also had to show them how to use an archaic system which would soon be replaced.

They didn't have a training centre in Dublin yet but at least it meant that they could have a tour of the UK offices. The rooms were already outdated and resembled their own work space. The desks were all but deserted, except for a couple of people talking on the phone. "The top floor is still in use but this floor has been emptied more or less," Louise told them. She introduced them to Gary who had worked in sales. He was seated at a computer, tapping intermittently and playing with a stress ball. He looked up as they approached and smiled, just barely.

"Gary's one of the lucky ones. He's just found a job. And it's still in sales, which is wonderful."

He nodded without saying anything, clearly embarrassed to be the centre of attention.

"Gary's always been good at his job." Louise said as they turned to move on. Gary gave a glimmer of a smile and went back to his work.

A blonde girl working on one side of the room looked at Gary sympathetically as the little group went upstairs. "There are some sales jobs within the company but not everyone will be kept on," Louise said.

Upstairs, the layout was the same with a group of people working at desks, all looking up as the group entered the room. "My goodness," Sorcha said at lunch, "it felt like a showdown. I thought someone might attack us with the looks we were getting."

"I was warned about this but it's not so bad. Just ignore it," Lorna said.

They were sitting in a nearby pub on the riverfront eating chicken and chips and baked potatoes. It was an old building tarted up to serve the needs of the local business environment. The floor leaned to one side and there was a row of slot machines in one corner. The clientele were young people in for lunch or business people having an afternoon pint. Piped music was playing recent hits in the background.

"One man's loss is another man's gain," said Gemma.

"I wonder what we should do tonight. I'm so tired now. I don't want to do anything."

"Save your energy for the shopathon tomorrow. We can go out tomorrow night."

They hurried back to the office block. Louise had been delayed in a meeting so they waited outside, strolling in the park for a few minutes. It was sunny now although it was October. A couple of worried-looking executives came walking out of the empty car park and entered the building. Louise beckoned them inside and they went back to the training room for another session.

Soon, it was time to leave. They were quiet in the taxi as it approached the airport again, this time dropping them at the hotel entrance. The modern glass building indicated luxury and they booked in quickly, using their company credit cards. They were staying on the same floor and tiredly went to their rooms.

"Call us if you're around later and we'll go for a drink" were the last words Sorcha heard as she closed the door to her room.

It was spacious inside and she had TV and a large bathroom to herself. She lit an aromatherapy candle in its holder and lay down on the double bed to try to sleep. She wasn't exhausted but could do with a nap.

Later, she woke at eight pm and checked her messages. No message had arrived from the girls. She ordered room service and looked out of the window as she waited. She could hear the muffled roar of planes flying overhead. It was quiet though and she switched on the television to watch the news on BBC.

―――◆―――

Next morning, the girls were downstairs having breakfast in the main room. It was full of business people or travellers passing though. She helped herself to scrambled egg and mushrooms from the buffet. Lorna was munching on a piece of toast. "How was your room, Sorcha?" she asked. "It's ok? This makes a change anyway."

She enthused about the facilities in the hotel's leisure centre, "I would love to try the sauna here but I don't think we'll have time so it'll just be some shopping, I think."

At lunch, they went to Pizza Hut which was having a special meal deal. This situated them close to the high street shops. They went in and out of Debenhams, Miss Selfridge and A-Wear and Lorna bought a couple of tops. Only Gemma had been to London before and she was nonchalant about the clothes shops. Inbetween all of the usual brand names, there was a small store selling natural soaps and candles.

The local library was open for business further down the street. They brought their purchases back to the office, shoving the bags into their coats, mindful of parading packages in front of the staff.

That evening, they went for a Chinese meal in the hotel. They ordered proper Asian food and had drinks. "I'm so tempted to put this on my credit card but we'd never get away with it. These have to go back when we go in on Monday," Lorna said.

"I'd love to have gone to a show or something here but we're too far from central London," Sorcha said.

The guys at the next table started chatting midway through the meal. "You're from Dublin, are you?" the older man said. "I've been over there a few times for work." He was in logistics and was bringing around his protégé Mark to show him the ropes. They had a project to work through in the area but lived in Gloucestershire. After the meal, they went to the bar for a couple of hours, the guys eventually running out of polite conversation. They began making lewd jokes as they ordered more pints from the waiter and then the girls made their excuses.

"They were tacky," Lorna said, later. "Imagine waving those notes around acting like he's so important. I'm not that desperate for a drink. I just thought we could meet someone if we were in the bar but no such luck." She made puking sounds as they went back up the stairs and separated.

They had one more day's training before the plane took them back home. Sorcha and the others walked right through Duty Free looking at the perfume and scarves and Lorna took out her card a couple of times. She couldn't resist.

They boarded an hour later than scheduled and the London suburbs were ablaze with light in the winter darkness as they flew home. It was late Friday night when Sorcha finally got back to her house. Jason was sprawled on the sofa after a night's drinking in the pub. She was careful not to make any noise. The kitchen was spotlessly clean as James was unashamedly houseproud. She made some tea and checked the phone for calls missed. There was a message from Isabelle, saying she hoped that everything was OK and that her birthday party was on in town the next weekend. Her brother was over from Paris and they were going to a pub near the Portobello Bridge.

Sorcha left a message for Isabelle, saying that she'd be there but might be late. The following Friday, she arrived for a meal with her workmates at a western style restaurant called Break for the Border. At ten pm she made her excuses and raced down Camden Street to meet the others.

"Hey, you made it," Isabelle said as she came through the door. The pub had the feel of an old watering hole with locals who eyed you suspiciously in case you took their pint. Sorcha ordered a Bacardi and sat on the edge of a seat beside Isabelle. She gave her a card with a voucher for the Body Shop. "Oh, *merci*, thanks very much," Isabelle took it gratefully. Her hair looked newly cut and glossy. "Have you met my brother?" Sorcha nodded at the thin French man sitting beside her, dressed in a casual suit and scarf, who smiled back. "He doesn't speak much English but luckily, my housemate has some French. So, how are you going? How is the job?"

Sorcha updated her with the details of the trip. Isabelle looked envious but remained interested. "We're very busy though," said Sorcha. "It's so hectic. I never get much time to myself in the house. But it won't last forever."

"Well, I'm still at the old office. I've stopped seeing Mick by the way. He's so busy with work that it didn't feel like we saw each other anymore. There are a couple of guys around but I didn't invite anyone to the party."

Sorcha recognised some of the faces and Gill had made it to the pub. "Have you seen her new flat yet? It's gorgeous inside although the complex is a very rough place," Isabelle said. "There have been some reports of muggings. It's very dangerous."

Later, she had introduced Sorcha to an old friend from her waitressing days. The girl had spent a couple of years in Prague and was back in town for a while. Sorcha had met so many people with foreign connections; she wasn't herself as she shook hands and made small talk. They were going onto the Gaiety again and went dancing in one of the rooms where they were playing samba. Marcel stayed in the jazz room. The girls took a breather in the main hall where people were chatting or making out in corners.

"I wouldn't worry about Karen. She has college work and her job," Sorcha said.

"I know, but I get bored on my own. I need some company. My brother is trying to convince me to go back to Paris."

"Is that possible?"

"Well, it's becoming more expensive here all the time. Last weekend, I had to check the total on my bill when I went to the supermarket. I was buying things for my brother's visit. And my contract is up soon as well. There's no more work there and the money will be used to pay creditors. I think the directors are looking for new jobs in the city."

"I can come visit you," Sorcha said.

"Ok, maybe. You know you could have been friendlier, Sorcha, to my mate. She's only over for a few days and she left for some reason. Well, whatever, I just thought you might like to get into town for a change, whatever, Sorcha," she said with a warning tone in her voice.

She had a couple of funny e-mails on her inbox on Monday morning. Karen had forwarded these from Rob's work e-mail. There were a couple of links to humorous websites and a giant smiley face with what looked like strobe lighting on one e-mail. She closed them hurriedly and went on with her work. Sorcha had been told that she would be working with Kathy, the executive in charge of recruiting for the financial services department. Sorcha was glad to have this new responsibility as she liked being busy. Lisa was often overwhelmed by the amount of paperwork coming her way to be processed and was glad when one of the girls offered to help out. They were already discussing the Christmas party which had yet to be arranged.

"One of my friends said that they were all taken to a hotel in the country last year and wined and dined. I know I'm just back from the UK but I wonder what they'll put on for us," Lorna said.

"They're not up and running yet. You'll be lucky to have a meal in a nice hotel and maybe a card to hang up on your mantelpiece."

Lorna decided to ask her boss but Lisa hadn't heard anything so she took on the job of dressing up their cubicles for the festive season. She draped tinsel and bell ornaments over their computers and was ecstatic when the tree went up in the main hall. The ground floor had been populated with staff divided into groups of ten, answering calls from all over Europe and escalating customer complaints. Their desks were soon covered with colourful decking too, and the sounds of tacky Christmas songs could be heard in the canteen as the event grew closer. The managers routinely took visitors from their European offices through the new rooms to show them the outline for the central headquarters.

"There's a real buzz in here," Sorcha overheard the General Manager say cheerily as he swiftly led another group around, chatting all the time, then herding the visitors into a meeting room for discussions.

Sorcha had become friendly with a tall, dark-haired Dutch girl called Dani who had moved over to work for the company and lived near the quays with two workmates. They drove by car to the business park early every morning; the vehicle had been brought in to the country from Holland.

Dani was fluent in three languages and worked in the customer service department serving the Netherlands. She answered calls from machine users who needed to order supplies or book a service. Each team had targets to reach and issued statistics to the centre manager at the end of each week. The company had provided relocation fees and she had been in the personnel department the week before to fill out a form to have these paid back now that she was settled. She had also been to the UK for training like the majority of workers hired.

"What does he mean by *buzz*?" Dani asked. Sorcha explained the term and Dani burst out laughing at her description of worker bees madly scurrying together in the hive.

"OK, it is busy but not in a good way. A couple of my team have already left and they are finding it hard to replace them. It has become really busy since they opened all of the phone lines but I need this job to get experience.

"I just thought it would be a change from Amsterdam which is so expensive now. I can't afford to live there on a graduate salary but it's not much better over here. With the changeover, customers are not getting the service they're used to and sometimes I have to deal with a city office that can't use their machines. It can be really irate conversation."

She said this with a resigned smile on her face. Dani had only been in Dublin six months and liked the nightlife but not the area she was living in. "It's near the clubs and stuff and don't get me wrong, the flat is fabulous but at the weekends, they have these weird markets at Smithfield. And you see horses around the area too, leaving their crap behind. The place stinks." She wrinkled her nose in disgust.

⇒◆⇐

"Gemma, check the website. Ohmigod, it's amazing inside. I've never been in it before. I don't know anyone who has," Lorna was exclaiming after they had been told the venue for the Christmas party, an expensive Italian restaurant in town, all expenses paid. Sorcha had heard of the place millions of times but it was out of her budget. As Lorna considered out loud what she would wear, Sorcha began to consider her options. But just for a moment. She had a lot of work to do and the event was still several days away.

As the year drew to a close, the team members were taking holidays that they hadn't used. This meant covering for them when they were out and sometimes she was working flat out. She left as soon as she could, waving good night to the security guard as she walked to the exit. On one of these evenings, she went straight to the shopping centre and used her own newly acquired credit card to buy an outfit she could wear to the party. The centre was thronged with Christmas shoppers looking for the best deals.

The winter weather had arrived with a vengeance and on her way to the restaurant later that week, Sorcha pulled her coat with a fake fur collar around her neck. It had been another necessary purchase. She could hardly see as she made her down the street to the entrance. She was nervous as the managers had all been invited and felt the responsibility of putting on a good show.

Lorna and Gemma arrived dressed glamorously in what they openly admitted were outfits borrowed from their mother's or sister's closets. Lisa had arrived with her boyfriend and they were chatting with the other guests. The girls were seated beside some of the staff working in the governance area so they didn't feel like they were centre stage. One of the accountants made jokes about his company car, which he had yet to figure out how to use.

"It's a great piece of engineering but I've just been too busy to read the manual. Somebody gets in that car and they may not get out. There's a central locking system which I managed to find by accident. God knows what kind of other tricks lie ahead."

He asked a lot of interested questions about their experience of the company so far and told them about his two young kids. They were still both in school and he was always in a mad rush to get home in the evenings before they went to bed.

The management team was ordering drinks like they were going out of fashion. John was chatty and seemed adept at arranging these get-togethers. He had taken a group of Spanish visitors to the same place just two weeks before and knew the menu very well. Sorcha chose something safe to eat. At least it was oriented towards the festive season and most of the dishes looked familiar.

There were a couple of announcements to be made and the team was thanked for making such a wholehearted contribution to the new venture. Sorcha could hear the manager talking in his heavy-accented voice about turning the centre into a modern-day *utopia*. He had worked in the human resources area in Europe for over ten years and was eager to ensure that his new project would become a success.

"It'll be difficult, won't it, with hundreds of people in different departments?" Lisa asked, eating her chocolate dessert.

John left his utopian dreams behind for a moment as he looked her square in the eyes and replied, "Now, that's no attitude, Lisa, I'm surprised at you." He grinned but they felt the cool atmosphere and changed the subject.

They had been invited to a nearby nightclub where other departments had also arranged to meet up and dance the night away. Sorcha arrived with her workmates and they threw their coats into the cloakroom. The main area was jammed full of partygoers and they struggled to find room to stand. Sorcha found herself wedged beside Lisa and sucking her drink through a straw. They edged their way to the side of the room and watched as John Xavier, their head manager, got into the spirit of things. He was dancing with a girl who had pulled no stops when deciding what to wear. "Isn't that Joan from Accounting?" Lisa said. "She went all out tonight."

The dress was floor-length and pink and Joan dealt with this by pulling the material around her as she danced around a tiny clutch bag. John Xavier was tapping his feet Flamenco style and at one point disappeared under his partner's dress as she threw back her head in oblivion. The rest of the group laughed and danced even more energetically. A tall dark-haired woman in a backless dress shouted comments from the side of the dance floor. Her face was heavily made up and she was sipping a bottle of beer. A number of handsome Europeans stood by her and heckled the group but it was all in good humour. These were managers of various new groups who had been working hard all quarter with the moves and wanted to enjoy the night.

John Xavier had a long-term boyfriend back in Spain where he spent his weekends and was well known for enjoying himself. The girls turned round to face the Irish service team shaking bottles of champagne around as security tried to stop them from wrecking the newly decorated room. Lisa pushed her way through the crowd to wrestle a bottle from one of the team and make the message clear that his behaviour would not be tolerated. She did not want to cause any more trouble that night.

"Isn't Utopia some kind of adult shop? I've seen one called that on Capel Street," Lisa's boyfriend said on the way home, making light of the situation.

"What were you doing on Capel Street?" Lisa demanded, jokingly. "Don't you work in County Meath now?"

"John is alright, you know," Lisa said, as they drove. "I don't know what to expect from the next year or two but he seems to know what he's doing. He very enthusiastic and likes his fun. He's probably still in the club right now, dancing the night away."

Sorcha had a train to catch the next morning. Most of the group had moved on to Renards around the corner. Sorcha said her goodnights at the house and went inside to pack. She was lucky in that she didn't have to get back to work until January and would be making full use of her time off to come back kicking again in the new year.

Chapter 4

Messages were crackling in to the bus driver as he navigated his way through the streets filled with slush to reach the main junction at the village. As they crossed over the bridge, the passengers could see a car crash scene on the motorway. The driver looked worried but held his breath as they drove towards the business park. The bus cast off layers of snow as it raced along the wet ground. It was January and the first snowstorm had arrived with a vengeance. It had started to rain and Sorcha rushed from the bus stop to the main door covering her head with a scarf. Just yesterday, the snow had been powdery and soft underfoot, though still dangerous. Dani met her at the front door, smiling but with a strained look on her face.

"If you were at home, you would be ice skating now," Sorcha laughed. Dani made a face and said, "Yeah, right. Only in the country, I'm afraid." She was wrapped in a cream lambswool coat and winter boots. "I wouldn't mind if the bad weather affected some of our customers and maybe the phone queues would reduce."

Sorcha was urgent to get to work. The bad weather meant unpredictable arrival times but she didn't want to get in anyone's bad books. Upstairs, Lorna was tapping her pencil hard on the desk, waiting for her computer freeze to end. "It's been like this all morning; I have so much to do." Her computer had been jamming and she would have to get a replacement, the technician said.

Sorcha was too busy to notice. She had met with Kathy to run through a few requirements and had been given a pile of information to wade through. Lorna and Gemma had been given the same from their recruitment contacts and the computer problem was giving Lorna a headache. Eventually, Lisa told her to take a break downstairs. She sat flicking through a magazine in the empty canteen. Lisa had to find her something else to do so she printed extra forms for the afternoon.

She had finally bought a car with the help of her dad who ran his own business. The vehicle was second-hand but she had customised it with a few bits and pieces.

"I feel like I'm getting somewhere now that I'm in charge of the admin for a whole department. It's a lot of work though. Hopefully the new guys will show up soon." The enthusiasm didn't last long. She complained of the repetition involved in typing innumerable details about the scores of new starters. Sorcha liked the job and was keen to reach the targets set by her managers. She looked to them for approval and there had been no major complaints so far.

"I'm glad you find it so interesting, Sorcha. It just seems to be the same thing over and over. I know that they're not going to let me move on until they have someone to take over my job." Lorna had her eyes on a management role.

"But I suppose that's not the priority at the moment. Once they have enough of us to process everything, they'll just focus on taking on replacement staff.

"Not to worry," Gemma said, sounding hopeful. "There should be a lot around eventually if you just stay put and bide your time, you impatient skivvy."

The girls amused themselves by joining the local gym at a reduced rate. They both had gym bags with the logo on and usually parked in the same places every morning. Gemma joked that she was the one getting the full value of the membership. "All she does is sit in the sauna. She tries a couple of things, like the bike, then she sits down in the sauna for a full hour and treats herself. Her skin will be as smooth as a baby's bottom in a month."

Lorna protested and demonstrated how her muscles were aching. "Not as much as mine. I could hardly lift the pen this morning."

The gym was situated close to the motorway. There were plans to build an even bigger one at the end of their road. There were other companies opening up for business and the area had one of the larger shopping centres which employed hundreds of people. The girls raved about its range and proximity. There were four car parks to chose from, each in a primary colour.

"That's where I got these from," Lorna said, holding up her new boots. "I bought them in a sale. They were half-price."

"They have all the health services down there as well so you can just pull your car into a space and get everything done in one go."

"Don't anyone get sick for the next couple of weeks. If I get any more work to do, I'll go crazy," Lorna said, only half joking.

The cavalry arrived in the form of Miriam, Seamus and Jeremy who started as the spring set in and the pace of recruitment intensified. Miriam was a petite strawberry blonde who lived with her boyfriend and they wanted to get their own place eventually.

The two guys were graduates but blond haired Jeremy was older and had travelled for a couple of years. Their section of office space was expanded to make room for the extra desks. They had changed their lunch rota although Lorna and Gemma still took the early break with Miriam. Sorcha took hers with Seamus, a dark haired Northerner, and Jeremy who was living in a large house in a new estate two bus rides away. A couple of German girls had taken the other two rooms. "The girls are like chalk and cheese. One is really quiet. Well, they're both really quiet in different ways," Jeremy was saying.

Zara was a spoilt rich girl from outside Berlin who wanted to work in Dublin to gain experience. She had a few friends in the area that had moved over at the same time. She said very little and kept mostly to herself when she didn't have a visitor around. Katerina was the exact opposite. She had never been away from home before and had spent the first couple of weeks crying in her room. Slowly, she had emerged and was now talking constantly. Zara had been resisting every attempt Katerina made at being friends and the guys had decided not to intervene. They were hoping to throw a party in the not too distant future and who knew, it might settle things between their German housemates.

The renovation activity continued for some months. As one section was completed and wired for action, it was populated with a list of new teams and management. The workmen moved on to another part of the building and commenced their work again. They had three large buildings to fill with rows of desks. As the plans were worked through, the company employed more and more staff. The personnel team processed the paperwork at each stage. Despite all the activity, there was no sign of new positions opening up.

"It's a tough job, hiring and firing staff," Gemma said. "I think I'm ballsy but I wouldn't want to get into that. So long as I get my cheque at the end of every month, I'm OK." She had taken on a mortgage and was spending her spare time on the internet, looking for cheaply priced furniture. Lorna had her eye on a development of apartments and had been helping out with presentations in her spare time. The presentations were on topics such as further education and college funding. The company hoped to have a training centre open on site in the next year.

Jeremy had worked in HR in an Australian company and had started helping out with the induction days for new starters. He also had to ensure that fifty welcome packs were printed out each week and nobody complained when they saw him spending up to an hour at the photocopier on a Friday afternoon.

"Rather him than me," Lorna said. "It's like working at Burger King with all the merchandise."

They had a drawer full of notepads, pens and stress balls all stamped with the company logo and Jeremy was obliged to ensure that this was kept stocked. He was at the office early each morning to collect everything and set up the systems in the training room. He usually returned some hours later with a wad of paperwork from the new starts to be processed.

Seamus was content to stay tapping on his computer as long as he got off early on Friday to get to the pub. Miriam had not used a computer on a constant basis before as she had worked in retail and was finding it hard to adjust. Every so often, a manager came past and smiled at the hard-working crew. There were also queues of employees checking on minute details regarding their personal information or to enquire when their team's move to a new building would take place.

"I wonder if they have any idea how much pressure we're under every day," Jeremy said as they took the bus home. "I came back here because it seemed like things were happening for a change. But this place is so busy. I just hope it all makes sense in the end."

He was happy to stay for the time being. The guys said goodbye to Sorcha when they alighted on the Castleknock road as they had to take another bus to their estate. She walked to her house from the stop. There was no-one about so she put some convenience soup on the stove and warmed herself by the radiator. Jason came in soon after. He said hello swiftly then went upstairs. Sorcha put some boiling water in a saucepan and made spaghetti. There was plenty left in the pot so she offered it to Jason when he came back downstairs. He took it gratefully and they went in to the living-room.

"James is working late tonight. He'll be back later on so we can leave the rest for him, if you'd like," Jason said.

He switched on National Geographic and sleepily changed channels from time to time. His small body was still perched on the couch when James arrived and had his meal with them. "Don't know how she does it but our manager Sandra goes to the gym every morning before work. Although she's earning so much that she could probably buy her own pool any day now." He looked at Sorcha. "She deals with mortgages and she's making a packet."

"Is that something you'd like to do?"

James sniggered and ran his hand through his greying hair. Jason started to laugh. "Sandra's in the peak of health, Sorcha, like I told you. She's not going anywhere. I'd have to really get my skates on to be like her. I'm happy doing what I'm doing. At least for now. This place is fine too and I'm not thinking about a place of my own just yet."

He paused. It's handy when I'm working late." He looked at Jason who had lost interest in the conversation. "They spring it on me," he said, half-laughing.

———◆———

Next morning, it was raining heavily. James gave Sorcha a lift to the village where she caught the bus as usual. The journey was a slow crawl and the driver cursed as he was caught at a red light. She saw the girls with Miriam in the car park and caught up with them, feeling sluggish. She had started to watch what she had for lunch and tried to eat soup instead of a main meal. But she had to keep her strength up. She didn't know how some girls managed to survive on a tiny salad.

Lisa announced that she wanted a complete organisation of work processes and asked the guys to come into work on Saturday. If they had plans they would just have to change them and these were orders from management. There was a lot of paperwork that had not yet been cleared and they would have to blitz the outstanding load at the weekend.

"It would be suspect if someone asked us questions about their profile, and the paperwork was sitting on a desk somewhere," she reasoned. "It's just a once-off then we can work in a more organised way." Everyone agreed to be in at ten am on Saturday, although it didn't seem like they had much choice. Miriam could only make it for a couple of hours as she had to babysit for her sister.

"I don't mean to be unpleasant but can't you change this?" Lisa asked. "It's not fair of me to ask the others to work the extra hours and have you leave early." They discussed it all morning and then it was agreed that Miriam could leave at half past twelve. The new girl left without saying a word and the others watched silently. They could do with the extra help.

They all arrived before ten on the Saturday. Overtime had been agreed but it didn't cheer up the disgruntled workers. They were given a pile of papers each and these had to be completed by the agreed finish time of three pm.

Miriam took hers without a word. Sorcha took a look at what she was given and reckoned she could finish the pile by the allotted time. Pizza arrived mid-way through. Miriam had left by then, to drive back across town. Lisa was still hovering about and supervising the work so nobody said anything. At three pm on the dot, they cleared up their desks and shut down their computers. They passed on the papers to be filed away and left as quickly as possible. Lorna and Gemma got in their cars and drove away at top speed.

Sorcha was left with Jeremy and Seamus. They called a taxi and got out at the village centre. The guys were on their way to the video shop. Sorcha went into the supermarket and bought some things. She was too tired to do anything else so she went straight home. Jason had gone home for the weekend and James was meeting a friend in town. She ordered Chinese: spring rolls, prawns and plain rice. She had developed a taste for this since her meal in London and it seemed like the thing to do after a busy day at the office.

When this winter wore away, she promised herself that things would be different. She would eat salad; she would propel herself to the forefront of the workgroup and would get involved in all kinds of clubs and activities. For now, she switched on the comedy channel and amused herself. The furniture was squeaky with age and needed to be replaced. There was a dining table to one side, which had seen better days. She flicked through the channels and caught the tail end of a BBC documentary and then watched some of a talkshow.

Later that night, she heard James return. He cursed in a low voice when his foot creaked on the stairs. She heard him use the toilet then he closed the door to his room.

In the morning, she was amazed by the stillness everywhere. When she gazed out of the window, she saw that the lawn was damp from the rain which was no longer falling. She took a quick look at the room: her small double-bed was in the centre; the CD player she'd bought cheaply in town was positioned in the corner by the window. A small stack of albums lay cloistered beside it. Her books had been rehoused in a small shelf over her bed.

Everything else was stored in the fitted wardrobe: her clothes, travel cases, shoes and a box of memorabilia. It wasn't much but she had thought of buying some furniture if and when she got a place of her own.

The bathroom was an old 1970s style suite with a huge mirror to one side. She got up and showered then dressed and went downstairs with her laundry basket. She took things easy on a Sunday but always found things to do. She used the last of the washing powder and poured in some conditioner then switched on the machine, watching her clothes spin round. She felt hungry so she grabbed a reusable shopping bag and went out of the front door. They had no alarm system and didn't feel it was necessary. There were houses worth millions just minutes walk away.

The local store was walking distance from the estate. There was a butcher's, a beauty salon and a pizza takeaway plus a pub, which she hadn't yet visited. The store was family-run and a little grotty like a shop she had frequented as a student but it had a certain charm. She got a basket and picked up some things: fruit juice, milk, eggs, bananas and the washing powder. She got the Sunday paper at the counter. The girl was very friendly and helped her pack the bag.

Back at the house, James was still sleeping. Sorcha made an omelette using leftover tomatoes and some cheese. They shared a lot of things for the house. She had had to get used to this but had been broken in while sharing the flat with Karen and Rob. It was laborious having to refill the fridge and restock the presses when everything was used up. They usually made a list of things to buy every second weekend but their diverse schedules meant that this system was not always used. She saw pork chops in the freezer along with bags of frozen vegetables. There was beer and mineral water and a packet of chocolate bars in the fridge. The bottom press contained a half bag of potatoes and a string bag of onions. Sorcha loved stew but had to learn how to make it from scratch. From time to time, they served stew at the work canteen but it had made her ill. She ate the omelette quickly and drank a glass of juice. She made some coffee and read the magazine section of the newspaper. She could hear noises upstairs and soon, James appeared. He yawned broadly then took a cup of coffee and took some bread out of a packet.

"Any plans for today, Sorcha?" he asked, putting on some toast. She shook her head. "How did yesterday go?" he asked. "Oh, fine. So I just came home and took it easy with a Chinese and some TV."

"You should come out with us sometime. We went to Temple Bar." He rolled his eyes at the memory.

"I drank far too much. It was good fun though." He went back upstairs with his food and Sorcha started to clear up. She scrubbed the pan clean and sprayed and wiped the worktops with a disinfectant. The floor had to be swept and mopped. She left the hoovering but polished the surfaces in the living-room including the mirror over the fireplace. It made a small difference, she thought, as she opened the window a little bit and looked outside.

The neighbours on either side seemed friendly. They had only greeted each other so far but it seemed like a nice neighbourhood. Later, she went for a walk towards the Park. She crossed over the bridge with the motorway below. There were houses everywhere and she got bored with her walk. She reckoned the house was situated inbetween two village churches but she did not ever feel the inclination to attend Mass. She had been too focused on work for months to give it some real thought. She shivered faintly as she stood on the bridge over the motorway and turned back in the direction of the house. There was a lot happening in the office at the moment and she would have to get a good night's sleep to be full of energy for the week ahead.

She had noticed a contrast between her home life and the chaos she encountered when she entered the canteen every morning. The teams in her building often took their morning break at the same time. There was a mad flurry for the coffee jugs laid out in a row and she had taken to using the coffee machine for a while. "Damn this Irish shithole!" a Finnish girl had screamed one morning as she stuck her blonde, jagged head down to check what was happening with her order. A couple of days of taking her own coffee to work and Sorcha gave up and went back to using the communal coffee jugs. By then, the rush had ceased a little. She never knew what to expect from the place. As soon as a problem was noted, management would be advised and would have to intervene if they could.

It was no better at lunch time. She had taken sandwiches for a while to cut back on expenses then one day, had tried the restaurant again. Lorna and Gemma had arrived back from lunch ten minutes late. "Be warned, it's very busy down there. It took ages." Downstairs, there was a queue going out of the door, waiting with their red trays to be fed. She had gone back upstairs in frustration. Lisa had passed on the information to the managers and soon enough, it was safe to go back again. They had extended the main hall and had put in extra coffee machines. She was relieved although she still had to be quick to make sure she was back at her desk within half-an-hour. The company would not look favourably on someone who wasted time when there was work to be done.

She was sympathetic to the canteen staff that had to prepare everything first thing in the morning. They served breakfast from the early hours to cater for the foreign language staff who took lunch an hour before the English language groups. It was the same with lunches when they served a menu of low-priced meals and desserts. The standard could vary from good to diabolical. They learnt early on to avoid the rehashed stews and tasteless vegetables that could appear in the strangest of incarnations like pizza toppings.

The couple of staff working at the sandwich bar were the ones who had it worst. Every day, between the hours of 11.30 and 2pm they had

About Turn

to make sandwiches to order for the queue of people who arrived like clockwork. They asked the same questions: what kind of bread, how many fillings, butter or not, have here or takeaway, and put it together in double-quick time. She saw the General Manager reach across and grab a plain baguette with a couple of fillings on the side as he swiftly paid and went back to his desk. Sorcha would briefly bump into some of the workforce but many of the foreign workers finished at 4.30pm. At least it meant she could get home safely as the company was still working on a dedicated bus service for its workers.

John's Spanish protégées were settling in well. They had already been invited out for drinks and were a well-known fixture on site. Unlike the groups of Spanish youngsters that had stayed in her hometown when she was at school and had travelled in a raucous pack, all of these had individual personalities. Manoli came from the North of Spain and had been dealing with her mother's death after a long illness. She was outgoing and a bit pushy though and had massive green eyes. Sorcha often saw her listening to music if she was on her own travelling to work.

Her friend Berta came from a small town near Madrid and seemed more conservative. They mingled with a couple of good-looking Spanish boys who were energetic and enthused when it came to setting up their team desks with bright red and yellow bunting. They called up to HR one afternoon as a group and made chatty conversation with the staff. The HR manager stood with them until all of their issues had been sorted. He seemed a little edgy and possibly worried about something. Sorcha knew that the company was spending huge amounts of money on the new centre but it was early days.

The Spaniards were joined by Paola, an Irish girl who came from a well off Irish family on the Southside. Paola had lived in Spain for years and had recently started at the company as a customer service agent. She had already made friends with John Xavier and had even been invited to his house. "Not for any horseplay, obviously," she said. But we've been to some of the places in Madrid so he's asked me to let him know next time I'm planning a visit. Anyway, I'm just getting settled back in the auld sod so let me know if there's any openings in the finance section, OK?" Then she continued conversing in fluent Spanish with her teammates.

John Xavier had picked a group of volunteers to start up a social committee to arrange events on site. Every employee automatically paid a fee out of their salary each month and the funds were used to pay for parties during the year. The committee had been meeting to decide on what kind of events would be popular. There were only a few pubs in the area, frequented by team members eager for a few drinks after work. It always seemed pretty lively but the conversation usually centred on the job. The employees were still in limbo for the most part as the company expanded bit by bit.

"But that's all they're going to do," one Irish guy commented. He was already miserable about spending every day on the phone wrestling over arrival times of the engineers and had applied to his manager for a transfer to the Technical team. Inbetween, staff were feted for high target achievements and best customer service. Representatives of the HR team attended a meeting in a city centre hotel for call centre staff where objectives were discussed and members of staff were picked out for awards and extra time off. Afterwards, everyone met up in the lounge and bottles of champagne were popped.

Sorcha was introduced to the manager of the UK financial services team at one of these gatherings. Dolores was a curly-haired middle-aged woman dressed in denim from head to toe and they chatted politely for a few minutes. At the moment, she was setting up the teams and was busy recruiting during the week for people to work on customer accounts. The financial services section was due to occupy the small distant building 2 with the IT department for the time being. On the other side of the driveway the company was erecting three large identical buildings to house the bulk of the workers.

"Hey, man, have you been watching the match?" a tall Belgian leaned over the table and chatted to the group. He took some gentle slagging about his favourite soccer team and drank from his pint of Guinness.

"Is that any better than Belgian beer? Now you're drinking the real stuff," his workmates shouted loudly. The conversation was halted by a middle-aged Irish man who had been hired to manage the Commercial team. The young man turned around and began chatting to a skinny dark-haired Spanish girl who had just started as a customer liaison administrator to get through college. She was wearing a plain t-shirt with patterned leggings and a matching handbag.

The curly haired manager walked through the group, eyeing the group of t-shirted lads with distaste. She had numerous staffing levels to fill and would be responsible for the move of financial operations from the UK to Ireland. She stood with a group of middle-aged English men who had run the operations in the old office and would be spending considerable time in the near future in the Irish capital. A moustached man in a v-neck nodded seriously as his co-worker, a bald ugly man with control over the leasing section, cracked a couple of jokes and looked around at the young girls in the room. He spotted one familiar face and shouted in greeting, "Oi, you getting me another one from the bar, then?" Shortly afterwards, he was surrounded by the t-shirts as they jokingly arranged a night in town.

The next morning, Sorcha was met by long faces. Management had wanted them to come to work on Saturday again but had made the announcement too late in the week. They had been given a gruelling schedule of work for the next week instead. She felt relieved but spent the day at her desk, taking only a small break for lunch. She got caught up in the whirlwind of work with so much waiting to be done. The team was equally busy and they left at five pm, gladly. Sorcha saw the manager approach and chat with Lisa as she left. He gave her a piece of paper, an outline of the following week presumably. Lisa said little and then announced she was gone for the weekend as well. Sorcha packed up her things and left the empty office.

She went home and sat in her room, listening to some late-night music on John Kelly's radio show, feeling bad about her situation and half-wishing she had not made the move to the company. It had been so easy just slotting herself in with the charity and enjoying her free time. At least she had a couple of days to re-energise, she thought, as she went to sleep.

On Saturday, Sorcha had decided to join James and his group for a night out. She was in her room, getting ready and listening to a dEUS CD. It always got her going and she was pulling on a pair of tights when James knocked. "Taxi will be here in ten minutes," he said through the door. "OK!" she yelled, fixing her skirt and spraying some scent. She didn't have a lot of party clothes but had been intrigued by tales of new theme clubs opening up in the city centre. The one they were all meeting at tonight was called Pravda and had been designed in a Russia style reminiscent of a Communist Party drinking hole. She took her bag and checked she had enough money then she locked the door and met James downstairs. They took the route through the Park again and ended up on the quays.

"It's just a little bit further. The bar's called Pravda. It's near the Ha'penny Bridge on the North side," James said to the driver. The driver nodded and stayed on the left and pulled in to the kerb for a moment so they could get out. "This one's on me," James said. "You can pay for the trip home. I won't be in good shape by then." He laughed and paid the fare, leaving a small tip.

They passed by the sculpture of two Dublin women having a chat and saw the entrance to the club, in the corner, near the Woollen Mills. She noticed the Winding Stair bookshop, a place she had frequented as a student. James saw the knitted caps in the window of the Kilkenny shop and joked, "You should have worn your fur hat. It's Russian after all."

"Don't be daft. It's almost summer," Sorcha said.

They queued for a few minutes. The assembled crowd was a mixture of well-dressed students and young people like themselves who were keen to share the new experience. Eventually, the doormen let them in with a small group to make a round number of ten. They went inside and there were already people sitting at tables near the entrance, drinking and chatting among themselves. They went past the first bar area to the next part of the club. The music was loud and the dancefloor was jammed with people and there was only standing room in the whole section. They squeezed past some people to find the cloakroom and James swivelled round to look at the design and to see if he could notice his friends. He noticed a message on his phone when he put his coat in. "They're not here yet. I think one of the guys wasn't feeling well so they had to take him home," he said, trying to listen through the noise. They managed to find a small space on the stairs, from where they could order drinks.

Sorcha took the opportunity to look around. There was a small line of tables across from the bar which were all occupied. A blonde girl she thought she recognised gave someone a hard stare when he put his drink on the table. He thought better of it and moved away. The walls were covered with paintings depicting Russian activism at the turn of the century. The hammer and sickle was the emblem of the worker's fight but here it was just the backdrop to the young people of Dublin letting go after a tough week in the office. James was chatting to a girl at the bar. He turned around again when he was tapped on the shoulder.

"Oh, Eamon, you made it," he said. Eamon and his workmates were caught at the top of the opposite staircase and were protesting that they could not get any further. James gesticulated back that he knew the feeling. It was like TV scheduling for the deaf and dumb as Eamon pointed to the exit and suggested they go somewhere else? James shrugged. They stood wondering for a moment and then a couple of people moved away, allowing the other guys to come down onto the same level. "It's great in here, isn't it?" James said. His friend rolled his eyes and shook Sorcha's hand. She was introduced to all three of the group who were looking like they'd much rather be someplace else. James and Eamon chatted for a few minutes, making jokes and shouting orders at the barman who was sweating. The little group made small talk and decided to move closer to the dance area to get some breathing space.

They took their drinks and went single file in the direction of the bright lights, James leading the way. Half-way through he announced that he was stuck. Holding his pint glass high in the air, his face grew serious as he realised he couldn't move. Eamon pointed this out to the people nearby who moved away a little, enough for him to be released. Now even James wanted to get out. "Christ, what a scrum."

Sorcha turned around and asked the two guys to move back. They edged their way back to the small row of steps, which now had a throng of people standing on it with drinks, who had settled in and had no intention of moving. "Just try to get past," James said. They did as they were told, apologising as they went along and they filed past the first bar to the door where they had entered. The entrance area had filled with people since their arrival. James went to retrieve their coats and came back in bad humour.

"That was a waste of time," he said, glowering. "Come on, I just want to get drinking."

"We should have gone to Vicar Street," Sorcha joked as they walked over the river.

"Where?" James asked.

"Vicar Street. It's a new venue near the Guinness factory."

"That's way too far for me," James replied, looking at her like it was the most preposterous suggestion. They entered the Temple Bar area which was bursting with activity. There were a couple of buskers playing on the street corners. The group walked along and checked each pub for any sign of spare room.

The doormen were being especially arrogant and regarding each approaching set of people with suspicion.

"That's it," James said, "no place to go. We should have stayed out of town." He looked crestfallen.

"It's the wrong time of night," Eamon said. "If it was an hour earlier, we would be OK."

The atmosphere had changed. They plumped for standing room in one of the late-night hotel clubs and stood in the middle of a group of twenty-year-olds drinking alcopops and chatting about Robbie Williams. There were a couple of hen parties at different locations near the bar and they watched as the bride-to-be had an assortment of shots poured down her throat. James got another pint at the bar and began to perk up. He started to dance on the spot to some tune and moved away to chat to a couple of girls standing at the water fountain.

"So where do you work yourself?" Sorcha chatted to Eamon's girlfriend who had arrived and was looking displeased at the young crowd she found herself amongst. She pulled Eamon aside and began a campaign to allow them to move somewhere else and Sorcha found herself watching the scene. She saw groups of inner-city girls who were wearing short skirts and high heels and accompanied by guys in runners and designer jeans. She grimaced as a girl walked past with a skirt just covering her bottom. She couldn't wish she was back in the other club but started to feel out of place. She noticed his single friends who had joined James who looked like he was fighting a losing battle.

He returned, holding an extra pint, and taking turns to drink out of each glass. Sorcha took a sip from her vodka mix and asked how it went. "Not great," James said, as the girls went off with his group to dance. "I'm too old for them or they're too young for me, not sure which."

Eventually, they went upstairs to join them and Sorcha got a buzz from the music as she danced for a couple of hours, taking a break every now and then. The girls had stayed on with their new friends and the small group scattered as they left in the early hours of the morning.

The excitement of city centre club hopping had soon subsided and Sorcha went back to work. She had settled in at her desk, sticking up a couple of pictures and using an old photograph of her favourite beach as her computer screensaver. They were not allowed to play music or use the internet during work hours and she found she was too busy to do this anyway. Kathy the financial services recruiter had a work ethic like no other and spent an equal amount of time trawling through her own recommendations for recruitment before passing the files for processing on the girl's desk.

"How are we coming along?" she asked, all cropped hair and dressed in a business suit.

Sorcha managed a smile. "Fine, no problem."

"Let me know if it's too much and I'll try to fit some paperwork in if I have time. I have meetings abroad next week so I won't be around but you can drop me a mail if you have any issues."

Sorcha had started to stay on a couple of evenings a week. She could stay on till half past seven and one of the team was usually leaving at the same time and could drive her home. She could make it in on Saturdays as well if she worked in the afternoon and left her plans until the evening. There were usually a few of the team around, catching up on work, and they could play CDs at a low level while typing. She noticed the difference in her pay packet and this spurred her on to keep working.

But she could not see the difference in the amount of work she had to manage on a daily basis. Even with the extra hours, she still had too much to do and the flow of paper seemed to be never-ending. If she did manage to process a set of files, she would be given another load to complete from someone else's pile which surprised her. After several weeks of working non-stop, she could feel the fatigue in her body. She could feel a recurring pain in her left shoulder as she worked through the day.

Lorna had noticed a similar pain in her hands and voiced her concerns, "This can't keep happening. The pain in my hands when I left the office yesterday was so bad I had to wait before I could turn the key and drive home. If they're recruiting so many people to work in these buildings, then we should get extra admin staff surely?"

Lisa was doubtful that the budget could stretch to more people working in human resources and pointed out that the capacity was full. However, she acknowledged that the team did not have to work overtime if they didn't want to. As the overtime dwindled, the amount of paperwork to be processed increased.

"Sorry, guys, but I'm afraid we are going to have to do a blitz once more. If everyone could show up at work on Monday at 8.30am and we will concentrate on the outstanding work to be done," Lisa said, as she was being urged by the senior staff to push on with the processing.

Lorna had had an appointment with an occupational therapist at this stage and had been given exercises to do at her desk. This improved her ability to work at a constant rate and it wasn't like she had any choice. Sorcha had figured out a good sitting position to ease the shoulder pain although she often found herself slumping as the day wore on.

Lisa announced a drinks night at the new bar in the village to make up for the heavy workload. Every department had organised a formal visit to the new venue, which was the largest bar in the area. They went there by car, and it turned out that the bar was not in the village, but across from the shopping centre. They were met by two security guards who looked at them for a second, greeted them and let them through. Inside, the bar was furnished in a very modern style. The bar was dead centre with cube chairs or couches and small round tables along the walls. There was a huge golden Buddha in the far middle of the room. The music was loud and blaring out hit songs from the year so far.

Lorna took a look around and nodded her approval. "Come on," she said, "let's go find the others." She walked around the room to the back, where the rest of the department was ensconced. Lisa waved to them and got them some drinks.

Sorcha was drinking Barcardi and chatting to Lorna, who suddenly came alive when she tasted her cocktail. Gemma was looking thoughtful. She seemed tired and didn't say much. People were sitting at tables that were scattered around the room and they took the first one that became free. Lorna and Gemma chatted quietly and Sorcha took a look around. She could see their most senior manager standing at the bar, watching his staff let their hair down, a beaming smile on his face. Seamus and Jeremy had shown up and were drinking pints at another table. The finger food had arrived and everyone was taking cocktail sausages or chicken wings onto paper plates. She got up and took a serving plate full of food and placed it on the table. The girls tucked in gratefully.

"I'm going up to take a look at the apartments on Saturday," Lorna said. "They're small but the block is only down the road. I can take a shortcut and I'll be in at work in no time." She turned to Sorcha, "It's going to be a village on its own eventually. They're building a shopping centre and a bar and everything."

"Have you thought of any colour schemes yet?" Gemma asked.

"I have some ideas. I know the kind of furniture I want so I just have to decide on the right shades to match. I can't afford a consultant obviously so I'll just have to look at the catalogues."

"Are you still planning on the two-bed option?"

Lorna nodded. "Yeh, I'll get someone to rent for a year and that should help me with the repayments until I get on my feet."

She flicked through furniture magazines Gemma had brought, trying not to make it too obvious. They were arranging to meet up at the weekend to visit a popular furniture store that Gemma had used to decorate her house. Lorna looked up suddenly and said, "Have you thought about getting your own place, Sorcha?"

She looked surprised. "No, I haven't," she replied. "I don't have the money to do that just yet."

"It's OK," Lorna said. "It just means having no life for a few months until everything's settled. I can't wait to get a tenant in and have my normal salary back again. Or most of it."

"I'm too tired to think about socialising these days," Gemma said, "so it didn't matter when I had to think about saving for a mortgage. We should go on holidays when we're finished with all of it."

The girls continued chatting about the best brands to use and Sorcha lost interest in the conversation so she wandered into the main room again to see what was happening. She saw James standing at the bar and went over to him. He smiled and turned round to introduce her to Sandra who was standing behind him. The short tanned woman barely moved a muscle as she smiled politely and extended a hand in greeting. Sorcha did likewise then turned back to James. He was waiting to be served and offered to buy her a drink. There was a line of old men sitting at the counter, nursing their pints and it reminded her of being in some old country pub.

"What are you doing here? Did you come down after work?" James asked.

Sorcha pointed to the private room and asked for another Bacardi. James was drinking Guinness. Sandra was halfway through a soft drink and was sipping silently.

"Have you been here long?" James wanted to know.

"An hour or so," Sorcha replied. "It's certainly different in here. I was dying to find out what it looked like. We've been talking about this place all week."

The rest of Dublin 15 had heard about the new bar too. There was barely standing room and they squashed together against the support. Further up, the golden Buddha glinted brightly among the commotion.

"Don't look too closely, Sorcha," James said, laughing. "It'll suck you in."

"I don't think so," Sorcha said, feeling unsure as the crowd surged to the bar. Sandra finished her drink and left. John appeared at the entrance to the private room, saying his goodbyes. He had a flight scheduled first thing in the morning and had to leave early. Lorna and Gemma appeared for a moment, holding their bags, on their way to the bathrooms. They were chatting and didn't see her.

"Those two girls work with me," Sorcha said, pointing.

"The taller one's very good-looking," James said, smiling. She watched out for them but they didn't return.

Eventually, the lack of space began to irritate them. "We can move into the room I was in before," Sorcha said. But the crowd had overflowed into the smaller space and they decided to leave. It took them a while to get to the exit and there was another queue of people waiting to get inside. The doorman saw them leave and said, "Ok, another two inside," holding back the rest of the crowd.

"That was fun," Sorcha said, as they walked to James's car. She hadn't been down this side of the centre before. The car park had been built specially for the club but would no doubt be used by the shoppers during the day.

"It was OK, but I'd prefer a smaller pub just to drink in peace. It was getting on Sandra's nerves and she was getting on my nerves. Did you bring your jacket by the way?"

"Yes," Sorcha had tied her cardigan around her waist. "She seems quiet, Sandra."

"Well, she can be demonic in the office. I think she just shuts down out of work hours." They drove home, past the block of apartments being built close to the major road extension at the village. It was just a pile of bricks and mud at the moment with a bare outline of the first two floors. The layout of the apartments looked small but the name was not the one that Lorna had mentioned.

"They look very small, the flats, like mini apartments," she said, as they stopped at the lights.

"It's probably all they can fit into that particular corner. I think there's a larger block going up just beside them. So I've heard."

She mentioned the name of Lorna's development wondering about the location. She had said it was more of a village than an apartment block. James recognised the name and said, "I think it's a much bigger site and it's near one of the train stations. But it is easy to get to and from by car or at least it is at the moment. They're planning to have a couple of thousand units at the end."

They arrived back at the house, which looked old and uncared for with its tatty piece of lawn at the front and went to their rooms. Sorcha lay awake, thinking of the possibilities. She was determined to make a go of her career with the company. Things would settle down and she would thrive. But she wasn't sure about living out here, so far from the temptations of town and full of housing estates where she didn't know anyone. She fell asleep, dreaming of paint and fine furniture and her own proper front door key.

Sorcha had accumulated some savings in the bank and, as she knew it was not enough to put a deposit down on the house, she thought about a holiday. Jeremy and Seamus had introduced her to a couple of friends who lived near their shared house. The estate was full of the company's employees who had travelled from Italy, Germany or France. Some of them bought cheap cars and could travel in a group to and from the business park. She had met lanky Denise who was Irish and had a bubbly personality and her housemate Monica, a serious blonde who was from Germany but had lived in Ireland for a few years.

They had found jobs in the company, Denise working in the UK call centre with ambitions to move up fast and Monica working in financial services, and now shared a house close to Jeremy's in Carpenterstown. They had met Jeremy at the local pub and were regular visitors at his home. It was at the boys' housewarming that she had the chance to talk at length about work and their plans for the summer. It had rescued her from a dreary conversation with the German girls with chunky Katerina chatting about her family and Zara, smartly dressed and dark, silently drinking a cocktail. Now she often bumped into them on the bus route to work.

"We're planning a holiday," Denise said, on one of those mornings. She was holding a handful of brochures for sun trips with pictures of tanned, smiling sunbathers on the cover. "It's been such a shit summer so far and it doesn't look like it'll improve."

Monica and Denise were planning to go together and share accommodation but a third person would make the cost so much cheaper.

"Where are you thinking of going?" Sorcha asked, half-interested.

"Spain, Tunisia, Cuba. Oh, just one of those places," Denise said. "Tell you what, I'll make some calls and I'll give you the figures when I have them. No obligation but it would be fun if you could come along."

That afternoon, Sorcha received a personal e-mail, with the full details attached. It was for a week's break in a resort on the island of Crete. The deals for Cuba and Mexico had been too expensive and the girls had already been to Spain and wanted to go somewhere new.

Sorcha replied saying thanks and that she'd sleep on it and would let them know the following day. They had provisionally booked it over the phone and could re-book if she backed out. She thought about it on the way home. She reckoned she deserved a good break and it would be her first decent holiday in a long time. The salary at the charity had not been enough for a foreign break and she had only been able to snatch a couple of days here and there on her budget.

James was full of encouragement. "Of course you should go. Jason's planning a break and if he can do it, why can't you?"

"I don't really know the girls that well. Plus it will cost me several hundred pounds and I'm afraid I'll be penniless when I get back."

He laughed at her teetering on the brink of blowing her savings on an adventure. "Don't worry about it. It seems like a good deal and you should treat yourself. Think of the alternative: slogging at your desk with the sun blazing outside and there's no contest."

"Are you planning to go anywhere?" Sorcha asked. She had spread out all of the information on the table in front of her and was highlighting the important parts.

"Not this year, but I've been away enough to know that you'll have fun and it'll be something to remember."

Sorcha took a closer look at the print out she'd been given which detailed the services at the hotel they would be staying in, the number of pools in the complex and the numerous expeditions they could go on while on holiday. She supposed she could go on some of these trips if she felt like she needed a diversion. The girls were OK and Jeremy had recommended she travel with them with no reservations. So she mailed Denise and took up the offer. They had booked a week at the end of August so she had a couple of months to prepare herself.

The tourist season had hit with a vengeance and everywhere she went in town, there were crowds of Spanish kids here to learn English, American tourists with their cameras attached and an array of foreign workers in the cafes and bars. She met up with Karen who had finished her exams and was working in the new cinema on Parnell Street. She arrived at the coffee place in Temple Bar in her uniform, looking dazzled. "This job is getting me down; I've spent the whole day promoting this membership deal they have, repeating myself like a mantra. I'm seriously thinking about going back to college in the Autumn, where it's safe."

Sorcha told her about the holiday she'd booked and she was delighted. "I'd love to go on one of those trips. But we'll be saving for a house in the next couple of years. Our bank manager talked us through a plan and if we both work, we can have our own home in the next couple of years. It's a serious prospect."

"Will that be here, or elsewhere?"

"Dunno. We might move back home. My mum told us about some companies opening up in the area. She's very keen for me to get a place of my own. Two years would give us time to organise, you know, a wedding and all that." She laughed at the prospect. "My mum is ok with the fact that we live together but Rob's parents don't know about it. They're very conservative. They would probably prefer if we tied the knot. Just as well they don't come into town much. It's our life at the end of the day and we're not hurting anybody."

Karen played with a piece of her hair and yawned. "So, maybe we could go round to Gill's later, if you're interested. I think Isabelle's housemate has some friends staying with her this weekend, so we're getting some videos and some food. I suppose we could walk round now, if you want."

They trekked through the busy streets, taking a look in the Laser video shop on South Great George's Street and picking out a couple of movies to suit all tastes. Sorcha felt tired by now. She had been out the night before and had not slept well and was already planning to take a taxi home later that night. They walked down the lengthy route of Camden Street with the vegetable markets and quirky stores and passed the DIT college at Aungier Street to cross at the lights connecting them to Wexford Street. They stopped at a nearby off-licence and bought some bottles of drink and nibbles. Gill's flat was close-by and Karen pointed out a grey block of buildings as they turned a corner. It was a corporation flat complex and they could see the lines of clothes hanging out to dry on the balconies as they approached. Sorcha was a little worried as they passed a group of guys with bikes but didn't say anything. They walked through the main entrance where a group of children played with their dolls. There were a few cars parked around and they followed the numbered buildings, smelling the hops in the air floating down from the Guinness factory.

"It's this one, I think," Karen said. "I haven't been here in a while and they all look the same." They climbed the steps to the fourth floor and rang the bell. Louise answered and let them in, hugging them both. They went down the narrow hallway to the living-room where Gill was sitting. She greeted them and said, "You can go out to play for an hour, Louise, while I chat to these two."

She opened the door again and Louise slipped out, clutching a Barbie doll.

"Oh my, you look great. Long time no see," she said to Sorcha, who was wearing pretty smart clothes considering she had been out all night. "How is the job going?"

"Great," Sorcha answered. "Although I could do with a good sleep. I was out last night. There's another new bar on the quays that we just had to go to. It's called Zanzibar. We got there really early and got a nice spot at a table."

"What's it like?"

"Amazing. Very exotic. The interior is very swish and it's got all these palm trees lining the floor. It was jammed by the time we left," Sorcha replied. "The flat looks gorgeous." She looked around at the neat room decorated in pale green with tasteful knick-knacks and shelving as Gill smiled. "All my own work," she said, "I did it while Louise was on holidays with her dad."

"Very nice," Sorcha said.

Karen nodded. "I'd have helped but I had exams. I can do the upcoat in a couple of years. Just joking."

"It didn't take that long, but painting isn't healthy for a small person with all the fumes," Gill said. "Here, let me give you the tour."

They left the living-room and went left to the first bedroom. "This is where Louise sleeps. It needs a good tidy but I think the rosy pink is a nice warm colour. I just need a rug for the floor."

They went next door. "And this is my room. I wanted a different colour but I got a good deal on some paint so I've just used the pink again," she said, opening and closing the door. They looked in at the small white kitchen where brightly coloured delph was lying in the sink rack to dry. There was a small oven and a tiny fridge freezer which Gill's mother had paid for. "We've gone healthy since we moved in here," Gill said. "There's no room to store frozen food."

The bathroom was beside the front door. It was a tiny rectangular room with just a bath and toilet. Gill had put soaps and bath salts along the window and the side of the bath to add colour to the room. "And that is it. It's small but it's a great location. I can walk into town in twenty minutes. And the school is close enough as well. I'm just going to make some tea. Anybody like some?" Gill asked, as she went back to the kitchen. Both girls said yes, and went to the living-room to take a rest. They were discussing the videos they'd borrowed when Gill arrived with a tray of things. "Here, put the bags you brought behind the couch for now. If Louise sees them, she'll want to stay up."

They took a cup of tea each and Karen mumbled through a mouthful of Kit Kat, "Did you know Sorcha's going on a big holiday to Crete with her new friends?"

Gill stopped pouring for a moment and said, "Oh, really?"

"Yes, she told me," Karen continued. "She's a lucky bitch. I'll be lucky if I get away for a trip home this summer. My parents' house is all full up as usual and I can't afford to go away anywhere else."

She turned to Sorcha, "It sounds great, that holiday you've planned. I wish I could come along. And it's one of the nice resorts. Show us those pictures again."

Sorcha passed round the colour print out she'd been given, showing a modest hotel surrounded by palm trees and sandy beaches. She was looking forward to it more than ever now that she'd seen the new club. The palm trees and cocktails had given her the feel for being in an exotic place. Gill looked at the pictures for a long time and read the details like a pro. "It does sound good. I think one of my friends from back home has been there. Was it pricey?"

"We split it between three so it's OK. I just hope I don't get the couch to sleep on, that's all," Sorcha said.

Gill was silent for a moment then got up and went to the kitchen. She came back with a cigarette and opened the door to the balcony. The girls sat drinking their tea until she returned. "Alright?" Karen asked.

"Yeah," said Gill, "I just wish I had a bit more money. The wages I get are enough to cover the expenses but we've paid a lot to get the flat up and running. I'm just hoping next year things will be better."

"Are you planning to freelance when you finish with the charity?" Gill was on her third year and it was unlikely that her contract would be renewed.

"Hopefully, but I'll have to get something fairly permanent. Thing is if I go back to full-time work, I'd lose a lot. Not just money, but also being able to take time off when I want to, like yesterday when we went to the park in the afternoon. Working is so dull, isn't it?" She broke off suddenly. "You've just reminded me. Mick is to call round later with some money. I bought some things in the market with Isabelle last weekend so he said he'd help pay for groceries."

She picked up the phone and punched in his number. He was out so she left a message. "Maybe he's already on his way. I told him we were meeting up tonight."

About Turn

Just then, they heard knocking at the front door. Gill went to open it. "Oh, it's you," she said, as Louise returned. She skipped down the hallway and went into her room. "You have half-an-hour, then lights out, OK?"

She went into her own room then came into the living-room with a bagful of clothes. "These are some of the things we found last week at the market. Remember I was telling you?" She took out a black jacket and a couple of pairs of boots. "I don't normally buy shoes secondhand but these look alright. Isabelle has the rest of the stuff at her place. She should be here soon."

She held up the jacket and tried it on, pulling it around her thin frame. "I just couldn't resist a bargain. It was only twenty quid. And the boots were pretty cheap too."

"They're lovely, Gill," Karen said, trying on a suede boot.

"I know, that's what I told Isabelle," she said. "They should last for a while. The heels don't even look worn."

They sorted through the rest of the items and then put them away. She went to check on Louise who had switched on her night-light to read. The girls got up as they heard Gill whisper and went in to say goodnight. Louise waved bye as they closed the bedroom door.

In the living-room, Karen took out the bags again and began to sort through the videos. "I'm just going to order some food for later. I'm starving. Can someone get that and when Mick gets here, I can pay my share."

They ordered takeaway food from the place down the street and it arrived just as Isabelle showed up with Mick. He gave Gill a few notes and left quickly. "No, we're not back together," Isabelle laughed when he'd gone. "I think he's seeing someone actually." She yawned as she announced she'd had a late night in town, one thing had led to another.

She spotted the bag from the market in the corner. "Oh, yes, I can't wear what I bought yet. It's a winter coat with nice fur on the….what is it?" She pointed to her neck.

"….collar?" Gill offered.

"That's it," Isabelle grinned. "Where is the little one? Sleeping? I won't disturb her."

Then she noticed the brochures which had been left on the couch. "Holiday already, Gill? What's this? Not without me surely?"

84

"Those are Sorcha's. She's going to Crete in a few weeks."

"Oh, well done. It looks like a nice place." She looked at Gill and they said nothing.

They got some plates from the kitchen and shared out the food. Gill took out the bottles of alcohol and mixed some with tonic in three glasses. Sorcha just had a mineral water with juice. They switched on the video player and put on the first movie, a comedy. Then it was a thriller. Sorcha couldn't help but be transfixed by the screen at least some of the way through the films but had her mind on other things. She went through a list of things she had done at work that week and estimated that if she went hard at it, she could get the rest of her inbox finished. The amount of paperwork had eased for a couple of days after their blitz but now, she could see it getting out of hand.

Isabelle noticed her attention was on something else and whispered to Karen who giggled. Sorcha tried to give her full attention but she felt her eyes glaze over. Later on, they cleared up the glasses and ashtrays and talked about what they could do next. "I really have to go," Sorcha said, "I have work in the morning."

"You're not going to stick around?" Isabelle said. "I understand. Let us walk you back to town anyway. They took their coats and said goodbye to the host. "So tell us," Isabelle said as they reached the main street, "any nice men in your office?"

Sorcha thought but couldn't think of anyone. "No, I've met just about everyone in the department. We had a good night out in December but that's it. Everybody's pretty busy."

She told them of the queues and the crush travelling to and from work every day. She was sure it would calm down eventually when the structure was fully in place. "I hope so," Isabelle said, puffing her cigarette. "It sounds like madness. It's not good when you're trying to get your job done."

"I think we both are close to finishing at the old office," Karen said. "It's fine because I have to finish my course in a couple of months and sit my exams then get some kind of job for the summer. There are loads of part-time jobs around so I'm not worried."

Isabelle was not happy about having to search for a new job with all the new workers in town. "Slave at some restaurant or bar? No thanks. But I'm not sure if I want to work full-time yet. It's not a pleasant prospect. I can't say that I'm feeling unwell anymore. I've been out far too much in the last few months for that to be believed."

They parted in town, Karen went south with Isabelle and they planned to meet up again. "Give us a call. See you soon."

"It's a shame we didn't get to stay out later. Next time we'll go to one of those shitty clubs we like so much," Karen said, laughing.

Sorcha walked sleepily to her bus stop. She sat back on the bus and thought of the events of the evening. Gill's flat was nice inside but she shuddered at ever having to live in a place like that.

She figured once she got back from holidays she could concentrate on building up her savings account. It wouldn't hurt to have money in the bank. She felt confident that the conditions at work would improve and she could start looking at places in a couple of years. Maybe by then she would have met someone, she reasoned, and it would be the smart thing to be prepared.

<hr>

Denise had mailed her with updates and asked for her opinion on what she should bring. Sorcha sent her the list she had found and Denise had sent her back a reply, typing in exclamations and adding smiley faces. She had tuned the girl out in the end and just read up as much as she could about the resort and its surroundings.

As she became consumed by the travel plans, she could feel her interest waning at the office. Most days, they had a number of employees visit the office to ask questions or deliver forms for processing. They recognised her face when she saw them around the site or in the locality and seemed to think she knew what she was doing, which made her smile. She had had a visit from two blonde sisters that afternoon, the younger girl had managed to get a plum job in training and her sister managed one of the teams in the UK market. It sounded like an important role but the blonde girl screwed her face up behind her glasses and just asked to get the relevant paperwork signed as quickly as possible. The girls had recently purchased a house together in a local suburb and were juggling the move with the pressure of work.

Jeremy had been joking to Denise that she had made a bad choice of holiday mate. "You know you're going to have to watch yourself the whole time on the trip. Sorcha is a stickler for time-keeping and cleanliness. Any foot wrong, it'll be the worse for you when your reviews happen."

Denise had looked pale but laughed it off. "I won't be doing anything your mother wouldn't do, Jeremy."

"Sorcha told me that she did a course in internet design before she came out here. Another reason to be careful," he joked.

The announcement came over the intercom that they would be landing in twenty minutes. Sorcha moved in her seat, half-asleep, as the plane began its descent. She looked out the window as the pilot prepared for landing. It was pitch dark outside and she wondered if she would be able to make it to the hotel before she fell fast asleep. The two girls had begun to stir and were tightening their seatbelts more securely as the airhostesses moved into position. Sorcha closed her eyes and could shortly feel the bump on the ground to indicate their arrival on the island of Crete.

Seconds later, Denise quickly unlocked herself and began scrabbling around for her hand luggage. "I can't wait, I'm so excited," she said, making for the exit. Sorcha and Monica followed, and they waited to dismount from the plane. It had been a pleasant journey with no mishaps and once they had found their baggage, they joined the queue for the taxis.

"I don't know what these guys are saying, I'm lost already," Denise said looking puzzled at a phrasebook. They were staying several miles from the airport so they pointed to a picture and the address, saying "*Thelo na pao...*" and the driver nodded and drove off. Sorcha had a phrasebook of her own with phonetic pronunciations of each sentence, and had been practising her basic language skills but knew that she would have to be careful not to leave the others. It had been alright for Shirley Valentine, her Greek boyfriend had been an English actor called Tom.

Studying a little bit of Greek and Roman in school had not prepared her for a visit to the region and she felt cowed by the unfamiliar atmosphere. But she was glad that she had come along. The hotel room was clean and comfortable and large enough for three to share. They went to sleep straightaway in crisp white sheets and woke up in the morning to the sound of waves lapping the shore. Sorcha turned over to sleep some more and vaguely heard someone get up and leave the room. She was relieved when she heard the door lock and snoozed in the morning sunlight. A couple of hours later, Denise woke her up by whispering in her ear.

"Wake up, Sorcha," she said.

She sat up suddenly. Monica was buttering toast at the table and looking at her with a smile. "You surprise me. On the way, you told me you would not be sleeping much when you got here," she said.

"Is it from all the hard work?" Denise kidded her. "Come on, get up. We have a ton of things to do today. We only have a week, remember."

Denise had already been downstairs and had brought back food for breakfast and some information on the best places to visit. They would have to go shopping later that day. But first, she wanted to sit by the pool and think about excursions for the week.

"There are loads of historical sites we can visit. They have buses leaving every hour. And we can go to the city if we want. And in town, there are lots of markets and designer shops. Hurry up and get dressed. You've got ten minutes."

Sorcha took the last bath towel and had a shampoo and a quick shower. She was still sweaty from the flight and came out feeling refreshed. She had time for a quick bite and then left with the girls. Downstairs, the air-conditioning was on and they walked through the hotel lobby to the outside pool. It was for hotel use only and the area was reasonably full so they sat by the pool for a while with their skimpy t-shirts and shorts relieving the heat, and put on sun tan oil and fanned themselves with a towel.

The beach was just a short walk away so they got up and followed the sandy paths to where the tourist population was lying and baking in the sun. They stopped to buy drinks at the local shops in case of dehydration then had to face the long walk to find a space among the crowd. There were kids playing in the water with inflatable toys and parents taking it easy on dry land. Further down the beach, there was a group of people their own age playing volleyball. Their shouts sounded like they were Australian and their colourful clothes highlighted their brown skins. "I feel so white," Denise mumbled as they walked along. Soon, they came to a secluded spot which was shaded enough to be ignored by everyone else. "This should do for the first day, I suppose," Monica said. "But we will have to get up earlier tomorrow."

This was how they spent most of the week, relaxing by the beach. From their spot, they could see faraway speedboats or cruisers or a guy in a wetsuit with a colourful board sail past on the waves. Sorcha had begun to think of taking up painting and Monica had a small camera which she used to take snapshots of interesting things or crowds gathering in the sun. They took it in turns to go for a short walk to stretch their legs or get a quick meal and always made it back to the hotel to dress for dinner in town. The first night, they spent a lot on cocktails and a meal in an upmarket brasserie serving French food. They had gone for pizza at night after that and were planning to go for an authentic Greek meal when they got to the city.

Denise had lost her early enthusiasm for the tourist sites but had gained a reputation for her karaoke talents in the local bar. They had taken a look at some of the local bars but Denise had insisted that they go to the karaoke night at least once. "Anything is better than listening to that awful guitar music sung by guys in mustaches," she said, her face full of horror. She had sung several songs to huge applause and had gone back the next night for more. "She's absolutely crazy," Monica said, "I think she spent a whole travel voucher in two nights singing."

Sorcha was afraid that she would want them to join in sooner or later. They had sang a couple of songs as part of a group but it was clear she wanted to use them as competition and the girls were having none of it. They made their excuses and decided to go island hopping.

They took a boat out on the water and went scuba diving in the afternoon while Denise gargled her throat in preparation for her night on the stage. They went to pick her up from the club at midnight and she travelled back with them, still singing in the back of the cab.

"Didn't I see you somewhere before?" she mumbled to the driver, who kept his eyes on the road. She had drunk a lot and they carried her to her room with the help of one of the Australians who were sitting sedately at the bar, after a day on the beach. Next day, they checked her before leaving for a day trip to the city.

"I feel so bad about it but I wouldn't miss this for the world," Monica said. She scribbled a fast note and left it by the table.

"I'm just glad our mobile phones don't work over here or she would be calling us all day to sing angry songs," Sorcha said. "Like a selection

About Turn

of blues songs or country and western to get back at us for leaving her like this."

"I don't think so," said Monica, striding to the bus, "she's out of it. Silly girl. Just as well there isn't one of these kinds of bars near where we live."

Sorcha thought of Denise singing her heart out in desperation at being left all alone by her travelling companions. Once she had sobered up, and realised they had gone, of course. Her expressions on the stage as she had belted out old classics had been something else. She couldn't help feeling disdainful at the girl who was such a sucker for these things. As the bus trundled along to the ferry port, she couldn't help laughing inwardly causing Monica to look at her curiously now and again. They chatted about work and such things as they carried on the journey.

"You like what you do?" Monica asked.

"Yes, before I worked for a small company so this is different. But it's been so busy. It's hard making time for other things outside of work."

"I know, I worked as a temp before though so I like the sense of security," Monica said. "They also like to look after their employees so that is a good thing."

She paused. "It is busy though. I'm not sure how they will handle it in future. Where will everybody fit for instance? They seem to be very focused on the service department to keep the customers happy. You know they have that new programme for machine fixes but I think they're still building it and it will take a while. Meantime, customers are calling up demanding attention. I don't know why they say it's so great with an international workforce because I have very little time to chat and make friends and it's likely to get busier."

"Denise says the call centre is getting more pressurised by the moment. You know they have added digital boards to the walls and agents are being monitored all the time. One of the service managers made a complaint about the behaviour of someone a couple of weeks ago. Said the girl didn't give enough to the customer. Now that all the lines are active and in the hands of the Dublin teams there is pressure on the managers to achieve the best."

They chatted about Jeremy and his housemates. "We are lucky as we have a quiet house but I think that there are a lot of arguments there. The two girls don't get on. I think Zara can be an awful person. I like the Italians that live next door to us. They helped us out with things when we moved in and they're great fun. A lot of the guys I work with are very serious and are over here for one reason only."

"I suppose when they decided to move the European base to Dublin, people were obliged to either give up their jobs or move over here," Sorcha said.

"That's right but they made sure the managers were cosseted so they wouldn't feel the changeover too harshly. These guys know what they're doing although not everyone moved here."

Monica worked on contract accounts for the German market. The company had thousands of machines with customers all over the country. She used SAP and a range of internal systems to solve problems. The teams had a database to log queries and thousands of serial numbers were logged on it with issues such as incorrect billing, wrong address and terminations. The system currently carried a lot of debt and there was a heavy load of workload but it was being managed and Monica didn't worry too much about it.

"It gets really busy on the phone and it's hard trying to manage customer calls and deal with paperwork at the same time. So it's fairly similar in that regard because a manager will always ask me to get back on the phone after a break even if I have things to do. At the moment I have 60 queries to resolve but there's no time to chase the problems with the German offices. So I get a call from the Customer Relations team or a salesperson who aren't connected with the department and don't know how busy we are."

They reached their destination and travelled to the city centre. Sorcha was feeling a thrill of excitement in the pit of her stomach. She was reading about all the wonderful sites to visit although they had been warned that the city was not the best place to see. Monica had been given some information about local markets so they had a look when they got there and bought knick-knacks. Monica decided to get her ear pierced again and chose a silver earring to wear. Sorcha bought some inexpensive jewellery and gifts for her family. They sent postcards then walked through the city streets, eating ice cream. They found a small Greek restaurant selling authentic food and tried a few things. It was hard work, making sense of the menu, even with a phrasebook. Sorcha went for a fish stew and Monica chose a salad. They had the house wine and checked out the décor as they waited for it to be served. "I love the tiles they use on the continent. So colourful," Sorcha said.

About Turn

She mentioned her kitchen wallpaper with its kettle motif, which had continued to peel away from the wall.

"That sounds cute. Although I like our house because it's new and hasn't been damaged at all. It's handy for transport too but I have a car. It's just an old banger but it hasn't broken down yet."

They had some fresh fruit afterwards. The owner sat a few tables away from them and read the local paper, which was incomprehensible to them. Before they left, Monica took a couple of snaps with her camera. "I'll get you copies of these, no problems," she said before stopping to chat with a German couple outside.

"Hey, they recommended we go to see the historical site that's open to the public. It's not too far from here. We can make it back before dark," she said earnestly. They got a bus out of town and went straight to the ruins.

"Wow, this is amazing," Monica said as they entered, each clutching a map of the site. Sorcha walked around the throne room and the royal apartments looking at the architecture which was hundreds of years old. A pattern depicting various historical scenes ran the length of the wall in each room.

"It's amazing how the king and queen got to live like this and their slaves toiled all day and slept in hovels," Sorcha said.

"It's a typical example of how the powerful lived," Monica answered, a slight smile on her face. "You had to be a king or queen just to have a dwelling like this. And it's wonderful how things have changed." She said this with a hint of sarcasm in her voice.

They looked at the frescoes decorating the walls and then went outside to the gatehouse with the amphitheatre beside it. As they viewed the private entertainment centre lined with tourists, they stepped out of their little piece of history and back into the commercial centre which formed most of the town.

The sun was going down as they returned to the hotel. They checked their room but Denise was not there. Monica suggested they go into town or call the club but they were too tired and were reluctant to use the phone in case a native answered. Denise came back an hour later and clattered into the bathroom on her high heels.

"Denise, are you OK?" Sorcha asked, from her corner.

Denise stuck her head out and whispered, "Oh, you're back. What did you do all day?"

Sorcha told her about the trip and she made a face. "I would love to have seen that. I got up at TWO in the afternoon and fell asleep in the bath. But some of the Australians woke me up and wanted me to take them to the club. So I got dressed at seven or so and went downstairs to meet them. We were singing Crowded House songs and Abba songs and Madness. It was great but my voice is gone. No more singing for me."

She went back to the bathroom and Sorcha went to sleep, smiling to herself. In the morning, they had breakfast outside on the terrace. Denise was back to herself. She had a stripey t-shirt and white capri pants and wanted to make the best of the rest of the holidays.

"Let's go on another day trip and we'll do some more shopping."

"You're not going to use this as a chance to source another karaoke bar, are you?"

"No," Denise said croaking. "I want to buy some things too."

"I've checked around and Rethymnon looks like a good place to visit," Monica suggested.

They found an inexpensive day trip taking them on a pleasant tour around the Cretean coastline and they arrived in Rethymnon in a couple of hours. The town had museums, a beach along the harbour, tavernas and a fountain in the centre that attracted a lot of attention. They spent the free time browsing in little tourist giftshops where craftsmen produced goods as they watched. Denise was laden down with wooden sculptures, more jewellery and tablecloths. They sat at a café and Denise pointed at Monica's new ear piercing. "I want one of those. I'd do my bellybutton but I don't have the guts."

"Then you'd really be singing."

Denise pouted and said, "I don't see anywhere around here that does it anyway. So I'll wait till next year."

Monica went to get napkins and Denise whispered, "I'm not sure it's hygienic but she seems OK after it." She peeled a banana and munched on the fruit for vitamins.

Monica had left them briefly to check her e-mails at an internet room and returned to suggest that they visit a local monastery. Denise made a face but was content when she thought of how her mother would react when she found out.

"She'll leave me everything," she said, gleefully, carefully choosing mementoes from the monastery site.

On the bus home, she leaned on Sorcha's shoulder and declared that she was wholly satisfied with her holiday. She had almost become a star on the stage and had bought everything she needed and had a tan to top it all off. "I don't think I could have dealt with the crowds in the city. Who wants to go and see an old palace anyway?"

She had arranged to meet the Australians in town for a drink. They chose another bar this time, not the usual club. The group was lively and made conversation, asking about Dublin and the nightlife. They were younger in age though and talked about volleyball leagues and their parents' careers, not theirs. They were enthusiastic about coming to visit and phone numbers were passed around. They walked back along the beach to the hotel and said goodbye as they went to different rooms.

Next morning, Sorcha and the girls spent the last day on the beach again and then packed their things in the afternoon. They had had to purchase an extra bag each to carry the new bits and pieces and they brought everything downstairs to wait for the taxi. The flight was a late-night departure so Sorcha finally got some time to read as she sat in the waiting-room. Denise was sprawled on a row of seats, leaning against Monica who was flicking through a magazine.

"Look," said Monica all of a sudden, holding up an advert for the company. "I'd almost forgotten about work for a while. There's no escape."

Sorcha laughed and went back to her book. It was strange how a person could get so taken over. She felt engrossed in something apart from work for the first time in ages.

"It just shows what a success this holiday has been," Denise grinned as their flight departure was finally announced.

Chapter 5

Sorcha was soon back at work, the familiar grey buildings a depressing sight after two weeks of sunshine. The traffic had slowly moved up the main road from the village and she had watched the time tick past slowly, anxious not to be late on her first day back. Lorna was asking a hundred questions about the holiday and wanted to see all of the pictures. The file of photos Monica had sent was impressive; Sorcha had included a couple of Denise in various stages of performance at the local karaoke club but knew better than to brandish the photos and potentially damage the girl's good name on site. Everybody gathered round to chat about the break and to view the pictures.

"She is such a daredevil when she's not at work. You know Jeremy's gone on a short break to Spain. His parents have a villa near Alicante. They're not expensive. I'm hoping he'll invite us over next year," Lorna said.

Sorcha revelled in the attention for a week then she forgot about it and got on with her job. The company had planned a huge launch of the training centre and had invited all of its employees to the opening. Sorcha and her team were working on the preparations. They had been to several meetings and the desks were covered in paperwork relating to the launch. The campaign had already begun and they sent promotional mailshots to everyone in the company the week before it all happened. The new centre was upstairs in one of the new buildings which had been transported from Scotland and put back together in the new location. The three grey blocks were interlinked and housed a large canteen, the bulk of the company's office space and meeting rooms.

Workers could apply for college courses or complete courses online at the training centre or at their desks. The HR manager John had been flitting in and out of the area for a couple of weeks. He had organised a centre based on a model used worldwide and it was of the very best standard. The whole team had a quick visit one afternoon as groups of site workers sifted through leaflets and put their names down for upcoming courses.

"I wish we were working over here," Lorna was saying predictably as they walked into the main building past the new reception and through the security check. A staircase in the middle of a plant oasis led upstairs to the training centre and they spent a short time filing through the small room with computers and shelves full of material.

"The ECDL is really popular but the CD-ROMs are fully booked up," the centre manager was saying to a dark-haired Spanish girl. The girl negotiated while one of the Irish welcome centre teams made their way around the room. One of them picked up a management manual and signed for it while picking up some promotional notepads saying 'Who do you want to be?'.

Lorna looked at the brochures interestedly but wasn't sure if she would take on something. "I've too much on already, with the job, the gym, the flat. Maybe another time," she said. She had put a deposit down on one of the apartments being built in the development she had mentioned. "You should see it. There's two bedrooms, my own shower, my own bathroom. And there's a bit at the back where I can walk out into the garden although I probably won't be using it a whole lot. "All of my free time has been used up on appointments and going to pick up things for the flat. I won't have any time to enjoy sitting outside until next summer but it'll be worth it."

Her dad had his own business and had paid her deposit, which amounted to seven per cent of the price up front. The property was on a newly developed part of land, some distance from the nearest village and they hadn't even built a local shop yet. Lorna had to pay the monthly repayments herself and wanted to put an advert for a flatshare on the company website.

The site had links to relevant departments within the company and detailed information regarding company policy and important information for the employee. It had a small adverts page for buying or selling items or renting places to live. Sorcha had been interested in using her course skills and enquired about getting involved but the company had hired a professional service. Two serious-looking English men in suits sat with selected employees and discussed suitable content.

She also had an annual review where she could chat to Lisa and discuss any issues she had with the job. Lisa had booked one of the smaller meeting rooms and was meeting with each of her staff for twenty minutes one afternoon. Sorcha was the first one on the list and she waited in the room as arranged. Lisa rushed in looking flustered and apologised for being late.

"So much to do, so little time," she said. She ran through the work list for the year so far and outlined a couple of problems and ideas for more effective team work. "Any questions?" she asked at the end.

Sorcha couldn't think of anything. She had made a short list of points to mention though, to show her interest in the job. Lisa jotted these down and then handed her a memo which was marked 'Important'.

"This is just something we're working on at the moment. We'd like to get a helpdesk up and running within the personnel department just so we can ensure that every member of staff has someone to contact if anything goes wrong with their salary, expenses, benefits. You name it. I hope you don't mind but I've put your name forward for it. You mentioned you had worked on the phone a lot in your last job?" Lisa smiled.

Sorcha couldn't remember but she didn't say anything. "It would involve being on the phone a lot. We're trying to diversify and offer members of the team an essential role to play now that we have almost full capacity," she continued. "Obviously, the employees we have are going to need a contact for any issues they encounter. It would make their lives easier. The manager was very keen with the idea. He's hellbent on making sure the workforce is a happy bunch. So what do you think?"

Sorcha looked at the piece of paper outlining the proposed helpline. She had always liked problem solving and had been bored tapping in repetitive information over the past few months. "Well, it can be a little like being cut off up here in the personnel department. I wouldn't mind getting involved," she said encouragingly.

"OK, well, I'll let them know." Lisa seemed relieved. They got up to go and Sorcha walked back upstairs. Lorna was next. She had been asked to work on projects in conjunction with the training department as the company was hoping on developing a new plan for the Dublin base. "I'm thrilled," she said. "It's a boring area to work in at first but they said I might get to travel, fingers crossed."

Sorcha was busy inputting paperwork for employee's reviews as most people had been there a year by then. She spent most of each day updating the system with the new pay figures and saving the information to the central system. The monotony was broken by a trip to the local cinema. Jeremy had returned and was anxious to see the next instalment of Star Wars. "It's the first of the whole series, number one. This is the very start of the story so we see where Darth Vadar…" He was like a little boy on his way to the centre after work. Lorna laughed at his enthusiasm. They had decided to celebrate their pay rises by this trip. "I can remember kids at school going to see that but it was years ago."

"I've seen the first three…" Jeremy began.

"I thought you said this one we're going to see was the first one?" Sorcha looked at him, quizzically. Her head was fuzzy after a week back at work. But she was happy to go to see the film anyway. The posters had been all over town for weeks. It was the end of summer and there was little else on so she succumbed.

The cinema was a nine screen chain complex and had a little ice-cream parlour to one side plus a Pizza Hut right next door. They had arrived in time for the first show of the evening. There was a cinema like this selling hot dogs and nachos in every shopping centre in the city like the one where Karen worked.

Sorcha and her group spent a couple of hours flying through the starlit universe and enjoying laser fights although the enthusiasm never took off. She remembered the stir the film had made even in Irish towns and laughed inwardly as the story simply rolled along. Afterwards, they decided to go for something to eat. There were half a dozen fast food restaurants within walking distance, all staffed by locals. "Not McDonald's again," Lorna said, "I've eaten there every weekend this summer."

They went to an American style diner in the end and ate bowls of fries with mayonnaise and burgers with all kinds of toppings. Sorcha just had the Caesar salad and crunched some salad leaves as the group made small talk. Sorcha travelled back with Jeremy who was tanned and happy after his break. He was planning to take extra courses and qualify in personnel management. "There's so much happening right now. Even if the company went bust, I could still find a good job in town. Or even around here, there are a few companies that look good."

Sorcha nodded. The village was being given a facelift and reflected the surge in the area's wealth. Some of the houses had been turned into offices for recruitment agencies or consultants and the old businesses had been transformed into auctioneer's offices with notices of houses for sale covering the windows. There had been a couple of new restaurants added to the area, which some people had sampled and raved about. Jeremy went to get his connecting bus outside the village and Sorcha went back to her house in Castleknock.

James had been spending his weekends in reliable bars since the fiasco at the city centre club. He had invited Sorcha along but she was happy to spend some time on her own for a while. "I'll let you know when I'm rich again," she told him as he prepared for another night in the local. Jason had been going home most weekends so she usually had the place to herself. She was often exhausted anyway after a week at work and spent her weekend relaxing in the bath and listening to some new music. The next day, she was travelling in by Parnell Street and was watching the posters for upcoming shows as she drove past. An African woman with her baby strapped to her tightly got off at the stop by the Gate theatre. This area had become known as the Little Africa of Dublin with centres offering cheap international calls and authentic food shops lining the street.

She met Karen at the last stop on O'Connell Street. Part of the street had been cordoned off for road works. "This could be the beginning of the renovation job we've all been hearing about," she said to her friend. The preparations for the tram development had been laid recently and the area looked like a Berlin construction site.

Karen nodded although her thoughts seemed far away. "I have so much to organise. I'm leaving next week and I'm going to stay at home for a while then we'll see about getting a place together. I think everyone would be OK with that if we had some concrete plans. I'm not keen to stay in the city. It's mental getting home every evening from work and we don't have the money to buy a property here now. We could stay in the flat but we'd just be renting."

They crossed over the bridge. "There are a few companies opening up sites at home. It's only 90 minutes from Dublin, you know."

"Now that you have your qualification, you can apply for things and I'm sure you'd be snapped up, right?" Sorcha said.

"My mother has already done that on my behalf," Karen said, rolling her eyes as they reached the southside. "The minute I got my degree, she had my applications sent to everyone she knows."

They decided to take a bus to Gill's flat. Winter was setting in and they would have to face the biting wind if they walked. Sorcha noticed the crush of leaves in the drains as she went past. The gold, red and brown colours added a seasonal feel as the street cleaner collected the rubbish.

"I think Gill wants us to cook something but she hadn't decided what when I spoke to her," Karen said. "It's like the Last Supper. But I'd love it if you guys came down to visit later on when we're settled."

Sorcha nodded. "Sure," she said, "what's the town like?"

"It's very historical and there's a river running through the centre of town. There are a lot of craftshops and the arts festival is on each year."

"That would be something to look forward to."

"We should have a place of our own by then. We're looking at some new houses in an estate outside of town. We have to buy before they get too expensive."

"Next year seems so long away. I'm just focusing on right now," Sorcha said, apologetically.

The bus stopped close to Gill's complex and they called her from the local shops. "She's saying to come up first and we'll choose a meal to make then we'll buy the ingredients," Sorcha said.

"Fair enough," Karen agreed and they went through the stone arch again and up the stairs of the block they now knew to Gill's front door. It was slightly ajar and they knocked before entering.

"Are you decent?" Karen shouted. Louise was dressed up in a party dress and holding a brightly coloured parcel on her way to a birthday party in the flat downstairs.

"Make sure you're back by six o'clock," Gill said as she kissed her goodbye.

"Hi!" she said to the two girls who were wrapped up in their woollen jackets and scarves. "Here, let me take these things and sit down and make yourselves at home."

They sprawled on the couch and Gill put on the kettle. "How was your break?" she asked Sorcha.

"Fabulous," she said. "Worth every penny. I'm just so broke now that I have to watch everything I spend. But I should be flush again when I get paid," she smiled. Gill was listening to her every word.

"Well, Isabelle and I have been spending our money at the markets in Blackrock. We took a train out there a couple of times and we spent a lot. Just buying French food – there's this amazing stall and its run by a French man and they have some really interesting pictures and bits and pieces for the home and clothes of course," she babbled. "You know that the local markets have all closed. Mother Redcaps is shut more or less and the Iveagh markets are all boarded up. I'm like, 'but I've just moved in!'"

She looked at Karen. "And what's worse is that Karen is moving out of Dublin. Did she tell you?"

Sorcha nodded. "Yes, she mailed me."

"So I'll only be seeing her once in a blue moon from now on."

"You can come down for one of the festivals and you're welcome to stay with us," Karen said reasonably.

"I love Kilkenny," Gill went into paroxysms of joy at the thought. "I just need some bloody money. Bah."

"You have until next May to SAVE. I'll buy you a piggybank and you can put some money away each payday. OK?" Karen giggled.

"I'm really no good at that sort of thing. But I will try," Gill promised. "Now what are we having for our main course today? We have a couple of hours to cook and eat in peace until Louise is back."

They flicked through the cookery book Gill had bought secondhand and drank cups of tea until they chose a recipe everyone liked. To make the vegetarian meal involving eggs, nuts and several types of greens, Gill took £5 from each person and went to the local store to purchase what they needed.

The girls walked around the flat while she was gone. "It's so quiet up here. You don't really get any noise and it seems to be young families living around," Sorcha observed.

"I think my mother would jump four floors if she caught me living in a place like this though," Karen said. "It would horrify her. I mean if both Rob and I work full-time, we can get our own place. I don't think Gill is motivated enough. She earns a lot with benefits and she's been getting child support recently, she told me. It's not fair.

"You put in the hours at your job as well, Sorcha, and the rest of us have to work for what we want. It just annoys me sometimes because I think you-know-who gets away with a lot."

Sorcha shrugged. She didn't know much about Gill's financial situation. "At least she's finally getting some money from Louise's dad." She paused. "My parents would not be happy with me living here either and I wouldn't like it. It's an ugly place to live with the surroundings and the guys hanging around outside," she explained.

Karen laughed. "Give it a while and you'll be looking for your own place with all that dough you've earned for your hard work. Any day now."

Gill returned with a bag of groceries. She had bought her own weekly shopping as well as the ingredients. She set them on the table: packet of eggs, cashew nuts in a bag, onions and seasoning. "There's a spare bottle of wine in the cupboard. I think we got that at the market last time. It's cheaper at the supermarket but it's good quality so we can have that with the meal." She busied herself getting the pots ready and put some water on to boil. "It's a fairly simple recipe. We just have to watch what we're doing so that it tastes ok at the end."

They boiled the eggs and chopped the vegetables, which had to be sauteed in a pan. The eggs were mashed and the vegetables and nuts had to be added to the finished mixture with seasoning which was then cooked in the oven for forty minutes.

"That's it, I suppose," Gill said, retrieving a bag from beneath the bowl she'd used to create the egg mash. "I bought some chocolate eclairs for after. Isabelle would love some of this but she's working this afternoon. Mick finally got her some shifts at the office and the hours are all over the place."

"What is she doing?" Sorcha asked.

"Just helping out," Gill said lightly. "They have a print run this weekend so she has to work with them for that. The deadlines are pretty tight. I'm not sure she is so suited to that kind of work. It's very intense."

"She had those problems with the change of lifestyle." Sorcha added.

"Change? Oh, you mean her depression? I think Isabelle just took a little bit more of something than she should have. She is a lot of fun when we go out but she went through a really bad period and she had to calm down."

Gill continued, "That's why I'm so worried about her with this new job. She's finding it very difficult to keep working at that pace but she's prepared to give it a go. I don't know how long it's for but she needs the money."

The timer on the oven went off eventually and they took plates from the cupboard and shared round the contents of the cooking dish. "This smells gorgeous," Gill said, spooning out the hot meal. "A little bit of training and I could go professional."

The food did taste good. Sorcha gobbled up half of hers and felt full. Gill was eating her plate clean and took some of the leftovers on Sorcha's plate. "Vegetarian food is very filling but there's not much fat. It's not like eating a plate of steak which sits in your system forever."

Karen had finished most of hers and they scraped the remainder into a plastic container. "I can have this tomorrow for lunch," said Gill, her eyes gleaming. "Éclair, anyone?"

They ate the luscious chocolate and cream pastries and had coffees for after. Sorcha noticed a new photo in a frame on the side table and asked who it was. "That is Louise's dad. He's back in my good books now that he's paying for his daughter." The photo had been taken inside a block of flats like the one they were in at that very moment. The block in the photo was a high rise though and they could see the profile of another high rise block of flats in the distance.

Later on, the girls were walking back towards Karen's flat and Sorcha said out loud, "I didn't know that Gill had lived in a flat like that in London. Surely there was no need for her to be living like that? Maybe here because she's on her own, but I was shocked when I saw that photo. It looked so grim."

"I guess it's a lifestyle choice. We said before that she should invest some money in a modern flat but she didn't want to," Karen said.

They said no more about it but took the turning over the canal and walked to the apartment complex. Rob was out so they switched on the telly and watched some music show. "There are so many good bands at the moment. I'm going to miss living in Dublin for that reason," Karen mused.

"Is Rob OK with the move?"

"Yeah, it was his idea in some ways. He thinks Dublin is getting too expensive and he likes the idea of living somewhere else. He's pretty stressed with work all the time. He should be able to get something at home too, I should think."

Sorcha ended up sleeping in the spare room again, bringing back memories of her temporary residence in the flat. They stayed up late watching movies and Rob came back eventually at 2am. He was in a good mood, having been paid a good bonus and was looking forward to moving back home.

"Come and see us any time you want. There should be things happening during the year if you want a break," he said.

Sorcha listened and promised she would take up the invitation.

On Monday morning, Sorcha was feeling the effects of a late night as she sat on the bus taking her to work. She had noticed Dani had left the company to take up another job but there were plenty of familiar faces around. Denise had been sitting upstairs and they walked to the buildings together. Denise worked upstairs in the next block of offices as part of the UK customer service team. There was a staircase on either side linking the three buildings together. "We had that work thing on Thursday night to raise money for Childline. It was crazy," she said. "Robert, one of the guys I work with, and his team won the quiz and got a bottle of champagne. He was trying to spray it around the hotel lobby like someone who had won the Grand Prix."

"Where was this?"

Denise mentioned one of the hotels off Merrion Square. "I'm used to wild nights," Denise said, "but this was just complete abandon. Everyone made use of the free bar. The managers just had looks on their faces. I don't know if we'll be having another one of these. Then we all had to come into work on Friday. I woke up thinking I was going to die. Now I have to go to work and deal with escalations for the morning. It's getting busier in there every day." She tottered off towards her office and disappeared behind a potted plant.

James was in the kitchen cooking dinner and someone Sorcha had never met was sitting at the table, reading the evening paper. "Sorcha, this is Yves, he's just moved in next door with his girlfriend. He works for your company." There followed a brief description of how James had met Yves when he had come in to open a bank account. He had recognised the address and they had started chatting.

Yves had recently graduated from college with a degree in business and had been encouraged to move to Dublin by the company at a local jobs fair near his college. His girlfriend was from a small remote town in Poland and they had met in London, before moving over when Yves had been employed as a trainee accountant through a jobsfair. He showed them pictures of her: a tall blonde with a pretty face. Yves was clearly in love but he had one slight problem.

"I have been trying to get her something within the company but she doesn't have a work visa yet. So we're just living on one salary, mine, at the moment."

"You don't know of anything that's available in any of the areas? I told him you were in the personnel department," James said, apologetically.

"Oh, I don't know. I can have a word if you want," Sorcha said.

"Well, we'll feed you then," James joked, and handed her a plate of food. It was fried potatoes and gammon steaks and she took some.

"I'm easily bribed," she said.

Yves was looking through the adverts and smiled faintly. "We are renting a double room next door at the moment," he said. "The flats here are so expensive. One guy I spoke to was asking for £800 for a one-bedroom flat and that would be reasonable at this stage."

Sorcha took the paper and looked through the listings. She knew some of the areas and saw an apartment in Karen's complex with rent at over a grand. She pointed it out to the guys. "I know some people renting here, and this place was four hundred a month when they moved in two years ago," she exclaimed. "I think I've been too afraid to look but some of these rents have shot up."

"It's not so bad out here but I know I was wary when I had to find accommodation here last year. Any closer to town, and you'd need a second job," said James.

"There are apartments in this area which may be cheaper although I'm not sure how long that's likely to last," Sorcha advised.

Yves went home saying that he would forward a copy of the CV to Sorcha's e-mail and Sorcha promised she'd looked into the possibility of hiring his girlfriend. Her name was Paulina and she had a degree in design but had little office experience. Her time in London had been spent living in a cramped old house with other Poles, fully aware that she was not legal and had to take what work she could get. She had had very little income and had cheered herself up by going to art museums or a party or two which is how she met Yves.

Next day at work, Sorcha received a friendly e-mail with Yves' contact details and location attached. She passed the information on to Kathy and had a quick word about the request. Kathy nodded and Sorcha thought no more about it.

The announcement came that Lisa was moving to a new department. Sorcha's group was to be managed by a new employee called Sharon who had previously worked in London. Sorcha met her briefly. She had been born in Dublin but had moved abroad after school. She was a chatty woman with a bob and seemed friendly enough. Her background was in training and she had helped out with the development of the training centre. Now she had been given the plum job of manager within the personnel department. Not even Lorna could complain that it was unfair as none of them had any management experience and could not have been promoted.

They decided to arrange a night out at the newly-opened restaurant in Temple Bar. Their different schedules meant some tussle over dates but eventually they agreed to book a table for a late time on Thursday night of next week. Meanwhile, Sorcha was getting regular e-mails from Yves who wanted to know how she was and if there had been any progress on the submission of Paulina's CV. Sorcha typed back that the manager of the call centre recruitment was away at the moment. She told him she would check back the following week and let him know. 'Sometimes, these things take time', she typed. He responded with a short ok and seemed satisfied with her reply, and she put it to the back of her mind.

She was reticent to approach Kathy who had a temper and was obviously busy with other things. She hadn't even met Paulina and had only met Yves once in her kitchen but soon she was seeing him all over the place. He took the same bus route as her and she often saw him around her work building, looking worried. He always smiled and said hello. By the following week, she had not had a response to her e-mail. Kathy was back at her desk and had been in and out of Sorcha's work area but had said nothing. One evening, she was sitting in her house and she heard a knock at the door. She answered and it was Yves and Paulina, looking radiant in a brightly coloured winter coat.

"Are you busy?" Yves asked in his foreign lilt, "I just thought you'd like to meet my girlfriend. I told her you were trying to help out with getting her a job."

Paulina was back from a holiday in her hometown, paid for by Yves' bonus last quarter. She had brought over some homemade jam, which her mother produced in her kitchen. Sorcha took it with a smile. It was her evening off and she didn't really know what she was going to say. Luckily, they didn't plan on staying long and left without entering the house.

Isabelle had left messages about Karen and Rob's going away party which was being held at the end of the month. Isabelle and Gill didn't have a whole lot of money and prices for hotel parties had risen so much, there didn't seem like much point. Gill had tried some contacts including an acquaintance who sometimes DJ'd and she thought could do with the work but he had asked for a couple of hundred and she had hung up on him in shock. Sorcha had called Isabelle and left a message to say she was happy to go along with whatever was decided and wanted to know if they were buying a present.

James came home late and she told him about the visit from the neighbours. He seemed surprised. "Don't worry about it," he told her. "It's not on your shoulders to get anyone a job."

Next day, she bumped into Kathy at the coffee area in the canteen. Kathy was by herself and Sorcha mentioned the application from Paulina. "Oh, I think I deleted it by mistake. Can you send it to me again?"

Sorcha went upstairs and resent the mail and its attachments. Kathy responded straightaway and called her extension. "Can you forget about this one? I can't take her on as she doesn't have a work permit. She doesn't have any relevant experience either. Sorry, but no can do."

Sorcha left a quick message for Yves before lunch and came back to find his reply. He had typed his response in block capitals and was unhappy for the rejection. She waited for him to call but no phone call came. She was relieved and tapped out a formal rejection letter. She did feel bad but there was nothing she could do.

On Thursday, she went to Temple Bar and met the others at the Thunder Road Cafe. One of the team started to kid her about Yves and joked she would be stalked from now on. Sorcha laughed but began to feel uneasy. She sat at the remaining seat at the table for twelve. There were her team of eight, plus Lisa and the new girl and a couple of others. The restaurant was only half-full but very noisy as happy hour had just started. They ordered fries and burgers and soft drinks and beer and more fries and dips and all kinds of creamy desserts. Sorcha had not eaten since lunchtime but struggled to finish her meal.

"Lets get some shots to say farewell to Lisa," Gemma said, her feet already on their way to the bar. The service was pretty fast and they knocked back a line of shots in unison. Lisa was given a present of vouchers for one of her favourite clothes shops. She was going on to manage some of the payroll staff and would be getting more money so she was happy. She chatted to Sharon about the role and what to expect in her new job. Sharon was looking at the nearby TV screen showing some current videos from Britney Spears and Steps. "They are fantastic," she was saying. "Look at those moves. I've seen them live ten times in London. Are they playing over here at some stage?"

Some of the group played with a motorbike in the centre of the room and took turns to have their photo taken. "I think this is going to be a repeat of the Friday night in the hotel," Sorcha laughed. Jeremy raised his eyebrows but didn't say anything. He had heard about the escapade of the call centre staff and was quietly sipping his drink across the table.

"Sorcha will be taking care of the helpline from next week, when the salaries are paid," Lisa was saying to her right. "It was one idea to ensure that employees had access to personnel if they had any problems. There's a bit of a lull at the moment so we're using our staff to help with any problems."

Sorcha smiled at Sharon who asked how the workload was at the moment.

"It's manageable," Sorcha said, truthfully.

"Glad to hear it," Sharon began talking about her nails which had been painted blood red and Sorcha could concentrate on the activity again.

Next morning, Sorcha was half-wishing she had brought her sunglasses with her. Her eyes were sore after the smoke-filled room last night and also, she had just spotted Yves get on the bus with Paulina. They were engrossed in each other and didn't notice Sorcha sitting in the back row. Paulina got off at the village and Yves sat with his back to her. Sorcha waited till the very last and crept off the bus when it got to the business park then walked very fast to her office.

She had some things to finish off before her role changed, and had to collate some files for Miriam who would be helping her deal with administration for the financial services departments as well as a number of other tasks. There was a fairly high turnover with employees leaving for a new role or new company after a few months and they had to replace them if possible. Often, the jobs were open to people working in other departments. In some cases, the job stayed vacant for a few months until they had the resources to recruit again. Sorcha didn't see much of the financial side of recruiting apart from having the finance manager sign the authorisation forms but the pay slips went out via their department. They spent an afternoon as a team folding each slip and placing it in a specific envelope.

"I hope we're doing this correctly or I'm going to have to deal with the mix-up on Monday," Sorcha said, half-joking.

Miriam laughed and kept folding. "This is such a boring job. There are hundreds of these to send off. So much for modern business practices. I could think of better things to do and maybe they could hire some monkeys to do this work. We should make it a recommendation at the next team meeting."

They had finished by four o'clock and Sorcha took a taxi to the village. Karen's party was happening that night and she had to go home and change. She dressed in black and wore minimal makeup and a pair of shoes she had seen in the centre. They were red with pointed toes and flat soles and very comfortable. Isabelle had indicated that they were giving the couple money for their retreat to the country. They had decided to hold the party in her house and it was kind of a surprise.

Sorcha had to go through town as usual and she met groups of people dressed in stripey tights and pointed hats, or well-known superheroes such as Robin and Batman. They were on their way to Hallowe'en parties.

"You wouldn't believe the difficulty I had, just getting her ladyship here tonight," Isabelle said when she arrived. "It was unbelievable. Now that they're leaving us, it's all 'oh, I'm too busy. I've got so much to do.' And I'm like, 'wait, we're your friends, dammit.'"

Isabelle was in good form but clearly hurt that Karen was moving away. She was dressed in an old cocktail dress and had had her hair chopped into a bob at the students' hairdressers.

"She seemed very happy with the surprise when she came through the door. We were all here waiting for her," Sorcha said.

"Oh yeah," Isabelle said, holding a cigarette in the air. She was drinking strong whiskey slightly mixed with water. "She was OK with that but I won't let her get away with it."

Karen had shown up just after Sorcha had arrived. Some of the work friends and a few people from college had attended and it was a cosy gathering. The girls had ordered a cake and Isabelle had been at home all afternoon making the preparations.

"My flatmate was not too happy," Isabelle continued. "She's been working all week and wanted a quiet night. I said she was welcome to share the party with us but she didn't want to intrude. More for us, that's what I say. I couldn't let Karen go without a farewell party."

"Did you get time off work?" Sorcha asked as they poured wine into glasses. She was trying to make herself useful and had stationed herself in the kitchen to help with food and drinks.

"Yeah, well, I'm not working for Mick anymore."

"Oh no?"

"It was too much. I was feeling tired all the time. Now it's OK. I have some shifts at a local restaurant and I go to the gym. I don't get much money but I can live."

Sorcha could see Gill downstairs chatting to one of Isabelle's friends. A few people had been invited but the residents were anxious not to cause any damage to the house. It would not be so easy to replace their home a second time.

"Well, lets go and celebrate," Isabelle said, pouring the last of the wine. "Have you got a glass of wine? And bring the plates. Good."

They lit the candles and brought the cake across the landing to the living room. Karen's face glowed as she blew out the candles and made a wish. "It's not my birthday but we need all the good luck we can get," she said.

"Don't be silly," Isabelle shouted. "You've got everything you want waiting for you."

Karen smiled and began to slice the cake into pieces. Sorcha handed out paper plates of sponge and cream and a fork for each person. Gill had come upstairs with her companion and they stood around chatting amid mouthfuls of cake. Karen was opening the envelope and inside, there was at least a couple of hundred quid. She was speechless and didn't know what to say.

"We're just hoping that you can buy something nice for your new home when you get it," Isabelle said. "Maybe a spare bed and some blankets so we can all come stay. We won't leave you alone!"

"Oh, thanks you guys," Karen called from the couch where she was sitting. "I don't know what to say."

"Any ideas, Rob? Are you man or mouse?" Gill joked.

"Anyone got a microphone?" Rob asked, half-seriously. The room quietened down again as he spoke. "Just want to say thanks to everyone for being so generous. When we get ourselves going, we'd love to have you all down for a visit. At least we have e-mail so we can keep in touch. Many thanks. Give Peace a chance. And all of that." He grinned.

Gill began to cry into her cake. Sorcha passed her a spare napkin. She blubbered away to herself as the party began to swing again. Isabelle turned on some music and people began to bop as they stood in the tidy room with the bottle of cleaning spray still on the windowsill.

Sorcha had finished her cake so she took a black bag and began to clear up the empty plates and forks. She recognised a couple of girls from the old office and said hi. She had met some of Isabelle's friends at her birthday and chatted about Karen's plans to them. Then she returned to the kitchen and tidied up. She was tired, after working all day.

"Alright, Sorcha?" Karen said, as she arrived with some things to dispose of in the bin.

"Yeah, careful you don't throw out your money," she answered.

"It's all safely with Rob and he's got it in his wallet just in case it ends up in the wash. How was your day?"

"Busy. It's the end of month so we had to pay everyone. You have no idea how much work that involves."

"I know the feeling. My mother has me harrassed about organisation and she keeps threatening to come up here and help me pack everything. I've got it all under control. We're leaving first thing in the morning. Can't wait."

Isabelle arrived and was trying to light up another cigarette. "Damn this thing. Oh, *merci beaucoup*," she said as Karen passed her a new lighter. "These things wear out so quickly."

"Have you thought any more about moving back to France, Isabelle?" Karen asked.

"Yeah, I have. I have some plans. I can't believe it's almost my birthday again. I'm feeling so old. You know it's not the same here anymore. Gill and I were talking about it the other day," she said. "I am seriously thinking of moving back to Paris. With the prices increasing all the time, there's no difference. I came over here to get away from expensive coffees and designer shops and now everywhere I go, there's one right there on the corner."

The girls nodded and listened. "And everybody is too busy to talk these days. Even you," she said to Karen, "and it's your party! And don't talk to me about Mick. He's just not the person he used to be. Well, in a way he's just as selfish." She laughed bitterly and took a swig of her drink.

"I have noticed it's changed in the past couple of years," Karen said in agreement.

"Yeah, I mean it's still kind of grotty but now you're dealing with a faster pace and I don't like it. There seems to be a lot of people when I go to the gym or the shops and a lot of people with money too," she said, making a face. "But you still have all the street people late at night. When I was coming back the other evening, I was taking a taxi to be safe."

Just then, Rob came to the tiny kitchen and beckoned Karen to the door. "Oh, we have an early start in the morning so I have to go. Thanks for the big effort and the gift. This is fantastic." She kissed them both goodbye and Isabelle and Gill took them to the front door.

"See what I mean?" Isabelle said, "completely selfish. I know they're moving but do they have to be so rude?" She leant against the kitchen worktop with her arms folded.

"Is it true about Paris?" Sorcha enquired.

"Yeah, look at this house. The kitchen is like a cardboard box, and everything is in the wrong place. That bathroom downstairs. I have to crawl down there to wash in the morning and hope no-one sees me. Mark my words, I'll be out of here shortly." She stomped upstairs and joined the crowd. Sorcha took sips of wine and stood in the kitchen for a while. The group was dispersing slowly while she spent all her time in an office block. She didn't know what to feel about the changes in her life: there was still so much she did not know. Gill called her from the living-room and she went upstairs.

On Monday, she was still recalling the atmosphere as she had left Isabelle's house. She had called for a taxi eventually as Isabelle's behaviour had gotten more and more out of control. "This is Sorcha, she used to be one of us but since she entered the corporate world, she hasn't had too much time for us."

"Don't take this out on me," Sorcha had said. "Talk to Karen if you're upset."

"Oh, come on, stand up for yourself," Isabelle had shouted, flinging her glass around. "Tell us how much you love money and all the egos you work with. She asked me if I wanted a job out there you know. It's like a cult."

Isabelle had turned her back and Sorcha could feel her face turning crimson with embarrassment. The other guests had no idea what was going on and were chatting among themselves. She realised she did not know anyone and Karen and Rob were probably in their own place, tucked up in bed. As she left, she could see Gill looking out of the corner of her eye and laughing to the guy she was with. She had already moved on.

Sorcha recollected this as she went to start her first day on the helpdesk. Isabelle had laughed when she'd told her. "Come on, you'll be driven up the wall, people ringing you every five minutes to complain. Not my idea of fun."

Sorcha had argued that the job would pay off in the long run. Isabelle had just scoffed and had continued drinking. She remembered the time she had gone with Isabelle to an all night party. It had not been intended but the girls had ended up in a rented house somewhere in the suburbs with throbbing beats in the kitchen and computer games in the front room. She had no idea what was happening upstairs but Isabelle had spent some time chatting with her waitress friend and had debated taking some drugs. Sorcha had left with Isabelle as dawn arrived and they had walked to the nearest bus stop. She didn't know the area and wouldn't have felt safe on her own. Sorcha had walked ahead with Isabelle chatting to her tipsy friend a few steps behind. She had been angry and couldn't understand why she had to sit in an atmosphere like that and they called it fun?

The helpline number went live at 9am that morning. Sorcha took fifty calls before lunch time from worried employees who had been put on emergency tax or had not received overtime pay. Each person was worried and insisted that their issue be prioritised. She logged each query on her system and forwarded them to the correct person, attaching notes and any paperwork she could find. At lunchtime, she wandered down the stairs and grabbed a quick bite in the canteen. There were still remnants of the Hallowe'en decorations from the week before. She saw Yves in the queue ahead of her and pretended to take interest in the fruit lining the glass sandwich counter. Wow, the bunch of grapes reminding her of her sojourn in Crete looked so ripe and juicy. Yves seemed too busy to notice her and she took her sandwich and scrammed.

Upstairs, she wiped the crumbs from her outfit and switched on her phone again. The call volume had dwindled but she was kept busy for the rest of the afternoon, answering calls as they came through. Sharon approached her once or twice with files to process when she got a chance. She repeated her greeting monotonously as the phone rang during the afternoon. "Hello, good afternoon, this is the HR helpline, this is Sorcha speaking, how can I help you?" They had kindly stuck the greeting word for word on her phone in case she forgot any part of it.

She left the office a little later than usual tidying up the stacks of paper on her desk from the day. The rest of the group had gone home and Sharon was in a meeting with some of the management. Sorcha picked up her coat and bag and walked down to the exit, beeping herself out of the building. She said goodnight to the security man and walked quickly to the bus stop. There were groups of foreigners standing there, waiting to go home. Some of them finished earlier but the home times were staggered and these were obviously the five o'clock leavers. A group was speaking in French and discussing their day in animated tones. She recognised some of the words "*toute suite*", "*donne moi la briquette*" as they lit cigarettes. The bus appeared at the end of the road and slowly made its way to them. She listened to a couple of Italian boys chat softly to each other, looking at their watches as they stood in the cold to wait for transport home. There were a few cars starting to leave now and the traffic line was growing. She noticed one of the welcome centre workers approaching the stop in a haphazard fashion, her skinny frame bent against the cold wind. Christine was partially deaf and had poor eyesight. She was wrapped in scarves and had a chance to make a call home before the bus arrived. "Just on my way now, Mummy. Yes, I see the bus. I'll be home in an hour."

This became the routine for Sorcha each day. She could feel the pressure of work start to mount again and did not even consider taking leave when there was so much to be done. At the next team meeting, Sharon took a moment to thank Sorcha for her hard work and diligence in dealing with the queries. "It's taking a lot of the workload from us and filtering it so we know what is important to deal with. Thanks for being so helpful. It's not easy being the first point of contact in any job but you're doing very well. I haven't had any complaints so far," Sharon said, smiling. The group gave her an obligatory round of applause then continued with the meeting.

Sorcha really did strive to meet the requirements of the job and felt obliged to get involved with every query that was raised. "I can't help it. Every time they call me, I just think 'what would I do if it was me?'. I understand that they feel frustrated. The company is so large that it's easy for mistakes to be made," she said to James, rubbing her neck.

"I know what that's like," James said, agreeably. "Some people are messed around with bank charges or they're refused bank loans for whatever reason. At least I have the bank to hide behind but I hate having to turn people away. You just hope it never happens to you."

"It's not like they're earning huge sums of money, either, so most of them need it, if you know what I mean. The company brought hundreds of people over here to work and paid them an initial fee to settle in with, maybe a grand or so, but they've had to pay that back.

"There was one guy who had been covered to travel to London for training and ended up with a credit card bill of £1400 so he's been brought into a meeting room every couple of weeks to explain why it hasn't been paid off.

"When I looked into it, it turns out that the Expenses Department has got a bunch of boxes for a filing system as they're moving offices so it's in there somewhere. Because we can't duplicate the paperwork in case he gets double, we have literally had to wait until the form is found and processed."

The guy had explained that he was not able to pay the amount on his own account as it was close to the equivalent of a month's salary. Sorcha's own salary cheque was about the same and she knew, like everyone else, that she was being made to work for her money. She was aware that those callers to the helpline had little time to spend on chasing their issues and often, tempers were fraught as they spent their precious time discussing the problem in detail.

She was glad of James's existence in her life as work became the primary concentration of her week. In the last quarter of the year, the activity on site heated up. Sorcha processed files for temps from New Zealand who had been brought in as extra financial staff to help achieve profit targets at the year end. The temps had no need of training as they would be assisting the customer relations manager as she weeded out the problems that could be fixed and tried to sort as much as possible. It was an unpleasant task and the temps would be her right hand men for a few weeks as she dug in and fought. The paper queries would go straight to the account owner and it meant everyone had to make maximum effort with team leaders stressing the importance of high value amounts. Every penny counted towards revenue in the end.

Sorcha had to meet with the UK operations manager who would sign off the salaries for each worker that month. The ground floor of building 2 was chaotic with mountains of paper on every desk. She noticed the majority of workers busying themselves on the phone or at the computer. Her denim friend greeted her and quickly signed the documentation, looking stressed as she spoke simultaneously to a billing agent about a difficult query. "I'm not getting involved with this now. This will have to be put on the list for Friday's meeting."

The customer relations manager was also in the billing area chatting with one of the agents. "We have to make sure that this goes out properly to the customer or they won't pay. There are five hundred machines on here so this will probably take a while. Just let me know when it's done so I can check it before we print everything."

At the exit, Sorcha noticed the leasing manager handing out joke leaflets for a free trip to Las Vegas. "Here, dahling, have my last one. We're planning a big blowout in the States next year all going well."

The HR team had been allocated new desk space in Building 4 and would have to move by the end of the week. The movers arrived and the team spent a couple of hours packing boxes and tagging their office equipment. Sharon left the stickers on Sorcha's desk and she had just enough time to do tag everything before tearing off to the bus stop. It was a tiny gripe but the new location meant longer for her to travel in the mornings and the bus service had not improved much.

The new space was on the first floor of the building and comprised of a number of desks surrounded by makeshift cordons to protect against noise and people traffic. The management team was located in separate offices down the hall and the training centre was just at the corner. "So you got your wish," Sorcha said to her co-worker Lorna. The girl looked unimpressed and ate her lunch, looking out at the gigantic carpark at the back of the building.

"All day I have been bumping into bloody call centre workers," she said, later. "They're two a penny over here. Where is all the finance staff? I presume we have someone working on all this debt. Oops." She stopped as John Xavier passed by in a whirl, laughing at her comments. "I hope you like the new space, girls. You'll feel much better being in the centre of everything."

As December was fast approaching, Sorcha took the bus to the city centre and stopped off at Henry Street to see what was hot or not. The shops were full of red clothes and she decided to buy a dress, putting the charge on her credit card which she could pay off later. The employees were due to be paid twice in two weeks: the end of November and mid-December to cover the Christmas period. She would have her hands full until the 23rd and didn't want any complications till then. So she found some bright and cheerful accessories and charged these too. Then she braved the busy streets to get herself to the bus stop and home.

Chapter 6

The Christmas party was being held at a venue close to the airport. It was one of the few places large enough to hold the hundreds of staff keen to attend the Christmas celebrations. Sorcha and the others piled off the coach which had taken them from the village to the large warehouse of a building brightly decorated with red and green bunting and balloons. The main room was full of round tables on one side and rows of tables on the other. There was a bar on either side of the room and the servers were limbering up as they saw the influx of people. The little group she was with moved to the right and occupied a table of their own.

"This seems to be fine. We're close to the bar," said Jeremy, putting his overcoat on the back of his chair. Miriam was sitting beside him with her boyfriend. Seamus had arrived with a friend of his and was sitting with his arm around her. There were a couple of others from the department who had just arrived.

Gemma and Lorna had arrived together and went to share a table, which had some spare seats. They could see the management and senior members of staff sitting together on the opposite side but it was too distant to make out every person's face. A woman came round and took their coats to the cloakroom and a waiter took their drinks order. The first drink was free and they ordered doubles. Bottles of wine were placed on every table and a cracker on each plate. Ten minutes later, more waiters emerged with bowls of soup and hurriedly put one down in front of each person. "There's about 800 people here," Jeremy said. "I'm hoping there aren't going to be any accidents. This soup isn't very hot though."

Sorcha tasted her bowl and it was watery vegetable soup with a bread roll. She ate it anyway and waited for the next course, which arrived just as quickly. There was no choice in the menu and the plates were uniform displays of Christmas dinner with a splash of gravy. The group looked at the food unenthusiastically and slowly began to eat. The wine was poured round and there was just enough for a glass each. They pulled the crackers, reading the jokes to each other, none of which were remotely funny.

The manager took a moment to welcome everybody and to raise a toast to all the hardworking people present. Everyone raised their glasses in unison and cheered. But there was already a line of people going to the bar to order drinks. Jeremy offered to go and made a quick list of what they wanted before disappearing.

"You look tired," Miriam said to Sorcha. "Is the food not up to scratch?"

Sorcha made a face and tried to stuff some tasteless food into her mouth. She made small talk with the girl beside her and wiped her mouth with a napkin. Jeremy had returned with the tray of drinks and Sorcha took her second double.

"No," Sorcha said, "that's one good thing. The phone line finishes at five on Friday and I'm off for the weekend!"

"I wish I could get some more work to do," Miriam said, "I could really do with the money. I don't think we'll be getting an increase next year from what I've heard. The company will give some excuse and freeze our salaries. You wait and see."

She got up to go and Sorcha sat, nursing her drink and wishing she had something more exciting to talk about. Her life had been empty of things to do recently and she was waiting until the New Year to make some changes. She put her glass back on the table as she felt a dizzy spell come over her. She would be comatose in an hour if she didn't stop.

The dessert arrived in the form of a slice of chocolate log and it looked like the kind to be bought in the local supermarket. She ate it with cream and finished her drinks. The alcohol was taking effect and she felt capable of dealing with the rest of the night.

"What have they got lined up for us?" she asked to the general group.

"Some covers band, I think, but it won't be on all night and there's a DJ here for later," one of the girls answered.

Sorcha took a look around at the room. There were a lot of people she recognised: some Italians, a lot of the French teams and German teams, the guys who worked in finance and people she knew who worked in service or product support. There were a couple of Spanish girls chatting together and one was wearing scary spiked heels, her friend had on a bright red cocktail dress. Most of the guys had worn suits of some description. Some were wearing smart designer or borrowed tuxedos or had taken the opportunity to wear something smart and outlandish at the same time. Sorcha had worn her new outfit and relaxed for a while as various employees came past to say 'hi'.

There wasn't much time to sit back, however. The tables were cleared and moved back to make room for the dancefloor. There was commotion near the stage as a band came on, dressed in luminescent 70s clothing. The two girls were dressed in blonde and dark curly wigs with short skirts like the ABBA women and were joined by their 'husbands' playing their instruments. "Hello, Dublin, are you ready?" the blonde girl called out. They broke into a version of 'Waterloo' and the crowd erupted onto the floor. The sound was tacky but infectious and Sorcha's group joined everyone else on the heaving dance area. "Here, lets hold hands," someone shouted and they danced in a circle with a group of accountants and people they didn't know.

The circle broke as some tall Dutch guys bounced around the floor and dangerously close. Someone else started a conga line which grew to a few dozen until this too broke up and people went back to dancing on their own or face to face. Sorcha found herself beside some guy who was letting loose and seemed not to care about anyone else's space. He was chatting loudly to a tiny girl in a party dress and was oblivious to everyone else. Eventually, she sidled off to the bathroom. She bumped into Monica and Denise on the stairs. Denise was jumping up and down and was delighted to see her.

"Ohmigod, long time no see. Let me guess, you've been busy. It never changes in that place. So have we, right?" she poked Monica, who swayed on the staircase. She was linking arms with a couple of German friends. "Have you been out dancing yet?" Denise asked.

Sorcha nodded. "Yeah, but it was getting rough out there." She smiled and waved goodbye.

"Great band," Denise shouted. "I just feel like singing but tonight I'll just DANCE." She walked off with her arm outstretched dramatically. Monica smiled and waved goodbye. They tottered downstairs in their heels and disappeared.

She met another girl upstairs. Melanie came from the Caribbean and was pretty laid back. She chatted as they queued for the bathroom. The line snaked around the corner and they soon made it inside the door where a group of girls were putting on makeup and checking themselves in the mirror. Sorcha thought she looked healthy despite the busy schedule. She pinched her cheeks and reapplied lipstick then went downstairs again.

Her half-finished drink was still sitting on the table. There was no sign of anyone she knew so she picked it up and sipped a little bit. Some of the tables and chairs had been left behind so people were sitting around, chatting and playing with balloons. Although she had processed a large number of these people's applications and details, she had had little time to meet them. Some of the groups kept to themselves and had held seats at tables for their mates. They moved between the seats and the dancefloor. Every so often, a few girls would come and cajole their friends out to dance. They were making up little routines for the well known songs such as 'Super Trooper' and 'Waterloo' which had been performed a second time.

Sorcha saw Jeremy chatting to a blonde girl she had seen around the office block and wished she could be more enthusiastic but in truth she was bored. Dancing in a circle and blowing streamers was the behaviour of a child and she didn't see any reason to do that. She nodded at Jeremy who turned his back and Sorcha was relieved when they announced the prize giving. There was a huge cheer as the ABBAesque left and went backstage.

Bottles of champagne were handed out to the holders of lucky tickets which had been distributed with the party invitation. There was a holiday voucher which was won by one of the Dutch guys. "It's run-of-the-mill stuff," Lisa had said at the bar. "In the summer, they're planning a fancy dress party with a competition for the best dressed." The DJ set up his turntables shortly after and began a serious set of popular songs.

Sorcha went outside to get some fresh air. There was nothing around but a carpark and a few flowerpots. Someone came out to take a phonecall and she went back to the bar which had the shortest queue and ordered a mineral. She was feeling queasy after the meal and joined a group of people dancing in a small group safely by the tables. The dancefloor had turned into a nightclub probably like something Isabelle would have frequented in her heyday. People were throwing themselves in all kinds of shapes. "Did you see John?" Miriam asked. "He had all of the Spanish team dancing around him in a circle." There was a hardcore group dancing in the centre while small groups bopped along in pockets of space around the room.

At 2am, the evening came to an end. The DJ played the national anthem and the party goers all stood to attention for the obligatory two minutes as the music was blared out over the speakers. A couple of guys at the bar were having difficulty focusing and one of them put his head down on the counter in agony. There were a couple of people sitting in chairs and their friends were trying in vain to have them get up and go home. Sorcha went with her group to collect their belongings and went outside. One of the guys she had seen inside was throwing up by the wall and his friend was beside him.

"Are you going into town, Sorcha?" Denise asked as they met. "I'm too tired, this night seemed like it would go on forever." She had sobered up and was clutching her winter coat. Monica was nowhere to be seen.

"She's staying with a friend tonight," Denise said as they got on the bus. It could drop them either in town or back at the village. They chose the village and they hailed a taxi from the local pub.

"That was a crazy night," Sorcha said. Denise nodded, half-asleep. The taxi dropped Sorcha at her house and then continued on with Denise in the back seat, too tired to wave.

Her hangover remained until well into the afternoon on Saturday. She had forgotten to take painkillers on her arrival home and was suffering as she walked to the shopping centre. She had met James briefly and he was bussing it to town to meet his parents. Sorcha walked along inhaling the winter air, her woollen scarf knotted around her neck. When she got to the centre, it was full of shoppers. There was a line of cars encircling the brick building and the car parks were jammed full. She took care at the zebra crossing and dodged the women with trolleys full of shopping bags. As they took calls on their mobiles and dealt with their kids, they were as dangerous as motor vehicles.

Inside, the centre was ablaze with Christmas lights and there was a queue of kids at Santa's grotto. She walked quickly to the escalator and went downstairs. She checked out Boots and some of the well-known stores for presents. She had a list and found what she needed within half-an-hour. It was easier than making the journey into town anyway. As she was walking past Dunnes, she saw Paulina at one of the counters, looking harrassed. She was totting up amounts and folding clothes into bags and the line of customers was getting bigger.

When she had enough of the record stores, clothes, books and general gifts, she took a welcome break in Bewleys, the dark interior seeming almost out of place in this glitzy arena. She bought a strong coffee and a scone and sat rifling through her purchases to make sure she hadn't forgotten anything. There was such a hullabaloo even in the café and she looked around at the tables full of people and shopping bags piled in trolleys and on seats. There was no piped music in here but half of the local population of children seemed to be out for the day, clutching hot chocolates and Santa presents. She was glad to get out of it minutes later. She splurged on a taxi and the driver slowly drove her back home.

They had one more week of work to complete before the Christmas break. As the last batch of salaries was dealt with and made ready for distribution, Sorcha's team was advised to catch up on the outstanding work. "You'll feel great when you come back here in January to a clean desk," Sharon said. She had sent them all Christmas cards and a gift token, thanking them for all their hard work during the year. They had each picked a name out of a hat and had been given a limit of five pounds to buy a quirky present. Sorcha had bought Seamus some festive socks and the group had opened little ornaments, joke hats and soap or candles.

Despite the festivity, Sorcha and Seamus were manning the helpline all week. Seamus was trying to make light of it, joking that he was Santa's little helper, solving the problems of the little kids at the end of the line. "Alright there, mate, that's sorted. Now don't go spending that all in one shop. I'll be up North this holiday as well so I'll be watching you."

"They're not very appreciative of my humour," he said, wearily at lunch. "Some of these guys work in finance so when we make a mistake in their pay packet, they sound like they're out to get us."

"Maybe you should try a different approach," someone said. "Pretend you're one of the three wise men. Wise enough to solve anything."

Seamus smiled for a second but rejected the idea. "I don't see the point. It's the same mistakes over and over. Thankfully I'm out of here on Thursday. They're such a ungrateful bunch of losers. Don't you think?" He looked at Sorcha who nodded.

"Yeah, we're getting fried on the phones every day because of mistakes that are made in the system. Although, that reminds me, I have to go to Dixons after work and complain because my new TV hasn't arrived yet," Seamus grinned.

Sorcha was answering the calls seriously but wished that payday had not fallen so close to the last one. She could hear herself repeating the same words to people with different accents: "OK, I'll log that one. It'll be changed as soon as possible, I promise." Or "No, you're not entitled to a refund, let me explain".

Lorna had been calculating in her head just how much of her furniture list she could purchase with the two pay cheques and her thin face was contorted with the strain. As the calls came in more rapidly, extra paperwork was passed to her to take the weight off the two teammates and she groaned, looking at the clock which seemed to tick so slowly.

"Did I introduce you to Courtney the other night?" she asked Sorcha as they walked back from a toilet break. "Do you remember the American girl? She's a new starter in the finance department. Her dad worked for the company for years and they've lived in Hong Kong."

Sorcha vaguely remembered a dark haired girl with braces dressed in Chinese garb grinning politely and smoking a cigarette. She had just been to see the Lion King in London and was raving about the performance.

"Myself and Gemma dropped her off at her flat on the way home at 3am after chatting the whole way back into town about where to go. She was pissed off, I think," Lorna said, laughing hard. "She was bugging me, talking about the apartment she's bought with her new husband. They've decided to rent for a while to get started." The girl put on a voice.

Sorcha wasn't really listening. She had been feeling woozy all week since her visit to the centre. She had recovered after her night out but had picked up a chill. She went to the canteen and bought orange juice and as much Vitamin C as she could find. She drank it in cupfuls at her desk and continued to work although she had by now lost her enthusiasm. The vitamins did not have their usual effect and she began to feel progressively worse as the week wore on. She was forgetting silly things and was having difficulty finding information on the system and even listening to callers made no sense. She said nothing as people were busy with projects and administration and somehow, she didn't feel ill enough to stay at home in bed.

One by one, the team left for the festive break and on Friday, there were a handful of people about. It was the same downstairs as most people had taken holidays a day or two early. Sorcha was due to travel home that day and had planned to leave at midday. She took her things with her and fought her way through the blustery weather to the office block. She was not feeling any better and had not managed to shake off her symptoms. Sharon asked about her plans for the ten days.

"I'm getting a train home this afternoon," she answered as the phone activity had died down at last. Seamus had left already, happy as a schoolboy to be off on holidays. "Probably stay with my parents for most of it and enjoy New Year's as well." She felt groggy as she talked.

"I'm flying out to Andorra this evening," Sharon said. "The ski trip is finally happening. I can't wait."

"Lucky you, have fun," Sorcha said feebly, as she went to book a taxi. She organised her desk and said goodbye at twelve. The taxi was waiting for her and she got in.

"Where are we going?" the driver asked.

Sorcha wondered why no-one ever seemed to let these guys know the destination of the person they were picking up. She hesitated for a second and then gave her address. She was feeling tired and figured she could rest for a while before moving on to the station. The driver calmly drove her through the wet muddy roads laden with traffic and took her to her house.

James and Jason had already left for home so she was on her own. She sat on the couch and when she tried to stand, the room swam around her head. Panicked, she knew that there were only a couple of trains going home that day and she had missed the first one. But it was no good. She could not motivate her limbs to move as she wanted. She crept upstairs to the bedroom and tried to sleep. This was no fun at all and she wished she had left earlier. She would probably be home by now beside an open fire with hot tea and biscuits. Just the thought of food made her feel ill and she lay in bed for some hours, unable to function. Slowly, she drifted asleep and was half-awake when she could hear the phone ringing downstairs. She was unable to move and was afraid to attempt climbing down the stairs in case she fell. She could imagine tumbling on top of her head and being found days later by a puzzled milkman or one of her housemates upon his return.

'Oh please let them ring my mobile phone', she prayed. She knew she had left her bag someplace close by as she had taken it upstairs with her coat. It was still on the bed, she could feel it, although it seemed her coat had been knocked to the floor. The phone was inside and sure enough, shortly she could hear the familiar ringtone. She pulled the strap of her bag closer and retrieved the phone as if on autopilot. Her dad's voice called out to her in the darkness as she sat up in bed.

"Sorcha? Where are you?" he bellowed. "You weren't at the station. Did you fall off the train?"

"I'm." She broke up. "... not feeling well." She whispered the words almost inaudibly.

"No?" He paused for a second.

"I...can't make it to the station." Her voice sounded very far away.

He gave a snort down the phone line and started to talk to her mother. They tried again to make communication but Sorcha was out of it. She could hear herself talk but she was at risk of slurring her words like an alcoholic. She had never been this bad. What could be wrong?

Eventually, she made her point. She had horrible flu and wouldn't be home that day. Or the next day, as it was Christmas Day. "Sorry," she said, knowing that they would be worried. "I'm just too sick."

Her mother came on the phone and asked without thinking, "Is there something wrong?" If she had been feeling herself, Sorcha would have wanted to wrap the phone line around her neck. She said nothing and felt too fatigued to even roll her eyes.

They hung up in the end, angry at her inability to explain what was wrong. She looked at the phone and then promptly went back to sleep. In the morning, she found a message on the screen. They wanted her to call a doctor and she did, once she had checked herself out for any rashes but there was no sign of anything. She could hardly focus on the mirror and slowly called the doctor's number. Thankfully, there was a doctor in the area who came round later that day.

"How long have you been like this?" he asked, in the living-room, checking her pulse and her temperature. Both were normal and he diagnosed severe fatigue as she explained the symptoms, which had led to her near immobility.

"You should take vitamins all the time. Working in these offices can destroy your immune system. Maybe you picked up a bug in the office or in the centre, like you said."

He checked the kitchen to make sure she had enough food and the presses had enough for a couple of days.

"Have you anyone to call on if you're feeling worse?"

She shook her head. Everyone she knew was either away or on the other side of town. Jeremy had gone back to his parents for the break and most people came from country towns like herself. There was nobody left.

"Well, I'd advise you to stay inside and wait until this wears off. It's not a cold and it's not a fever so do whatever you can to make yourself feel better, OK? And call my office if you need anything." He smiled at her woebegone face as he left and shut the door behind him. Sorcha went to the couch and lay down. She called her parents again and briefly told them what the doctor had said. She was feeling a little braver now following his investigation but the curious feeling came over her again as she switched off her phone.

Her family had been about to start dinner and she could imagine her father sitting in front of a huge plate of meat and vegetables, dying to tuck in and stuff himself. She thought that even if she had been caught up in a freak whirlwind up here, he would still have to have his Christmas meal and would leave the clean-up work till later. The meal would have been the highlight of his life as a youngster when there were few delights to be had. She thought that he had not really moved on much from that part of his life.

She didn't have the energy to watch television and it seemed like too much of a blaring noise in the corner anyway. She went to James's press and took out a sleeping tablet. He had used them a couple of times on the advice of his doctor.

She went back upstairs and tried to relax, allowing the tablet to take effect. She slept for hours and woke still under the same cloud of dizziness and blur in her mind. She was unable to think and decided against moving, except to go to the bathroom. Travelling home even after the bank holiday was unthinkable. Even going outside was a chore. She opened the front door to look at the snowfall and quickly closed it again. She sat in the living-room for a couple of hours looking tiredly at the snow falling constantly on the ground. Aware that she needed to eat to keep her energy levels up, she had made some soup and had boiled potatoes with butter. It felt like her appetite had disappeared and she chewed the monotonous food wordlessly. Inbetween, she took naps on the couch, which no longer left her feeling refreshed.

She woke with a start when she heard knocking at the window. It was Yves from next door. Sorcha had forgotten all about him and Paulina. She had thought they would have gone home for the holiday. She went to open the door and he cheerily said 'hi' as he stood there in the snow-covered path. He came inside and she closed the door with a bang, almost falling over in the process. Yves' face grew anxious. "What's wrong? Is something wrong?" he asked.

Sorcha could feel tears trickle down her face as she struggled to explain what was happening. Making human contact after having been on her own for the past three days, she became suddenly emotional and she could feel herself lose control.

"Come next door with us. You're obviously ill," he said, as Sorcha swayed from side to side. Every little thing had been such an effort since she had left the office on Friday. She nodded and pointed upstairs. "What do you need?" he asked. "Shoes," she mumbled, smiling weakly. He went upstairs and got her usual pair then she bundled herself together and went next door. Paulina took one look at her. "I was surprised to see the door open today. Yves went over to check if everything was OK when he got back from the shops."

"She's very sick. There's no fever but she's dizzy all the time. I told her she could stay here. I think Daniel's room is open, right?" Daniel was their flatmate and had gone away for the break. Sorcha began to feel a little better surrounded by the neighbours.

"I thought you two had gone for the winter break as well," she said slowly. "And I don't know the people on the other side. But it's cold when you go out of doors and I had food to eat." She wasn't making any sense.

"Did you call a doctor?" Yves asked with concern in his voice.

"Yeah, and I've been told to take it easy and allow this bug to clear out of my system." She could feel the faintness in her voice as she spoke.

Yves nodded with relief and gestured for Sorcha to sit down on the armchair.

"Is it warm enough for you?" Paulina asked, checking the fire, which was blazing. Sorcha nodded and took some tea. Yves went next door with her key and got some spare clothes and a toothbrush. She had her phone and bag beside her that she had dropped on the floor. The house was decorated with cards and they had made a good effort with a bright tree in the corner and lights around the ceiling. They watched some movies in the afternoon but Sorcha was unable to concentrate so she went to sleep in the spare bed. Paulina came in and out during the day and Sorcha took soup and drinks when offered.

"Sorry about this," she apologised.

"It's no problem. We couldn't afford to travel this year. My mother is coming over soon for a visit so I don't feel so bad," Paulina had sat on the edge of the bed. She had a worried look on her face as Sorcha's face was expressionless.

"Are you feeling any better?" she asked.

"No," Sorcha said. She put down her cup and went back to sleep. She faintly heard Paulina leave the room. She had taken a couple more sleeping tablets as her system felt out of sorts and she could not get proper rest. When she woke, she felt well enough to get dressed and sit downstairs.

"That was quite a knock-out cold you got," said Yves. They had made a meal of leftover chicken and rice and Sorcha felt OK to have some, albeit small portions. "You should take something to support your system this time of year," he continued. "It's easy to get rundown."

"I don't know where it came from," Sorcha said. "It came out of nowhere. I've been so busy lately." The dizziness had eased somewhat and now she was starting to feel embarrassed about being such a burden during the holiday. As soon as she felt capable, she went back next door and had a quick hot bath being careful not to disturb her delicate sense of well-being.

Slowly, she got back to normal. She was just grateful that she didn't have to deal with New Years parties. The boys were at home, probably having a whale of a time. She called home and her mother answered. She wondered if everything was alright and could not understand why Sorcha had not shown up for the holiday.

"You wouldn't believe how I felt. My neighbours thought I was close to death. They just happened to find me and I stayed with them."

"Hmmm," her mother said and gave monosyllabic answers for the rest of the conversation. She didn't seem convinced that there was anything wrong. Her dad was not at home. He was out visiting some old friend or a family member, Sorcha supposed, as her mother chatted haltingly here and there. Her brother had called over for a week's break from his flat in Galway and was probably being doted on by the parents.

Sorcha hung up and watched the New Year's celebrations on the television. She saw the fireworks in Australia first and thought of her holiday, which had been so much fun. But she would have to focus on purchasing a new home this year and it would be her last break for some time. The gathering in Dublin city centre was tiny in comparison as she saw familiar TV faces show themselves on the screen for the occasion and link arms for Auld Lang Syne. Paulina and Yves had gone to a party in town and would be back in the morning. She dragged herself upstairs and went to sleep. She had made one resolution: only to survive the next week and get well again.

Chapter 7

Still feeling a little under the weather, Sorcha went back to work after New Year's Day. Her illness had subsided enough for her to travel to the office and do a day's work. James had been horrified and apologetic when he'd found out what had happened. "You mean you were in that house all this time on your own?" he said. "You should have called. I would have come back early. It would have meant leaving Finola at this early stage…"

"Who?"

"This girl I met when I was out at home. She was in Belfast for the Christmas visiting some friends and we bumped into each other at one of the clubs. She's just my type: blonde and good-looking. But she has a nice personality too."

He looked pleased with himself and Sorcha was glad that she hadn't called for help as it would not have been fair. She was just glad that it was all over and she would just have to get back to normal. At least she felt capable of working and there was no shortage of things to be done. She thought of Paulina and her and Yves' kindness and decided she would push again for Paulina's sake when she got a chance.

Lisa was sitting on Sharon's desk when she arrived and they were chatting with a friend about the ski trip. Sharon's partner had twisted an ankle on the second day so they hadn't spent much time on the slopes. "It was so infuriating. But we made the best of it. I've had so much alcohol inside me these past few days," she said. "And of course, I now have my brand new car. Things are looking up!"

They pointed to a blue mini jeep parked outside and visible from their office quarters. "That is big enough to fit a small family," Lisa joked. "Are you trying to tell us something?"

Sharon giggled but denied she had bought it for any reason. "Haven't you bought something new too?" she asked Lisa.

"Yeah, it's just an upgrade of my old car. I thought why not, I'm good for it," said Lisa. "Anyway, we'd better get to work. John is back and raring to go."

They left and Sharon chatted to the team about their holidays. They had all done the usual round of parties and celebrations. Sorcha felt like the child who had only eaten one Wonka bar when it was her turn to tell all.

"A bad cold, was it?" Sharon asked. "I had to lug a man twice my weight through the airport on the way home so I know what suffering's like, don't worry."

They got on with their work eventually and enjoyed the slow pace of the environment as a lot of staff had taken a couple of extra days. Sorcha got on with sorting the problems she had raised the previous month and was making some good headway. She could hear Sharon chatting on the phone about the lobster meal she had eaten during her holiday and how that had almost landed her in hospital high in the mountain peaks. But she had not succumbed and, as Sorcha tapped, she could hear Sharon's voice drop to a whisper while gossiping about the other people they had travelled with and couples they had met during the break.

Within a day or two, everyone was back to the rigorous routine they had been so glad to give up in December. Sorcha had to action a number of e-mails from employees who had also started back to work and had decided to start off the year with investigations into better pension rates or a different level of health insurance. She made notes of each request and passed the details to the people on her team and mailed each person with a response. She filled out numerous forms and mailed the relevant persons to please come upstairs and sign them at their convenience. Then she got on with the rest of her work once she had cleared her desk of festive decorations for another year. She sent her cards downstairs to be recycled and got some clean stationery from the cupboard. She could feel a remnant of the weakness still in her body and made sure to wrap up well and take it easy at the weekends, keeping a supply of vitamins handy.

The company had recommenced its hiring drive for the New Year and, as well as keeping current employees happy, Sorcha found herself processing new applicants' paperwork when she had spare time. There was not a free moment between 8.30 and 5pm except for half-an-hour's lunch which she didn't enjoy. As Seamus had to man the phones while she was on her break, she usually went downstairs and sat with whoever was available.

"There isn't really a lot of satisfaction from this job," Seamus said. "Do I really care if we have employed another 100 people this month? After a while, it grates on your nerves. Some of the questions are stupid and unnecessary. I just wonder where this is going."

Sorcha had nodded in recognition. When the American girl Courtney appeared to sign some starter forms, she chatted with her about the job and could feel herself drooping with tiredness. Courtney herself looked a little annoyed as she waited her turn. "Yeah, we're busy as well. It's a little too busy if you ask me. But at least they're agreeing to pay us our bonus no matter what."

Lorna had been asked to survey each department to measure their training needs and had to collate this information and design a training plan with the managers of their resource centre. She had little experience of the processes involved and was learning every day. She had been obliged to find her way around some computer packages which allowed her to process the statistics and create charts for the eventual presentations. "I'm enjoying it mostly but the figures are a pain. Imagine trying to collate all of this information for over a thousand people. I've been up and down to the girls in the centre asking them for help since I started this," she said. Her desk was a swamp of paper and she had spent numerous extra hours after work sorting through the debris.

Gemma was hard at work processing pension plans for new and existing employees and saving the information onto disc and on her computer hard drive, careful not to make a mistake. She was responsible for maintaining the records of the workforce and was lucky enough to have the essential computer skills to process the information quickly and securely. It was a boring job but might help her gain favour with the managers. She was often in early in the morning already working when everyone else arrived, and left at 5pm exactly to visit the gym before going home.

Jeremy had continued to take part in the early morning induction sessions before the new employees went on to their learn-at-work training schedule. He had spent the early part of the year preparing the necessary paperwork for new starters and had also helped to put together a handbook for employees, covering every aspect of personnel and what anyone on site needed to know regarding their jobs.

Sharon had spent most of her time so far in meetings and this didn't seem likely to change. She trusted her team members to work on their own time. As the helpline had been a new idea submitted by the manager to help workers adjust to their busy environment and was not a usual part of personnel activity, Sorcha had no one to refer to if a problem arose as Sharon had little experience of these things. The busy atmosphere meant that there was no time for discussion and she dealt with issues as best she could. She had no idea if what she was doing was helping the workforce or not as the calls were not monitored and they had no feedback from management yet. One thing that was certain was that the project looked likely to continue for some time.

She often had employees come up to her desk with issues and found it immensely hard to close a conversation. She usually made some excuse about a heavy workload or was saved by the person having to return to his/her desk before the issue became too heated. With all the new faces arriving, it was hard to maintain professionalism at all times and sometimes she found herself stumbling when asked about a specific team or to explain minute details of a contract. The head manager had not found reason to complain, however, and often walked past on his way to or from a meeting with a smile on his face, sometimes whistling as he went.

As the new season of Spring arrived, Sorcha had to arrange a meeting with her mother to explain face to face what had gone wrong those weeks before. She picked a quiet day and arranged to meet her in the village around midday. Her mother would be driving the three hours from home and was feeling more confident about the trip now that the Winter was finally over. The afternoon of the day before, Sorcha bumped into Alicia, the manager of one of the Spanish teams in the financial services sector. She had brought a list of issues her team was having with their work environment and asked Sorcha to have a look – she spoke rapidly in broken English and simultaneously chatted to her deputy team leader who looked expectantly at Sorcha with his dark eyes.

"You see, it's like theese, I have a group of twelve peeple who have come over here from Madrid, Galicia and all over Espain. They're not happy, I'm not happy. I want a response by the end of the week and I would like you or somebody else from this department to come to where we work and meet us and explain what is going on, OK?"

The woman had a blaze of curly hair and a skinny, sallow face and had clearly been hounded for some time to sort out the problems she had listed on a sheet of paper: insufficient transport, crowded facilities, and issues with administration. The items on the list were familiar and Sorcha took it politely.

"Tell your senior manager if I don't get answers this week, I will create some problems for him and his organisation. I have my staff to think of and if they're not happy here, they don't work!" she said, dramatically. "It's not your fault but please think of the people, downstairs, TRYING to do our jobs."

"I'll make sure he gets this and I'll let you know his answers as soon as possible," Sorcha said. Alicia seemed satisfied with that. She smiled back as she went downstairs accompanied by her deputy and disappeared. Sorcha left the list and a quick note on top of Sharon's desk as she had not returned by the time her day had officially ended. She would be interested to find out what had happened to the note when she got back in the office.

Sorcha went to meet her mother in the village the next day at twelve pm. She noticed the familiar registration as the car pulled onto the main road. It stopped where Sorcha was standing at the vegetable store and the lights were switched off. Her mother, a thin woman with a wavy bob, sat inside motionless except for the unlatching of her seatbelt. She hardly reacted as Sorcha waved cheerfully.

"Is this the place?" she said looking around, as she got out of the driver's seat. "It's not much, is it?" There was no traffic that time of day and she took her time getting onto the footpath. She looked at the vegetable stalls with some interest although they had plenty of fruit and veg stores at home. "I hope you buy these sometimes," she said, thoughtfully. "It's better for you than trashy junkfood. And cheaper." She looked at her daughter for a moment conveying nothing.

"I didn't want to travel all this way today," she sighed. "I have so much to do. This is only reminding me of how much I have to do at home. You get a little break for Christmas then it's back to business."

The store also sold garden tools and fertiliser. An array of well-kept gardens either side of the street attested to the benefit of such a store in its locality. "Have you got shopping to do?" the mother asked. "Now's the time to do it as you don't usually have a car, do you?" Sorcha mentioned that James sometimes drove to the centre if they had time. Her mother did not reply. "Lets go back to the house," Sorcha said, "I have everything we need."

They got back into the car and drove off through the village centre. The mother did not notice anything; she was too busy watching out for traffic lights and oncoming cars. The interior of the car was spotless as usual. Sorcha sat in front and gave her directions. They went over the bump past the train track and turned right into the estate. There was no-one about as they unloaded the boot.

"Here," her mother said unceremoniously, as she handed her bags of vegetables. They had all been handpicked from her garden and ferried to the city. She had done this before once or twice and it was a common occurrence when her mother travelled on a holiday to a friend's house or to visit family. She always brought some fresh produce with her to share. Sometimes, if a caller came to the house, she would send them off with a sprig of lilac or a sample of some shrubbery that they had admired.

"I didn't bring any flowers with me today," she said, as they entered the house carrying her heavy jacket. "They wouldn't have lasted the journey. Three hours on the road and the traffic is just getting worse." In the kitchen, Sorcha switched on the kettle and rummaged for some teabags. She went through phases and had not been making cups of tea in the evening anymore. James worked late most evenings and went home at the weekend. Once a month, his new girlfriend came down for a couple days but their schedule varied and they often spent time out of the house. Eventually, she found what she needed at the back of the press.

Her mother hovered around the kitchen, checking presses and looking at cloths to see if they were clean. She looked at the bin, which had been emptied the night before and took a look outside at the garden. "You can go in and sit down," Sorcha said as she got things ready. Her mother was annoyingly quiet and she knew that it wasn't just the journey. She didn't know what the problem was and maybe there wasn't one, but she went ahead with the charade and poured the tea into cups and put biscuits on a plate. She made triangle sandwiches and put these on a separate plate.

Her mother was in the living-room and had found a copy of one of Jason's trashy magazines. Sorcha took it from her and threw it in the bin quickly then she put the things down on the rickety coffee-table and sat down herself.

"Is this where you spent all of the holidays?" her mother asked, taking her tea with no sugar and just a dash of milk.

Sorcha nodded. She poured in milk and took two sugars and stirred her cup.

"How sick were you?" her mother asked suddenly, looking at her. "You weren't vomiting. You just had a cough or something. Is that it?"

Suddenly, her illness and seclusion over Christmas seemed piddling. Her mother continued on, talking about a list of people she knew who had spent the holiday either coming out of or going into intensive care.

"At your age, there should be nothing wrong," she said. "What you were doing up here on your own all that time, God knows."

"I had neighbours next door. They called on me and brought me things," the girl said.

"And where are they from?"

"Poland. And the guy is French," Sorcha said.

"Are they married?"

Sorcha shook her head. Her mother made a face and said nothing for what seemed like an age.

"I'd really prefer if you got a place of your own," she said, eventually. "I don't know what's taking you so long. There are plenty of girls you went to school with who have bought homes by now. You should take care of yourself. Buy a property and buy a car and don't be spending money on travelling to crazy places. I'm surprised you came back in one piece."

She filled both cups again to the brim and helped herself to a couple of sandwiches. "If you need money, we'll give it to you. But we'll have to inspect the place first before we buy anything. This house is a bit tatty. Look at the furniture. He's a cheap fellow who rents a house in this condition. Some of this stuff is falling apart."

She moved forcefully in her seat, which groaned and squeaked under the weight of her movement. The floorboards made similar noises underneath. Her mother smiled satisfactorily at having proved her point.

"You should do something about it as soon as possible and quickly before everything's snapped up. It's a good investment, you know."

Sorcha nodded in response. She was already starting to feel the weight of her mother's presence and suggested that they go for a walk. Her mother took a look upstairs at the rooms before they left the house and Sorcha gave her the bag of presents which she had not been able to use. Her mother took them wordlessly and gave the bathroom and the bedroom a quick scan.

"These look comfortable," she said, approvingly. "Although the bathroom's a little old. Have you got enough of everything?" She checked the communal hotpress and slid her finger down the banister as they went back downstairs. She held up a dusty digit and looked at Sorcha who remembered that there was a cloth and polish in the kitchen. She decided to leave cleaning it till later and ushered her mother out of the house.

They walked back into the village, over the hill past the green and the train station. The afternoon sunshine was welcome and they walked along the tiny footpath. Her mother was chatting about an old schoolfriend who had been poorly and mentioned the annual party they had held for the senior citizens last year. They passed a young woman pushing her baby in a stroller, the child bouncing in her seat and holding a toy rabbit. Sorcha walked ahead a bit and turned round to see her mother stealthily pulling a flower from a private garden.

Sorcha went back to get her. "No," she scolded. "you can't touch these things."

"But it's growing over onto the public street," her mother protested. She took the flower anyway and smelt it, before squashing it into her pocket. It was a small cream flower and that particular garden was full of them. They walked away quickly and Sorcha took a left to the church which had been decorated with flower baskets to celebrate spring. They went inside and her mother knelt as Sorcha walked around looking at the Stations of the Cross and the drawings children from local schools had made in religion class. She sat at the back of the church and watched her mother who had slowly drifted into oblivion and was mouthing the words to the Hail Mary over and over.

There was an elderly woman on the other side with her prayer book and her rosary beads passing through her fingers. Her lips didn't move but she remained still and did not move while they were there. Eventually, her mother stopped and bowed her head then she got up and genuflected and walked back along the aisle of the old church.

Outside, at the end of the church avenue, there were a couple of auctioneer businesses on each corner. The windows were full of notices for houses in the area. Her mother looked at them and gasped at the prices. She linked arms with her daughter as they walked along the street. The traffic had built up with people on their way back to work from lunch.

"Are you still busy at work? That's the way to have it," she said, as Sorcha nodded. There was little else to see in the village apart from a holiday shop and a couple of restaurants. Sorcha suggested visiting the shopping centre but her mother declined.

"I came up here to see what the problem was. I can go shopping if I want at home," she said, as they made the return journey.

"There's no problem," Sorcha insisted.

"Well, you had us worried for a while. And we were at the station waiting for you. You shouldn't do that. You can be so thoughtless sometimes. That's what happens when you live like this. You forget about other people and concentrate only on yourself."

Sorcha rolled her eyes and wished it was already 4pm. As they approached the house, she noticed Paulina on her way home and waved. She explained who it was and her mother looked disgruntled as Paulina turned her key and closed the door.

"Does she come over often? What is she doing in this country anyway?" she reeled off a list of questions when they got back into the house. Sorcha fended off all the comments she made and offered more tea. She didn't feel like defending the immigrant population that afternoon. From time to time, she felt twinges of the old flu that had kept her bedridden for days although she was watching her diet all the time. Anyway, she couldn't really explain the influx of foreigners just yet. It would take some time before everything settled down and made sense, if that ever happened.

Later that night she sat in her room, quietly listening to music on her headphones. She had fed her mother again before putting her on the road for home. Her mother had eaten boiled eggs and more bread between mouthfuls of tea. "Have you got any friends around this area?" she asked. "Whatever happened to that girl Karen?"

"She moved home last year," Sorcha told her, chewing on a ham sandwich. Her mother ate a very plain diet and it was too early to cook which she hadn't done much of lately either.

"There's not much point living somewhere if you don't know anybody," her mother had said, having clearly given it some thought.

"I do know people in the area," Sorcha said, "and there are clubs around that we go to sometimes." She smiled and now her mother looked at her disapprovingly. She had never had much time for places like that and preferred a day out at Knock to a night in the pub. Sorcha thought wearily that she would have preferred a day in the basilica to spending time with her eldest daughter. She would have brought Maeve, Sorcha's younger sister, but she was at school. It would have been nice for the chat on the long journey.

She had tidied herself up and the kitchen, giving the banister a quick wipe, and had driven off just before four o'clock. The traffic would be crazy if she left any later, she said. Sorcha had opened her belated Christmas presents when she was on her own. It was the usual batch of toiletries and household goods picked up from a new shop which had caught her mother's attention or had been recommended by an acquaintance. She put the bits and pieces away. There was so much to do and she had switched on her CD player to block out the noise of the television downstairs. Eventually, she went to sleep, half-wishing she was at home and didn't have to bother with all of this nonsense while knowing that she would be driven stir-crazy if she had to spend any part of her adult life in her parents' company.

Chapter 8

Once again, the threatened outbreak of fury within the workforce had been quelled by the intervention of the senior manager John when he received a number of complaints from the departments on site. He decided to arrange visits to each team leader that had contacted his office during the week and made a promise to look into devising new methods of dealing with the issues. The helpline was unable to deal with everything that arose and he had to look outside of the HR team and liaise with the transport company, the facilities team and other relevant organisations to help with the difficulties facing his workforce. He listed a number of new measures that had been taken on board to help with the crowded conditions. Many of the teams had been working flat out to achieve good targets and put in a good performance for the company's end of year results. Their managers had taken the opportunity of a new quarter to request appropriate conditions.

The social committee did their bit for morale by organising a special trip to town to celebrate St Patrick's Day. Groups of enthusiastic workers started the evening in the local bar then were transported by the busload into the city centre for the opening ceremony. The tricolour led the parade amid the sound of drum beats and whoops. It was the start of things to come as an assortment of colourful groups announced the beginning of a long weekend of revelry to celebrate the national saint. Sorcha stood on some grimy steps on Dame Street to get a better view as some of the Scandinavian managers stood politely in attendance to one side. Paola and her team were bouncing up and down beside John Xavier. Sorcha got bored and slowly made for home.

Karen sent her an e-mail for St. Patrick's Day. She had started work at a local insurance company and there seemed to be lots of opportunities and the pay was good. When are you coming to visit? she asked. Sorcha mailed her back telling her how busy she was and was looking forward to the bank holidays for when she could plan a break.

She did eventually get somewhere with her quest to employ Paulina, even though she felt it was because the particular department had trouble keeping staff and constantly requested backfills. They sorted contracts for new and existing customers and dealt with leasing issues. "It won't be till summer," she was told, "but there should be some vacancies at that stage with the way things are going."

Sorcha told Paulina who was delighted. She was still working in the local shopping centre and the pay was OK but she wanted something better. She looked at Sorcha, her eyes full of gratitude. Sorcha immediately felt bad as she knew that the job could be difficult, dealing with contract payments. Paulina's living room was covered with swatches of coloured material as she worked on some design pieces from a handbook in Polish, a language that Sorcha had never seen before apart from in news headlines. She had only called in for a quick update and left as she could see that Paulina was busy. "So I just need a copy of your CV again to make the application."

Paulina said sure, no problem, she would drop it over. At the door, she touched Sorcha on the arm. "You know, I'm so pleased. I spent so much time in London living in a horrible house and never really got started. I thought this would be better. It was taking so long I thought I might never work in a real job. There's lots to do in the house when the guys are at work. I'm always ironing or cooking but I was getting really tired of the routine. Thanks so much."

Sorcha was pleased but knew her own path had become difficult. Her life had become like a triangle with her leaving home first thing in the morning, going to work and then travelling to the nearby centre in the evenings to study or have a drink in the bar. They had discovered a secluded area at the back of the building, which had a private serving area and they could chat about work in the evenings without fear of being seen. Sorcha usually tried to make it once or twice a month to keep up with the gossip and changes in the office environment.

There were pockets of workers from the company dotted around the floor: she recognised some French people she had met before and some familiar faces at the bar. Sorcha got up to go to the toilet and joined the queue of girls waiting to use the facilities. It was a tiny space and she rushed in and out of the cubicle as quickly as she could. When she got back to the table, she could see a couple of the guys from the service department had joined their group. The guys were from the Scandinavian and Benelux teams and Lorna had dealt with one of them for her project. He was a tall blond from Norway and managed one of the service teams.

"Hi, how are you?" Sorcha said, shaking hands as they were introduced. He seemed friendly enough and she sat down and retrieved her drink.

"This is the girl who deals with our helpline. She's taking a well-deserved break," Lorna said.

"I'm surprised that you guys have time to do this, you seem so busy with work," the Norwegian said, in accented English.

"Well, it's part of the job that we socialise together. We come down here to spy," Lorna said, making a joke.

"Well, I really have to complain about the way that the department is run. You know, last week, I tried to call about problems we had with payroll and I was left hanging on the line for ages. I'm a manager and I was doing it as a favour for the people on my team who were affected by the mistakes."

He waved his pint glass around and looked hard at the group of girls. "I don't understand it. We're offered the jobs to come over here and work and we just get treated so badly. I had to run upstairs in the end to get the problem fixed. That eats into my time as a manager", he said.

"It gets really mental sometimes, doesn't it?" Lorna said, looking at her co-workers for assistance. She was starting to look uncomfortable.

"If it was last week, then it was very busy," Sorcha said. "There's just two of us and if someone's out, then it's hard to cover every call. You got it sorted in the end."

The blond looked at her without blinking. "Yeah, I got it sorted. In the end. I don't think it should happen again."

"Do you guys find it OK living here? It's not a lot like Norway." Lorna tried to change the subject. "What's the nightlife like over there?"

"It's very expensive. Most people drink at home to save money."

"At least we can drink fairly cheaply here," Lorna said, smiling.

"Yeah, but there are a lot of problems living in Dublin," the blond's friend interjected. "The public transport is a joke and there's no difference in the rent we pay, here or at home. So this is maybe," he said holding his glass aloft without smiling, "maybe the one advantage for us. Cheers."

The guys left and Sorcha felt the atmosphere of the group change instantly. She made a face at their departing figures and looked at the girls.

"Not very charming, are they?" Lorna was angry. "I think I'll be giving Norway a miss although I can't bloody afford to go anywhere right now," she chortled and fixed her bracelet.

The site numbers had swelled close to capacity with hundreds of Europeans working on three floors in each of the buildings. Sorcha had some idea of the pressure they were under as the company fought to maintain balance. The amount of money involved formed part of conversation on the top floor. She could at least be glad that she worked in a small section and was not lost in one of the larger departments. The company prided itself on its ability to communicate with its employees and treat everyone equally although the survey had thrown up glaring inequalities and a lot of dissatisfaction.

"It must be hard going to work every day and switching on a phone when you're in one of those cubicles on the third floor somewhere. At least we have desks and we're not easily forgotten," said Lorna. "I wouldn't be surprised if they found a couple of skeletons in the darker corners of the office block in years to come." She laughed darkly at the idea and Gemma gave her a disgusted look.

"Don't be daft," she said. "They have everything charted and mapped out. You couldn't lose a body."

"You wait and see," Lorna said, waving a finger in mock-warning.

———◆———

With the bank holiday looming, Sorcha booked a trip to see Karen and her new abode. She didn't have much time to check train times and took advantage of a lengthy meeting on the floor to make a travel schedule. It was easier than she thought and as the weekend approached, she looked forward to it. Her co-workers were planning weekend breaks out of town and she was glad she had made the effort. It would be a talking point when they got back to the office after the long break.

Sorcha perched an apple on the armrest of her seat and continued reading the magazine section of the newspaper, flicking between articles on popular tv programmes, cookery and interview pieces. There was a mention of the festival she was going to attend, the writer suggesting that they take in the event which had potential to grow in an annual occurrence. Sorcha was relieved; the write-up made it sound like it was part of mainstream culture. There had been a resurgence of interest in rootsy music recently and bands playing new songs with the country verve. Johnny Cash had even recorded some new albums. If it had not been for the office notepad she was doodling on with a company logo pen, she would have been like Huckleberry Finn on his way down the river with an apple close to hand.

Sorcha had an education and knew a good song and she also wanted to avoid the clichéd popular country bands that proliferated the radio shows. On the phone the night before, she had advised Karen that she didn't want any line-dancing or dodgy clothes the entire weekend. Karen had laughed down the phone but had sounded horrified, "Do you really think I would do that to you? I would hardly wear that stuff myself. You'll be surprised by how good the festival is when you get here, honest."

Nonetheless, Sorcha was sceptical. The train carriage was full of middle-aged women with their young sons coming back from a day's shopping or families off for a weekend in the country. No-one seemed dressed for a roots festival. The travellers chatted among themselves, talking about the bargains they had found and the nice weather they were having for the Bank Holiday weekend. It was nothing she hadn't heard before and she went on reading, pausing to look out of the window every so often at the green fields and the farm animals: cows chewing grass, baby lambs dancing around their mothers, sometimes a horse or two. The relevance of this was not lost on her as the train sped past on its way.

Her arrival at the destination did not improve her outlook on the weekend. As she was walking from the platform, she could see nothing but green fields and what looked like an old convent with a cross at the main gable. She took her travel bag to the car park and was met by Rob who had taken a break from work to meet her. "How are you?" he asked with a grin, giving her a quick hug.

"I'm just fine," Sorcha replied, looking around at the desolate outskirts of the town.

About Turn

"There's not much here right now. But it's all happening in the town centre. Where did Karen book you in?" Rob asked, as they went to the car and put her luggage in the boot.

Sorcha sat in the passenger seat and gave him the name of the bed and breakfast she had printed off the web. Rob nodded as he saw the name, and they drove through the street into town, over the river then through the town square and back out.

"This is handy for getting home after the shows," he said. He dropped her at the house and said 'See you later' and Sorcha went to check in. She left her bag in the double-room which was hers for the weekend and went into town for a walk. At least the journey had not been a long one, and she felt ok about going out to explore that afternoon. She had on her walking shoes, light trousers and a small backpack which she normally brought to work. The walk to town took almost half-an-hour, she noted. She would have to get back to the house later and change for the night out.

The town square was gleaming and she passed through the commercial centre, she thought amusingly. The activity was mostly to her left so she took a walk down the street which was topped off by lines of bunting and banners announcing the festival. There were shops either side selling handcrafts, clothes, kitchenware. She was hungry and crossed over to an old-fashioned tearoom. There were mementos of times gone by and old-fashioned delph on the windows and inside, a few people sat at tables having coffee and cakes.

She ordered a main meal and this was served at a leisurely pace, the staff seemed at home here and was friendly as they put the plates down in front of her. The wall was covered with old adverts for tea and soap and she felt uplifted by the charm of the old place. A couple of women were having a chat at the other occupied table in her section. It felt pleasant to be away from the rush of business.

Back on the street, she passed by two guys dressed in leathers with a band name she recognised emblazoned on the back. They were tanned and their hair was bleached; obviously American. She giggled to herself and walked down to the end of the main street to the festival office. The office was a tiny room at the top of some stairs over a pub and the walls were covered in press cuttings for the performers at the upcoming shows. She read the timetable again and noted when the acts they were planning to see were scheduled to appear. It was a fairly loose arrangement but they were going to see as much music as possible over the next three days.

She noticed the cathedral and went inside to get some cool air. She walked around the Protestant building and sat for a moment before continuing her walk in the grounds. There was a carnival coming to town and she could see colourful vans in the distance, the carnies setting up for the weekend. It was typical small town stuff. She ducked into a small pedestrian street on her way back and visited the supermarket. The aisles were mostly empty this time of the day but the shelves were well-stocked and she brought what she needed back to the house.

Karen and Rob called for her later that evening and she locked the front door behind her. The landlady had checked if she'd needed anything and had even offered her use of the kitchen but Sorcha had eaten a quick sandwich while getting dressed. She had chosen another pair of trousers and a light, colourful top with a zip-up cardigan just so she could blend. She skipped to where the car was parked, narrowly avoiding some muck at the front gate.

"Wow, Karen, you're looking very smart," Sorcha said, as she got in the back. Her jeans had embroidered pockets and her hair was shiny. Karen gave her a big smile. "How are you enjoying the town so far?"

Sorcha told them about her afternoon, seeing the band jackets and the carnival and the shops. "Oh, I love that place," Karen said, when she mentioned the pedestrian walk-way. "There's a really old pub up there and it's always packed."

"Are they going to have any shows on there?" Sorcha asked, thinking ahead.

"No, nice for a visit though. We should go tomorrow."

They drove into town and parked at a vacant spot near the centre. The night was still bright and they walked down to the town's theatre where the festival's first big show was taking place.

"Are you glad you moved back home?" Sorcha asked.

"Without a doubt," Karen said, holding Rob's hand and linking arms with Sorcha as they walked inside. They had plenty of time for a drink before the show and went into the nearby pub. It was full of locals drinking as groups and there was a little room near the door. Rob went to the bar and the girls leaned against a pillar to secure themselves against the incoming and outgoing crowd. Sorcha told her friend about the crush in the bars she'd been in recently in Dublin.

"I really do love it here," Karen said. "When I think of travelling on smelly buses that rattle your bones, I'm glad I made the move. We're still really busy and there isn't the choice that you get in a big city but with the internet, no-one needs to be in the capital anymore."

Rob agreed and they made a toast to country living as he returned with an armful of bottles and glasses. He had bought the local beer and Sorcha was drinking cider. Karen was the designated driver and had lemonade with ice. Sorcha was glad to be back in the circle again. The couple introduced her to all the people they knew from work or school. "I know her from the weekly Mormon meeting," Karen joked. "Just kidding. I've met her a few times when we've been out. I think Rob knows her brother."

The crowd moved slowly across the street to the theatre as the start of the show neared. Sorcha's little group had swelled and they marched across and took their seats. First up was a Northern Irish singer-songwriter Sorcha had seen perform on a tv show recently. She didn't know the songs but the delivery was good and the singer made easygoing banter with the audience. At the finish, the crowd cheered appreciatively and the girl walked off with a smile and a wave. The main band was American and they coolly walked on one-by-one to loud applause and began playing their instruments. Rob had warned they had quite a following in the area although they lived near the Mexican border. They improvised without the back-up of a full band and played around with the sound. They had invited along a musician friend to play keyboards and towards the end, the singer stopped and asked, "It's a little quiet up here. Anybody want to come up and help us out?"

There were shouts from the audience. "Some of these guys were here last year," Karen whispered. "They came with a whole brass section and started their European tour here. They were brilliant. I'm not sure I like this lot." She scrunched her face and smiled. Rob was listening intently to the band play.

The set was a short one and they still had plenty of time for drinks in the bar. Sorcha squashed herself up behind a couple of guys ordering heavy-duty lists of pints and shorts for their friends. She got the same again and went back to where Rob was standing. He was raving about the concert to a friend and then introduced Sorcha. "Phil, this is a friend from Dublin." They shook hands and Sorcha joined in. Phil was a short bloke with light blond hair that curled at the ends. He was dressed in a cool shirt and seemed to be an authority on the histories of most of the bands playing that weekend. He chatted enthusiastically about where the band came from, holding a pint in his hand.

"I saw one of the American country bands on the main street today," Sorcha said, laughing. "It was like being in Nashville of something."

"Oh yeah?"

"Do you work in the area?" Sorcha enquired.

"Of music?" Phil looked hopeful. "Oh, in town? I moved down here just before Christmas. I worked in Dublin since I left school, you know. But I got tired of it recently."

"So what are you doing down here?"

"Not much," he replied. "Actually I'm glad that the festival came along. I was getting bored."

"Karen and Rob both found jobs though."

"Well, I don't want to work in an office anymore. I'm taking a career break for a while and I'll find something else." He looked unimpressed by the prospect of finance management and left to go to the bar.

Rob was chatting to one of the band members who had all convened in the bar post-show and were surrounded by locals and fans wanting to chat about the music. Karen was leaning on Rob's shoulder and Sorcha went over to them.

"There is another really good show on later at 11pm in that restaurant further up the street. You should come down and see them play. I know a couple of the guys. They play here all the time," Rob said to the lead singer whose name was Mike. He was dressed in jeans and cowboy boots and had a full beard. Although he was clearly jetlagged, he had a charming grin on his face. Mike nodded in appreciation and went back to his bandmates who were signing autographs, looking embarrassed to be the centre of attention. The support singer had left as she had another show in Waterford the following night.

Karen was yawning as the pub became crowded once again. She finished her drink and nodded at Sorcha. "Lets go outside. This place is great but it's hard to breathe when it gets this full." They stood outside and waited for Rob to join them. The next show was starting in twenty minutes and it was at a late-night bar. Karen knew the way and they started to walk up the street.

"Have you heard from Isabelle?" Sorcha asked.

"No, nothing. Gill has been in touch a couple of times but I get the feeling now that I'm down here, it's a case of 'out of sight, out of mind'. She's met someone new, you know."

"I didn't know," Sorcha said, "I called her last week but there was nobody in the flat. I left a message but she didn't call back."

They entered the restaurant and got a table by the window. They had recovered by now and ordered some food. "Try the nachos," Karen said, "Lets order some wine. One drink is not going to hurt. It's the bank holiday weekend, for God's sake." Rob arrived with Phil and some friends and the band came in with their sound crew. The restaurant owner scrabbled for a few free chairs in the back and eventually gave up even the footstool to accommodate the guests. The festival manager was hovering around and ordered drinks for the band. They perched bottles of beer on the tiny makeshift stage as the performers arrived. They played a mixture of bluegrass and country songs and everyone listened attentively. Sorcha could feel a buzz in the pit of her stomach and was getting into the festival mood.

During the break, Sorcha was introduced to some of the Americans: John played drums and said little as they shook hands, he just smiled politely. Shawn was younger and outgoing as he asked them their names, listening intently to their comments on the show. "It's just one of the projects John and I are working on," he said ambitiously. Karen was apologising for her lack of information on the band. Shawn laughed as if he'd heard it all before. "We're maybe obscure but we have worked with a lot of people," he said as he reeled off a list of names.

"What do you think of the town?" Sorcha asked.

"Love it, it's a great festival" the American smiled broadly. "I have family living in this country. But we're touring right now so I can't take a break unfortunately." He broke off to welcome another person to the table. It was the festival publicist, a young brunette with a fresh face. She beckoned to him to come back to his seat as she had someone for him to meet. John had already returned and was quietly drinking his pint.

The show ended at one am and they stayed on for a while. Phil was reluctantly going home as they left. "Get some sleep," Rob said. "You'll have more fun tomorrow." They went back to the car and saw the band drive past in their tour bus. "They're staying in one of the hotels overnight, courtesy of the festival organisers," Rob said. Then they drove out of town and dropped Sorcha at her little holiday home from home.

Next day, Sorcha met Karen in town. It was Saturday and they had no work to go to. Sorcha wanted to go to the teashop again but Karen suggested they go the pub on the pedestrian street. They sat in the stone building, eating banoffi and drinking coffee, with the sun shining in the large window. "No sign of any bands so far. Those guys are probably asleep. They travelled all the way from LA yesterday," Karen said.

"No kidding," Sorcha said. "This dessert is delicious by the way." She gobbled up the homemade bananas and cream treat as the afternoon sun shone through the large window.

They went to the local craft centre at the top of the street and looked at the silver jewellery and handcrafts on display. "I'd love to buy something," Karen said, "but we're saving for our furniture. This festival is our big blow out before we put everything into bricks and mortar."

Sorcha bought a silver necklace and wore it with her blue dress that evening at an impromptu performance the band were giving in the back of a pub. "It's used as a theatre sometimes," Rob said, "For local productions, that can't afford the main theatre."

They all squashed into the tiny room and the band were setting up, tuning their instruments and checking the mikes. Sorcha was standing beside a dark-skinned woman who had a case of CDs for sale. She noticed the girl trying to get a closer look and began chatting. "This is the tour CD which they made specially for the summer months. It's a mixture of instrumentals and some songs which didn't make it onto the studio album."

Sorcha took a look at the homemade album cover and Rob handed the woman a ten pound note. "It's a present," he said, and Sorcha protested then tucked the CD into her bag, smiling thanks. The woman patted her hand and said, "Would you mind these for me while I go to the toilet? If anyone asks any questions, just show them a CD. You don't need to explain."

Sorcha nodded sure, and the woman got up and squeezed her way back to the exit. "I think she's one of their girlfriends," Rob said. "She was here last night too. I think she might be Native American."

A couple of people edged their way to the stack of CDs and picked up the items to have a look. The room was too crowded for it to happen and the woman crept back to her post as the band came on and performed a shorter but more professional set of songs. One of Rob's friends jumped on stage and played mouth organ for a couple of songs.

"So that's what they were chatting about last night," Karen said. "Our Mike is so chuffed at getting up onstage."

Mike was a local though and when his moment in the spotlight had ended, he went back to being just that. It was different for the band, especially Shawn, who Sorcha noticed was surrounded by girls at every step.

"Is he taking phone numbers?" Karen said, giggling. "This is becoming very rock-n-roll."

They carried on to another show in a venue nearby and were emerging from the bar just before midnight when they saw the band's bus pulling out of town. Rob said, "On their way to the ferry port to get to the UK. And then they're touring the rest of Europe for a couple of months. Nice of them to drop by though." They stood in the street for a few moments wondering what to do next.

Phil had caught up with them and was looking a bit down but cheered up as they decided to go back to the restaurant for another late-night show. During the interval, Sorcha noticed him sit beside her. He was half-way through his pint and had put another down on the table. She looked at his duck-like features in disgust and noticed he was making himself comfortable. Karen kicked her under the table and said loudly, "We'll be dropping you back at your place tonight. The landlady's very strict about visitors so we won't stay."

Sorcha looked at her intensely. Did she really think that there was a remote possibility it would come to that with this leech beside her? Sure, he knew his music but otherwise he left a lot to be desired. She made her excuses and went to freshen up. When she got back, Phil was deep in conversation and she escaped out the door.

"Didn't get lucky this time round?" Rob joked, as they drove out of town.

"Those musicians were nice, weren't they?" Karen said although she had absolutely no intentions of deserting her boyfriend. "Don't worry about Phil. He thought you were nice actually but doesn't mean, you know." She smiled back at Sorcha whose eyes were closing shut despite her efforts to stay awake. She was happy dreaming of a clover field, sunshine and her own festival happening nearby. The thought of Phil kept entering her head and she had to admit he had kind of repulsed her. It was the only blight on what had turned out to be a great weekend.

Back in Dublin, Sharon was busily typing at her desk for a few minutes. She had been distracted all morning after a short meeting with Seamus. Seamus came back to his desk, looking ruffled but determined. He had been offered a job in his friend's dad's company, it turned out, and had negotiated a better salary packet. But he was obliged to stay on until the end of the month at least. The HR manager had tried to coax him into staying but he had refused. The hours and repetition had taken their toll and he wanted to go.

"Just so long as it wasn't me," Sorcha joked. Seamus didn't even respond and she realized he had probably stopped joking a long time ago. They had never really socialised that much but she had put it down to the age difference and different lifestyles. That evening, she was sitting with the girls in the budabar. Courtney had decided to join them with friends of hers from the UK financial services. There were a few managers from the same department on the rip that night. Plus some new hire London graduates who had been handpicked to work on finance projects with the Leasing manager. The projects were talked about within the department as most people who had been there a year or more could apply to work on new stuff and it meant a getaway from the usual customer service role. An unused room in the building had been designated as the Projects Room and the graduates and their Irish co-workers were getting to know each other.

"Will you be going for that role?" Lorna asked Courtney. The American had ordered a large cocktail from the menu and was sipping the red liquid, looking at the group seated around her.

"No, I don't think so. It sounds pretty hot though. I think I'll stay where I am with my friends. We're a tight bunch down on the concessionaire's group. And it's not the worst place to be at the moment. The direct accounts are in a total mess apparently." She stopped as the Londoners approached the group and the two neatly dressed girls were introduced around. They made small talk before moving on to the bar. Courtney looked serious. "To tell you the truth, I'm not sure that there's money in the pot to pay for these projects. They're just in start up right now. Doesn't mean they'll get off the ground."

Sorcha noticed one of the London girls with a soft perm, dressed in a navy business suit, chatting animatedly with her manager. She seemed happy to be here and smiled in a friendly way to the group as they were surrounded by drinkers. The girls were being put up in a hotel until they found suitable accommodation.

"Who is that guy? And what is his t-shirt saying?" Jeremy asked, nodding towards a middle-aged, balding man with a beer glass clutched firmly in his hand. Sorcha recognised him from before.

"That's the Commercial team manager, Mr Popular. Although that's not what it says on his shirt." Courtney said, looking embarrassed. "It looks like they're having lots of fun tonight. They're celebrating."

The group was tightly packed together on the other side of the room. Every so often, a new round of drinks was ordered with the management team putting up a credit card as payment. The group had won a competition for reaching its targets in the last quarter and the London girls had been caught in the moment. The curly haired girl said her goodbyes to a tall Englishman in a waistcoat and beard. He was the Operations manager for the UK market and had been involved in the changeover from the start. He left the group and struggled towards the exit as the bar once again had filled up.

Sorcha took a break to visit the toilet. She noticed the t-shirted manager on her way back to her seat. He was speaking to his wife probably, explaining when he would make it back home. A group of foreign workers were watching the TV intently as Sky Sports played the latest soccer game with added commentary. There was a couple making out with some intensity against the wall as she edged past to the main area.

"Lets join the crowd," Lorna said, when she got back. "Well, I'm going over. Come on Courtney." She immediately engaged in conversation as she hit the lively crowd of workers. Courtney made small talk with the managers as Sorcha noticed the English Leasing manager limbering up to dance to the music. He threw some shapes to the chart hits and egged on the rest of the crowd to join him. Lorna had begun chatting to an English guy around her age who was looking at her perfect face with interest. They were momentarily interrupted by a small conga line that started with the Leasing manager and snaked around the available space in the bar. Sorcha had some reports to make for a meeting the next day so she crept out of the bar when no one was watching.

Outside, the last of the shoppers were driving around and out of the centre. Sorcha walked past the new library and arts centre to get the bus home. There were a few company workers on the bus, laughing and joking. She didn't know their names but they still had work badges hanging off their necks as they rode home in oblivion. She thought that they were part of the French team who had moved to a prefab while they waited on their office space to be allocated. But there was more than one language being spoken and some English thrown in too. The guys seemed fairly happy with themselves and got off at the Bell pub, clattering down the stairs.

Sorcha endeavoured to jobhunt for a while, partly due to the traffic chaos she often ran into in the mornings. The development of the extension through the village had been completed and now there were loads of buses going to the business park which resulted in jams. There was a train service into town just beside her and she looked around for other options. "That's a pretty full CV you have," the girl said at the agency, "lots of experience. You like working in the personnel department?" Sorcha nodded. "We have a few vacancies at the moment with some of our clients. Just let me go through our files and I'll make sure to pick out a couple of things that would suit." The blonde-haired girl swept Sorcha's particulars into a folder and scribbled a few notes on the front.

"I will have a look and will contact you as soon as I can. There are a couple of big clients looking for new staff at the moment." She mentioned a couple of names and explained the types of roles available. Sorcha was keeping her options open so she tried to keep the mood light and friendly while focusing on her achievements so far.

"Is there any particular reason why you want to leave your job?" Melanie had asked, during their meeting. Sorcha gave honest but controlled answers to the questions. She didn't want there to be any doubts about her capabilities. The girl scribbled notes as she spoke then looked up and smiled.

"OK, well, thanks for coming in," she said, "you'll be hearing from us soon." Sorcha got up to leave and the blonde handed her a card with

About Turn

her contact details. She walked her down the stairs of the city centre office block into which her recruitment agency had just moved. They had organised a recruitment day to highlight their move and attract new customers. Sorcha had seen that there was an open evening for full-time workers already in employment and had left work on time that day to attend. This office was full of young people probably fresh from college, all dressed in a uniform of dark skirts or trousers with a plain blouse. She knew she had to start somewhere though and put the impression to the back of her mind.

There seemed to be a glut of these open days over the next few weeks; all popping up like seasonal fruits. Sorcha had given herself some time to get to some events. It was the same routine each time: show up, fill out a form, chat to one of the office staff about her experience and the opportunities available then leave with another card to add to her collection. After all of this, she was tired of talking about herself and just waited for the results to show. She did get a call from Melanie's office but it was another girl, the Senior Business Recruiter, who passed on details of an interview taking place on Thursday evening after working hours. Sorcha made a note of the details and arrived slightly late.

The interview was in the IFSC buildings and she had to make it there on foot from O'Connell Street. She tore along by foot to make it to the venue on time. 'I don't think this is really who I am', she thought doubtfully, as she walked through the revolving door of the office block in which her meeting was scheduled. The reception was a plain room with a potted plant in one corner and a painting on the wall. She gave her details to the girl at reception and took a seat. It was just after six o'clock and she waited patiently as a couple of other hopefuls arrived and did the same.

Shortly, a woman emerged and greeted the group. They went inside and were given clip holders and forms to fill out. It really meant copying the same personal details onto a piece of paperwork to be filed. The woman collected each file and introduced herself as being from the company's HR department. She asked the group to move into an adjoining room, a sparsely decorated meeting room with a wooden table and chairs in the middle, where they sat with answer sheets in front of them. Sorcha looked at the sheet in surprise; she hadn't expected an exam of all things.

"Can you just fill out this list of questions? It's an aptitude test for the job and will influence whether or not you're called back for interview," the woman said. "There's no pressure and no time frame but if you could complete the sheet as quickly as possible, I'd be grateful."

Sorcha did as she was told, finishing the test in a reasonable time and answering practically all of the questions correctly. She handed the sheets back and left the office in wonderment. She had missed the quarter past seven train from Connolly but there was another train leaving shortly. She walked past the high rise blocks of offices and apartments to the station, avoiding the pockets of tracksuited guys and girls that hung around the station entrance. It was after nine when she got back home. She bumped into James who asked her how she'd got on.

"It was just a test," she explained. "I have to wait to see if I'm called back."

Her housemate took a look at her weary face and warned her to take it easy. Sorcha nodded, secretly wishing that she had a choice in what she could do in the next few months. The workload had become severe since Seamus had left and showed no signs of easing so she was ploughing all her hopes into getting another job as soon as possible. She was relieved when the agency called back on Monday and asked her to attend an interview at the same place that following Thursday. It was a different girl again so she could not mention the mix up with the exam that had not been forewarned to her.

"It's an early morning meeting. You should be there at 9.30am but try to be a little early. Ok? Good luck and let us know how you get on."

Sorcha woke early on Thursday and looked at her clock to check the time. It was just after six am and quite dark in the room. She lay still for another twenty minutes or so; if she got up now, she would be left with plenty of time. Her first day off in weeks and she had to prepare for an important interview. She had lined up a couple of appointments to get a taste of what was out there and hoped that this would be the first of many. 'I doubt as if they would miss me at work if I left,' she thought to herself. 'They would just pass the files on to the next dummy.' She smiled inwardly as she pictured herself leaving the company and defecting to a position with a better pay packet, city based offices and plenty of prospects. That would be one in the eye for Sharon

About Turn

and her bunch of cronies. She might have to do some work for a change if Sorcha was no longer around to cover all the bases.

Then she thought of all the work she had left sitting on her desk; the tasks would be building up even as she lay here in bed. It seemed like magic elves arrived in the night and left even more work for her to do. She sank into despair momentarily then checked the clock again and got up quickly, noticing the time.

She had showered and dressed in half an hour and she swiftly put on a layer of make up which she normally did not wear and dried her hair. There was no time for breakfast as she had a long journey ahead of her and could not be late. She was wearing a plain blue suit with a white shirt and flat shoes, which she wiped with a damp cloth before leaving to catch the bus. It sped into town then crawled along the quays and Sorcha made her usual dash past her old haunts to the familiar office block.

She sat again in the plain reception room and was ushered almost immediately into a smaller room this time, decorated the same way as the rest of the building. She focused her eyes on the potted plant as the interviewers arrived. There were two of them: a serious man of about forty and his co-worker, probably a few years younger and a look of determination on his face. She congratulated herself later as she walked along the quayside, quaffing a fruit drink. She had answered their questions as well as she could but their expectations seemed too high for anyone to reach. They weren't interested in listening to her issues with a heavy workload and the moody younger one outlined their working methods:

"We run a shipshape office, Sorcha, and we need our staff to be able to maintain our standards. Do you think you can do that and be one of our accomplished crew?"

She had answered yes, and he had asked for more details about her previous work prior to her current job. He looked at her doubtfully as she described her experience with the charity. When it was time for her to ask questions, she enquired about the day-to-day routine of the office to compare it with her own job. The older man gave her a quick rundown of the duties and answered her other questions and then his colleague called time, and left the room in a hurry.

Sorcha sat in a café in Temple Bar, eating a sandwich. She was feeling bummed about the interview and walked around the area,

Deirdre Haugh

checking out the museums and galleries for their exhibitions and briefly checking her e-mails in one of the internet centres on a side street. She was looking for a mail from one of the agencies she had registered with that month. The agency had organised a meeting for her with a company based in some temporary offices in the old Guinness factory, now a Digital technology hub. She had mailed the girl straight back and arranged to attend a meeting that afternoon.

It took her a while to find the exact location within the maze of brewery buildings that comprised the Guinness factory. She felt tired and was relieved when she came to the right place. She had been briefed about the company before the interview and the job sounded exciting. She would be working as a recruiter for an online company if successful.

The shared offices were within stone block buildings that been modernised to facilitate the companies taking refuge there as they waited to move into permanent bases. She chatted to the elderly security man at the front gate before getting permission to go inside. There was nobody at reception this time and she waited in the empty room before being greeted by a small friendly girl with dark hair, obviously on her way home. "He's just on his way," she said, smiling. A tall man in a creased suit entered, carrying a folder of papers clumsily gathered together. He shook her hand briefly and led her through an interior maze of orange coloured walls and glass doors.

"There are quite a few companies in this building but we hope to leave soon," he said as they came to the correct room at last. He unlocked the door and asked Sorcha to sit at a seat. He described the company and went through the details of the job. The company organised online gambling, he said, to her disappointment and Sorcha looked at him with distaste as he went through a list of figures and scratched his back with a pen.

"So, what do you think?" he asked, finally, leaning back on his chair against the faux brick wall design.

Sorcha tried to sound enthused and questioned him about the resourcing requirements of the company. The man looked uncomfortable and stuttered his answer. "We…d-don't have any jobs in that area as such." He looked through his notes.

"I t-think all of those positions are filled actually."

About Turn

He looked up at her. "It was a recruiting job that you wanted, was it?"

She looked at him straight and replied, "That's why I'm here."

"Sorry, no can do, we have plenty of telephone based jobs though," he said, hopefully.

"Not interested," Sorcha said.

The man shrugged and she took her leave. Back in the corridor, she tried to remember where the exit was and eventually got back to the reception. She left by the security entrance and hurried to the main streets, aware of the fact that there were several council housing blocks in the area. She could see a queue of people lined up to get into Vicar Street. As she checked the upcoming events, she got a bleeping sound on her phone and listened to the message. It was one of the girls calling her IFSC job: "Sorcha, can you call me when you get this? I spoke to one of the interviewers you met this morning and they thought that you didn't seem very interested in the job. I could have slotted you in somewhere else if you know what I mean. Thanks." The girl stood on the pavement in surprise and thought about calling back but instead purposely deleted the number from her phone. She hadn't been given a lot of information about the job and the interviewers had given her just a basic outline of the role so she didn't feel she was to blame.

The next agency arranged for her to attend two consecutive interviews for a job based in a business park on the southside. Sorcha negotiated a reasonable meeting time with the company but had difficulty finding the location. The park was new and she didn't know where to go. After several calls to her contact, she arrived late but sat through the interview. She agreed to attend the second one in the hopes of getting the job but a couple of weeks went by and she had still not heard anything. She called the agency and eventually got through to her contact. "Oh sorry, but the company decided not to fill the vacant role in the end. We'll call you back if anything else comes up."

Sorcha looked at her phone in shock. All of that effort for nothing? The development of her local area had led her to believe she could get back to town with not too much effort but maybe there wasn't as much out there as people thought. She went back to her day job. She had taken precious annual leave for interviews and had felt confused and angry at the letdowns but resigned herself to the work at hand as the phone began to ring.

Paulina was settling in well at the job downstairs although there had been a few difficulties at the start. The company had inherited a lot of problems from its UK office and was trying to solve these as quickly as possible. Paulina had tried not to work overtime but sometimes she found herself staying after finish time for a half-hour to catch up. The girls met for lunch one day and Paulina was looking stressed.

"How are you doing?" Sorcha asked sympathetically. "Kept busy?"

Paulina nodded, tucking into a salad, her blue eyes looking tired. "I had no idea it would be like this," she said. "At the interview, they said it was a busy department but the workload…" she rolled her eyes "it's phenomenal. I've found myself saying 'I can't do this.' Everybody is so helpful so it's OK and I don't really have a choice, do I?

"There are so many problems and the systems are outdated. It was funny at the start but it's tough when you get a call and you're searching for information through these old programmes. I just hope it gets better. After all, there are so many high value contracts on the system but at the moment they can't afford to do upgrades.

"There's just such a distinction between how I live in Poland, no job and no money. Or I live here and have a job and money but so stressed. Even yesterday, I was thinking of sitting in the sunshine in our garden at home and doing absolutely nothing!" She laughed at the notion.

"A holiday would be nice, but they go so quickly," Sorcha said, "I haven't planned anything this year."

"Neither have we," Paulina said wistfully. "Although my mother may come over later in the summer but she has to get a visa first. You went with friends last year?"

"Yeah, some people I met in Carpenterstown. I've no idea what they're doing this year. They don't work with me but they're in the company. What are the people like in your department?" she asked curiously.

"They're a mixture," Paulina said. "Some of the people left but the people I trained with are very nice. One of the girls is Spanish and one is English. And the trainer is from Ireland; he works on the team and he's been there a long time. He's very easy to talk to and can answer all the questions. I was hoping I would be sitting near him but I'm at the very opposite end! The girl who sits with me is Rachel; she takes a break with me in the mornings and we found our way around together."

"Have you met anybody else from Poland?"

"No, I'm the only one! Hopefully, if we get to the EU, there will be more. They have started selling in the Eastern countries but most of my co-workers are English or speak English. My English is improving because I use it all the time so that's one good thing.

She sighed. "We would like to stay here. Maybe get a house in the near future. Although it will be out of town, I should think. So I'm happy to stay here.

"There seems to be a lot of bad news about the company's plans. I think the accounts teams have a lot to work on in the future. There's a backlog on the system."

"What kind of backlog?"

"Well, they had to focus on a certain kind of debt, the big amounts, to meet their targets last year so the correspondence has been building up for a while. There is a lot of information which needs to be addressed. Now they're discussing ways to work through this but there aren't any plans to hire extra staff. Most people work on the phone so will probably have to do both jobs at the same time.

"I use the same system to check for archived material but I don't have access to what they use. Apparently, there are hundreds of items which were never opened or dealt with. It could be an important letter about a large debt from one of the customers like BT or BAE. You know if addresses change or a purchase order or a customer refuses to pay.

"Often, I get a call from a contact in the company who has a maintenance contract which hasn't been paid. Their contracts are very expensive if they have high volume equipment and they might refuse to pay over a mistake or a price increase. There have been conference calls with the customer relations manager but it doesn't always get worked out."

"The problem is," Paulina continued, "if customers have a lot of machines like hundreds on an account the outstanding figure can increase really fast when they refuse to pay. Like the normal cost of a quarterly bill of £250 or £500 multiplied by 1200 machines equals so much. It's hundreds of thousands. And they have their management staff put up in B&Bs during the week. The customer relations manager stays in a very nice place in Castleknock and goes back to the UK every weekend. Yves knows about this because he is dealing directly with the income and expenditure figures."

Sorcha shuddered although the problem didn't directly affect her and she didn't feel the full impact. She wondered where all of this was heading. Rumours had begun circulating that the company was going to pull out altogether because of the massive costs involved in the new site. If so much debt was sitting untouched on the computer systems, it didn't look good for year-end revenue.

Chapter 10

Sorcha met up with workmates that weekend when she was at a loose end. She was feeling too tired to venture into town and arranged with Jeremy to call on Saturday evening and go for a drink. He had just finished showering and let her into the living-room while he went back upstairs. She flicked on the TV but couldn't concentrate so she lay back on the sofa and waited. "OK, ready to go?" he said, bouncing into the room.

"Where do you get your energy from? You're like the bloody Duracell rabbit." Sorcha got up and followed him out of the front door.

"Sorry," he said. "I suppose I have to be lively when I'm meeting people all day long. This is my day off so I'm going to enjoy it and drink as much as I want. Tomorrow I can sleep it off."

They walked round the corner to the local pub, the Carpenter, which had a beer garden outside. The sun was blazing down and they sat in the shade of an unoccupied table with an umbrella overhead. Sorcha ordered drinks at the bar and brought them out on a tray.

"Think you could do with a holiday when you see this weather?" Jeremy said.

"Who needs Crete when it's splitting the rocks in Dublin city?" Sorcha joked.

"I'll be going to Spain for two weeks next month," Jeremy said. "It's a good time because the recruiting will be less heavy and one of the girls will take over for me while I'm gone. You should do it, Sorcha. It'd be good experience."

"I don't think so. I think my destiny is at the end of a phone line for now. I'm trying to conserve my spending and save some money for a property before things get completely out of hand."

Jeremy took a large swig of his beer. "I suppose. Despite what anyone says, my parents aren't going to fund my life either but I'm just kicking back for now and I'll worry about house prices next year when I have developed a nice tan." He leant back on the seat and put his hands behind his head in a restful position. "It's nice to just kick back. I never see you guys during the day anymore."

"Work is a little overwhelming but don't lets waste our time chatting about that," Sorcha said, avoiding the subject. She discovered that they had not much to talk about when this was taken out of the equation. "I know," Jeremy said. "We'll give Denise a call and see what she's up to. She's always good for a laugh."

He flipped open his phone and called her number. They chatted for a while and Sorcha could only hear snatches of the conversation. At one stage, he turned away from her and she sat drinking from her bottle of alcopop until he had finished talking. He put the phone away, wiping it clean with his finger where the glass had smudged. It was a top of the range moby and he was very proud of it.

"She's in the shopping centre," he said, smiling. "Just coming out of McDonalds when I called. She said she'd be over later with a bag of chips so sit tight." He looked around at the handful of benches fenced off from the rows of housing in the area.

"There's not a lot to do around here, is there? Sometimes I get very bored. I'm too old to go to all-night parties. It's weird how when work finishes, a person can end up with two whole days on their hands but nothing to do," Jeremy mused.

"Which is why you're looking forward to Spain," Sorcha ventured.

"Yeah, but my point there is there are so many houses but I don't know anybody out here. If it wasn't for Denise and yourself and a few more, I'd be lost. My family doesn't live out here. I'm not really into sport so I don't have any clubs to join. So what do I do at the weekend? Watch a few videos, go drinking or go to a friend's house. I just get bored, that's all."

"Yeah, it would be nice to have a little outlet. This is how come all those guys get into drugs and crime, although that's not an option for me." He paused for a second. "You know, if our house in Spain was a little bigger you could have come along, if you had two weeks to spare, that is."

Sorcha had heard him mention the same thing to Lorna at work on Friday and realised he was probably just bullshitting. She said nothing and waited for Denise to arrive. The girl arrived in a pair of shorts and high-heeled espadrilles.

"You like them?" she said, "we have booked another holiday for September. This time its Tunisia and I am psyched, people!" She went inside and pushed her way through the crowd at the bar and brought new drinks to the table.

"We didn't ask you this time, Sorcha. Haven't seen you in an age so that's why. But we also got a really good deal for two sharing so we didn't want to miss our chance. So it'll be camel rides and hopefully more karaoke."

She passed around sheets of paper advertising the forthcoming Charity Day. "I entered the competition we had at work for charity, remember? There are a few guys in the departments in our building who share my interest in singing very loudly in front of a screen with a mike in my hand. I'll expect to see all of you there."

She clinked her glass very loudly against the others on the wooden table and stuck on her sunshades and smiled. The charity event was obviously practise for her big adventure in North Africa. Sorcha didn't mind not being asked. She had been hoarding her money all year with the possibility of getting a property at some stage.

"So, any holidays planned?" Denise asked loudly. "I know you're going to Spain, Jerms. What about you?"

Sorcha shook her head. "Too busy. I went into overdrive a few months back and now I'm kind of stuck there."

Denise looked disappointed. "That's a pity. I want to have a nice break before I move back home." She shifted in her chair. "I told Jeremy that I'll be moving to Cork before Christmas. I don't like it up here. It's too noisy and there's a lot happening in the real capital, you know. Better weather, too. I have to wait all year to get a day like today and top up my tan."

The girl sniffed as smells from a barbecue filled the air. "Oh, that must be lovely. I'm amazed I'm still alive after eating that canteen food for so long. And sitting at that desk all day, I'm surprised I can fit into my shorts! There really is no reason for me to stick around. After all the promises they made about better conditions in the call centre, it has just gotten worse. Even with a hundred people working flat out, they can't hit their targets. How are you supposed to fill out paperwork when you have a line of calls waiting?"

She started to get animated. "This is exactly what happened just yesterday. I took a call, began to fill out my paperwork then I was told that the form didn't matter anymore. I just had to take the next call or the stats would go down. They said that there was absolutely no argument. I'm picturing what, the stats go down for the team and next thing I know, I'm fired?"

She fanned herself with a beermat and slugged her drink. "I don't see how I'm supposed to do anything when most of the problems are linked to the customer accounts or service control and I have nothing to do with those. So if I can't even fill out a customer chase form, what's the point of any of it? Then some bitch ring back looking for an update on her escalation and I have to tell her nothing's happened because I haven't filled out the form. At one stage I got really angry and then I was called into the meeting room to explain what I'd done."

"In any case, who needs the bustle of Dublin when it's all happening in the south? And that dumb manager can sit on his ass for the rest of his life for all I care! It's not worth the effort."

"That will mean a going away party. You should have a big bash before you go," Sorcha said.

Denise perked up at the thought. "Yes, absolutely. Just wait until we get back from holidays and we'll organise it too."

They stayed till early evening when the serious drinkers arrived and it was no longer warm outside. Jeremy walked back with the girls to his house and they went inside to watch a movie. Katerina joined them on the couch for a couple of hours and they could hear Zara stomping around upstairs. "She's been in a bad mood all weekend," Katerina said. "So she just talks to her mother and tries to feel better."

When Sorcha arrived home on the last bus, she found the kitchen in tatters. Jason had been cooking and had left all of the dirty utensils in the sink. She checked them and they were caked with food. 'Just what I need' she thought as she climbed the stairs to go to sleep. She saw the light was left on the landing and in his room so switched them off before closing her door.

⋙◆⋘

The dishes were still there the following morning and there was no sign of her housemate. She presumed he was at a friend's house. She avoided the dirty things by washing vegetables and making a salad.

About Turn

She found the chopping and preparing therapeutic after a long week at work.

"This is not how I thought things would turn out," she said out loud to herself. "Two years ago, I joined the company thinking it would go somewhere. No sign of that happening."

She had a bunch of certificates of achievement in her bedroom, mostly from short training courses she had done like spreadsheets and office management, which were just gathering dust at the moment. She had checked with Sharon for a possible move but no roles had become available and she was indeed stuck in a rut for the time being. She didn't want to hassle Sharon again as it could mean a black mark against her.

She checked through lists of housing as she ate, groaning at the amount that she would have to pay as deposit on a potential home. It would probably mean taking on at least one renter and she shuddered to think of how that would work. Years ago, she would have been earning enough to own her own place but not anymore. The figures on the page in front of her were stressing her out so she looked at a holiday brochure instead. She thought about visiting home for a few days to get some rest and called home that evening.

"We'll be away for a few days ourselves the end of August so keep that in mind" her mother suggested.

Sorcha made a note of that particular weekend. She would make some excuse and turn up and would have the house mostly to herself. If only she could get away with a ruse of that kind and have some space to herself for a change. But she thought her sister would probably be around anyway. She had kept her old bedroom while she did some training courses. Maeve had had developmental problems. Sorcha rolled her eyes at the memory of that time several years ago when she had great screaming rows with her sister and mother who would not listen to reason and understand her need to study for exams or just enjoy her own space.

———◆———

The bombshell came shortly afterwards without warning. Sharon announced one morning: "Guys, we have to go downstairs for a meeting."

Her face looked genuinely worried as she stood up and leaned across the desk partition. Sorcha stopped typing and her manager whispered confidentially that she couldn't divulge anything. The small group got up and went into the main office space downstairs. A microphone was set up at one end of the room and the workers had gathered to listen. Moments later, the General Manager entered and took the stand. He was flanked by the other managers who stood silently.

"Good morning. How are we all doing?" Alan said, his large frame looking slumped as he read from a set of notes in his hand. "I'm afraid I have some bad news to impart and the news is this. We have just had word from our counterparts in the US that they have decided on the basis of the performance of the company last year to revise their operations in Ireland.

"This means effectively no expenditure unless absolutely necessary. We don't have concrete information but a number of our teams will be returning to their home countries following review of the situation. And I'm afraid for us we will be cutting any plans for projects within the department. We will also be cutting back severely on any expenditure on a daily basis, meaning stationary and any unnecessary business costs. We will be outlining this in greater detail in due course." He finished amid gasps and boos and stepped down as John switched off the microphone. Alan left the room, looking apologetic, on his way to the next group to announce the bad news. John stood and chatted with the department managers before leaving.

There was silence on the way up the stairs. The girls knew that their jobs were safe but the announcement meant a lot of extra work in the near future. As usual, they didn't know exactly what was going to happen. They quickly got back to work and Sharon popped her head over Sorcha's desk to ask her to put on her headset.

"Let me know if it gets really busy. There should be lots of questions from workers after today's announcement. We'll be focusing on contract terminations from now on where paperwork is concerned."

They held a quick meeting in the afternoon and the team turned attentions to the selected employees whose jobs were being returned to the countries of origin. There were official letters to be sent out and paperwork to be processed which would take some time.

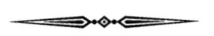

About Turn

In the bar that evening, most workers had congregated to complain about the news. There had been clarification regarding specific countries that would no longer be based in Dublin and other countries were sure to follow. Sorcha saw the red-haired Corkonian discussing the issue with his girlfriend. "I've been here since the start but they have just let things get out of hand. The customer calls up for a service, often having debt on an account, and even if they don't it's a disaster. The service managers worked with us for months and we could hear them telling the callers to hang on, that the engineer was on his way. Then we would get the same calls the next day or someone demanding a recall because the machine was out of order.

"Customers hanging on the lines and being bounced around when all they want to do is order supplies. They've lost millions by losing packages and not delivering on time. Those service agreements are a joke. I'm not surprised at the announcement. Now we'll see just how badly they treat us when we're given our dismissal letters. There's no way I'll be going back to Austria to work. I've been looking around and I'm pretty sure I've got other options."

The technical teams were the least affected by the news. The well-trained staff were settled in the new buildings and the company was hoping to keep this part of their business running.

―――⋄―――

The office was busy for the next few weeks with workers keen to arrange their final payments before leaving the company or going back home. Each leaver was granted a few minutes with a HR rep to discuss the final details and fill out an exit interview form. The feedback had been fairly negative so far. Sorcha noticed the skinny Spanish girl from the pub spitting fire at Jeremy. She was letting off steam about the situation as some of her close friends had been relocated home. "I don't have a lot of time right now to make small talk. I have two minutes to drop off this stuff then I have to go back to my office and try to make sense of the garbage on my desk. What kind of treatment is this?

"Anything you've been hearing is absolutely true, believe me. I have to stay here and finish my exams but I want to leave as soon as possible. It's going nowhere. All of our hard work came to nothing and the managers just sit back and do nothing." She glared at the managers' office when she said this then joined her friends to go back downstairs.

They went to the canteen which was deserted in the afternoon. Now that most of the teams had moved to the new buildings, building 1 was quiet and civilised. The catering staff had moved to the middle block and part of the old building would be sold off in the coming months.

The finance teams were the only groups to reside in that building. A team of 100 UK workers had taken over the welcome centre space and the German team were in the next section. One of the UK finance team arrived during lunch to complete her exit interview. The blonde girl had been working on projects with the London recruits and was reluctant to go back to her desk and pick up a headset again. "A year in that place tells you all you need to know about what's coming. They'll be pulling out all the stops from here on in. I just said no way when they offered me my old job back. I'll find something in town, I suppose," she said resignedly, as she carried her going-away gift to the cubicle for the interview. The girl lived in one of the nearby estates and would have a long trek into town each day.

She was joined by a horde of finance staff who had spent the past year struggling to deal with customer complaints. Many of them had worked on the Commercial team and they had managed to find work elsewhere, some had gone back to their old jobs. One of them joked with his teammate. "Not up to scratch. Sure you did your best." He turned to the admin staff member who was dealing with the paperwork. "Check her for lates now and make sure you put it all down in her reference."

He burst out laughing. "Shouldn't you be somewhere, Paul?" his ex-teammate said, laughing. She looked relieved to have her exit interview over with and handed over her ID badge. Paul walked downstairs, looking glum and patting her on the back as they left the building. He had just bought himself a top-of-the-range car and had put a downpayment on a house with his fiancée and didn't want to back out now. The finance staff were due to meet their management team at the Citywest conference hall later that week and it was hoped there would be some good news announced.

The Spaniards had been selected to go back home as well and the girls came upstairs, looking worried. The workers had the option to stay in the company in a different capacity but most had decided to leave. Paola came upstairs with her face looking upset. Despite her language skills, she had minimal education and had not been able to climb the corporate ladder sufficiently to have a safe landing. She was wondering whether to stay and continue working as an agent or take her chances on the jobs market.

Eventually, the clamour of activity began to subside and the finance department started to advertise their charity day which would be happening in July. It was the first time for this to happen and the UK staff had had to request a day away from their phones to ensure it ran smoothly. There was a day of scheduled events to be held on site in aid of a children's charity: car washing, raffles, cake sales, sponging and games. Sorcha was too busy with work to attend but snatched a few minutes at lunch to visit the casino downstairs and purchase some tickets for the raffle. There were a number of hampers lined up and she picked five tickets for a good cause. She noticed out of the corner of her eye that guy Paul who had set up a mini golf tournament in one section. "The very woman," he said to a short dark haired woman with glasses. "You're not going to contribute?"

His workmate tittered as the woman passed by without a word. "It's not my fault his girlfriend left him," she said and rolled her eyes. Outside, the sponging was well underway and Sorcha noticed a familiar face from the Scandinavian market getting pelted with wet soaking yellow sponges. A list of managers had been selected and they were scheduled to appear at twenty-minute intervals or face a fine. There was a good atmosphere altogether and it was heartening to see the activity. But Sorcha was too tired to join in the fun. She noticed Lorna making an effort at the cake stall when she was really pissed off with the situation.

Lorna had decided to go to the bar that night with Courtney and some other staff members. There had been an open invitation but Sorcha decided it would be better not to go. In any case, it would just be full of football fans after the charity matches that evening. The American was delighted to have another round of cocktails at hand. The department had moved to building 1 and occupied the bottom floor with the German team. Her team had been the only one to reach its targets for the second quarter and she had a chance to celebrate. Her Irish co-workers had been tackling Commercial problems and had barely gotten any percentage of a bonus. "Not their fault but I don't think Paul is very happy about it. They were way behind. I suppose they'll just have to work through it and maybe restructure the teams eventually."

The management staff had opted to hit their workers hard by focusing on query logging and resolution. UK management were still around but had survived the setup and only had minimal input now. The leasing manager had returned to London with his Vegas winnings and the large new location was quiet as the department got on with the work. There were two new Irish heads of the department and they had set up a list of all outstanding debt to be tackled. It meant dealing with a huge backlog of correspondence, especially for multi-machine commercial accounts, where ownership had changed, machines had moved location and bills had not been paid. In some cases, workers had little clues and had to work the query back to its origin. Often, the callers were abusive as they either had sales to make or they had to sort out a mountain of incorrect bills for their own CEO. The Irish managers did little about pleas for better working conditions as their remit was to sort the billing problems out once and for all.

———◆———

Sorcha took the train for a few days break at the beginning of August. It was surreal travelling through the countryside in the early afternoon on a weekday when everybody was at the office. She sat back and read about a recent immigrant from Nigeria who had spent three years in a crappy flat waiting for housing. Angela had a small son soon after she arrived and was hoping to restart her life by going to college to study. She already had a degree in history from her country's university but found juggling motherhood and a job didn't work very well. "I just want my son to have a future. It's really urgent that we get a place and that my son goes to college," she said. The woman had been offered a place in the new development where Lorna lived and she was worried about childcare and commuting.

The other interviewees had similar stories, Julia had arrived from Zimbabwe and had lived in a houseshare with three other people in south county Dublin until she had managed to save enough for a proper flat to bring her children over. Since then, she had met her husband and had managed to restore the lifestyle she had enjoyed in Africa as PA to a company director. The story engrossed Sorcha for most of the journey. She had some music tapes in her bag but didn't really feel like listening to anything.

As it happened, her mother had decided to go away for the weekend. She had gone to the pilgrimage at Lough Derg in Donegal and would be away for a few days. The weekend involved a series of religious ceremonies, fasting and walking the stony ground just like St. Patrick had done centuries before.

"Why on earth has she decided to spend her summer holidays in such a place?" Sorcha wondered out loud.

Her dad shrugged and made excuses. He didn't mind as she had frozen a few dinners for him before leaving and had cleaned the house from top to bottom. She would be back next week and they could then go on holiday together, and he'd have a travelling companion on his trip to their rented beach house.

Sorcha was starving by now and checked the directory to see if she could order something. There were a couple of Chinese and Indian restaurants in town but no pizza service. It was the first time she had ever ordered anything like this at home. The delivery car pulled into the drive and she handed him a note and a few coins and put the paper bag on the kitchen table. She pulled out prawns in sweet and sour sauce and fried rice with beansprouts. Her dad was sitting down, eating his second main meal of the day, a badly made fry which he had scrambled together with food from the fridge.

"What is that?" he asked incredulously as Sorcha emptied most of the contents onto a dinner plate.

"Chinese food. It looks quite nice. I think this is good quality."

She tasted the fluffy rice and took a mouthful of prawns. Her dad made a face and turned away from the table, still eating his bread and rashers.

"Do you buy that a lot when you're above?" he asked. "It must cost you a fortune."

Sorcha shook her head. "It's just I'm on holidays," she said. "It's just seafood with sauce and rice. What's the problem?"

Her dad finished his meal and took the greasy things to the sink to wash them by hand. "When are you going back?" he asked, abruptly.

"In a few days," Sorcha said. Her dad nodded and went inside to watch television. Sorcha scraped her plate clean and then went to her room to read. It was always like this. She had spent virtually all of her teens sequestered in her room, reading Shakespeare, Dickens and then more stuff as she got older. Her parents were stuck in their ways and nothing would change them.

They lived on the outskirts of town, near everything but the countryside was just a quick walk away. The nearby housing estate was full of people her age but she had learnt that it didn't necessarily mean that they had anything in common. After hanging around with various neighbourhood kids in primary school, she had resigned herself to schoolwork and leaving home as soon as possible. Her parents regularly gave her updates on the news of the area or she heard things from friends of hers.

There was one boy, Joseph, who lived a few houses away who had taken to drugs when he went to college and had been well and truly hooked. He was getting treatment and making progress. She remembered him from when she used to visit the house to hang out with his sister. He was a tearaway even then and just laughed whenever anyone tried to discipline him. One of her primary school friends had gotten pregnant shortly after leaving school and had married soon after. She now lived on a farm in the country with her husband's family close but she never called. Sorcha had always liked the country and could bike it to the girl's house for an afternoon if she was free and they would listen to records and go for walks.

It was a better option to sitting at home or chatting to Sheena who lived in one of the first houses of the estate. Sheena had always been polite and well-mannered when she had visited their house and came from a good family with both parents in full-time employment. She had always been a little rebellious and the first to have an opinion but had spent most evenings after school on the town when she got to her teens, and neglected her schoolwork to the point of almost being expelled. There had been a group of them who listened to hard metal and dressed in post-punk look and talked about rejecting the system although it was mostly just a chance for her to meet boys.

Looking back, the lack of interaction had been hard. The girls had chosen one path and she had had to go elsewhere. However, Sorcha had been the only one to make it to university and the city and she liked to think she had plenty of opinions and get up and go. Things weren't exactly rosy at the moment but she had hopes for the future. She thought of the people she had met since starting work: Jeremy who came from such a different background and was so career-oriented; Denise whose party attitude got on her nerves. As a whole, the environment offered little in the way of friendship.

It was quiet without a group of friends to call on and she spent the first couple of days walking to the local community centre or sitting in a café and seeing for herself the changes in the locale. There were still parts of the town that needed a facelift but she could see that development taking place all over. With young adults like her old friends coming into the environment, it was easy to see how businessmen got the upper hand. Most of the girls who had listened to the Clash in their teens just succumbed to an easy life of suburban living and motherhood and didn't get involved as shopping centres and retail outlets were built. Sorcha didn't think she had many options but to stay in the city, like many of the company's employees.

By day three, she had had enough of town and went with her dad to the local fishing grounds for the day. The lake was a mile out of town and her dad often came out here to catch a bite or two. He parked the car and went promptly to the lake and set up his equipment. Sorcha walked within view of him along the manmade pathway to a small ruined church that had long since lost its roof and had grass growing in among the stones that served as a floor. There were memorials among the ruins to various priests that had died in the parish and she knew that an elderly couple often came here to check on the old buildings for vandalism.

She walked through the church grounds and through a field of grass to a nearby waterfall. She sat on the rocks as the water gushed loudly onto the rocks and the river below. She paddled her feet in the water for a few moments, glad of the coolness as she playfully splashed her feet. It was a warm day and a few people were about, taking pictures of the site. It felt luscious to sit by the side of the fall on a warm summer's day and have nothing to worry about. She almost forgot about work as she lay back on the grass, mindful of the cameras circling about. She didn't want pictures of her ending up on some John Hinde postcard or an internet site later on.

Her mother's family farm was situated a few miles away and she could see the familiar hills which hid the farmhouse from view. It was just a few minutes drive in the car and she had enjoyed staying out there during summers while at school. The idea of living the country life was still in her head but she knew it was just an idealistic notion and figured it was the same as building several office blocks and expecting the workforce to dance in the aisles. The reality was that they just spent their time working on the phone, trying to meet targets by quarter end and juggling their personal lives.

"What have you been doing with your time?" her mother asked her that evening. She had arrived on the afternoon bus from Donegal, having starved herself in the pursuit of what, nobody knew. She didn't really seem to benefit from these religious excursions, just became irritable as the outing came to an end. Sorcha told her about the week so far and her mother asked about work, before going to her room to sleep. She looked worn out sitting on the edge of the bed.

"You shouldn't do these things if they have such an effect and make you tired," Sorcha said, leaning on the doorjamb.

Her mother said nothing, just got ready for bed and pulled the curtains. Sorcha could feel the familiar sensation she had when her mother was around. She agreed with the concept of family and could appreciate its benefits but she could never feel comfortable with her mother. She decided to have one more day of fun then leave on Friday. She could have a weekend in Dublin and get back to work on Monday.

"What are we going to do with you?" her mother asked, quizzically, the next day as Sorcha sat reading the newspaper for something to do. She was eating a piece of fish caught the day before and picking the bones out with a fork. "Have you met anybody in the area? Are you going to do anything today? " Both parents had seen the news report on the job losses in the company and mentioned it unnecessarily at times she could not predict.

Her parents didn't seem to understand the complexities facing her and had never understood why the girl had failed to make a neat group of friends. They still asked after her old buddies which made her angry and made her laugh at the same time. She had tried to figure it out before. She was apparently too well-behaved to be friends with a bunch of girls who had really just been pursuing popularity with the boys in town but this made her a social outcast in her parents' blinkered eyes.

Her mother had exclaimed at how Louise, who had always been chubby, had lost so much weight when she got to her teens. Sorcha hadn't told her that it was because of the thirty cigarettes she smoked every day. She had been kind of envious of the girl's social status and

About Turn

popularity and still wondered if her life so far had really proved to be successful in comparison. But this meant that she was letting her mother's words get to her. She had noticed the forecast for the economy looked good and something positive was bound to happen.

———◆———

Back at work, she found that Miriam had covered for Jeremy while he was in Spain and Sorcha had to deal with the overflow of work. She had been receiving e-mails from the blonde manager whose sister worked as a trainer in the main building. The woman had been put forward as representative for the UK finance department and had been haranguing Sorcha to provide the training places they needed. She was getting more desperate now in case the company decided they had no money to do this. Sorcha had an inkling that her e-mailer felt she was inexperienced and an easy target. She decided to have a word about the situation with her manager and Sharon eventually found space in her calendar to have a chat.

"I don't think I can help," she said, when Sorcha broached the subject of changing job roles. "Everybody has their part to play and it's all perfect for the company right now. If we started to switch people around, we could end up making the whole situation worse. I think the whole team works really well in this configuration and we're at our most productive. Don't you like your job?"

"But it's pressurised," Sorcha explained. "I don't feel like I'm getting anywhere." She could think of so many ways her job could be made better like if they had extra staff and put some thought into the organisation of work, but knew if she criticised her work too much she could be fired. Each time she raised an argument, it was batted back and she no longer felt like she had a point to make. When ten minutes had gone past, Sharon went to get up and said, "I'll make a note of this on my personal diary to remind me that we talked. Just hang in there, Sorcha. You're doing a great job."

The girl wondered as she left if she had felt even a pang of hope at that comment and was careful to just take the compliment as face value. She was tired of spending so much time taking care of other people's business and some of the issues were so simple, the people could easily have sorted them out by doublechecking their information. It left her an excess of items to check and the whole process made her feel like she was pursuing a pointless goal. The list of items had not diminished since she had started and she felt it would never end. She was starting to understand how the Finnish girl had felt. Simple things like getting a sandwich if she chose to work at the weekend could be really complex especially if the machines had not been refilled and she was miles from the nearest cafe. She often saw Yves on these weekends, walking upstairs with his briefcase and looking glum. He had extra hours to work as well with no extra pay to deal with the massive expenditure of the site. There was no chance of hiring extra staff as the budget wouldn't stretch.

Lorna had booked a holiday in the Canaries to have something to look forward to in the Autumn. It was just a break from work and was all she could afford as she had been spending money since moving into the new flat and could not afford to leave her job either.

"I'm on to my second credit card at this stage. I had to pay for the furniture for the flat and all of the different bits and pieces. Plus I needed new clothes and my car has to be paid for. It's not funny. Once this holiday is over, I'm not spending a penny.

"The girls were planning a holiday all summer and I just gave in when they told me where they were going. I'm going to have to take out a bank loan to pay off all my debts. There's no way around it. My dad won't pay for everything. He has his limits, too." She grinned sheepishly at the thought of the mounting debts while she dreamed of sunny Gran Canaria.

Miriam had been able to take a couple of hours off work to arrange her meeting for the mortgage approval and had been looking for properties with her partner.

"It is so difficult to arrange these things because we work such different hours. He works as a bus driver. I had to drive all the way back home on the southside to meet with our bank manager. So we got approval and now we have two properties booked for visiting next weekend. We've already seen the information sheet and I think we know the one we want. Just a matter of getting it and putting the money down."

The house they chose was in an older estate on the outskirts of Dublin but within commuting time of their old haunts and parents' homes. The couple living in it were planning to move out as soon as it was sold and Miriam had been given a move-in date of just before Christmas. "We went over to see it," she said, "and they had all these

About Turn

kids' toys in one room and the décor isn't very nice but we can do it up in the new year, fingers crossed. They were happy to sell to us and we weren't going to say no. You can't be too choosy these days."

As they left for the day, Sorcha noticed John, her head manager, on his way back to work in short sleeves for a few more hours. He had no major ties and didn't mind doing 60-70 hours a week. He had a smile on his face as he whistled his way back upstairs. Someone had joked he spent most of his time surfing the internet to add another apartment to his string of properties in European cities. But most people knew he had worked his way up from a psychology degree through call centres in Spain to his current position within the company.

———◆———

She bumped into Yves on the bus that evening. He had left the office on time for once and was sitting with a friend called Rosemary. The girl was in her late twenties and had recently joined the Commercial team in UK finance. She got off in the village and immediately pulled out a packet of cigarettes. Yves laughed and nodded goodbye. "She's so stressed at the moment. It's horrible but she has no choice because she had her CIMA exams this year which she didn't pass. And she has to do a customer visit in the UK next week. The company has lost the records of some of their machines and the bills have been unpaid for two years. It's very serious."

Jason was in his usual spot when she arrived. He had stayed up late the night before to watch something called Big Brother, a show which featured twelve different people sharing the same space and all of their actions being relayed to the public via television. They had normal broadcasting as well but BB could be viewed late at night as the cameras were never switched off. The occupants were evicted one by one until the last remaining person who would then win a cash prize.

Sorcha sat down to have a look. "Have they voted anybody off yet?" She tried making conversation with her housemate who was eating a toasted sandwich and had the remote control in the other. He shook his head, not willing to miss any of the action. The girls at work had been chatting about the different characters that had been plucked from the ordinary population and had the potential to become stars if they avoided eviction.

She watched the colourfully dressed participants dress up in wigs and outfits for a game that had been decided by Big Brother's management. If they scored enough points, they got to choose what they wanted to eat. It was a lame show and she felt her nose wrinkle again at the TV screen.

"They're not allowed books or anything from the outside world", Jason helpfully explained the experience, which sounded like a nightmare to her. "James was watching this last night as well and he'll be dying to know what happens."

She felt like she was living her own version of the show having to share so much space with people she didn't know or with whom she had much in common. Her situation didn't feel too different, living in a house which was full of other people's belongings and not having very much control.

A van pulled up next door and Sorcha recognised some of their neighbour's friends. They worked in low-paid jobs around the city but were able to send money home from their savings each month. She saw Paulina and Yves come outside and waved. The vehicle pulled out of the driveway and she remembered that Paulina had mentioned they were looking for a new place to live. Now that they had two proper incomes, they could afford to maybe look around. They had not been resident long enough to purchase a home but wanted a bigger place to rent.

She went upstairs and looked at her face in the bathroom mirror. There were already bags under her eyes and she felt tired and lethargic. She decided to have a shower and used a new scrub from The Body Shop. She could feel the anger welling up inside her at the situation. The weeks, months and years just seemed to yawn in front of her with no end. She would be stuck like this forever, it seemed, but she had no idea how to change her life.

She went back downstairs to have a word with Jason just as James arrived in the door.

"Would you mind if we watched something else for a little while?" Sorcha asked, with menace in her voice.

Jason looked at her with surprise and James joked, "Look, I made it home early so I could sit and watch this tonight."

"Very funny," Sorcha said, stomping into the kitchen in a fury. James followed her after a few minutes as she busied herself with cleaning up.

"Sorry," she apologised. "This place is starting to get to me."

"Watch whatever you want,' James said. "Jason is going to help me move some stuff over to my girlfriend's."

"Are you moving?" Sorcha asked, in shock.

"No," James laughed. "Just some things she asked me to buy for her. Don't worry, it would take more than that for us to move out. I'm from Belfast remember."

He lowered his voice. "If Jason bugs you, just tell him. He can be quite understanding but he's one of the most immature people I've ever met."

Sorcha nodded. She took a drink and went back to the living room when the guys had gone but didn't really feel like watching anything. She felt like she was suspended in air and none of the elements around her made sense anymore. She didn't like where she was stuck but everytime she tried to move, nothing happened. It was a weird sensation and she felt dizzy again as the TV ranted about inflation and the crisis in the Middle East. The aim of creating a utopian dream had taken a strange turn, and she wanted out.

Chapter 11

"Sorcha, these will have to be done again. I know we're busy right now but can you please watch what you're doing?" Sharon handed the girl back a bunch of papers that had been crossed out. "There's no excuse for this behaviour. And you were late this morning as well."

She said in a lower voice, "If there's a problem, can you let me know? We're having an audit of the department this week, and I don't want anybody to let us down, OK?"

Sorcha went crimson as the rest of the group looked at her. "Sorry," she muttered and went on typing, knowing her mind was not on her work. The bus service had marginally improved but to catch the shuttle bus from the shopping centre, she had to walk through the village and it was tiring.

"I am really starting to hate this business," she fumed, as she ate another lunch at her desk. It was a droopy sandwich with cold ham and coleslaw, which she washed down with a coffee from the machine. She also had to train her new co-worker Mark on the systems and this was nowhere near as fun as she had thought. She had made a couple of mistakes on the main computer system in the first hour and he had noticed when the files were handed back to her.

"How long have you been working here?" he asked.

"About two years. We've been pretty busy since then," she added, by way of explanation as she flew in and out of the different screens. He watched her and nodded as she explained how each file was created for an employee. She chatted about some of the people she had met and the issues that had arisen.

"There can be a lot of complaints, particularly at the end of the month when people get paid. Or we get requests from managers to

About Turn

improve certain services and there are round table discussions on a regular basis."

"I would have thought that most of those things would have been ironed out by now," Mark said. "Is that not the case? Surely you would be primarily responsible for highlighting these issues?"

Sorcha felt herself getting defensive and didn't like her job being undermined by a new arrival on the floor. She pursed her lips and went on, lightly discussing the job role. When he left to get some phone training, Sorcha was relieved and settled down to work. She felt restless and unenthusiastic and just went through the motions to complete the administration.

Sharon came over to her desk before she went home and asked how the training had gone.

"Fine, I think," Sorcha said, wearily.

"Did you cover all of the systems with him?" Sharon enquired.

"Yes, I think so."

"Ok, I asked him about our databases and he didn't know what I was talking about. Could you make sure next time you have a new recruit that you put your work aside for the time being and ensure you cover all of what we do, OK? It saves us valuable time."

"Yes, sorry." Sorcha stammered.

She left the building in shock. Sharon had been behaving in such a strange manner lately and she felt like she had been transported back to the classroom, being tapped on the wrist for childish behaviour.

"The managers are expecting big results next week in the audit and Sharon is very nervous in case it goes wrong," Lorna said the next day. "She's not very happy about the promotion prospects here either. There doesn't seem to be anything around on site. She'd only be able to move sideways which would not mean a pay rise."

Lorna told her not to worry and Sorcha went on with her paperwork, careful not to make mistakes. She was annoyed too about the lack of opportunities. Although her job sounded good on paper and she was proud of her achievements, the reality just meant a lot of repetitive inputting and chasing around for signatures while dancing to someone else's tune. She was involved in hundreds of people's lives but did not ever get to meet these people socially or go to their houses. She could feel the weight of responsibility resting on her shoulders and didn't see why she had to shoulder so much at such a young age.

Deirdre Haugh

The work atmosphere had changed within the group as well. It was busy enough but Sorcha got the impression that people were just bored and unmotivated by the lack of movement. They still had nights out but most people were too stressed to make interesting conversation and often made excuses not to go or to leave early.

"What do you think of that new guy Mark?" Lorna asked. "He's not very talkative, is he? Where do they get these people? I wouldn't be surprised if I come in some day and they just have a robot sitting at one of the desks. I asked him to come down but he was talking about driving home in the traffic."

Sorcha would usually defend the person being derided, but was too tired to talk, having worked solidly all day. She sat and nursed a drink and said nothing. Eventually, the girls moved away from her and went to sit by the bar. Sorcha looked around at the crowd of heaving bodies and wished she were anywhere but here. She had a friend working in Chicago and thought about possibly moving over there to work. It wasn't that weird and she finally had some money together to relocate. People did these things all the time. Lorna had been chatting about a move to Spain where everything was so much cheaper but she didn't speak the language well enough to work there.

She realised that she needed to make some contact with people, at least to stop her going mad in a city that was exploding with money and traffic. She was keen to retrieve some of her old connections and called Isabelle's house out of interest but got a curt message that Mlle. Isabelle had departed for France and she would have to leave her name and details to get a forwarding address. She decided against this as she knew Isabelle would have contacted her if she had wanted to remain friends.

She had not heard from Karen either who was probably living happily in the country and not bothered about her friend. She was still attracted by the busyness of town though and ended up in Mao's in the city centre for something to eat one weekend. She looked around at the pop art pictures of the Chinese leader that covered the walls. There was nothing else to look at apart from a menu. In the old days, she would have really wanted to go someplace like this for a treat. Sorcha started to eat her meal, which had arrived piping hot. She hunted around in the soup for noodles and pieces of chicken but left most of the meal behind her. She could feel her heart pumping from nerves as she sat in a restaurant where she didn't recognise anyone and tried to engross herself in the magazine she had bought.

Couples and groups filled the room, upstairs and downstairs, and she felt conspicuous as she got up to leave. She paid at the counter then ran to the exit. Outside, the sky had become cloudy and she bought her first umbrella of the season just in case. She packed it into her bag for an emergency and strolled down Grafton Street, looking at the shop windows. There were a few Romanians walking about, selling copies of the street magazine and she responded with a terse, cranky 'No' as they approached, trying to wheedle change out of her and their gold teeth glinting. An African woman with a kid strapped to her back pushed a wheelie bag full of shopping to the edge of the pavement to cross the street. Her partner and two young sons played a game of tag and their actions drove Sorcha crazy. She dodged their small bodies as they zigzagged in front of her. They joined the crowd as they crossed at Dame Street and Sorcha scuttled across to the first taxi in line.

"Hard day shopping?" the driver asked, as she stepped in and scrabbled for the seatbelt.

"Not really," she muttered.

He took a look at her in the rear view mirror and said nothing more. She was glad for the silence as they drove through the park and didn't feel any concern for the deer that might possibly jump in front of the windscreen. 'Fuck them', she thought, completely out of character. She was sick of trying to create a life for herself with no support. As she paid the driver, she could feel tears welling up in her eyes and hurried inside.

―――◆―――

She woke up on Monday morning with a dread of sitting at her desk that day or any day, tapping endless wads of information into a system, which gave her nothing back in return. She felt like she was fuelling some monster and there was no end in sight. She made sure to get to the bus stop in time and was at her desk just as her watch showed 8.30am.

"Good news, guys," Sharon said. "For all our hard work with the audit, we have been allowed lunch out of the office this week. Can you decide among yourselves where you want to go and we'll book a table?"

"There aren't any nice restaurants within a mile's radius of this place," Gemma moaned. "Anyway, all of you vote and I'll haggle for a table."

They decided on a local pub and, on Wednesday, the group drove without much enthusiasm to the venue. Lorna took Sorcha and two other girls to make a carshare and they listened to a boyband's CD as they went. Lorna was talking about their latest concert and Sorcha could feel herself cringing in the back seat.

"I can't believe you listen to this stuff," Miriam said. "I thought this was just for teenyboppers."

"They're really great when you see them live," Lorna protested. "Some of the songs are fantastic. I'd love to book again next time they're in town. They put in such a lot of effort."

"Oh, OK." Miriam picked up the CD and looked at the cover. "I'm always trying to find new stuff to play in the car on the way to work."

"I'll make you a copy," Lorna promised.

The bar had just opened under new management and the staff, who told them about the meals on offer, greeted the group. They got sandwiches or hot meals and sat on high stools in the bar area, but no alcohol was allowed.

"Did everyone bring money because this one is not on the house?" the manager asked. "And we have a strict one hour lunch, that's all."

"Can we not just have a little one?" Gemma asked. Sharon shook her head. She looked at Sorcha who was standing close by and, without apologising, directed her tray in the direction of Lorna who made some room at her end of the table. She picked at her meal as she discussed property prices with Gemma and Jeremy and didn't speak to the rest of the group.

Sorcha ate silently, without much appetite for the roast potatoes and meat she had picked from the selection. It felt like enforced socialisation. She half-expected some researcher to be standing around with a board and pen, taking notes as the group made small talk. Sorcha felt so unhappy and all she could think about was the amount of work she had to do when she returned to her desk. Sharon tapped the table as their hour out came to an end and they got up to leave. Sorcha turned to get off her stool and suddenly felt panicked. She held on to the table and

About Turn

Miriam took her bag as she got down. She saw stars in front of her eyes for a moment as she struggled to maintain control of her actions, then walked out of the room with the rest of the group.

She realised how bad things had become when the department went for a drinks night in the local bar with the giant Buddha still shining on its pedestal near the bar. She walked like a zombie through the crowds of people and felt like she was on her own planet as everyone chatted around her. Lorna and Jeremy were swopping holiday stories and Miriam was looking pleased as punch with her new home ready to move into.

"At least Spain means a break from all the immigrants that have moved here," Lorna was saying. "Everywhere you go, there are hordes of them. I don't know where they all come from. I was just saying to my dad that if any of them moved into our complex, I would move out. I've paid a bundle to have that flat decorated the way I want it and the idea of having to see blacks at the shops when I go out to get milk would kill me. I don't want these guys to break in and to have to pay to have it all replaced. Just the idea!"

Jeremy made some sarcastic, faux-sympathetic comments about the poor little rich girl dreading the fantasy apartment world being swept away in a wave of crime and immigration.

"AND," she continued loudly. "AND, before, it was bad enough to listen to some idea they had about giving ten per cent of the houses and flats to social housing?? I mean, come on, I work every day and I don't want to have to share my space with a bunch of welfare families."

Jeremy started to get embarrassed. "But wasn't that for affordable housing?" he said. "Isn't that something different? I mean, I've never taken social welfare but I don't have the money to spend on a house right now. I don't know if I ever will. I'd like to have a home of my own someday and not just some newly built slab of concrete in the middle of nowhere. At least some of these schemes give people the chance to buy and trade up, right?"

Lorna nodded and admitted he was correct. "But you know what I mean," she said.

On the bus home, Jeremy was looking worried. "It's not my favourite topic of conversation. The minute I came back from Oz, I had my family on my back to be more responsible and settle down. I can't afford a property on my own and when I hear someone talking like that, I just tell them to shut up.

"Anyway, nice to have a couple of drinks even if we all have to assemble in our spots tomorrow and continue working for the greatness of the company in the world without any sign of any dividends coming our way. If I had known, but then would I have had any choice?" he groaned.

He filled her in on the gossip that Lorna had been seeing her English friend from the UK market for a couple of months now and they had become very close. Stephen had gained notoriety for taking part in a Robbie Williams lookalike contest in London and, apart from being a really nice guy, it seemed this was all he really had to offer. "The job itself is not brain science and Stephen wanted a new scene so he came over here from London for a while. Don't know how long it will last."

They waved goodbye as they came to the familiar turn just outside the village. Sorcha walked to her 1970s housing estate and Jeremy travelled on to his modern house a few stops ahead. She saw him get on the 37 bus and take a seat towards the back, putting on his headphones and listening intently to Radiohead. He had been talking about moving back home for a few months to get the deposit together for a starter flat nearby. It wasn't just that simple. Then he needed to pay for insurance, furniture and all the other bits and pieces required. With some help from his old man, he might just be able to do it.

Tony was trying to decide if he had enough money to get engaged. He walked around the house, uncharacteristically seeming like his thoughts were elsewhere for a while as he mentally calculated the costs of a romantic engagement and a wedding to follow.

"You should go for it," Sorcha said, encouragingly. She plodded home from work evening after evening knowing that people all around her were moving in the right direction or some direction but she was just stuck. She called home that weekend to chat to her parents but her mother just repeated the same conversation over again and she couldn't continue.

"The weather is getting cold again," she said in a miserable voice. "And the winter is so long. What do you do with yourself for all those evenings above in Dublin? You must be bored out of your mind."

"I get out and about," Sorcha said.

"You shouldn't go out on your own. I told you that. What if something happened? Think of someone else for a change."

"OK, I'll stay in."

"And do what? You'll never get anywhere if you don't mix with people."

Sorcha rolled her eyes and put down the phone, feeling more miserable than ever. She had facts and details reeling around in her head from the week in the office and knew that she would have the same to start into again on Monday morning. There was no respite from the pressures and she could feel her body shaking with fear at the thought. It wasn't anything personal to her co-workers but she felt responsible for the endless mountain of work that waited to be done and there was no way out.

The winter weather had arrived with a vengeance. She spent most evenings trying to get home before the torrent of rain fell. One evening, she was not so lucky. The bus was late arriving and she cowered in the bus stop as the rain lashed against her and the other workers. When she finally could clamber onto the bus, she sat soaked for half-an-hour until she reached the village then had to fight her way through the busy street as she rushed home, splashes of water hitting her from cars as they drove past.

Miriam suggested that everyone go to the Hallowe'en party that took place at the end of the month. Sorcha listened to the conversation without much enthusiasm. "Are you coming, Sorcha?" someone said. She hated to say no and would have been enthusiastic if she had been feeling better. She found herself under pressure to commit to donning a costume and booked an outfit with a rental company in the city centre. Eventually, it was the night of the party and she sat on the couch with the package upstairs in her room, unopened.

Tony had started talking about his wedding again and was leafing through a booklet of rings, debating how much to spend on the engagement jewellery. Sorcha had spent the day dealing with the UK finance manager for their move back to Building 1 and had spent a lonely half-hour in the local shops afterwards. She was not happy to spend her free time discussing some else's plans. She watched as he ticked off certain items and made a list of reference numbers.

"Which one do you like, Sorcha, or is it OK to ask?" he said, politely. "You don't have to get involved. I'll probably pick one that she'll hate anyway."

"No, it's fine," Sorcha answered. "It's hard to know so maybe you should give her a call."

"Are any of your friends married?" he asked.

"I think we're a little young yet, but in the next few years..." she trailed off.

"Yeah, there's quite a few of my old college friends that have paired off, except for the guys you met in town. Which reminds me I have to give Eamon a call; his brother has some ideas for a wedding venue." He got up and went to use the landline. Sorcha sat on her own in the living-room, realising that she didn't really have a coterie of friends from school or from college either. It was coming to a bit of a crunch time for her as she thought about what she had been doing with her life. So she had been working intensely for a couple of years but what about before then? Her head was confused and she couldn't work out an answer. She called Miriam and was glad when she got the girl's messaging service. She left a message to say that she wouldn't be going to the party that night.

"Aren't you supposed to be going out tonight?" Tony enquired as she brushed past him in the hallway.

"Change of plan, don't feel like it," Sorcha said.

He put his hand over the speaker, "My girlfriend's calling round later. I could arrange to go to her house if you want the space, but I thought you were going out?"

Sorcha said nothing and shrugged as Tony looked at her quizzically.

"I'm not going out," she said.

He nodded and went on talking. Sorcha went up to her room, feeling like she was letting everybody down. She was too tired to think but knew that the girls would get on fine without her. They were all bringing partners or had someone to collect them afterwards and she didn't want to be the only one having to call a taxi home. It wasn't just the feeling of being an outsider – she had no energy and despite a good night's sleep the night before, she was tired and irritable and wanted Tony to stop talking and laughing within her earshot.

She had already been in trouble that week with an oversight regarding her house key and didn't like the feeling that she was the one in the doghouse. She had been trying to finish some work in the office and had absent-mindedly left the key in the lock on opening the door and had gone upstairs upon arriving home. When Tony called her downstairs some time later, she had been genuinely surprised when he had handed her the key and raised an eyebrow. Even one incident like this could have caused serious security problems so she apologised and promised that it would not happen again. She had felt bad all week and knew that she had to do something.

In the evenings, when she arrived home from work, she had noticed her lack of focus as she made something to eat. Her mind was all over the place and she couldn't settle, dropping cutlery and glasses on the kitchen floor. It was from a tiredness that never seemed to go away.

"Maybe it's the time of year," she said to the doctor the following week. She had called in sick first thing Monday morning, using the phone in the doctor's appointment office, which was walking distance from her house. She had been half-confused on her way there and almost went to the bus stop instead. The doctor took one look at her and signed off a permission slip, giving her six weeks off work. Nervously, she took the piece of paper and went to call her office. Sharon was surprised but took the news pretty well.

"Take it easy, Sorcha," she said. "Let us know when you're feeling better."

Sorcha decided to give the letter containing the doctor's cert to Tony to post for her, and had to organise a trip home. She didn't want to sit around the house and thought that perhaps some space would make her feel better and give her head peace.

Surprised but aware that Sharon was OK as long as she was not in trouble and didn't have to answer to her own manager, Sorcha sat on her couch in the house which was empty as the guys had gone to work and thought about what she should do. She didn't leap or jump about but sat looking at the slip of paper the doctor had handed her, noticing that her hand was still shaking slightly.

Even the picture of her manager being angry, hurt or confused at her absence did not deter her from calling 'time' on her months of suffering. She had to call her parents and dialled the number. Her sister answered and she let her know that she was on her way home. Maeve didn't object or ask questions for once and Sorcha hung up and went upstairs to pack a bag.

She grabbed some warm clothes from the wardrobe and folded them and stuffed them into her travel bag. She had a couple of jumpers and pairs of pants from last Winter as she hadn't bothered to buy anything new this season. There was a train leaving at lunchtime so she called a cab, anxious not to take any chances.

She sat waiting for the cab to arrive, drinking a cup of tea. As she drove to the station, she sent Tony a text explaining where she was going.

———◆———

Sorcha woke just as the train was passing underneath the final bridge before reaching her hometown. The carriages passed through the stone walls swiftly and the train gradually came to a slow as it neared the station. She did not move as the other passengers began to put on coats and gather bags to prepare for disembarking. Her eyes felt heavy and although she had slept fitfully throughout the journey, she did not feel the required energy coursing through her body to make that final effort. A woman in the next seat looked at her momentarily as she got up to leave.

"Are you OK?" she asked, as she moved towards the exit.

Sorcha nodded and half-smiled. It was more of a quarter-smile really; she did not feel anything as the train came to a sudden halt and she could see the newly painted fencing and stone walls of the platform. She looked for her bags reluctantly and went to pick them up by the handles. One, two, three and her fingers were around the first handle, then the next one and she stood up and edged her way out of the seat. She pulled her bags with her and caught herself slightly at the exit doors. She yanked the bags to the outside and slowly put her feet on the ground. Her head felt heavy and she had pains in her joints although she had made sure to wrap up well. The platform was full of people who had come to meet their visitors but there was no one she recognised this time.

The house was just around the corner but there was no sign of a car to collect her. She had made sure to tell them exactly when she would arrive, hadn't she. It didn't surprise her and she resigned herself to walking home. She trudged through the wet ground mingled with old leaves and gravel and clutched one bag to a hand, feeling braver now as she noticed the familiar surroundings and neighbours' houses in the area. As she walked on the footpath over the station bridge, she could see the train below with steam rising above the blue-green painted rooftop. The station manager took an armful of parcels back to the sorting office and the train's departure was OK'd by his colleague in a jumper and jacket, waving his flags at the end of the platform. She stood looking at the sign indicating the name of the station for a moment. To some people, this would represent a rustic setting with the cosy station nestled on the outskirts of the town. She tried to get a different perspective on the place but to her, it was like the back of her hand and all too familiar. As she walked down the hill, the train chugged beneath her and around the bend to its next stop.

Sorcha crossed over the road and opened the latch on the garden gate of her parents' house. She checked the front door, which was locked, and rang the doorbell. There was no answer so she went round the back of the house. The back door was firmly shut although she noticed the washing basket left outside which indicated some sign of life.

"This is all very strange," Sorcha said, but knew deep down that it was to be expected. She could only imagine what was to happen when she finally did encounter some of her family members. She found the back door key in an old box in the garage, the usual hiding place. She had thought that this had been changed but they must have made that little concession in acknowledgement of her arrival before they had all skipped town. She knew her father was at a meeting out-of-town and would be away till late evening. Her mother had any number of opportunities to spend her time of an afternoon and was probably a little closer to home.

Inside the house at last, she put her bags away in the guestroom, a small extra room converted for storage and a spare bed. It was the only free room in the house: her sister had taken over their room and locked it every time she left home. The walls were covered with posters of boybands and she had a collection of teddybears covering half the floor space, or so she had heard. Her brother had occupied the front room.

He was in his final year at college in the nearby city and usually linked by wires to his computer games when in the house. She tried the door of his room and it was also locked. There was a picture of some soccer star attached to the paintwork and a note saying 'Keep Out'.

"They grow up so fast," Sorcha mused to herself sarcastically, as she went to the kitchen. She had managed the challenge of the key search and was feeling hungry. The tiny freezer was empty apart from a half-eaten block of ice-cream. The routine was to use the vegetables grown in the garden and these usually sufficed to make dinners each day. Throw on some potatoes, carrots and meat bought at the butcher's, or some fish perhaps and there was no need to go hungry ever. But Sorcha had not cooked in a while and did not feel in the humour to go to the trouble. She made a quick sandwich and toasted it under the grill while she waited for fate to show her the family's response to her travails. The cup of tea made with real tealeaves warmed her up as she bit into the sandwich and wondered how long she had to wait. Hours or minutes? Maybe days, who knew. She felt an overwhelming sadness as she stared at the wall, not knowing how it all had come to turn out like this.

She was OK to pull herself together for now and she cleared up the dirty dishes and went into the living room to switch on the television. Her mind could not concentrate on the programme she was watching although the beach setting caught her eye and held her attention. It was a chatty show with English people running around a chosen holiday location and picking new places to live. She had seen this one before. Some of the people had a lot of money to spend and others were scrimping to save every penny to buy their new home.

"No, I don't think we've found what we're looking for," one woman said, holding a cocktail, as the presenter nodded enthusiastically before wrapping up the show. The woman and her partner and the presenter smiled from some faraway location as the credits began to roll. "Better luck next time," said the announcer, who moved on to the next programme. Sorcha lost interest and switched off the TV. She went out to the room and lay down on the bed. In truth, she did not know what to do with herself. She wished she had some sleeping pills and she could drift away for a couple of hours. Slowly, she nodded off and slept in a comfortable position with her shoes still on her feet.

About Turn

She woke up cold, with the clamour of voices in the hallway outside. It sounded like everyone had returned. She could hear her sister arguing with her brother.

"She's not sharing my room, that's for sure," the girl said. "Tell him, Mam. I don't want her in the room again. I've just spent ages putting all my things away."

It sounded like he had been making fun of her again. Since Sorcha's departure, Maeve had taken over ownership of their once shared domain. Maeve's voice was rising to a shrill whine in protest at the new arrival. Sorcha reluctantly opened the door of her room and made an appearance. The combatants took one look at her and dispersed. Maeve sloped off to her room at the end of the hall and Liam nodded at Sorcha then went into his room and shut the door. Sorcha went to the kitchen where her mother was listening to the radio full blast. It was the local station and she cringed as she heard the familiar jingles advertising the local funeral parlour and the town beauty salon back-to-back. There was an hour-long show in session where the presenter read numerous requests for cool songs but only ever played the most dreary of those requested. There were people in the locality asking to hear Suede or something by Ash and he read each one before choosing an old country air requested by an elderly lady living in some pocket of the county who wanted to be reminded of times gone by.

Her mother stood at the sink, sorting through a bunch of red berry branches she had just picked. She had washed out a glass vase and was expertly putting the branches in place, one at a time. She turned round suddenly and said, "Oh, you're up. Help me with these, will you? I got them when I was out last week."

She looked down at the vase and finished the job as Sorcha held the remaining branches, handing her the best ones first. She stuck the last ones in willy-nilly to use up the whole bunch and then took the vase to the window-sill, saying nothing. Sorcha had been silent as well. She didn't know what to say. She remembered when she had lived at home as a schoolgirl when speaking just made things worse if she got into trouble with her parents.

"How was your afternoon?" her mother said, without an expression. She stood with the sweeping brush now in her hand and made a face as Sorcha stood in her way. "You've no work today?"

"I told you," Sorcha said. "I've been advised to take some time off. The doctor said it was best."

Her mother looked at her. "Did the doctor say it was OK to eat red meat on a Friday?" she asked. "No, I didn't think so."

She opened the fridge and took out the package of ham Sorcha had used to make the sandwich earlier. She flung the ham back on its shelf and swept the floor. The radio was still blaring as Sorcha left the kitchen and went outside. She didn't want to stay long but felt that the fresh air would do her good. There was little difference between the atmosphere either in or out, she reasoned, and she barely noticed the cold evening air as she walked down the garden path to the cluster of trees at the end. She felt dizzy as she stood there amongst the trees, the branches of which had been used to hang swings or climb upon. She walked slowly around the baby trees and small blades of grass that had been set to encourage growth and noticed a snail's shell attached to one of the rocks beside her feet. Birds chirped as they flew in and out of the upper branches of the trees and she watched the larger ones caw to each other on the fence before leaving.

Her mother was on the phone, chatting to one of her sisters. She didn't mention Sorcha's name so the girl felt guilty about her presence. It was OK to show up at Christmas or Easter or for a short break during the year but it was November and this could not legitimate her presence.

She didn't care and rustled around the kitchen for teabags as she felt her mother's eyes on her continuously. She found nothing and went back to the living-room and sat in the armchair by the fireplace, her head leaning against the wall. Her mother had finished her call and followed her inside.

She warmed her hands at the fire and looked at her daughter questioningly. "Are you tired, is that it?" she said. "You can stay here, I suppose, but make yourself scarce if anybody calls. They'll only be asking questions. There can't be much wrong, can there?"

Sorcha nodded as she noticed her dad arriving. He walked in the back door and his footsteps could be heard in the kitchen. He nodded at her and walked down the hall to his bedroom. He spent what seemed like an age in the bathroom before appearing again. In the meantime, mother had prepared his evening meal of fish and two veg. "Do you

About Turn

want some of this?" she said holding the remains of the pot in her hand and the girl shook her head.

The mother put the food on the kitchen table wordlessly and crossed her husband in the hallway as she went to their room. She had taken her large prayer book stuffed full of mass cards with her and Sorcha could imagine her repeating the Hail Mary over and over just as she had done in the local church a few months back. It was part of her daily routine and she usually made up for it if she missed a day.

The parents seemed to having one of their spats again but it would not be long before her mother broke, she felt, and complained about Sorcha's transgression with the ham sandwich. The girl sat in the living-room, glad to be out of the office but not feeling quite at home. "When did you get here?" her father called from the kitchen. He was a stocky man with dark hair graying in his middle-age. Sorcha looked at him, his mouth open and full of food, and answered, "About four o'clock. I was asleep for a while."

Her father nodded and went back to his meal. The clock on the wall was ticking ever so slowly and it seemed like forever before her mother reappeared, lost in thought but not saying anything. She cleared up the dishes as Sorcha's father went to put on his boots.

"I have a couple of jobs to do outside," he said. "See you later."

He closed the back door and Sorcha watched as he got the toolbox out of the garage and picked out what he needed. He wheeled the lawnmower out of its corner and turned it upside down to begin tinkering at its underbelly. She had noticed that the lawn had been cut recently and supposed that it was just some maintenance work. During the winter, the garden did not need to be tended as often and she felt her dad got bored. The faulty lawnmower was an excuse to spend some time out of the house. Her mother was humming off key as she emptied the laundry basket into the washing machine and switched on the cycle to start. She closed the kitchen door and came back to sit across from Sorcha.

"I suppose you don't do much of this housework in Dublin, do you?" she said with a frown.

"As much as I have to," Sorcha said. She had lived away from home for so long that she no longer knew how to operate things in her parents' house and had to re-learn something every time she visited.

Her mother made a face as she looked out of the window. "It looks like it's going to rain," she said. "I'll have to hang those clothes in the garage. If he's out of the way by then."

Her sister coming in dressed in a mismatched outfit with heavy eye makeup and lipstick on her face broke the awkward silence that followed. She said nothing and went straight to the closet to get her coat. Her mother's eyes followed every move and missed nothing. It was only when Maeve had her coat tightly buttoned up and her coloured hair in a scarf that her mother said, "Are you going out like that?"

Maeve just looked at her and said goodbye as she marched out of the back door. Sorcha could hear Liam shouting out of his window, "No burgers tonight, young lady!" as the gate slammed shut. Liam followed shortly. The skinny lad was on his way to a friend's house and left with his ears covered by headphones.

"Look at those two," exclaimed her mother, "leaving without eating a bite!" She was half talking to herself at this stage and Sorcha was relieved when her dad arrived back in and switched on the news. She had felt like she was imposing herself and didn't want to be seen watching television in the middle of the afternoon. Maeve was so predictable, she had insisted on taping Big Brother results while she was out and wouldn't let anybody else touch the tape.

They watched the headlines and the financial reports and some light stories from the day's news. Sorcha sat in the comfort of the living-room with the fire blazing and the entertainment shows that ran throughout the evening's schedule. Her dad said nothing and read the paper while simultaneously watching the TV. She looked across at her mother asleep in the chair and wondered what she was going to do with her time for the next couple of months. At least she still had her salary and didn't have to sign on. She just wanted to rest and went to bed early, lying in the darkness with the wind rustling outside her window until she went to sleep.

The next morning, she woke to hear a tractor rattling past on the road and cars following it as they tried to avoid the grit thrown up in its path. Then she listened to the early morning birdsong as garden birds flew about in the cold sunshine. She got up and had a shower, carefully brushing her teeth and shaving under her armpits. Her siblings were still asleep in their rooms and her parents had already left. They usually went grocery shopping first thing on a weekday morning when the shops were quiet and she imagined them in the car, not speaking but going to the familiar places all the same, like clockwork.

She prepared a bowl of cornflakes, heating the milk in a saucepan and standing over it thoughtfully in case it boiled too much. She had no idea what she was going to do today and the day yawned in front of her. Now that she had so much time on her hands, she couldn't think of any way to use it. She was trying to be upbeat and thought of a possible schedule but realised that she was only at home on her parents' say-so and at this stage, didn't think that a day in town would help matters. She flicked through an old magazine as she ate her cereal and had an orange and coffee. At least she could try to take care of herself while she was on a break.

Her parents arrived back together an hour later, chattering as they left the car. Her mother brought in what she could carry and left the boxes of food for her dad to transport as she came bursting into the house. She was chattering non-stop so it seemed that her parents were back on speaking terms.

"Yes, I was right," she called from the front room. "It will fit perfectly between the wall and the door." She looked at Sorcha who had followed to see what all the fuss was about. "We're getting a new sideboard and a dining table for the front room. I saw just the one we need."

She put her overcoat away and went back to measure the space in the front room again, this time with a measuring tape. "Yes, it'll fit perfectly," she said with relief. "Sometimes Liam puts his things in here and I have such a hard time getting those two to stay in their own rooms. No more than herself who's back again and we thought we'd seen the last of her." She sighed as she re-measured for accuracy's sake.

She sat down in the living-room with satisfaction and thought for a second. "How long are you planning on being here for, Sorcha? A week? Two weeks?" Her mother looked exasperated and Sorcha knew she was thinking of her daughter's college experience when she had found it tough going and sometimes needed to be home.

"I have time off until January, if I want it," Sorcha said. She scrabbled in her things for the doctor's note.

"January?" her mother exploded. "That's..." she counted on her fingers "... two, three months away yet." Her mother made an ugly face and tapped the tape against her knee. "I see."

She got up and went to the kitchen. Sorcha felt incapable of responding as her mother began to take out her cake-making equipment, saying nothing. She grabbed the girl's arm as she went past. "You can stay here till Christmas but I can't cover for you after that. You'll have to get on your own two feet and get back to normality. Can't you see that we have enough to do? I wouldn't mind but there's nothing wrong with you. Anyone who can get up in the morning and take care of themselves like you've been doing does not need to be sitting in her parents' house, waiting for something to happen."

Sorcha was too mentally exhausted to respond to her mother's reprimands and directions. She helped put the things away slowly, feeling like her own independent life was further away than ever.

After a midday meal of potatoes and lamb, Sorcha went for a walk on her own. She went past the station again and walked along the tree-lined footpaths that took her to town. There were a couple of neighbours about whom she greeted with a smile. Some of the kids in the area were tearing around on bikes and horns beeped as they threatened to swerve onto the road. She pottered along with no great plan in mind. The last of the leaves were clogging up the gutters as she went. She had stuffed an umbrella into her backpack but there was no sign of rain. The town green was empty apart from a couple of people taking a shortcut. She walked straight across it and crossed over to the main street. The town centre was full of traffic and people pouring in and out of shops. She blocked it all out and went to the local arts centre, which had opened recently.

The centre offered a quiet oasis from the hullabaloo in the busy streets. The town had developed a couple of shopping arcades in easily accessible pockets and Saturday afternoon was peak shopping time. She had a look at the exhibition upstairs which was a mixture of sculpture and paintings produced by local artists. She had a coffee in the downstairs café and had a look at the upcoming events. There was a little magazine on sale offering news and a schedule of performances and exhibits. She noticed an interview with one of the artists whose work was displayed upstairs. The woman talked about her experience of hardship as a child but that she had used her painting talents to realise who she was on the inside, her true self.

She went back home by foot and her mother looked up as she came through the door. She had her prayer book on her lap and her rosary entwined in her fingers.

"Back again?" she enquired. "Did you meet anyone?" Sorcha shook her head.

Her mother reacted by setting her mouth in a straight line. "I don't know what you're doing coming down here like this. Wandering about with no one to talk to. There's your brother to think of when he graduates next year. If you're going to waste your time and turn into some loony case, what will he do with a sister like that? You should be showing an example."

Liam put his head around the door. "The minute I leave school, I'll be going on a permanent world trip, Ma. So leave her alone. Can't you see she's already developing stress lines and she's not even thirty?"

Later, Sorcha looked at her face in the mirror. If she looked at herself from a certain angle, she could see a couple of lines snaking across her cheekbone and one between her eyebrows which worried her for a second but she put it out of her mind. Liam had been only joking and if she had the money, she might just join him on his world travels.

She felt the overwhelming despair when she went to the cinema the following night. She went to see a so-so comedy and could feel a wave of depression cover her as she sat in the row of seats. She could feel tears rolling down her cheeks but managed to control them as she walked out of the building. One of her neighbours passed her by with a smile but she just walked, hunched, to the main door.

Afterwards, she went to the ATM outside and when prompted for her PIN, she stood for a couple of minutes unsure of what to input. She tried to remember the correct digits and their order but her mind was a blank. Luckily, there wasn't a queue but the formation of numbers did not come to her as it had dozens of times before. She had her home phone number on her mobile so she pressed the dial and asked her dad to pick her up.

He arrived ten minutes later and she got in the passenger side. "What did you go to see?" he asked, trying to make conversation while watching the road.

"A comedy," she said, her eyes glistening again.

Deirdre Haugh

When they got home, he busied himself tidying the car seat cover then the mat at the front door while Sorcha let herself in and went straight to bed. She wanted to avoid her mother's questions and as she lay there, she could hear her parents whispering in the living-room. She couldn't be bothered listening but had some idea the hushed conversation concerned her and her future. If her dad had said anything, it wasn't obvious the next day as her mother spent the afternoon preparing her Christmas cakes. She usually made several cakes of different sizes for friends and handed them out the week before the big event. She had already bought the ingredients and had kept them in a large box: extra eggs, bags of flour, sultanas, cherries and icing and marzipan plus some whiskey from the drinks cabinet.

Sorcha had left the house to get out of the way after calling the bank to send her a new PIN number and her mother barely noticed. She had always demanded that the kitchen was hers at this time and nothing had changed.

"Where are you going?" Maeve asked, as she met Sorcha in the driveway. She had on a scarf of multi-coloured pom poms and was chewing an apple.

"Town for a while," Sorcha said. "I'll be back later."

"I won't wait up," Maeve said sarcastically.

Sorcha knew full well what her sister was implying, that she didn't have a social life. At least she didn't have to babysit her sister anymore. When they were both living at home, she had often to accompany Maeve to birthday parties or outings with neighbour kids in case she got temperamental. Maeve had been easily angered as a child and often took this anger out on random people if she thought she could get away with it. Sorcha had felt like her own identity was marred by this constant attachment she had had beside her and had felt embarrassed by her sister. But she felt she was too grown up to respond to the girl's sly needling and said nothing.

She was bored with small town life: the roundabouts outside town allowing people to bypass them, the graveyards and churches strewn about with little to do inbetween. She had noticed the addition of the leisure centre and thought about bowling some time but she couldn't go on her own. She ended up in the library, which was fitted out with new computers, and she could surf the net for a while. She hadn't done this in ages. At work, she had been too busy and she had lost her habit of checking information this way.

Her membership of the library had expired and she discovered that it was a full three years since she'd taken out any books. Sure, she had bought books but not enough to start a collection; she hadn't spent long hours reading for pleasure in ages. She persuaded the assistant to let her use the computer for free as she temporarily didn't have any money but she would have to pay for any print outs. There were six computers in all and she bagged the last one at the end of the group.

Sorcha sat, idly checking her hotmail account. She had found it hard to adjust to not having a barrage of e-mails to answer every day although she did have a lot of unwanted junk mail. She deleted the files plus the ones asking her to choose between various brands of fast food and perfume. She opened up the Windows Explorer and inputted the word 'counsellor' and the name of her hometown. She only had an hour so she checked through the listings and came up with a couple of names that looked hopeful. She jotted down the details and scrolled through some other files for information. She went back to hotmail for a moment and sent a quick mail to Karen who had not been in touch for a while. She didn't want to sound miserable so she kept the content light and friendly.

Towards the end of her session, she fidgeted for something to do and for no reason, inputted the name of the band she had seen at the festival those months before. Shawn's band seemed to be doing pretty well: they were working on a new album, had an American tour already underway and were headlining a concert in their town before Christmas. The show was to raise funds for a local charity which helped old or sick musicians to pay their medical bills. They seemed like a bunch of top guys with an interesting take on life. She scrolled down some interviews with Shawn who seemed to be the most talkative member of the band. His words indicated his powerful ambitions; he dropped names all over the page and was enthusiastic about the high-profile shows on the tour and various names they were planning to work with the coming year. No mention of a girlfriend but there was maybe one name that cropped up again and again. She was touring with them and had spent some time working with them on her own album.

She could hear parts of their songs playing in her head as she scrolled through the comments section, a drum beat or violin part. There were posts from all over the globe: well-wishers sending messages of thanks for a great show; fans agreeing to swop copies of live shows or unheard songs that were played at low-key shows. She clicked on photos of the band's concert in Germany that summer and their guests, a percussion band that played back-up.

Sorcha closed the session down as the bell began to ring prior to the library closing. She walked home through the estate taking her off the main road. There was a pedestrian path linking her to the station road at the end of the estate. She walked quickly and made it home just as the rain came down in bucketfuls.

The following week, she checked her financial situation. She had access to her bank account again and was relieved. She paid for the computer use this time and noticed Karen had replied to her mail. 'Hey Sorcha,' she wrote. 'What are you doing at home? Hope everything is ok. We are moving into our new house before Christmas and are having a New Year's party. Let me know if you can make it. Would love to see you again. K xxx

Sorcha mailed her back, pleased at the invitation. 'I'll try. Just have to figure out travel plans. Hope we don't have a blizzard by then. In the confusion, I forgot my bank details. It feels good to have money again! I don't think my family would accept my forgetfulness as an excuse not to buy presents!'

She could feel her old sense of humour returning little by little and knew she was the only person who could pull herself together. She hoped that this was the start of a renewal and she would have something to celebrate in the new year. Although each day she felt she was dealing with an uphill battle. Her mother had gotten used to her being around but still made comments about her returning to the city as soon as possible. Maeve was being typically unsupportive and the two men kept to themselves and their activities.

Sorcha couldn't help but get into the Christmas spirit. A couple of weeks before Christmas Day, she found herself in town, rooting through shelves of clothes for presents for her family but not feeling remotely heartened by the sounds of festive songs playing in each store she visited.

She had stalled the visit to a counsellor as the holiday came closer and she knew she would be facing the various members of the community, her family included, that came to visit.

On her way home, she rationalised that the holiday wasn't necessarily fun for everyone. The music website had no mention of the garrulous lead singer who seemed to be out of the picture for the moment. He was resting at home, having to sort out a divorce, and had mentioned a vague notion of starting a solo career by releasing an album of covers. Ironically, she was finding herself in the same position, which caused her some concern and she knew when she had recovered from her exhaustion, she would have to consider her own options or be left behind. The lifestyle so far away from bright lights appealed to her though and gave her cause for thought.

Her mother was pleased as punch to take delivery of the new dining room furniture in time for the celebrations. The morning it arrived, she spent a couple of hours pushing the sideboard into place and filling the shelves with china and glass. Then in the afternoon, she took out her box of decorations and began to assemble the artificial Christmas tree.

"Can you hold this while I balance the stand beneath?" she said.

Sorcha held the fake tree in place and helped to twist the branches into place. They had purchased a couple of real trees when they first moved into the house but the needles had shed into the carpet so this 'tree' was the third in line of ones they had bought in a box. It came with its own fairy lights and they had numerous home-made and shop-bought ornaments to attach to each branch. "There," her mother said as the tree took shape, "that's a start. It looks good, what do you think?" She said this to nobody in particular.

Sorcha nodded, still offering up tinsel and sparkly bells for consideration. Her mother took or rejected each one and sighed at the tree as she tried to decide where to put everything. Eventually, Sorcha left her alone and went into the room. She had decided to look through a catalogue for presents to get ideas. When she emerged again, her mother had finished decorating the tree and was tidying away the wrapping and boxes. She put everything in the closet and placed the tree in the hallway, where its lights could be seen twinkling by passersby late at night.

"All that fuss for nothing," she could hear her mother muttering to herself. "Same nonsense every year then we all eat ourselves sick and it starts up again next time."

She put her fake crib on a stand in the living-room so any visitors would get the message of what the holiday was really about: religion. The assembled group of weary travellers looking for a safe place to rest reminded Sorcha of her situation and the tenuous grip she had on life right now. She still felt dizzy and had limited herself to one hour per day to get out and about. She remembered the homeless people she had helped give a party for three years previously, and was glad she at least had refuge of some kind.

They went to church early on Christmas morning. It had snowed a little during the night so Sorcha braved the cold and went first thing in the car with the rest of the family. As they reached the entrance separately, Sorcha could hear the familiar Latin hymn refrain "*Gloria. In excelsis Deo*" and felt ill. The service was over in half an hour and they exchanged goodwill wishes of peace with each other before going to look at the lifesize crib. The Three Wise Men were hidden at the back of the Nativity scene ready to make their appearance at a later date. There were little kids kneeling to get a closer look at the baby, which had been added to the cast of characters overnight.

Her mother eventually blessed herself and they could all go back to the car. The town was silent as they drove through the deserted streets and took the road for home. All of the shops had closed for the holiday and the kitchen had been stocked full of extra food, which was off-limits until it was time to be used.

Sorcha took her small stash of parcels and distributed them around to the family in the living-room. "You shouldn't have spent your money on us," her mother said, sitting down to unwrap her gifts and promptly putting them away. "I'm surprised they're even paying you when you're not working."

"The company pays you while you're down here?" her dad looked at her in surprise. "I was wondering what you were living on."

Sorcha was too busy looking at Maeve who was putting away her presents. She looked bored and complained loudly about having nothing to do. Liam suggested a spell in the kitchen might help. She got up and

About Turn

banged some press doors and came back with cutlery and table settings and busied herself putting everything in the right order.

Sorcha had a couple of book tokens and put them on the mantelpiece with her Christmas cards. She was out of the loop this year and had only received them from close friends. A lot of people did not know her city address so she was sure she had not missed any lying on her mat in Dublin. She thought again of what her workmates were getting up to and presumed she wasn't missing anything. Another new bar with three floors had opened in the area and she imagined the girls enjoying the new venue.

The meal began early at 12.30pm and Sorcha found herself sitting at the top of the table, underneath the framed picture of a depiction of the 1916 Easter Rising. The painting showed a street of buildings in flames and revolution fighters in green uniforms rushing about with rifles. Women and children stood in the foreground looking horrified, as their homes were destroyed by the blaze. Her dad had bought this on a trip to the city and had hung it up in memory of the people who had fought to make his country free.

Now the time was veering closer to a new century and her dad said Grace in the Irish language before he tucked in to an enormous plate of food. He had been eating very light meals all week and allowed himself free rein as he ate a second helping. Sorcha sat eating her free-range chicken and stuffing and drinking lemon and lime. She pulled a cracker with her brother and they read the jokes while her mother ate brussel sprouts and stuffing and checked the table umpteen times for any sign of imperfection.

Maeve picked at her food, leaving most of it behind on the plate. She was wearing a new jumper bought for her by her mother and the makeup on her face matched the cranberry sauce, Sorcha noticed. She smiled in spite of the situation and Liam smiled back. She admired him for maintaining his good nature in the middle of this humdrum household. There was no mention of any misdemeanours on this special day at least and Sorcha was beginning to feel a little better.

When they had cleared their plates, Maeve and her parents took the empty delph to the kitchen for cleaning. Sorcha was sitting at the table when she heard screaming.

"Damn you!" she heard her mother cry loudly.

There were shouts and she could hear her dad's voice rising. Maeve came back into the hallway and went to her room in floods of tears. The parents appeared again after a few moments, carrying bowls of mushed up trifle and a jug of cream.

"She knocked it on the floor, the stupid bitch." Sorcha's dad did not like to see food wasted and was trying to eat the trifle salvaged from the kitchen.

The mother placed a bowl of the dessert in front of her son who ate it politely. Sorcha refused a portion and looked at her dad eating hungrily. It was just like the old days. In an hour or two, he would go for a walk and then settle down by the fire to read for the evening, switching on the TV to get the news updates or out of boredom.

Like her brother, she was trying to make the best of the situation and that evening, Sorcha went to play cards in the kitchen with Liam and a friend of his who had moved in to the area. They had met at a concert and were now fast becoming best buds. As they sat betting coins on each game, the snow began to fall and they watched it through the uncurtained windows, cascading silently in the darkness. Liam was making whispered jokes about his mother, talking in a low voice about the fact that she had put her foot down about the annual Christmas party at her husband's company.

"Last year, she came back and complained for weeks about the food and the music, how it was only for young ones, and she hasn't worn the outfit she bought since. I think she's packing on the pounds in her late middle age and she feels a lot happier around the old folks who won't mention the spare tyre." He giggled to himself and Sorcha could feel her body shake with laughter.

———◆———

By morning, the snow had covered the garden and the roads outside in a blanket of white. Sorcha watched from the front window as her parents reversed the car out of the driveway on their way to church for St. Stephen's Day. "They are crazy," she said to herself, before snuggling back under the blankets for an extra ten minutes. She got up eventually and had a quick power shower under steaming hot water then got dressed and went to the kitchen. Her brother was tinkering with his CD player – the door had jammed open and he was trying to free it again.

"Have those two lost their minds?" Sorcha asked.

Liam looked up and shrugged. "I think Dad thought it was safer to drive to church through the snow than risk a day listening to the wife narking at him. She was planning for this last night. I heard her insisting she would go, no matter what."

"Do you want some breakfast?" Sorcha said, putting on the frying pan. She took eggs out of the fridge and cracked them into the pan with some olive oil. She put on some toast and made coffee in a mug. Liam shook his head and rattled his CD player in frustration. "When you start making some money," he said, "can you think of me and send me some? I really need a new machine but I couldn't afford it this year."

"Where did all your money go? You should have quite a bit saved."

"I had to buy a present for someone. Someone very special," Liam batted his eyelids. "Well, it's true, sort of. She is special. And she needed some new clothes. Her old stuff was diabolical," he said jokingly. "I kept telling her then I just decided to buy the new wardrobe myself."

"Who is this? A girlfriend?" Sorcha asked.

"Her name's Clodagh and she works in the same record shop as I do. I've known her for a while. It's just you haven't been around so I didn't get a chance to say anything." He lowered his voice. "We went on holidays as a group during the year and now we're actually living together. It just made sense. We both work and she finished studying last year so we can live better by sharing the rent and things."

Sorcha sat down and ate her eggs silently. Liam spoke again, "The parents don't know. They know about Clo but not about the living situation. So don't say anything. You're welcome to come and stay with us next year if you need a break. You just seemed busy so I didn't ask before."

"What's she like?"

"She's from the area but lives away from home. With me! And she's perfectly fine. We get on like a house on fire. I'd have asked her up here for Christmas but her parents wanted her home. And of course there would be questions from the Bean an Ti in this house about a young lady staying under the same roof.

"They did say she could stay anytime but we'll see. This is not an ideal situation, not with Maeve the raver around." He paused. "It's kind of early days but I'm missing her. I've been sending texts since I got home. Discreetly, of course," he said, smiling. "It's a nice feeling. You should get yourself a young man."

He got up and took his things with him, leaving Sorcha to finish her meal. She looked out of the window and noticed a robin hopping from tree to tree in the back yard. She opened the window latch and shook some crusts of toast onto the ground. The robin watched for a second then swooped down and ate hungrily.

She didn't get a chance to mention the news to her mother as there were visitors arriving, having braved the bad weather, during the day and her attention was elsewhere. That evening, they visited a nearby museum which had just opened out of town. They drove through the village and over a small bridge to the old Victorian Gothic house, which had once belonged to a local landlord. The building celebrated the social history of the country and had become a real tourist attraction. Sorcha noticed the red berries growing in clusters on the roadsides as they drove along with her mother looking innocently ahead. Her mother reversed the car into one of the free spaces in the car park and turned off the engine. She turned to look at Sorcha and smiled. "So, what do you want to do? Have a look around or go inside out of the cold?"

Sorcha took a look at the frozen river and the icy paths and said, "Lets go inside. There's a café somewhere, I think."

They walked up the main road leading to the house, careful to avoid the slippery parts and enjoying the cold winter air. Lanterns lit up the grey walls of the house, creating an atmosphere as they went inside. They walked through the few rooms on display downstairs: the drawing room, the library and the main hall before reaching the little shop and café which had probably been the old kitchen. The main museum housing all of the artefacts was in a different building: a modern construction on the grounds just a walk away. They got hot chocolates and sat on the long wooden benches in the café. There were a couple of families having lunch and two older ladies having tea at one of the tables.

"So this is where it is for you. You should speak to your manager if you're not happy. Tell them what you want to do." Sorcha's mother came up with a bunch of solutions but none of them seemed like the right answer. Now that the strain of the holiday was over, she was able to be human again. Sorcha wasn't comfortable with the conversation so eventually she changed the topic. They crunched their way over gravel to the modern extension to look at detailed exhibitions of country life in Ireland with a fake shopkeeper offering jars of sweets or rolls of material for clothes.

"I already saw this last week after the official opening," her mother said as they drove home in the car. She had grown up around most of the stuff and seemed equally comfortable and hesitant around the exhibits. She revelled in the woollen outfits and pretty flowers that girls wore on May Day. Sorcha could recognise some of the items like an old churn or lamp that had been donated from personal collections. The area had been controlled by the people in the big houses though and their possessions had always been off limits till now. A museum was one good way to bring in revenue for an old unused estate. She remembered from local history that the landlord in the neighbouring estate had actually sold some items and had gambled the proceeds to raise funds for his tenants during the Famine, losing all of it on a horse.

Back home, Sorcha stepped up the driveway and opened the front door with her key. The hall was a blaze of coloured decorations arranged neatly in place. She didn't feel like she was coming home anymore and wasn't even sure what she was doing here. The other option of staying in Dublin would have been unthinkable so she had had to plump for being at home. But it was nearly time for her to go. She could feel it as she walked into the living-room. Her brother had moved on, her sister didn't have anything in common with her and her parents treated her like she was a distant relative. They barely looked up as she entered the room.

She still made an effort though. She noticed her mother getting antsy as she looked out of the window at the snowfall.

"It'll be like this for the evening," she said.

"I think it's OK to drive," her dad said looking at the layer of wet snow on the ground.

"I want to go out and walk around. I have places to go," the mother said.

Eventually, she took the car keys and gathered a couple of Christmas cakes that she had not yet delivered.

"I'll come with you," Sorcha offered.

Her mother nodded and they took a cake each to the car.

Sorcha looked out of her window as they drove through town. Her mother stopped the car at a familiar house past the church. One of her mother's elderly friends lived alone here and was often brought deliveries of vegetables throughout the year. The garden was filled with wooden boxes of flowers, garden seats, gnomes and decorative trellis on the walls. Festive scenes of Santa and his reindeer had joined these and were lit up in the early evening. The snow just added to the scene as Sorcha's mother got out and walked to the front door, which opened after a while. The parcel was handed over and then the two women chatted for an age. Her mother plodded back to the car and put her hand on the steering wheel for support then got going again. "That poor lady all on her own," she said, turning on the ignition. "Ah well, she likes the chat."

She seemed like she was in a world of her own as they drove to the outskirts of town and delivered another cake. Sorcha waited in the car and watched the local kids tobogganing on a nearby hillside. The hill was covered in snow and there were shouts as they took their man-made sledge to the top then slid down the slippery slope all the way to the bottom, screaming at the top of their lungs. It looked like fun as she waited patiently, listening to the radio on low volume, for her mother to get back and drive home.

That night she couldn't sleep. It was partly PMT and she had a lot going through her mind. She tried several times to fall asleep but woke up with a start at 3am. She lay awake in the darkness and listened keenly; there was no sound to be heard. So she got up and walked to the toilet. Then she remembered the storeroom which she had so far ignored this visit.

It was a tiny walk-in closet at the end of the hall, beside her old bedroom and her parents' room. There were boxes of photos and paper cuttings that had been kept over the years. She liked looking at some of the pictures that held memories and sifted through some of the older photographs for a start. She picked out one of her standing in the snow at Christmastime – it was part of a group of pictures but in this one she was standing on her own. Her small face looked radiant as she had been snapped playing in the snow, holding twigs for a snowman and standing beside a small bush with berries that had long since disappeared.

She was all wrapped up against the cold and could make out a couple of white teeth that showed as she smiled. That year, she had received presents of books to read, colouring pencils, probably a toy like a bear

About Turn

or a doll and an umbrella for the bad weather. She was wearing a home-made jumper and scarf as well as her plaid winter coat and tights with her boots. She couldn't remember much about what had happened around that time – she had only been two to three – but she started to look for more pictures and took her small collection back to the guest room.

Her parents had enjoyed the family thing at the beginning. On holiday, they had coped with not so busy shopping centres and uncongested roads and had taken pics of their kids for the benefit of the grandparents who could not travel. But the expansion of the town and other towns in the area had meant loans for new houses and preparation for college. It often meant double standards of spending while craving a more simple life. Sorcha's recent experience had demonstrated how someone could lose a feel for life while just working for a living.

The evening before she left again, they ended up watching a video version of a book about a mother/daughter relationship set in California in the sixties. Sorcha had taken it home on rental and was engrossed in the story. Her mother finished what she was doing and watched more intently, her face becoming a blank as the story developed. Sorcha tried to explain that the woman and her teenage daughter held very different views and were unable to get along and the director had thought it might be an interesting topic. It was based on a true story.

Sorcha hardly noticed when her mother floated out of the room and rewound the tape when it finished for when she brought it back to the shop the next day. The film had seemed very much like a book simply pasted to screen although it had held her attention. In this case, the daughter had a sense of morality while her mother spent time in prison for what she thought was a just cause.

She tried to understand that her mother had grown up in a time when sitting and watching a film was not to be taken for granted. She had been brought up on a farm and would have been kept busy with the demands of being self-sufficient. They were very different: her mother had left school early and had worked in the local hospital before marrying. Plus she just wasn't that bright to take an interest in something that was outside of her range of experience.

"So, you've checked the train times and you know the one you need?" Her mother was chattering as she put the finishing touches to a Christmas decoration which had been damaged. She was spraying the wooden log with silver paint and adding some multi-coloured sparkle to cover its cracked side. Sorcha had made dozens of these at school and was dabbing bits of glue and sparkle onto a piece of card absent-mindedly.

"Leave that alone," her mother said. "If you were right, you'd have kids of your own by now. Or something like it. And you wouldn't have to come down here one hand as long as the other." She looked at the new gadget Sorcha had bought in the sales.

"I don't know why you spend your money on these things. That is what young people are like these days. Spend everything on themselves and no thought for tomorrow."

She sat back in the chair as the doorbell rang. It was her aunt and cousin Tara on their way back from town.

"Merry Christmas," they called in the door. They got on very well together and had been out buying in the early sales. Sorcha waved in response. Her mother fluttered about as she got tea and things and they gathered in the sitting room as Sorcha wished she had changed her clothes. She was starting to feel like a bag lady who had worn these pants so much.

"When are you heading back Sorcha?" asked her aunt, making conversation. "You've been around a lot lately. I saw you in town about a month ago. Have you been visiting since then?"

Her mother rattled the teapot with annoyance. "Have we got anything else to talk about? I thought you were here to discuss the engagement."

Her aunt brightened up and said, "That's right. Tara got engaged just before Christmas. We've only told a few people but she'll probably be letting the cat out of the bag on New Year's Eve. So we said we'd better let you know in case you hear it in town and wonder why we never said."

Tara held out her hand and showed them the small diamond ring she was wearing. Her mother took a good look at it and said how pretty it looked. The proud aunt took a drink of tea and continued, "We haven't made any plans yet but we'll keep you posted. Are you coming out to the house to have a look at the designs for the new place?"

About Turn

The women continued chatting and Tara and Maeve sat beside them, listening to every word. Sorcha liked her cousin. She had travelled for a couple of years after leaving school and was working in a local office. They had lost touch but Sorcha left her congratulations and went to her room to pack.

She had just finished a laundry wash and neatly folded her clothes into the bag again. She dreaded the return journey and was glad that she had New Year's to enjoy before starting back at work. She put her new CD walkman into the side pocket and gathered up the rest of her things. She hadn't had a chance to get to the family home this year although it was just a few miles out of town. She could hear the women gossiping and discussing wedding styles and felt out of things. Her grandparents were long gone but she had looked again at the old sepia photos of them on their wedding day and in New York, where they had lived for some time. She wasn't allowed to take the pictures out of the house as they were the last few mementos of the couple.

She was knocked out of her train of thought as she heard her mother's voice at the door, "In our day, we spent our money on sensible things. I sometimes think that I've brought up a very selfish bunch of children, one in particular. Some people think that they don't need to work."

Her relatives left hastily and Sorcha stayed in her room, not inclined to get into further discussion. "What is the problem anyway?" her dad said now, in an exasperated tone. He had taken her mother's side as usual in the argument and was eager to show that he didn't support layabouts.

Next day, as Sorcha lugged her bags to the car, her mother was still talking. "This is exactly what we had to do at your age. Get on with our lives. We can't mind you forever, you know." Back on the train, she had to travel back across the country in time for work the following week. She rolled her eyes at the thought of her mother closing the front door, still giving out and anxious to start work on the dishes. The parents would stay in tonight and go to bed once they had watched the New Year ceremonies on television. The trip to the station was so short that they didn't have time to chat. Her dad just helped her carry the bags to the platform then drove back home, glad of the relatively peaceful atmosphere now restored.

The train was empty apart from a few subdued travellers. She looked at the guy opposite who was listening intently to music on his earphones. He had a sixpack of beers on the table beside him and was drinking from one can while reading the inlay notes of a CD. Sorcha continued reading her magazine then heard a question being asked in her direction.

"Are you on your way to Dublin?"

She looked over at the guy who had removed his earphones and seemed in the mood to chat. She nodded in response, happy to talk back.

"I'm going there myself. Just to stay with friends. Do you know the Southside?"

"Yeah," Sorcha said.

"Are you from the Southside?" was his next question.

"No, I don't live anywhere near it."

He pummelled her with questions, finally holding out his own can and offering her a drink. She turned away and ignored him for the rest of the journey, which suddenly seemed long. The guy seemed like a throwback to maybe five, ten years ago when this was all you could expect from a social encounter. All notions of a move to the country were instantly dispelled by his presence and she focused on getting to and out of the station as quickly as possible.

Finally, they were in Dublin and she collected her things and walked to the taxi rank. The scaffolding around Heuston station had been removed at last and she gazed in awe at the newly-restored 1800s building which had remained encased in wrapping for so long. The taxi drove over the decorative historic bridge and through the Park to the shared house in Castleknock. "This area used to belong to the Guinness family at one time," the taxi driver said as they drove through the village. "The only houses out here were their big monstrosities. Now all the green land is full of housing estates. But you can still hear the trains bringing the Guinness out of town late at night." Now Guinness was owned by Diageo and subject to the fortunes of the company on the international scene.

He helped her with her bags and she opened the door, not knowing what to expect after being away for so long. There were a couple of cards on the floor with her name on them. Nothing from work apart from a letter about her health benefits from BUPA. She walked into the kitchen with the funny wallpaper, still peeling from the walls. The cupboard had been cleared before she'd left so she went to the store around the corner.

The owner grinned at her and she noticed a sign saying 'Under New Management – Sorry for Inconvenience. We are Refurbishing.' It looked like Centra deal with the estates was opening up and the area would be getting a facelift. She bought all the essentials, stocking up on fruit and yoghurt although she bought a readymade pizza as she didn't feel like cooking. The house was clean but a little dusty. She heated up the pizza and cleared up the remnants off her plate and wiped the surfaces clean before going upstairs. The bedroom reminded her of all the times she had crawled in here after another hectic day at work and she shivered, thinking of the rat race that was to start all over again tomorrow.

Tony had left her a note, updating her on bills due and wishing her a happy holiday. She had sent money each month to cover the expenses in the house, as well as paying her rent so she didn't have much money saved despite her long absence. It was a relief that she had not left her job totally. She had been tempted to just leave but it would have been the wrong move. So what was she to do over the coming months? She didn't know and as she sat in the room, a wave of apprehension crept over her.

It took her twenty minutes to put away all her things. She put on some music enjoying the peace and quiet of being on her own in the house; she could get used to this. Liam had burned her some CDs as a present and she put on a jazz music CD that had appealed to her on its first listen. She liked the brass melodies and let the music enter her consciousness, refreshingly cerebral as it was.

Chapter 12

Sorcha walked nonchalantly to her desk first thing on the start of a new working year – 2001 had for decades symbolised a futuristic time and had always seemed so very far away. She was already on the second day of the year as she approached her old desk in the middle of the small cubicles on the first floor. The place felt as deserted as the moon landscape as she hung her bag and coat in the locker but before she could feel that she was spinning through space in a white suit, she heard noises nearby as other workers arrived. It had been touch and go for a while but now she was back to familiarity and she could feel the slight carpet and hard floor beneath her feet as she tapped her name into the computer.

She sifted through various envelopes that had accumulated on her desk during her absence, some already opened in case they were important. She felt a tinge of panic as she fingered each item and put it back in its place but she clicked into work-mode and began to sort through the small pile, checking for relevant markers as she went along. Her desk had been mostly cleared apart from a couple of piles stamped 'complete' or 'to do'. Jeremy was the first to arrive: a gust of winter coat and scarf blowing into the office just before 9am.

"How are things?' he smiled interestedly. "You remembered where we were." He said this with an apologetic look on his face as if he didn't intend to offend her.

"How could I forget?" Sorcha gave him a weak smile.

"Back for good?" Jeremy asked and she nodded. She glanced at the cup of coffee he was holding in his hand and stood up to fetch her own.

"You look well. Hope you're feeling better," he said, as she left the area and disappeared downstairs. When she returned, he was already collecting files and bundles of forms to prepare for a morning meeting. He swept past, still holding his mug of coffee.

Sharon appeared, looking tired and under the weather. She smiled as she sidled into her seat. "Welcome back. Don't mind me; I have a cold. It's not contagious, I hope," she said, tugging at her coat. "And not life-threatening although it certainly feels like it today. I spent the weekend in bed trying to beat this."

Sorcha nodded and tried to look busy. She watched as Sharon filled a mug with boiling water from a flask and poured a satchet of Lemsip on top. She knocked it back and stared groggily at her desk. "I'm not going to be much use today. Let me know if you need anything. Sorry," she said.

The rest of the team trickled in, wearing long faces. The girls made pleasant conversation about their holidays before everyone got on with their work. Only Lorna walked around, looking agitated. She sat at her desk and looked fed up with the situation. She had been asked to draft a survey to assess which areas should be focused on during the year following a drop in morale on site. The survey would be issued in March and the results would follow soon after plus a list of actions to be taken.

"I think people are just unhappy with the salaries. We're working so much harder but are not getting any benefit ourselves. That refers to every department on site at the moment," Lorna said, as they left that evening.

"I can hardly live on what I'm being paid. If they had some ideas or projects to develop, it would be something but they're putting all the resources into growing the business at the moment. I'm really feeling the pinch, I can tell you. You can't even get a notebook out of these guys."

They were driving home and Lorna took a detour to the shopping centre. The traffic crawled along the busy road creating a blaze of taillights in the darkness around the business parks. Approaching the shopping area, they joined the circle of cars moving slowly around the centre, eventually pulling into one of the four car parks, each in a primary colour. Lorna drove around the almost full enclosure, looking for a free space.

"This is ridiculous," she said, as she swerved into what was probably the last space in the Red Zone and backed her car into place. She scrabbled for a bunch of papers that looked like bills in her bag and they got out of the car and walked to the entrance.

"Thanks for the lift," Sorcha said, by way of goodbye, once they got inside and joined the milling crowds out for another evening of shopping. Lorna waved briefly and walked along, her head bent over the papers.

Sorcha got entangled in a line of people waiting for the bank machine. She knew she had enough for the next couple of days and walked along the shop windows, reading the sales prices for music CDs and bargains in household goods. The supermarket was full of people pushing trolleys and carrying bags full of shopping to the exit doors. She avoided the throng and went to the ground level health store for shampoo and vitamins. There were people she knew from work at different stops along the way, engrossed in bargain hunting. She noticed some colourful tops on sale and made a note to come back at the weekend. The shoeshop had slashed their prices for the first week of the new year but she couldn't allow for a new pair so soon.

The escalator took her to the upper floor and she looked down at the indoor waterfall gushing noisily but at this point, drowned out by the bustling shoppers laden with purchases on their way to McDonalds for the evening meal. Three girls in glitzy jeans and tiny tracksuit tops were flicking their highlights around in front of her and one of the girls, in side profile, popped gum as she chatted excitedly and played with a diamond hooped earring. The descending escalator was crowded with shoppers intent on spending money. One middle-aged man passed by, licking an icecream and tapping his fingers nervously on the railing as his wife looked set for a battle ahead. People were checking their wallets and checking their cards at the cash registers.

Upstairs, there were young women reefing through the railings for discounted outfits with fervour. Sorcha saw a glamorous mixed-race couple standing at the jewellery store and looking at watches through the glass. She spotted Lorna eating a fruit and gazing at the perfume counter before moving on to the Body Shop. Families passed with the youngest in a pushchair, usually holding a brightly-coloured balloon. Slightly older children walked through the fray, holding on to their parents' hands. The HMV record shop looked like it had no spare room to stand and she narrowly missed a glob of indiscernible food that had fallen to the floor. The upstairs section was grubby from the crowds that had swarmed in and out all day. She made it to the exit and walked into the cold air as the automatic doors slid back for the millionth time.

Outside, the situation was the same with queues waiting to access the fast food restaurants, which lined the exterior of the centre on that side. The exit was lined with Christmas decorations. She stood at the pedestrian crossing as buses and cars and taxis drove past and behind her, pulling in to let down passengers and gather new ones.

Sorcha wandered from the yellow brick building of consumerism to the opposite side of the road. The new arts building had closed for the day but she could see the inaugural exhibition of paintings through the front window. Current events were advertised in the posters at the entrance. The library was still open as she walked past. Sorcha passed a few moments looking at noticeboards advertising services in the local area. 'Let us help you to quit smoking' one poster said. There was an advert for a book club which met during work hours. She read about an improvement in waste disposal for the community before picking up pieces of literature on the shelves.

Outside, she caught the first bus home. They left the bright light of commerce behind as they drove through the newly extended roads to the old village. Sorcha got off at the pub and crossed onto the footpath. She rushed up the hill in a blur and was almost off the main road when a car came speeding over the hill, stopped abruptly with a screeching of tyre rubber, and turned at a full 180 degree angle to the path. She stood there dazed for a few moments then as there was no sign of damage to the vehicle or injury sustained, made for home.

The HR team ended up in the local bar their second week back. Although the Buddha was still gleaming on its stand, the bar had become worn and tired and only a few people were about. Lorna was chatting about the great deals she had found in the city stores at the weekend while spending her Christmas vouchers. It was definitely sale season and with the sound of the great bargains to be had, Sorcha half-wished she had spent some time rummaging through the racks. She went to the bar on her own at some stage and was distracted by a guy her own age who was hovering nearby. He had a few empty glasses lined up on the bar and as Sorcha gave her order to the barman, the guy leaned towards her and tried to speak. Sorcha said 'Excuse me?'

and he repeated the movement. He was obviously legless and too drunk to make sense. She looked at his crumpled clothes and a work badge hanging round his neck and left as quickly as she could.

The group conversation turned to celebrity bashing as the girls slagged off the worst dressed famous singers. They tapped their hands to the usual chart songs being played. Nobody really questioned Sorcha about her time off and they just assumed she was better now and ready for action again. Some of the UK staff were standing in a corner by the bar and she could see Courtney sitting in the group. Mr Popular had taken over the running of the entire department and seemed more sober as he stood chatting to his PA. There were still some French teams in the prefab but it wouldn't last forever. As the last of the selected teams relocated home the French workers would finally be moving to a proper building.

Sorcha ended up thinking about one of the cards she had received from her friend Valerie who had moved to Chicago post-college and was working for a pharmaceutical firm in the city. Valerie was planning a return to Dublin very soon and was hoping to meet up when she got back. Her family lived in the country but she was hoping to make Dublin her base. Could Sorcha give her some ideas of where to live, what it was like job-wise and had the nightlife changed?

Sorcha was enthused by this project and had answered back with as much information as possible. She offered the girl a temporary place to stay if she needed it or she could check for accommodation if that was ok. She had been checking the rental adverts just in case and the city centre was no longer the haven for single people who just wanted to rent a cheap room. Most of the ads were for flatshares and it was hard to find anything for less than €100 a week. It was all done by website now and west county Dublin seemed like it had all the reasonable deals. She sent her friend the addresses for some companies and mentioned some of the clubs she knew about. "Where's your head at?" Jeremy asked. "You look like you're miles away."

Sorcha apologised. He continued talking about the party for Denise which had happened before Christmas. "It was a great night, one of the highlights of the season for me, I'll say. Monica put on a great spread and we had loads of fun but not too rowdy. Monica didn't want to end up being kicked out of home."

"That's right, I missed that. Did she leave a contact number?" Sorcha asked.

"I have it at work so I'll send it on to you. I think Denise is still jobhunting at home if I remember correctly." Jeremy was still house hunting and had moved to new accommodation for a while. Katerina had stayed on in Dublin despite all the changes and Zara had left for home, leaving a parting gift of tiny insects in Katerina's bed. They had finally emptied the bugs out of the window but Jeremy had moved anyway.

The group dispersed rapidly as they all had to get home and get some sleep. On their way to the bus stop, they passed a couple of local lads, one was getting furiously sick on the footpath.

"Looks like the vomit brigade has moved in," Jeremy said, looking disgusted as the noise became unbearable.

They had a year start meeting at the end of January. Sharon had shaken off her cold and was keen to outline the plans for the year and ensure that her team was fully motivated.

"There are going to be quite a few changes this year. First thing is that John is leaving us after starting this whole project from scratch. He's been offered contract work so he can base himself at home and travel around for different clients. Lucky him," she said.

"We are trying to improve the services we provide bit by bit so that will probably happen after the survey results come through in April. It should be interesting to see the ideas that we come up with. In the meantime, it's business as usual. We did a very good job with the audit last year...."

She continued in the same vein for some time. Sorcha heard nothing about job possibilities and was not surprised. She was keen to stay out of Sharon's bad books but she was not interested in pushing her limits anymore, only trying to do her job. Her manager handed round a couple of boxes of sweets as a thank you and the group groaned slightly. The new currency meant prices were bound to increase and everyone needed more money, not chocolate. A video featuring their new CEO was played at the end of the meeting. The blonde woman who had had to do without a million dollar dividend for the year greeted the group and promised to make everyone's lives easier in the coming months.

She thanked everyone for their hard work and spoke about the efforts to increase profits and cut costs to get back on top. She warned that there would be challenges ahead. The speech did not affect anyone and as soon as it ended, the group filed back to their desks.

"So where do I sign?" the dark haired woman asked. Yvonne had come to sign a part-time agreement as her baby daughter had just been diagnosed with a rare form of cancer and would need intensive treatments over the next six months. The slim woman was dressed in a neat suit and was holding car keys and a mobile phone. "Thanks very much for letting me do this," she said to her manager who walked her back downstairs. She passed by a tall dark Galwegian with glasses who had come to get the precious training kits for the UK team. Daire had also signed up for a Masters degree to better his chances of getting a promotion but for now he was obliged to run short classes for his co-workers on a weekly basis as well as doing his own job.

Sorcha was eager to do some socialising and paid a visit to her neighbours next door. Paulina's friend from Poland worked as a childminder in the area and had called over with new photos of her charge. Paulina was cooking some stew and was busily checking that her vegetables were heating properly. She seemed like the average housewife, complete with oven glove and an apron tied around her waist. "*Alez piekne dziecko!* What a beautiful child!" she exclaimed as she checked out the pictures. "*Czy ona chodzi do szkoly?* Does she go to school?"

Her friend nodded and Paulina ooohhhed as she stirred the stew. Thinking about a family of her own helped her to go to work every day. "I have an American manager now, who is a nightmare." She made a face. "Always talking so loudly at her desk. They brought her over here to help us improve our figures. We haven't had very many lates or sickies since then but that's because people are afraid that they'll lose job."

Her friend Maija asked about their plans to buy a house. "We're hoping to get that sorted out by this year. But we have to deal with the banks and that's another thing about this country. The banks are not used to dealing with so many customers." She laughed as she continued, "The local rep seems like he's from the country. He reminds me of someone I went to school with years ago."

The girls burst out laughing at her description of him and they began talking in their native language, Paulina taking care not to let her pots boil over.

"How about you?" she asked Sorcha. "Everything OK? Yves said that you had been ill again last year. I hope it's nothing serious."

"Just overworked, I suppose. It got so busy last year," Sorcha felt foolish trying to explain herself and became embarrassed. She knew Yves had been very busy as well.

Paulina seemed immersed with the chores and was more comfortable talking in Polish anyway so Sorcha made her excuses and left. She had fallen into a routine of easy meals and TV watching and imagined that Jason would be chastising her any day now for her terrible habits. She had given up on chasing new jobs or making contacts and the workload had eased off. She usually got home in time to collapse on the sofa for the evening to watch all of the comedy shows and did not feel inclined to make any effort to stop.

The team was obliged to have a goodbye party for their manager, some were actually sad to see him leave. The bar was already full when they arrived for drinks after work that evening. Some early finishers had gone on ahead to book tables and they waved their hands as Sorcha's crowd entered. The women held different management roles on site and were in their element, having free drinks so early in the week.

"Order something at the bar," Sharon said, as they filed past her seat. "Just give them the name of the company and they'll put it on the tab."

She was engrossed in chatting to her friend, and John sat with them, chatting and laughing with a drink in his hand.

"Have you any idea where he's going?" Sorcha asked, as she lined up beside Jeremy to order at the bar.

"He hasn't said anything. I do know that he is going back to the continent. That's all he's willing to tell us, humble workers as we are."

"I think he's going to freelance, take on contract work for companies and organise deals for probably twice as much as he's been earning here," Lorna said, flicking her newly-highlighted hair and catching herself in the mirror opposite where they stood. "Now that he's successfully put this site in place, he's off to capitalise on his career achievements. Nice work if you can get it."

Sharon had announced her plans to take a round-the-world trip in September. "They're holdin' interviews next week for someone to replace her," Lorna said, grinning from ear-to-ear. "I've got mine scheduled for Thursday. There's not a lot to know but it's just the extra responsibility of running a team. Sharon will be around for a couple of weeks to get us up to speed on everything. Or I could try out for that Lean Six Sigma programme they have decided to introduce. Plus I'm looking at cars again. My old one's such a botch."

"The nice blue one?" Sorcha said. "But it's so comfortable."

"Well, I'm sick of it," Lorna said. "All my friends have got top-of-the-range new cars that only came out in the past two years and I'm still driving around in something that's four years old. I can't ask my Dad again for money and he has other things to pay for at this stage."

Sorcha smiled sympathetically and turned as Sharon stood up to announce the gift presentation. Sorcha had not contributed but most of the managers had done over the past week. Some of them made a short speech, thanking John for his management capabilities, and his input into helping the site develop since startup. And the manager did likewise but then he was speaking to an easy crowd, most of whom had stable jobs and good incomes.

"This is an unusual situation. I'm not sure that there's anything we can say about what happened," Jeremy said. "He has some weird energy, that guy, hard to describe. I never really got to know him although he was around so much. What did you think of him?"

Sorcha shrugged. "Just with our different roles, I didn't really get a chance to chat with him."

"Me neither. I think he's gone back to his boyfriend, the plastic surgeon," Jeremy sighed. He had a lot of things to organise in the next few months and did not want to get involved in a campaign against the company and its practices.

Lorna was chatting with a couple of guys in the corner and Sorcha looked closely at them to see if she recognised their faces. As she listened, their accents were Irish, one of them obviously being from the heart of the Northside, and his friend speaking with an affected Southside tone. They were an unlikely pairing but on introduction, she realised that their personalities explained everything.

About Turn

Noel was from one of the nearby suburbs and had just bought a house close to Lorna's flat. He was working as an engineer in town and shook hands in a laid-back, good-natured manner. His outgoing friend was a different type of person. John had recently launched a brand of mobile networks on the market, featuring a range of new gadgets and possibilities for the average mobile phone user.

"We've just spent the last six months working on the design and the marketing. When it goes live, I will be worth my weight in gold. I've lost a lot of weight with all the hard work but you know what I mean."

Lorna was listening, agog at the figures being spouted by John at every turn. He was telling stories about the manager of his company who liked expensive wines and travelled to China on business regularly, eating dog and local delicacies as a matter of course.

"I'm hoping to get a trip in this year. Otherwise, I'll have to go over to Noel's house again and chew on his labrador for something to do. Go in to work on Monday and tell them, yeah, I had dog and fried rice in Blanchardstown at the weekend. Very tasty!" He made a sucking noise with his lips as Lorna burst out laughing at his antics.

"So where do you guys work? Are you working locally?" John asked, getting serious again.

Lorna told him and he scoffed at the mention. "I'm surprised you're able to buy a flat with that kind of money. Busdrivers get paid better wages, don't they? Me and Noel here don't have to worry about anything, thank God.

"So, what kind of flat is it? One bedroom? Do you even get a bedroom or is it kind of fold up bed sort of job? Noel's mother did that for long enough when she split up with his old man." He started to laugh, holding his can of beer ever closer to their faces, with a cigarette dangerously close to Lornas' hairsprayed head.

"Come on John, work in the morning," encouraged his friend. "We only came in for one. Sorry." He made an apologetic face as he led John away. Lorna was looking flushed and sat down, miserably.

She had to admit that she felt some regret at the possible promotion of Lorna to team manager and tried not to show any emotion. She had not considered it but it was like insult added to injury. One of the main gripes in the company was a lack of career path which was even more relevant now with the cost of living increasing and company cutbacks. How come she was so far down the pecking order?

Sorcha wrote this down in an e-mail to Valerie in Chicago. They had been roommates in college and she had kept in touch when she could when Valerie had relocated to the States after getting her science degree. They had started by writing the traditional letters sent by post and not forgetting a card at Christmas or a birthday. Now, they both had a hotmail account and corresponded by e-mail. Valerie was working in a lawyer's firm in the city and liked to keep up with what was happening at home. They had often confided in each other while living in Dublin and Sorcha now described her experience in the company, mentioning titbits about her family's reaction. She kept it light and humorous for the most part but knew that Valerie would understand.

Sorcha sent an e-mail to Monica. She was partly embarrassed about having had to leave so dramatically and, as always, had since wondered if it had really been so necessary. During her schooldays, she had rarely been ill and had never had any fainting fits or times when she felt unable to breathe and had to be taken out of class. She had been well-behaved and it was shocking for her to have to admit defeat after such a short time in the company.

"It has never happened to me before," she said to Monica when they eventually met up. They had booked tickets for the theatre on a weeknight and the bar was half-empty so they went for something to eat, having gone in straight after work.

"I just felt jaded, spaced out, like an out of body experience," Sorcha continued. "It just got worse and worse to the point where I couldn't function anymore. I know what it's like to be tired but this was different. I kept trying to remember when my dad was working like was it the same for him? I suppose he had some off-days but then again he worked close to town and there wasn't a commute involved. I'm the first one of the family to really make that break so it's not surprising to hit a problem."

Monica was listening intently while gazing at the menu. She had already eaten so just wanted soup and some fries. Sorcha ordered a sandwich and a side order of salad. The German girl looked at her for a moment and then said, whispering, "You're not the only one to end up like that. My workgroup is a tough bunch but I do know that we've gone through a pretty hectic time trying to stay profitable."

"When they announced the cuts last year, they slowly introduced a new work plan whereby team members had to work through every iota of correspondence to make sure no query was outstanding. We have this electronic system which meant every item could be checked so if we had not logged a query or archived it properly, it reappeared. They went from focusing on high debt and aged stuff to just prioritising everything. So instead of it being just really busy like when I started it became maniacal."

"I think it was a common thing when they started the finance section to just leave certain customer correspondance on the backburner and then last summer, they brought it all back, put it on the shared system and asked us to work through everything. So I had the phone, my existing queries and all of the new stuff. Plus at one stage they suggested I help train up some new starters who only lasted a few months."

Sorcha looked surprised. Even though she worked in personnel, she didn't know much about the workings of the individual departments. "And did you manage to do it?" she asked, sipping her drink.

Monica nodded. "Yeah, most of it anyway. There were some things that I couldn't personally deal with but it was either work them or don't come to work. At one stage, I was going to come up to your department just to complain. But they made some persuasive arguments like, 'If you get all of this done, then we can concentrate on making the department work a little more smoothly' which has been true, I suppose. Not very reassuring though for a company of that size to be so disorganised."

The waitress arrived with their food and knives and forks and Monica stuffed fries into her mouth as she talked. "Before I worked here, I was in the bank in town like I said before and they never had enough time to deal with customers and deal with paperwork so things would be left in files and they would have to put aside time to do that. But this was on such a huge scale.

"I had to pull out pages and pages of files regarding one big account and just fax it to a sales manager in Germany and ask them what was going on because the customer had charges for software when they'd signed a different contract. I think they just did hard sales to boost their profits which just added to the problems. There were drinks companies with machines that had changed ownership several times and the paperwork trail was a mess. You could spend days sorting through something and get nowhere. That was another argument the managers had: once all this mess had been sorted, we would have cleaner accounts but it wrecked my head. Just as well it was only for a few months or I would have been sharing your room at home," Monica joked.

"And the sales people were calling up with the customer on the other phone line asking why is this not done? They have such double standards. They create this mess and want us to annotate everything and clear it up so the account history contains all of the information. I had to allocate the files so I know how much there was on the system. It took forever to clear it down and the managers just hassled us to meet the targets.

"At first, people were annoyed at not being able to reach the targets then they changed things around so that the targets could be met but only if we worked our asses off and we did. Part of the reason I didn't chase the mail I sent so much was because I spent the last three months of the year constantly working. Even on Saturday, you know, I was up a little later but I still had to come in to work just to get through my backlog because if some work had not been done by Monday I would have been in trouble."

Sorcha sighed and sat back, her sandwich half-eaten on the plate in front of her. It sounded familiar and she suddenly had an insight into another department's operations.

"It has spoilt my experience at the company," Monica said, "I think that I will probably spend another year here then do some world travelling. There isn't a lot at home so I'm just staying where I can work for the moment."

"I know what you mean," Sorcha said. She didn't have anywhere to go either but hoped to go abroad. It was hard to explain her family life to the German girl so Sorcha changed the subject. "So where to from here?"

"There have been a few changes, they announced the new overall manager for Germany and for the UK before Christmas. You know Rocky? He's an idiot but nobody else wanted the job. The managers left one by one last year and they waited ages before appointing someone. So now they've redistributed the work so nobody gets lumped with too much stuff. We're being trained to do the same tasks. I'm not sure if it will be ok because the billing is very important and you need to have certain people working on the large accounts but they're obviously trying to make life better. Just a little too late for some of us."

Sorcha asked about the party for Denise. "We had a good time. There is still some of the booze left in the house so I might have a party at St. Patrick's Day or some weekend when there's not much on. I haven't seen Denise since then but we're planning to keep in touch. She was a good housemate and I've found it hard to replace her.

"I think she was tired of having to fit into the tight work mode at the centre. She has such an upbeat personality and there were only so many jobs to go around. We were at a team night out in Temple Bar before she left and I've never been so bored. Lots of tedious office workers looking lost and nobody willing to make decent conversation."

Monica was easy to talk to and at least offered a different approach to life, unlike her settled friends and family. She chatted about her feelings over the Christmas period.

"I was the same," said Monica. "You should give yourself a break and not worry about having to fit in and get a mortgage. Maybe the company is not right for you? Think about other options although things are so expensive these days with stamp duty. Maybe you should look into changing your accommodation. You should take a look at the flats around here. Or your parents could help you get a mortgage/deposit?"

They went in to the performance of the Grapes of Wrath, which was on a short tour, handing over their new euro notes at the ticket desk. The audience was silent as the small cast portrayed a family's struggle for survival as they moved west to make a living. The stark set had only a stationary beat-up truck which the characters used to get to their destination. They were dressed shabbily with their belongings stacked in the vehicle. The family discussed their options and debated what they could do as they ate their meagre rations from tin cans and tried to stay hopeful.

Monica was enthusiastic about the show and mentioned the arts centre as being one good thing on the horizon. "When I was last up there," she said, "there was a performance of dance taking place and I walked around the foyer and had a look at the art exhibition in the studio. Makes a change."

In the morning, she could hear voices next door. Paulina's mother had arrived for a short visit. The tall, thin woman had travelled from her home two hundred miles from Warsaw to catch her first flight and had been on the go for 24 hours. Sorcha noticed a skinny face with a frown peering out of the window as she left her house for the day. She noticed boxes in the living room and was just waiting for the couple to announce their departure.

When she got a spare moment, Sorcha checked her account and saw that Valerie had replied to her e-mail. She had checked out the jobs market and was setting up interviews with a couple of practices hoping to get a permanent job in Dublin. She had heard about the new clubs that had opened and wanted to know more. Sorcha had felt enlivened just reading all her requests for information and typed up her lengthy response when she got home. She checked the web for ticket bookings and was able to confirm a cheap return, which would give her a week in Chicago the following month. She made a provisional booking knowing that she would have to book time off work first.

Chapter 13

London was a blaze of light as the plane swooped into the air after takeoff that evening. A couple of hours in and Sorcha was wondering what all the fuss was about when it came to trans-Atlantic flights. The film was a badly-made comedy, the food was awful and the journey seemed to take forever. She fell asleep as the pilot made some announcement about poor weather conditions. Every couple of hours, she woke with a start, wondering where she was as the plane bounced its way up and down across the ocean. But soon she was about to land in the midst of the onion fields of Chicago as the pilot announced touchdown at O'Hare airport.

The plane drove slowly along and was manoeuvred to a parking space where it finally came to a standstill but Sorcha felt like she was still moving. She raised her head and looked out the window. American airports looked just the same as European ones, grey and impersonal, disguising the fact that they were launch pads to destinations all over the world. Not sure what to expect, she joined the small queue of people leaving the plane and, bleary-eyed, followed the signs to baggage reclaim. Her bag in tow, she joined the next queue of people waiting to get through Immigration.

It seemed like half of Mexico had descended upon O'Hare that morning. People were lined up with summer shirts and big smiles, even at this hour. She gave her passport to the checker who looked at it and handed it back without changing expression, he seemed unimpressed with having to work the overnight shift. Through the doors, the waiting area was full for a moment of people on their way home and then suddenly empty apart from a couple of people who had decided to spend the night there, waiting for a flight. A girl was wrapping herself up in a sleeping bag in one corner of the seating area, her luggage strewn around her. She looked tired, about as tired as Sorcha felt, having spent eleven hours on a plane.

So this was her arrival. Before she left Dublin, she had mailed Valerie that she would be in town and a rough idea of her schedule but the flight had been delayed and there was no welcoming party. In a way, she was relieved that she didn't have to encounter anyone just yet. There was no one about at this hour; a couple of employees exchanged small talk across the room. A couple of times, a group of newly disembarked passengers rushed through the double doors and through the waiting area and exited to the big world outside.

She sat at the edge of a row of seats near the giant glass windows and put her bag underneath her feet. Outside, she could see that it had been snowing heavily and early morning traffic drove slowly past, the kind of American vehicles she had seen on TV. Big trucks and long, flat-shaped cars. She read her book, 'Accordion Crimes' by E Annie Proulx, the Pulitzer Prize-winning author. She'd liked her book Postcards and this new work outlined the history of immigration in the US by using a small accordion of Sicilian origin as a tool.

She imagined what everyone at home was doing right now: Tony had decided to move in with his girlfriend to save money so she was glad to be out of the house while a new flatmate was chosen by the landlord. It was an avoidance technique which meant that she didn't have to push herself into finding a new home or moving all of her stuff just yet. She could enjoy her freedom while it lasted.

A dark-skinned woman started up a floor polisher and moved it steadily across the room, catching a look at Sorcha and smiling ever so slightly. The sky had grown lighter outside and Sorcha decided that maybe it was about time she got moving. She was anxious to get into the city. A shuttle train took her to a giant cavernous building, the interior of which was dilapidated and stank of neglect and disrepair, wherein lay the 'El', a commuter system that served the city of Chicago.

The building was empty apart from a couple of grumpy employees who seemed to have the early morning blues. She asked a large, moustached black man behind the booth about trains for the city. His face barely moved as he motioned towards the stairs and said, "Take those, take the train at the platform on your right. That will take you there." She did as he told her, the train was waiting patiently at the rundown platform and she sat on a blue plastic seat with her bag perched carefully on her lap. A few others joined her just before the train moved out of the station, a muffled announcement telling of their destination, and as it moved towards the city, more and more people got on until the train was almost full.

They sped past old churches and houses, which reminded her of what she'd heard about Chicago's architecture. As they rolled into the city, the buildings became modern and majestic. She'd forgotten that it was a working day, and as the train came to yet another stop, she joined the crowd of people who were getting off and climbed up the steps to the sidewalk.

Snow covered the ground; the footpaths and cars drove slowly past in the slush. This unnerved her. She could imagine falling and being covered by a snowdrift and never being heard of again. But she continued on, almost losing her balance several times, until she came to some streets showing signs of life. She spotted a small deli, which was almost empty. Although the menu was in English, she suddenly remembered that American English was different and the choice on offer was fairly limited once you got past the unfamiliar terms and the fifteen ways of ordering the same thing in different sizes. She asked for a basic cheese sandwich and a coffee. The sandwich was basic and the coffee was served in the usual paper cup.

Sitting by the window, she chewed her food until a middle-aged man sidled along and asked her, "Are you finished with that?" pointing at the half-eaten sandwich in the wrapper. She was startled and didn't answer. He shuffled off and approached a couple of other people without much luck before going outside to lean against the wall. Sorcha had lived in Dublin for some time but could never recall when someone who was so obviously hungry came up and pleaded for a bite to eat. She handed him the rest of her sandwich as she took her bag on wheels and went up the street.

The giant MusicStore across the street reminded her of the Megastore on Dublin's Aston Quay, rows and rows of CDs upstairs. But downstairs, there were all sorts of musical instruments behind glass cages: double basses, clarinets, and pianos. Upstairs and next door, there was a university bookshop with mainly black authors on display like the bookshops back home, which featured Irish writers.

By now, her bag was practically an appendix so she looked around for somewhere to put it, to free her up so she could explore. She found

Union Station, a giant building in the middle of the city. It conjured up images of the railway, stretching across America. Inside, the building was clean with rows of empty seats. Most passengers were running towards the platforms to get their trains. A down and out was sitting on one of the benches until an official came by and ordered him to move. These Chicagoans were grumpy.

Sorcha went downstairs to a room full of lockers. The girl at the desk was possibly Russian and unhelpful; she waved her hand towards a coin box and watched Sorcha struggle with the mechanics of the locker room system. A slight glimmer of a smile only crossed her face when Sorcha eventually managed to open and close the impenetrable locker, her bag safely inside.

Back on the street, Sorcha checked her phone with its newly acquired roaming facility that allowed her to make calls on it while abroad. She sent Valerie a text message and thought that the girl was probably just getting up and wouldn't appreciate an early morning call. Nearby, beside a small green park that was covered with snow, stood an impressive building with the Stars and Stripes flapping outside. It was the Art Institute and the interior was equally grand; she could feel a few pairs of eyes on her as she entered. It turned out today was free admission but she still needed a pass so she got one and entered through the gates, manned by a couple of well-dressed officials, one of which was an elderly man who looked like he'd worked here all his life. The ice melted slowly in the building as she was granted access.

A large black woman with curly hair said, "Alright then" as she held out her pass. The Institute housed an amount of artefacts and exhibits to put Dublin's National Gallery in the shade. Some black and white photos by Alfred Stieglitz, upstairs in the Institute, captured a time when New York was young and under construction. A finished skyscraper stood in the foreground with plastic taped coverings over the window while behind it, stood another half-constructed giant building.

On the stairs, she stopped in front of a huge painting depicting a blue and white cloudscape. This was 'Clouds' by Georgia O'Keeffe, who had lived with Stieglitz in New Mexico. She stood gazing at the paintings lining the staircase before hurrying for the exit.

Outside, it had begun to snow again. Sorcha pulled her collar around her neck and crossed the street. There were very few people about and the grid system gave welcome relief from the gridlock chaos that characterised Dublin traffic back on the auld sod. She noticed an old cinema with film notices tucked away underneath an old, statuesque building, which looked deserted. No one was at the ticket booth. Two girls clicked their way past in dancing shoes; they must have come from the performing arts school upstairs. The girls rushed past on their way somewhere.

The by now busy streets were starting to tire her out so she went back to Union Station to rescue her bag and read for a while. In the afternoon, she decided to call Valerie who sounded flustered and busy. "Oh, Sorcha, you made it. Welcome to Chicago. Where are you?"

"Union Station?"

"Wow, you know how to get around. Look, I'm up to my eyes here. But if you want to come over to the office, I'm sure my manager will let me leave."

Valerie gave her directions to an office building that had an ornate entrance but, upstairs, was just like any other office with files and computer screens from wall-to-wall.

"Sorche!" Valerie came flying out of the lift and threw herself at her friend. The girls hugged and stood back to take each other in for a moment.

"You look great," Sorcha said this with feeling but thought that Valerie looked tired. "And tired too."

"Yeah, I feel tired. We've had a load of projects to work on the last couple of months. But it's good experience, as I keep telling myself." Valerie smiled weakly. "Anyway, lets get you home." Valerie picked up her work folders and threw on a heavy cape.

She was wearing sneakers and could smartly hurtle along the busy streets to the train station. Her flat was a small studio on the northside of the city. Sorcha recognised a lot of the artwork and posters of the Flatiron building in New York which had adorned her student apartment. Ruth had made this her own home. She rarely came back to Ireland. "Unless there's a death, and I'm needed," she had often said jokingly.

"OK, what would you like to eat? I can make a stirfry. It's healthy and fills you up?"

Sorcha nodded gratefully. She left a small parcel of goodies on the counter worktop and sat on the couch, which was to be her bed for the next few days. Valerie had draped a fur throw over the back of the couch and Sorcha felt its warmth straightaway.

"Where did you kill this one?" she asked.

"Lets see," Valerie faked a thought for a moment. "Maybe that one's from Alaska. No, I bought it in Canada. They have such lovely household stuff here and I can afford to buy things once in a while. If it brightens up the place I say why not?"

They chatted over dinner, discussing old friends and their social circles. Valerie was horrified to think of Sorcha's experience at the company and couldn't believe it.

"You were always so bright at school. It's shocking to have to leave like that. I did hear that the company was going through a bad patch. It just shows that they don't tell you everything in the news."

"I felt so angry at times," Sorcha said. "It just came out of nowhere. One minute I was a valued member of staff with perks then I found myself attached to a phone eight hours a day and feeling nauseous to have to sit and repeat myself so often. I ended up feeling like I was worthless because they didn't really acknowledge that there was a problem. They were too busy trying to figure out how to stay in business.

"It was like in school where you have a bad teacher who won't help you to learn. And you know I can be a very motivated person. But there was nothing I could do about it."

They sat drinking Irish coffees until the small hours of the morning. Then Valerie yawned, her mouth becoming her entire face for a second, and announced she was going to sleep. "I hope you'll be ok on the couch," she said. "I can't afford anything bigger than this and I know some people who live in smaller rooms, believe me."

When Sorcha woke the next morning in a strange room filled with books and skiing gear, Valerie had left a note for her telling her how to find her way back into the city and to have a nice day in that feel-good American way. There was even a smiley face in the corner of the page.

Sorcha took the train back to the city and got off at Van Buren. She plodded on for a bit through the streets, stopping for a slice of pizza which seemed to be the main staple over here. A young black man fell into step with her at one point and asked her if she was going for something to eat. She quickened her pace and broke off down one of the side streets. The well-behaved traffic quietly drove past as trains rolled by overhead. She walked over one of the many bridges and found herself in what seemed to be no-mans-land. Most of the older buildings had been destroyed and some new theme cafes had been constructed in their place. There was the Rainforest Café, Planet Hollywood and across the same street, there was even an Irish theme pub called Fado.

She went inside curiously and the layout was exactly the same as an Irish pub like O'Neill's but the room was spotless and the clientele sat politely in booths, discussing work and chatting. There were old-fashioned etchings of Irish city scenes on the walls in small, modern frames. Sorcha sat at the bar and ordered a sandwich and listened to the sounds of Irish flute music gently playing in the background. This place was too good to be true.

Valerie left her a message that afternoon. She had arranged to go to an Irish night on Navy Pier and gave Sorcha a time and a meeting place, which could be easily found using a city map. Valerie had a friend with her and they were going to drive out in his car.

As the offices finished for the day, Sorcha rushed to the office again and waited for Valerie to appear. She came out chatting with a tall, skinny guy. "Joe, this is my friend Sorcha from my hometown. She's staying with me for a couple of days," Valerie said. Joe shook her hand lightly and said hello. They got in his car and drove through the middle of the city, in the stock exchange and markets area, impressive buildings lining the streets on either side.

"Joe works for a hospital as a social worker," Valerie said. "He's getting married very soon so he's working a lot to meet the mortgage but he's agreed to be our chauffeur for the evening."

Joe laughed at this as they came to the traffic lights. "Have you got a property yet, Sorcha?" he asked, and looked at her in the rear view mirror as she shook her head.

"I've been browbeaten into it just when things are going crazy over here. You know, I get to the apartment block and there's all these kids who have no problem coming up with the money. The flats are six figures and more than I can afford," he said.

"I'm just a lowly medical employee who wants to settle down but I'm finding it very tough. It just seems so wrong. I really wanted to work as a health professional and this housing crisis just came out of nowhere.

At least it means there will be plenty of work in my area if you know what I mean."

"I think you really need to be settling down with someone. I don't have a partner so it's not an option for me either," Valerie said.

"What about Dublin? I've spent some time in Ireland and it was such a different experience. I wasn't sure at first.."

"What do you mean?" Valerie pretended to be offended.

"But – let me finish – when I had a chance to look around, I realised that it wasn't too different to here. I often think about maybe moving, I don't know." Joe thought out loud. "What I'd really love to do is learn the guitar and play with other people, like, communicate. There's more of a facility for that in a smaller country."

"Uhhh, I don't know." Sorcha thought of the amount of times she had sat in a bus in rush hour traffic, dying to get home but not moving anywhere. "You have good qualifications as a health worker, you would be OK."

He seemed satisfied with this information. To perk himself up, he suggested they collect his girlfriend who was working as a graphic designer nearby. They parked outside a skyscraper with had rows and rows of cars parked precariously from top to bottom. A car park skyscraper! Mia's building was nearby and she came out just as they approached. Mia looked like the Canadian actress Sandra Oh. She was friendly enough and sat in the back seat with Sorcha as they drove to Navy Pier.

It was dark and the scene on the pier was not so visible. Inside, a crowd of people had gathered to celebrate the weekend and a stage had been set up at one end of the room. She was introduced to a whole bunch of people, one girl whose grandmother had been born in County Cork. She had never been to Ireland and had no real plans to go. Sorcha had only been to Cork once in her life as a child but she listened as the girl chatted about her family. The band played a mixture of blues and some jazz ballads with people dancing in the middle of the room. A few guys began to get really drunk and throw themselves about. The hours slipped away and soon, they were taxiing their way back to the flat.

"Ho hum," Valerie said, as they let themselves back in the flat. "Sorry about that, those guys just drink and talk bullshit. No different from Dublin in that regard."

"Yeah, it did seem very similar," Sorcha said, relieved to get away from tacky cover bands and feeling good after the long car ride home. Valerie seemed tired and didn't want to stay up so they went straight to sleep.

Next morning, Sorcha woke up when she heard the phone ring. Valerie was calling to say that she had organised a trip out of town for a couple of days at the weekend. They were staying with her mother's cousin Maggie in a suburb and she had arranged to meet them at the local train station.

"Maggie joined the workplace late in life when her kids were grown," Valerie said as they travelled out of the city. "It really shows with her kids, the eldest girl is a housewife but the two younger girls are in management for different sales companies. I've been meaning to call her for weeks now to organise a visit."

They got to the suburbs within an hour and Maggie was waiting with her Mercedes. Her home was a large detached house on three-quarters of an acre. In the hall, Sorcha noticed a dining room full of fine furniture and expensive items which was only used on special occasions. Upstairs, the girls were sharing a room which was pleasant and bright with a vase of flowers were on the dressing table. "These are for you," Maggie said. "Come downstairs when you're ready."

An unused computer sat on a chest of drawers. Sorcha noticed that the other two empty bedrooms had been filled with gym equipment. They freshened up in the bathroom and went downstairs. Maggie was bent over a notebook and her face was twisted in frustration. A deal that she had been working on was not going according to plan and she would have to drive into the office to work it out. "It's only for a couple of hours, dears, and then we can do what we want."

"Hers is the largest real estate company in the area," Valerie said. "It's a big block of a building and swamps the other companies in the park. She bought her daughters homes in the area once they got married."

"Would that be a possibility for you?" Sorcha asked.

"No, I am dead set on going back home soon. I've been over here long enough. I haven't really had a chance to get to know my relatives because they're always busy."

Eventually, Maggie returned from the office but a cloud had descended upon the happy atmosphere. She started to make dinner and the girls helped set the table. "It's just us tonight," she said. "My husband is at a conference and won't be back till Sunday. I'm hoping you'll both get to meet my daughters while you're here." They chatted over dinner about their work and ambitions. Sorcha said little about her experience at the company and hoped that her age would give her some excuse for not reached a management position yet.

"That is just one more reason," she said later in the bedroom, "why I dislike my job. I wish I could be enthusiastic and waffle about how much I love what I do but all I could think about was paperwork and being hassled and the stress."

"You really don't like it there, do you?" Valerie said.

Sorcha shook her head. She knew from her efforts at job hunting that she had little chance of a move. "The work itself isn't so bad. Just the level of work is or was the problem."

"Tell you what," Valerie replied. "Hang in there. When I get back, I might just feel like investing in a property but wouldn't be able to do that on my own. We should go into ownership together. It would probably help until you had found what you wanted to do?"

Sorcha looked doubtful but promised to keep it in mind.

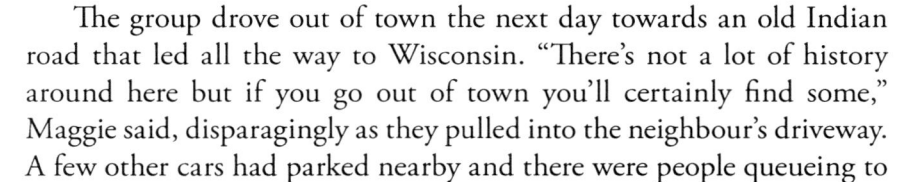

The group drove out of town the next day towards an old Indian road that led all the way to Wisconsin. "There's not a lot of history around here but if you go out of town you'll certainly find some," Maggie said, disparagingly as they pulled into the neighbour's driveway. A few other cars had parked nearby and there were people queueing to get inside the large two-storey home.

"There are actually two events happening here today," Maggie told them. "One is a sale of clothes and the other is a sale of goods belonging to my old friend who passed away here a few months ago. The family is selling off whatever is in the house to make some money."

Maggie brightened as she recognised her besuited daughter who was waving from beside her car. It was her youngest daughter Liz who shook their hands firmly and gave Sorcha the once over. They joined the queue of people looking at items laid out in the various rooms of the house, each marked with a price: $25 for an ashtray or $250 for a set

About Turn

of books. It was like a funeral at home where people would file through paying their respects to the dead but here they just wanted to buy their belongings! Having strangers pick up and handle each personal piece in the hope of a sale was unknown at home but it all made perfect sense to Maggie who was checking out a piano sitting in a corner.

"That would be lovely for your house, don't you think?" she said to her daughter. "Oh mother, not that one, it looks so tatty," Liz said. "We're thinking of getting a piano... just to have in the living room." She said these over her shoulder to the girls. Maggie said nothing but looked disapproving.

Outside in the garden the process continued: a set of summer table and chairs had a tag of $2250. Everything had its price. She could just picture someone carefully listing and assessing each time to gain maximum profit.

The small group made their way to another roomy house. Liz strode up to the door at the side of the building and greeted the woman inside. They all trouped in behind her. Two elderly and well-groomed women were sitting in a roomful of clothes, mostly designer but on sale. The girls looked at the rows of clothes as Liz passed by with an armful of t-shirts and sweaters. Downstairs, there were more racks of clothes. Sorcha picked out a dark blue and grey fleece, which was maybe too big, but she liked it. "I've been doing this for years," Maggie said. "The girls often work weekends and we don't have time to go to the stores."

Back in the car, Liz was discussing Ireland and travelling in Europe. She had been to Europe only once as a college student, and spent some time in Italy. "And did you learn any Italian?"

"*Grazie*", she replied and made a face.

Her mother laughed knowingly.

"Sorcha, when is a good time to come to Ireland? I've already asked Val that question," Liz said, passing around photos of her new red-brick home. Sorcha had spent plenty of summers avoiding tourists on the ancient streets of Dublin during the months of July and August so she said that later in the year was probably better. "And is it true that people just drink Guinness over there? Because I tend to drink lighter beers."

Sorcha couldn't remember the last time she had had a pint of the black stuff. "Well, there's also Bulmers, which is a cider. And there's Bailey's, it's a liqueur." Sorcha was racking her brains to think of other traditional tipples. Liz was talking about plans for their new house, a huge redbrick effort that had been sourced by Maggie. They had been trying to decide on the décor for their living room. "Isn't it awful when your husband starts having an opinion?" Jean said. Sorcha wasn't sure if she was joking.

"Did you say that you lived in Dublin itself? Wow." She seemed impressed by that, having no doubt read the ubiquitous TIME magazine. "Val might be leaving us soon so we have to make the best of her while she's here."

"It's not much fun for the girls at the moment," Maggie interjected. "I seem to have gotten myself caught up in a deal that is going nowhere. We painted the house that I'm trying to sell but I'm not sure if it will work. If not, then I don't know where to go from here." She sighed exasperatedly as she clung to the steering wheel.

They stopped at the ubiquitous drive-through McDonalds on the way back. Then they went back to Maggie's home. Liz took a look around then said, "OK, I have to go. I'll be over to pick Sorcha up tomorrow and take her to the airport." She kissed everyone goodbye and her mother looked at her gratefully. "Thanks for doing that," she said. "I have to go to church first thing then I'm out all day working. You can drop Valerie off at the station on the way back. She knows her way into town."

―――✦―――

"Wow, we have you dressed up in designer gear," Valerie said later that evening when Maggie was in her office. "The cousins are alright but they remind me of well-heeled girls I've met at home."

"It's nice that they have such a close family. It made me think a bit harder about mine, that's for sure," said Sorcha.

"Well, it's not all rosy. Maggie's family lives in a working class suburb on the other side of the city and they don't really see each other. There's a bit of animosity because of the two different lifestyles but they try to get on, I suppose, at family gatherings. Maggie's niece and her husband both work but their income is limited. Joelle is their daughter and they were hoping she'd get a college scholarship but she did some secretarial stuff instead."

―――✦―――

Next day, Liz arrived bright and early. "I drive pretty fast along the motorways so be prepared." When Sorcha told her they had motorways in Ireland, she looked genuinely surprised. Their conversation was broken by the arrival of a couple of girls who pulled into the drive in a jeep. The driver was a tall brunette wearing sunglasses and a bored yet focused expression on her face. Her friend was wearing casual jeans and a home perm.

"Why, it's the girls come all the way from the southside," Maggie said, watching the scene. She kissed her brother's granddaughter and introduced her to Sorcha and Valerie to whom she was related. They had met before.

"We were just in the neighbourhood," Joelle said. "We were out last night and crashed in some boy's flat. So I have to take the car for a check and then we're going into the next state to go shopping. Oh, you're leaving so soon?" Liz was already grabbing the bags and sitting into the car. They pulled out of the driveway and Maggie was by then making her way to her car.

They said their goodbyes at the airport car park and Sorcha went inside to check in. She gave her papers to the man at the counter whose expression changed from a defensive scowl to an interested smile when he saw the Irish passport. He must have seen that TIME article as well. Sorcha thought it funny that he seemed so impressed to see an authentic Irish person from the now gloriously hip capital of Dublin at his desk.

Valerie walked to the ticket check and promised to keep Sorcha updated with her plans to move back home. Sorcha handed her some dollars to get a gift for Maggie and they hugged goodbye. She joined the queue waiting for hand luggage checking and, as she passed to the departure lounge, noticed a young woman being interrogated by one of the Immigration officers. The woman was dressed head to toe in hot pink and was gesticulating madly, trying to explain her situation. There were hordes of people of every skin colour walking around the departure area, some looking suave and cool in light-coloured clothes while others walked past looking worried or miserable. An elderly man wearing a shirt and a fez wandered around the bookstore looking lost.

Sorcha flew back to Dublin with no hitches, reading another novel she had picked up at the airport. She had rediscovered her interest in reading and was planning to make use of this pastime. As she exited the arrivals hall, she felt a lash of rain on her face and the shower fell as she ran to the taxi rank. The journey back home was quiet; the only noise was the window wipers as the vehicle sped down the motorway. It stopped as they entered the village and the car dodged pedestrians shaking their umbrellas as they drove out of town and into her estate.

She paid the driver as drops of water dripped from the roof of the house in the otherwise silent air. The scenario inside was no different. She noticed the carpet had towels all over it to mop up an overspill of water. She checked the roof for leakage but it seemed that pipes in the kitchen had collapsed and leaked all over the floor while she was away. She checked the rusty innards of the press beneath the sink and saw the pipes bent out of shape and wrapped in a temporary cover of cloth.

"This place is a disaster," she thought to herself as she backed out of the kitchen and squelched through the hall to go upstairs. "Bloody rental property. I've had it with this place."

She put her roller bag on the bed and took out her belongings: clothes clumped together and magazines creased at the bottom of the container. She was relieved to be back but did not feel much closer to solving her own problems.

Chapter 14

Lorna was enthusiastic the next morning, asking questions at the coffee machine and Sorcha tried to humour her while she struggled to deal with work again. "I have friends who have travelled to Chicago and they went to Canada after that," Lorna chattered. "The weather was bad but they had a lot of fun in the bars. You must tell me where to go because we're thinking of booking a trip. Once I get all my loans paid off, of course! Courtney was over there recently looking for a new home, checking out the market but they can't afford to buy anywhere near New York state so they're staying put."

She smiled broadly as she went to her desk. Her credit problems had been fixed and she had no reason to worry. Sorcha had other issues on her mind: her message minder had contained a message from her dad who had been told where she had gone. His tone had sounded angry so she had called him on her way to work to get it over with.

"Where are you?" he had said, gruffly, down the phone.

"It's OK. I'm back home, on the bus to work," she had said, trying to calm him down. They chatted impersonally for a few moments and then he hung up. Strange, she thought, how he was so demanding of her attention when she was far away but that over two months at home, he had barely said a word.

She mulled the experience over in her head over the next few days. There was precious little else to do. She thought of the two of them going about their routines and just about going out of their way to avoid crashing into her as she coped with little things like making breakfast and deciding what to wear. Her dad had sounded like he had been made to call her by force; as if it had been against his will. She could hear him on the message, putting down the receiver in exasperation and wishing his wife would do the calling for a change. She remembered what her sister had said one evening while she had been at home. Ever tactful,

Maeve had blurted out in a rush that their dad had been to the city to visit an old family friend during the year and had been several times in fact, without her knowledge. He hadn't even called her to meet for a coffee.

Sometimes, Sorcha had to pinch herself that she had gotten so far. With the use of a library and natural curiosity she had taught herself to read some of the great stories from Victor Hugo and Alexandre Dumas and had stretched her mind to learn about art and sculpture, not just traditional Irish interests. Her family had no real artistic leaning so it was a constant surprise to her that she swayed in that direction. Her brother had a reasonable interest in music and always got good marks in exams but he was younger and involved in a different sphere. He had opted to study science when he left school and wanted to get involved in environmental projects.

That evening, the bus service had huge delays due to roadworks at the village. Sorcha waited for a while then decided to walk home. The entrance of the hospital led her to the main road and the village. She listened to the cacophony of bird noises in the trees as she walked along. It reminded her of walks she had taken as a child, picking bluebells along the way or dodging a shower of conkers falling from the trees. She could remember wandering the streets on warm summer days in the early days, eating an apple or an ice lolly and feeling worried about the future when there were so few jobs about and nothing that paid any kind of decent money. The big, bad world could be a real challenge and she wondered if anything had really changed. Some shiny, new buildings had been constructed in the area but had not opened for business yet. There was evidence of money trickling into the area to create amenities and resources for the community even if she had little in her pocket.

She knew that she had to wrestle with some issues that had been bothering her for some time. The issues mainly concerned her parents. She could remember coming home from school with severe stomach pains a few times over a two-year period. She had crawled into the house, looking for painkillers. Her mother showed little emotion as she pointed towards the cupboard, surprised at her daughter's outburst for no reason.

She thought that her parents did not have high opinions of themselves and were a bit doubtful about their place in the world. She had seen a couple of photos of her parents as children: her mother just a scrawnier version of herself now with the same miserable pout and her dad looking small and disinterested. She hated to say it but she could see where her sister had come from. They had never really professed much of a liking for Sorcha and she supposed it was because she was the eldest and expected to be responsible.

She imagined that her brother would be getting at least three more years of college fees and it was doubtful there was money for a flat for her during that time. Maeve would probably be dependent on her parents for some time to come and would only ever earn a minimal wage when she had finished her training courses. This meant she had to be self reliant and it was hard with an average salary and no chance of a new job to imagine how she could really make it all happen.

Sorcha had always been interested in people: what made them tick, how did certain behaviours take such precedence in modern societies and the history of thought. She liked even the simple examinations like surveys to find out if a certain section of the population liked to read a newspaper or had voted in the last election. She was always interested in the family and the highs and lows of human endeavour. Maybe she should think about applying to finish her course from before. She still had notes from her philosophy classes and the company still offered part-payment once exams were passed. But even as she walked, she knew that adding a trek into college two or three evenings a week could be detrimental to her health.

She was distracted by the approaching figure of an Asian man dressed in medical gear. On his way past, he smiled very warmly and said, 'hello' which took her by surprise. She nodded 'hi' and the doctor looked at her again, before walking back to his open heart surgery, she thought. She felt a little glow inside and wished this would happen on a more regular basis. She had used her time in the morning to carefully wash and condition her hair, which had also been brushed. Her skin looked better now that she was getting a chance to eat properly again and her eyes were glowing and healthy. She took the friendly advance from the doctor as a good sign and wondered if he was interested.

Waking up on a Saturday morning, she felt a sudden but real loneliness as she lay on her bed and waited to get up with no real plan in mind. This must be how millions of people feel all over the world, she thought. Her trip to the States had just shown her how similar they were behind it all and both countries faced the same battle these days. The paper ran a story about the current spate of house building and the growth of immigration with many people moving to live in the suburbs to get decent homes. She'd always thought she would be settled by her late twenties and it bothered her.

She had remembered Paulina's dad lived on the east coast in the US. She hadn't seen him in years but he sent money home on a regular basis. The States had a lengthy history of immigration and some of her cousins were out there. Her grandfather had started out on a similar journey at her age. There was an old photo of him dressed in army gear and holding a rifle, looking young, well-built and determined in 1920. He had joined the IRA, ready to take on the British and their domination. The Irish people had suffered the brutal treatment of the executed men shot by firing squad after the Easter Rising but had come back to fight again. The group had been captured shortly after their first attack and taken in a convoy to Cork city, the Irish soldiers at the front where they would be first to burn or be shot in an attack. The notion of him sitting in such a dangerous place as the convoy moved along was hard to consider, his friends sitting side-by-side not knowing what would happen. When they got there, the city was in flames from the Irish flare-up.

The men spent eighteen months sequestered in a camp surrounded by barbed wire with minimal contact with the outside world. Inside, they had tried to occupy themselves with cards and using money tokens for currency. They had slept on rough beds on hard ground during this period and Sorcha knew only too well how harsh the weather could be in this country. The soldiers guarding the camp had a different perspective: they were protecting their queen and country against a bunch of rebels and would not hesitate to shoot any troublemakers.

A trip to any stately home showed how the landed gentry had lived until then: room after room of fine furniture, extensive grounds and many servants. The landlords focused on production and profit for the Crown and the Irish locals could be imprisoned for stealing an egg. The IRA had burned some of these homes to the ground during the War of Independence. Even in her mother's time, there had been plenty of Irish families that had eked out a living with little option or variance. They had simple basic homes and could only dream of fine things. Sorcha could only experience these periods of history through a museum. But for her grandfather, it had been very real. She knew the spot where just a few years before his internment, men with similar intentions had been taken from prison cells and executed by a firing squad.

A second photo showed the same man a couple of years later and a little older, this time wearing an inexpensive suit and holding a hat in his hand. He still looked the same but she thought she detected some look of upset after his ordeal. He had been on his way to New York city with his brothers to find a job and a future. She wondered whose idea it had been to have these portraits taken, maybe his mother's. She couldn't remember when he had met his wife, her grandmother, but they had grown up in the same area. She was a goodlooking woman and there was a picture of their wedding day, dressed in plain clothes and Grandad at 32 had a happy smile on his face.

In the next photo, her grandfather stood in the store he had managed on Staten Island with an array of foodstuffs and storage barrels around him. It was New York in the 1930 and he stood looking at the camera dressed in a long white apron, looking older now and more handsome. His wife had moved to the city at that stage and had had a miscarriage during that first year. Grandad's brother had died in a fatal accident in one of the first skyscrapers. The Crash had meant poverty for many families and the Irish immigrants in the Bowery suffered with little to show for their efforts yet again. So they had moved back to Ireland during the Depression, taking a local boy with them who had no way of paying his fare home.

Even when Sorcha had visited their home years later, he would earnestly stand to attention as names of the fallen and dead were read out at a memorial ceremony. He would greet an old comrade with a handshake and they would gather on a grassy verge and reminisce about the old days. Her grandfather had gotten involved for the right reasons but his friend also took a hard line: his personality determined his approach and he had no sympathy for anyone who was British and died via a bomb or a bullet.

Sorcha knew the story by then and would take his hand as they went back to the car. He patted her head and called her 'darling' and 'sweetheart'. Back at the cottage he had had built for a farmhand with no other support, she could take a look at his War of Independence medal and listen to his stories. He had been through so much and could still reach out and be a friend. He had felt pride, courage, companionship, fear, terror, loneliness, the unknown, the spirit of adventure, worry, pain, love. She had gone through such a range of emotions in the past years. She didn't really know what he would have made of her experience and wasn't sure how to put it altogether. He had probably been subjected to similar busy days in NYC feeling the weight of responsibility as he worked while many starved and he was helpless to do anything. He would often work until 10pm and deal with poor transport, high crime and stress as he travelled back to their house. Her last memory of him was his corpse lying in a box covered by the tricolour, thankfully having made it to his nineties.

Now that her workload had eased, she was putting a few feelers about looking for some way of getting involved in the community again. Monica had mentioned an environmental conference, which was taking place that weekend in Temple Bar. She got up and made herself eat some breakfast in the cold kitchen then put on some warm clothes and caught the bus to town.

The cobbled streets were livening up in the early afternoon and she took the chance to visit a photographic gallery off one of the squares, mingling with the market stall sellers who had brought their wares to town. She spent some time looking at the main exhibition and browsing through the books they had on display: black and white photos taken in France after World War 2 or more artistic shots taken in the modern style.

The market was buzzing with shoppers, keen to buy organic produce or homespun jam and cakes. A few people sat in a makeshift section close to the gallery, eating oysters out of shells. Mostly, people ate on the small wooden benches or on upturned boxes, tasting the vegetable quiches and seafood on offer. Sorcha was hungry by now and stood at the entrance with a couple of geezers as she ate a slice of quiche. One of the guys was talking about a play he had seen the previous night at the Project.

"It was so much fun. One of the best things I've seen this year. The guy who wrote it also did that show we were talking about at the

Festival in October. There was a fight scene that went on for ten whole minutes. It really made me feel like I wanted to get on that stage and get involved…"

Sorcha gobbled down the rest of her food and cleaned off the crumbs on her coat. She would have preferred to sit down somewhere but the smell of food had been too good to miss. She passed the Project theatre on her way to the Green festival and looked at the posters. It couldn't do any harm so she jotted down the times and dates and thought she could book a ticket later. The Clarence hotel was just across the street and she walked past the shut entrance to cross at the Porterhouse on Parliament Street and into the older part of the historic area, which was still under development. The developers had found an archaeological ruin at this site and it had been boarded off for years while they unearthed the remains of an ancient age.

She found the environmental centre nestled among the council offices and a street of little shops and an internet centre. There were apartments on the upper floors and a bakery open for business. The centre had a surprising number of people visiting on its open days and Sorcha joined the crowd of colourfully dressed mums with young children and students eager to learn about green things.

"Gotcha!" She could feel someone poking her back right beside her shoulder blade and turned around. Monica was standing beside a giant sunflower plant and holding a wad of pamphlets. "You made it," she said. "I thought you might have taken the day off and stayed in bed. It's cold but this building is feels warm and cosy."

"I made myself do it," Sorcha smiled. She was glad to meet a friend.

"Have you seen everything?" Monica said. "I really like the way you can learn about the projects being run and buy some goods at the same time."

They rummaged through some items for sale on the wooden shelves nearby. The centre sold a lot of environmentally-friendly items such as washing powder, food and toiletries and also sold books and magazines on environmental topics. "Do you need anything?" Monica asked. "I bought some household stuff last time I was here. We could go upstairs to the exhibition. I think that the talk starts at 3pm."

They took the winding corridor which led to the converted church next door and went up the stairs to the main room filled with stands outlining the development projects ongoing around the world. "I'm meeting someone here later on. He said he would try to come to the event. Robert is a student and his girlfriend works here as a volunteer sometimes. She can't make it but he said he'd come along and take notes for an article. He does some writing for the student paper," Monica said in a low voice as they walked along, looking at charts and reading the information boards.

"This is like what we used to read about in school. When we left college, there were notices everywhere asking us to take part in volunteer programmes but I never signed up," Sorcha said. She had hesitated at a stall selling plants and seeds to grow your own vegetables and had decided against in the end. "I've no idea where I could put these. But we used to do this all the time in school. Grow an apple tree in a jar of water or set some flowers in the soil. I don't know where I'll be living when I move so I don't want to buy anything just yet." So she filled in a form allowing an amount to be taken from her salary each month by direct debit, feeling like it was a way to contribute to the project work.

The exhibition continued in the large room with stained-glass windows at the end of the wheelchair access ramp. One half of the room was set up for a conference and the girls took their places. A skinny guy with sloppy jeans came tearing into the room as the speakers prepared to approach the dais. He looked around through thick-rimmed glasses then came over to their row and sat down on a spare seat just in time.

"Sorcha, meet Robert. I've already explained who you are," Monica whispered. They shook hands and settled down for the speeches to begin.

"That was an unusual way to spend an afternoon," Sorcha said, afterwards. "I liked the way they kept referring to us all as being part of this symbiotic force and whatever I do could affect the rest of humanity. It's my choice to live a good, healthy life although the prospect scares me."

She had realised that green issues were not just a fad and that the eco groups were not just clubs you could join to show your leanings to other people. The issues were real and involved everybody – it was easy to make a difference.

"So, who's going to be joining up for the eco-village experiment?" Sorcha joked. "I think I have a long way to go before I qualify."

"It's a great idea but I'm a coward when it comes to things like that. I like to be in town and do what I want," Monica admitted.

Robert had his head in a leaflet about green energy and how to conserve water in a household. He stuffed the paper in his bag and picked up some seeds to buy.

"So, are we going to get a drink or what?" Monica wanted to know at the exit.

"Shame on you, Monica. It's just like the old days," Robert joked. "We just come out of the church and you want to go to the pub."

They decided on avoiding the bars near the Central Bank which were all full with the usual holidaymakers and football fans and went up Fishamble Street instead, to an old bar across from Christchurch which was empty apart from a couple of regulars smoking at the bar. They were relieved to find a spare table in the corner and sat down on the red velvet seats, throwing their bags onto the dark wooden chairs. Monica ordered drinks and they sat down to quench their thirst with beer or a juice.

Monica was chatting enthusiastically, "I would love to get involved in a cause or something like the green movement but I have to work full-time if I want to live in Dublin. There aren't too many jobs going in the area and not many that pay well. I've sent my details to the manager of the centre so I can volunteer next month during the festival.

"They will have stands where people can learn about certain organisations or green-related research and they will need people to hand out fliers and just direct people about. It would mean getting access to lots of talks on economic issues and the environment for next to nothing. This is what I studied in college for a while. Until I got tired of living as a student and wanted to work. Now I'm back where I started."

"I'm shocked," Robert said in a joking tone. "I didn't think you would take on a nice, easy number like that. Why not go the whole way and organise a demo on the main street? Plenty of rock-throwing opportunities and great if you like a good fight."

"You're talking about the eco-warriors or something?" Sorcha asked. "I've read about these guys but I didn't think it would be happening here with all the money pouring in."

"Well, eco and economy," said Monica, "it's not just the sky and sea that's the problem. Part of the reason that we have so many foreigners in Europe is because of the fuck ups being made in their home countries over the years which make these places unsafe."

"And people in the West want more control over their futures. I think most of them will be in Genoa in a couple of months time," Robert said. "I'd half-love to be there myself but my girlfriend would kill me. We're planning to get a property together in a year or two. As she keeps telling me, I want you to be alive and not just to have your remains in a jar on the mantlepiece."

"It gets kind of violent at these things?"

"It does at the big demonstrations. The centre will just have a weekend of events and it's very civilised," Monica assured her. "But when the world leaders have their summits, like they're planning to do in Genoa shortly, there can be riots. People are very angry about the lack of interest in putting the world to rights so they make their voices heard. There are lots of organisations that focus on profit before workers as we well know."

"So there's a lot of security?" Sorcha said. "I've heard about it and the police just go in with batons. It looked benign on TV, like the state trying to protect its citizens, but the protestors seemed very determined. They really hit back." At the time of viewing the footage, she had not been overly concerned but now she wanted to know more.

They chatted about the state of the world for some time then Robert announced that he had to leave as he had to catch a bus home. They walked him to his stop and then caught a bus back to their village. "You should think about coming in at the weekend for the festival," Monica said. "I've put the word round with some people I know. There's a big party at the end with lots of musicians playing from all over the world. You don't have to sign your life away but if you weren't doing anything on Saturday or Sunday, you could come in and volunteer. Now I have to do some shopping…"

She smiled as she got off at the village stop and Sorcha went on further feeling glad that she had been in town for the day and hopeful that this would lead somewhere. She didn't feel she was the biggest rebel ever born and didn't like the idea of having her head smashed in with a truncheon on some Italian street but she wanted to take part in a movement that meant something and would allow her to get to know

About Turn

more people. It would pay dividends in that she would feel she was doing some good for the country.

As she passed by the train station, she saw two young boys pull their pants down and moon at the passing carriages. Even this area had its rough elements. She was scared and knew her only housing option in the future would be to purchase an affordable unit in a rough area or over-developed new complex. It was like the CEO had said, there would be trouble ahead.

About the Author

Born in 1973, I have always enjoyed stories, characters and language. I moved to Dublin in the early 1990s to study sociology. *About Turn* is my first foray into novel writing although it has been an ambition of mine for some years. I have a qualification in journalism and have previously written for a number of magazines including The Big Issues and have also tried short story writing. My main influences would be Barbara Ehrenreich, civil rights movement and biography. I would consider this work to be the first of at least two novels that are based in Dublin and draw on my experiences over the past several years.